APOTHEOSIS

D1712351

DEAD FOREVER

BOOK ONE
Awakening

BOOK TWO
Apotheosis

BOOK THREE
Resonance

APOTHEOSIS
DEAD FOREVER BOOK 2

WILLIAM CAMPBELL

Glyd–Evans Press
Portland Oregon

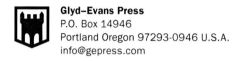

Glyd–Evans Press
P.O. Box 14946
Portland Oregon 97293-0946 U.S.A.
info@gepress.com

APOTHEOSIS: DEAD FOREVER BOOK 2

by William Campbell

ISBN 978-0-9717960-5-8

Also available in electronic form for most e-readers.
For more information visit www.gepress.com

1   3   5   7   9   10   8   6   4   2

WE REMIND: THE MISSION IS
INTACT AND WILL PROGRESS
NOW THAT WE HAVE RESTORED
MEMORY AND REASSEMBLED THE
TEAM. AT THIS TIME, WHAT
WE SOUGHT TO ACCOMPLISH
WILL BE EVIDENT. PROCEED
IMMEDIATELY TO THE
COORDINATES INDICATED BY
TIIE DIAGRAM. GOOD LUCK.
ADAM.

1

A LONE IN THE DARK THERE IS NOTHING TO SEE. BUT A CERTAIN warmth is here, the warmth of others. Projected onto a wall, an image glows brighter. Flashes bounce back and lend shape to this space, a square room with a tall ceiling. The room is full of people seated in rows.

The people laugh like someone pressed a button. The image on the wall is an animated cartoon. A giant rooster stands in a farmyard, hiding a ridiculously large hammer behind his back. Three black cats run in circles around the rooster, teasing him while he decides which one to pound first. What am I watching?

A young girl is seated beside me. She fidgets, bouncing one knee that flaps the hem of her skirt. I brought her here to see this cartoon, something for kids. She asked me to bring her.

I whisper, "I'm going for a snack."

She stops fidgeting and angles her knees to let me pass. Others in our row do the same and I make it to the aisle without landing in anybody's lap.

Outside the auditorium, the brighter light hurts my eyes. The corridor is carpeted by goofy designs, red and blue stripes in the shape of lightning bolts, pointing out the entrances to countless other auditoriums. Farther along the hallway, the stripes converge to become two thick bands that lead into the lobby where the carpet is divided, one half red, one half blue. Dead center is the concession stand.

While I wait in line, someone from behind taps my shoulder. When I turn to face him, he throws a teasing punch and smiles. I know him, he's family, but he's not my brother. Or he was, but not now. Something is wrong. This guy, the little girl, even the others I left watching the cartoon—they're all family. But I can't remember any of their names.

As the snack line inches forward, my relative tells all sorts of stories about himself and his latest escapades, all of which are boring and likely self-applauding exaggerations anyway. I may not remember his name, but I know his personality well—the tales grow taller the longer anyone listens. I order some popcorn and hurry away.

My egocentric relative follows, demanding to know where I left the little girl, and he claims to be here looking for her. He further demands that I reveal what the two of us have been doing outside of his supervision.

"She's safe, don't worry," I assure him, then work at making a distance from the creep. Two galaxies away wouldn't be far enough.

He chases after me. The red and blue carpeting leads to—which auditorium? Every door looks the same. I choose one and step into a black nothing. After a moment, my eyes adjust. The seating is wrong. Instead of straight across, the rows are semicircles bending around the screen. And the movie is no cartoon—a real-life sword fight. The two challengers thrust and swipe, their blades crash and clang, a ruthless, bloody contest. No child would ask to watch this.

I try the next auditorium. And another, my relative is right behind, breathing down my neck. Every theater is different. One has no seats, and the audience is spread across the floor on pillows. In the next, the seats are staggered like bleachers. And no theater shows the cartoon. Every movie is dramatic, violent or mournful, the most disturbing a tale of global war that annihilates entire populations.

My relative demands to know what I've done with the girl. He accuses me of losing her and warns of others coming to punish me after they learn what has happened.

In the next auditorium, high strings shriek a woeful ballad sure to bring us all to tears. Two lovers hold hands, gazing into each other's eyes, then they fall into a kiss, perhaps their last. Kids don't like this stuff. Again the layout is unusual. The audience is seated on stools at round tables. They hold cocktails in tall glasses, some drink pounders of amber ale.

Somehow, I know she is here. I dart between the tables, sail past one and knock the edge. A drink spills across the lap of a plump older woman.

"Hey!" she scolds. "Watch it."

I halt and steady the table. A bit late for that.

"I'm terribly sorry. Please forgive me."

She wipes off her dress, then reaches down for the spilt glass. She raises it high, ready to crown me.

I hunch lower, arms angled overhead. "I'm sorry, really."

She freezes, glass held high, and just stares at me. Her scorn melts, and her eyes grow round with amazement. She lowers the glass. "You are…"

"Sorry."

She shakes her head once. "No, not that. Your eyes."

Hers are locked on mine. Wrinkles fade as her expression transforms to pure adoration—for me. The change of mood alters her appearance. She is pretty despite her age. She stands and reaches out to embrace. I reluctantly join her, indulging in the soft, pillow-like texture of her plump, round body.

"It was only an accident," she says, her voice soft and comforting. "You're not like the other mean people in the world. Most would have done that to me on purpose."

My relative pulls us apart. "Quit talking to this old bag, she's no help. Besides, she's fat and ugly. Don't waste your time on fat, ugly people."

That wasn't very nice. A shame being related to someone not only a braggart, but rude and without compassion for others.

"You see?" the woman says. "That's why you're different."

I didn't say anything. Can she read my mind? I move closer to her, hungry for an answer. She has no fear of me. I search her eyes, but there is so little light, so little color.

On screen, the lovers are pulled apart in a flash that bathes the auditorium in white light.

The woman's face is wrinkled and worn, yet her eyes sparkle with color.

Tender blue eyes.

The same blue—like the little girl we lost.

✳

I'm floating above a field of dandelions. Down below, she is surrounded by the flowers and staring up at me. But now she's the adult I've always known, not young or old.

I am something but I don't know what. Lacking something—a body. This state is odd. It feels like I should fall, but I just hang here in the sky.

There is nothing to hold on to, and nothing that holds me. I have no weight, no shape, no substance. I am nothing.

My bodiless nothing is sucked into the clouds. Endless white, lost in vapor, I cannot gauge my position in space. There is no telling what is up or down, near or far. I toss and turn, tumbling through a foggy otherworld. But worse, I am alone. The thought alone gives me the shivers, even though I have nothing to shiver. I need to find others. Who? What I really want is my attention captured by something.

I'm just being dramatic. There is nothing to me. I have no weight, no shape, no substance, nothing that could tumble or fall. I'm making up all that motion, something a body would do. I'm not a body. I am simply a viewpoint capable of decision.

Back in control of my bodiless nothing, I drop from the clouds and swoop down like a bird, descending on an oceanfront of towering red cliffs. Subtle variations blend rust and copper, cinnamon and coffee, amid salient blades of sheer rock that meld a high plateau with crashing surf below, bursting salty mist.

Across the plateau, a highway winds between rolling hills and slips from view. A vehicle has pulled over to the side of the road. I select a better vantage point and assume it instantly, putting my bodiless nothing just above the tall, brown van. Double doors on its backside are flung open, and inside a man is rooting through boxes. He wears shorts and a shirt the same brown as his truck. Outside is another man uniformed the same, approaching the rear bumper.

"Did you find it?" he asks.

The man inside eases out, cradling a small package in both hands. He reaches one leg to the ground, gingerly steps off the bumper, and sets the box down at the side of the road. "Now let's get out of here," he says. "We don't want to be around when they hurt themselves with this stuff."

The package is wrapped in tan paper secured by white string. It has no markings, address, or any kind of label.

The men climb aboard the delivery van, tires kick up gravel, and they speed away. The van grows smaller, heading around a bend obscured by rising land, and should reappear on the distant stretch of highway following the turn, but it never does.

The package just sits there doing nothing. How could it hurt anyone?

I put myself inside the box.

Overwhelming white energy singes every perception. Unbearable light and shrieking so intense the sound alone is searing, though I lack ears to hear, eyes to see, or skin that could feel. From every direction comes scorching white and pure noise, as if shot into a blazing star.

I can't get out.

✳

"Relax," she says.

"Let me out!" The burning white penetrates my skin. Clawing at the sleeping bag only twists the poly fabric into a strangling cocoon.

"Settle down, Adam. It's over."

Boiling blood rounds four laps a second. My lungs scrounge for air but there isn't enough to feed the hammering in my chest. My skin should be crispy if not greased by sweat. The scalding heat fades to the tingle of a bad sunburn, then gives way to a chill. I open my eyes to see hers, tender blue staring into me.

Christina is close, wrapped in a wall-mounted sleeping bag the same as mine. Our berthing compartment. A black border separates the space in two, panels above polished smooth, and below, the floor is brushed steel. Or ceiling, depending on which direction you care to situate yourself. The floor at the moment.

She loosens the straps and wiggles out of her bag, then begins loosening the straps of mine. She floats before me in a billowing white tee, trim panties and stocking feet. Her rusty hair drifts loose, reaching out in a dance of wandering strands.

"You were fussing quite a bit," she says. "Bad one this time?"

"Are any good?"

She stops loosening the straps. "You dream of me, don't you?"

I push her away, finish the straps myself, and begin sliding out. Oh hell, naked again. I slip back in. "Could I have some clothes?"

Floating away, she says, "Maybe once you answer me." She reaches a wall and rebounds to soar back.

"I have," I tell her. "You know, had dreams with you. Now give me something to wear. It's cold out of this thing."

"Do we live happily ever after?" She pushes off, glides across the compartment, and reaches into a cabinet.

"Not in a certain dream I've had too many times."

She twists fast, her hair a silky twirl. "Why not?" In her grasp is a blue jumpsuit, like pajamas with built-in feet.

"The particular dream I'm talking about doesn't have a happy ending. More like a nightmare."

"I'm a nightmare?"

"Not you, baby, what happens. You're the good part, why I knew I'd find you."

She reaches up to corral her wandering hair. "So the dream came true." She smiles.

"That's the problem—I don't know." I pull the sleeping bag tighter around my neck and keep the cool air out. "I can't tell if it's a memory, just nonsense, or maybe even the future."

"What happens in the dream?" she asks.

"We're in a craft out of control, and you're telling me to put out a fire. But I can't, we burn, and we die. Then there's this ring on the floor, blinking, beeping…"

That got her serious. The gathered ponytail slips from her fingers.

"You think it's a memory?" she asks.

"I'm not sure. I figured it was before we were captured, what led up to it. You said something about how we wouldn't survive, they'd get us if we burned."

She falls into herself, searching the memory, and instead of handing over the jumpsuit, she strips off the tee, panties and socks, and while floating away naked, slips into the outfit I had thought was for me.

"I never said anything like that." She looks puzzled. "It doesn't even sound like anything I would say."

"So it's not a memory."

"Maybe not a real one, but that doesn't mean it doesn't draw on any."

"Then it's both," I suggest. "Memory and nonsense, mixed together."

She sneaks closer, swimming on air. Her stare is difficult to read. Hoping to comfort—if she could—but too busy gauging if it's really me.

I ask, "Could I have some clothes now?"

"That's how all dreams are," she says. "You remember that much, don't you?"

"I'd like to. Something to wear, too."

She angles back, hovering cross-legged. "Dreams *are* memories, just mixed up. Some from long ago, others just the day before, or a jumble that seems like a memory except none of it happened yet. The fire might be one memory, and someone telling you to put it out. The dream replaces that person with me, someone you're close to or know more recently. The burning and crippled craft are likely cross-referenced with capture, so your mind pulls it all together, and while you're sleeping it works out the possibilities. A game minds like to play. What if?"

"So it didn't really happen."

"We didn't die in any fire, at least not in this life. These are the same bodies they captured, I think during land battle, nothing in any craft. They brought us in from there, I'm almost positive."

"You make it sound like you remember getting captured. I don't. Only waking up in the hospital after they stuck that thing in my head."

She winces. "Yeah, I remember too."

"When I was in the hospital?"

"No, you goof. They did the same to me."

"But that was afterward. I thought the implant suppressed memory. So how could you remember getting caught?"

She straightens up and zips her jumpsuit, then slides her fingers beneath strands snagged by the collar and flicks them loose. "Because, what I know about dreams." From a cabinet, she pulls out another blue jumpsuit, something more my size. Prancing on air, moving some but not much, she twists like a corkscrew and pitches the garment. "Get dressed, my king, we have a workout." Her acrobatics have flung her horizontal, into a pose of lying on her side with elbow out, one hand cradling her head. Next she'll have me feeding her grapes.

"Don't start with that royal crap." I begin wiggling out of the sleeping bag, then reconsider and stay wrapped in it.

She swings to vertical. "What's the problem?" She tilts her head and begins braiding one side of her hair. "Nothing I haven't seen before."

I point to the compartment door. "That locked?"

She looks at the door, then back to me. "David's the only other person on board, and he's plenty busy in the cockpit, like you told him."

"Told him what?"

She keeps braiding. "You remember."

So annoying when she does that.

"In a single day I might tell him a hundred things. Think maybe you could help me out, narrow it down some?"

"If we cross a cargo lane?" One side complete, she begins braiding the other.

"He gets his ass kicked." Then I realize, "Oh. What I told him."

Head cocked and busy braiding, she grins success.

Smart-ass.

I slip out of the sleeping bag and hurry into the jumpsuit. "Anyway, back to us getting captured. How do you remember? I don't."

"I told you, I'm good with dreams." She completes her second braid and flings both like whips, testing they are secure. "I know how to sort through and put things where they go."

"You make it sound like a clerk, filing papers."

"One way to look at it. If you don't know the alphabet, you make a lousy clerk, right? Everything's a mess and no one can find anything."

"But not you."

"They may have blocked my conscious memory, but they could never erase what my dreams had to say. After a while, I began to figure things out. It's not like I remembered everything all at once, but clues kept popping up. I knew I was in danger anyway, especially after the interview." Her eyes flare. "When things really changed."

An experience I'd rather forget. Heaven, Hell, God and eternal damnation supplying a fresh injection of terror prior to roasted alive and sentenced to a frosty cell of ice. A load of crap. And those evil creeps, gloating over how they had tricked me. I'm still going back to kill them, someday.

She swats my tight fist. "Isometrics aren't enough. It's time for a workout."

"I'm in great shape. The best shape since... well, since I can remember."

"I remember better." She moves toward the hatch.

"Queen of Dreams, is that it? Okay, so let's hear your answer."

She turns back. "What's the question?"

"My dreams. What are they telling me?"

She comes close. "I don't know, Adam, only you do."

"But that's the problem. If you call this knowing something, I don't know anything. I want answers."

She reaches a hand to my cheek. "And your answers you will have, in time." She withdraws, and her emerging grin has me questioning her sincerity. "But just think," she says, "once you do, won't that be a little dull, having everything figured out? Then what will you do?"

They call it life, the search for answers. When every riddle is solved, the game is over.

"You're right, like always."

I hate it, yet I love it.

Her teasing grin blossoms to a full smile. "At least you know that much."

Smart-ass. Though I shouldn't complain. An adorable smart-ass with equally gorgeous smarts and ass.

"Now come on," she says, poking my thigh. "I'm not turned on by space-men with muscle atrophy." She pushes off and glides to the compartment door.

"What about the interview?" I ask. "When things really changed. What happened?"

She thinks a moment, then looks at me. "They asked what I know about god."

In a jolt, I'm back at my own interview, reliving the cold sweat and pounding heart.

I proceed carefully. "What did you tell them?"

"Only one thing came to mind." She smiles. "I thought of you."

A horrible thought.

"No, Christina, I'm not a god. You know that."

Her gaze wanders. "I don't know why, it just happened. I had no memory of you before that, but when they asked the question, there you were, like magic." She focuses on me. "It's not that I think of you as god, it's just you're the one person who demonstrates the force of god better than anyone else I've ever known."

"I'm not a god, don't talk like that."

"Well, you can be my god. And my king. I don't think anything's wrong with that."

"Don't start worshipping me, I'll have to kick your ass. I hate that shit."

"You always were a dreamer."

"Huh?"

"Like you could kick my ass. Let's see you try, buster. Now's your big chance." She strikes a panel and the hatch whooshes open.

I push off to join her. "Maybe after some coffee, if you ever find the damned stuff. My head's still full of cobwebs."

She eyes me with concern. "You know you can't have caffeine out here."

"Why not?"

She gives me that look again, gauging if it's really me. "When will you remember everything?"

"At this rate, maybe another ten-thousand years." I push off into the hatchway.

She grabs my ankle and pulls me back. "Remind me to be there when you do."

✳

Deep space makes for the strangest dreams. What effect might gravity have on my dreaming habits? Even the minuscule force between planets must have some influence. But out here, far from any system, any solid mass, hurling through the endless void of open space, my dreams go wild. That awful box, the burning white, and left to forever wonder, who will hurt themselves.

Reality is more sensible, but declaring something a good idea that makes sense doesn't necessarily make it pleasant. For a trek across space that spans months, travelers must fight to preserve their bodies. Life without gravity can be enjoyable, at times similar to gallivanting outside the body, light and free. However, once setting foot on a planet, these legs may fail. If only there were an anti-atrophy pill.

Soon we'll know the result of our time without gravity. Now that our journey is well past the halfway mark, our thrust has long since shifted from infinite acceleration to equally infinite deceleration. A tricky aspect of space travel—the delicate balance of when to stop going and then start stopping. If off by the smallest measure, we'll overshoot the target by months and be stuck in this coffee can that much longer.

Along the cramped passage, we tug at wall-mounted rungs, propelling our bodies through the maze and its stale air, bound for the workout compartment. A puzzle now committed to memory, having navigated this winding route at least once each day since our journey began. Not exactly a difficult puzzle. The passages throughout this craft give the illusion of freedom to roam, when really, following any one leads back to every other in little time. It might fool hamsters.

Another day in space, an odd notion since the interval is meaningless, so distant from any star we might orbit, or ball of rock to stand upon and go round. Yet we force the habit, counting off the hours and calling it a day, even while sentenced to a perpetual absence of sunny sky or moonlit night. Nevertheless, the lack of familiar intervals doesn't stop Christina. She sticks to her workout calendar with religious zeal, some days running inside a wheel like a caged rodent—a fair description of space travel—and other days sparring with me, far more exciting than my solo workouts, left to yank on contraptions strung with thick rubber bands.

Another supposed day navigating this maze, like all the days past, again my thoughts drift back to the onset of our journey and how it all happened so fast. Fast like not thinking, just doing, and getting swept away by the moment. Or swept away by yourself, how a person reacts to a situation without thinking, and next thing, can't think of how they ended up where they are now.

And now here we are, traveling in an Association craft, the last thing I expected at this point. But that's what the plan called for. Whose plan? That's the real question. After escaping Orn-3, I might say that I felt in control for the first time since… well, since I could remember. We would travel to the Restricted Zone, but how, I hadn't a clue. More of that not thinking.

We escaped the enemy, I had the diagram and found Christina, maybe even unlocked another clue to my identity. After accomplishing so much, my thoughts turned to what I could do and wanted to more than anything else—go home to Idan. Crack open a beer, kick back on the deck and watch the sunset, listen to the ocean roar, taste the salty breeze. For days, months, even years, with Christina by my side.

But it was not to be. We would not return to Idan, even had I denied the mission and chosen dreams of the good life. Farther into space, safe from enemy harm though well before we might reach home, we encountered an allied Theabean warship. The transport docked and once aboard, another mysterious note was delivered, instructing us to transfer immediately to the provided interstellar craft, ready for launch with fuel enough to reach the Restricted Zone. Precisely what was needed to continue the mission. But the craft, provided by whom? An Association craft, with enemy insignia intact.

Troubled by this, I queried crewmembers as to the source of the instructions and the craft. Their responses were incredulous stares and at times laughter, as if the answer should be obvious. Dave and Christina were no wiser, but it seemed the crew knew something. None of them had an explanation, only more of their tricky Theabean logic, always answering questions with more questions, their favorite of which was to ask if I was joking.

Now months later, and still without an answer, again we plod through this maze in search of rituals to preserve our bodies. In a minute, we're almost there. Just past the end of this dank passage, as is the rest of this miserable craft, like all craft spawned by the humdrum minds of Association engineers. Intolerably plain, free from variation, not to mention a creature comfort or two. Our craft even lacks a name, given only a number, as they label every planet in range of conquest. Our enemy, the ultimate utilitarians.

Another trip through this winding maze, again my thoughts drift and keep scratching at the mystery. Not only who the mysterious provider could be, more nagging is how they knew one detail—the fuel required. Who else would know the distance? Of course the Association would, dispatching countless transports loaded with frozen rebels sentenced to the Restricted Zone. But no rebel knows that location, not until I broke into the enemy computer and printed the star-chart with exact coordinates. However, in the time since I stole that secret, I have shared its details with only one other person. Who else would know?

✳

Today we're doing sticks. Christina is feeling feisty, says it's time to spar. Sometimes we use short sticks, one-handed like swords, other times long staffs and plenty of acrobatics. Her choice today.

The workout compartment is padded, the walls, ceiling and floor puffy white, even the cabinets where contraptions of physical fitness are stored. A mild gravity inducer lets us pretend we're not in space, rather standing like normal people. But it's weak, so we have to strap on harnesses that keep us from being hurled too far. From waistbands we each wear, rubber cords extend to tracks in the walls that allow the tethers to follow our movements, controlled by sensors that scatter thin blue rays. Like being a fly caught in a spider's web.

Christina snaps a cabinet shut and tosses a wooden staff, then twirls hers, testing it. "Ready?"

Whack!

I've barely caught the thing when she strikes. I counterattack, whap whap, left right left. The tan shafts meet at right angles, forming a cross. She leaps and summersaults, staff twirling, tethers whir and squeal. I shift and meet her assault.

She pauses to stretch warming muscles, then launches at me like a banshee, braided pigtails slapping like whips. Her staff weaves in a hypnotic pattern that alternates side to side each time up and over.

Not a blow penetrates my defense. I dip, keep the stick low, and sweep to catch behind her knee. I spin her head to toe, and the swivel mounts squeal. Her staff comes out of nowhere and bangs my ear.

"Ow, that hurt." I stop to rub it.

Her twirling slows and she plants her feet in the puffy floor. She offers a gaze of possible sympathy, but it's just pretend. She grins and jabs my belly with her stick.

"Pussy."

Whack!

I strike so hard her stick goes flying, bounces off the wall, and returns to her like a boomerang. Back and forth, sticks blurring, tethers whir and squeal. We settle into a heated rhythm, sweat rising, and dive further into another good workout.

As we spar, I mention, "You never did tell me who rescued you."

"I did," she says and lands another blow. "With a little help from you, of course."

I counter, whack whack. "Me? I wasn't with you."

"You always help me," she says. "All I have to do is think of you."

"What," I tease, "that I'm a god?"

She smirks. "No, you goof, not like that. *You.* Remembering you brought with it everything we know, all we've talked about. That makes me powerful. The instant I felt your presence in the memory of you, I was transformed."

"You escaped all by yourself? I mean, just you and the memory of me."

"Sure."

Our sticks clash. We shift and strike again.

"But you're just one girl."

Her stick comes fast. *Whack!*

"Just because I choose a female body doesn't make me weak."

All efforts to parry barely keep up. "Sorry, didn't mean it that way. It's just, you know, hard to believe, one against…"

"Maybe hard for you. Takes an army to rescue your ass."

"No it didn't. Madison came to—"

Do I want to talk about that?

Her eyes pinch. "What did Madison do for you?"

We trade a few blows. "She came to get me, you know, along with Dave and Matt. No big deal."

"I never said it was."

Whack whack.

"It's not, she just helped me—"

"Helped you what?"

Whap whap, thwack.

"Just, uh, get away, that's all."

"Then what?" she asks.

"Then? You know, we came, ah, home, and…"

Crack!

"You fucked her!"

She snapped my staff in two.

"Not right away, it happened later." I toss one half and use what's left as a sword.

"Sure, that makes it all better." Her staff over one knee—*crack!*—she matches my feeble sword, though hers bristles with splinters that may draw blood.

I dodge her swipes and jabs. "Yeah, I mean no, I mean I'm sorry, she just—"

"So it's her fault."

"No, baby, it's just one of those things. It just happened."

"Nothing *just happens*. It happens because you make it happen."

"They screwed up my memory, I didn't—"

"That's a lousy excuse."

She's impossible to argue with. She always wins.

"I didn't mean to."

She postpones further assault and steps back. "You're not even a good liar. You intended to have sex with her, you wanted it to happen, and you *made it happen*. And you don't regret it. Am I close?"

She knows I can't dodge any question so blunt. What am I to say? Honesty, all I have left is honesty.

My weapon droops and I hang my head. "Yes."

"Good," she says, surprisingly calm. She comes closer, nudges my chin higher, and makes me look at her. "That's all I wanted to hear. I don't like what you've done, but I can't change the fact you did it, and neither can you. But denying your intentions is worse than anything those intentions make real, and it scares me to think you've forgotten that. I don't want you consumed by guilt, it will destroy you."

"So you're not angry?"

"I didn't say *that!*" A hold of my chin, she flings my head like a rock. I bounce off the wall and right back to her, then she smacks me around like a rag doll. "I'm totally pissed!"

Her stick bangs my ear—hard. Now that one hurt, more than anyone deserves.

"I said I'm sorry."

She pitches her half-a-staff. "I shouldn't be surprised. I know what a horn-dog you are."

Not sure if that makes me feel better or not. If only she would smile, now that would be good. No, more like a miracle.

"Christina, you don't need to be jealous."

"Too bad, *I am!* Why I'm so mad! I don't want to be jealous but I have no choice!"

"Of course you do. You can blame me for what I've done, sure, but you can't blame me for how you react to it. That's a choice, your choice, only yours. Don't argue, you know what I'm talking about."

It's difficult to gauge her hollow stare.

"Baby, please," I say. "I don't want you consumed by jealousy, it will destroy you."

She scowls something wicked. "Don't you try that turnaround trick on me, you bastard."

"I'm not! It's true, you don't have to be jealous, you know that. *It's a choice.*"

She stews, piercing me with a sharp glare, then she moves off to fetch her broken staff. "I know," she says, lips tight, fury restrained. "I don't have to be jealous, but I am. I can deal with many emotions and keep them from harming me, but jealousy is difficult, especially when it comes from love." She returns with her two sticks. "You have to understand, Adam, my love for you *is* that jealousy, and I'm not strong enough to fight it." She pushes the splintered halves together, trying to make her staff whole again.

"Christina, you are strong enough. You can manage this."

"Adam, if it was anyone else, I could. But you're not anyone else, you're my one and only Adam, forever. The thought of you desiring another kills me, and my love has nowhere else to go, only to jealousy. I don't like it any better than you do, but that's how love works."

"It doesn't have to work that way. It's a choice."

"Turn it around," she says. "What if I was with another? Hmm? What would be your choice?"

I pick at splinters of my broken staff, sharpening it for the flesh of anyone who dares to touch her.

"Yeah," she says, "about what I thought."

"Christina, you mean the world to me, you know that. You always have, you always will. I never meant to hurt you. What I have done will haunt me forever. I feel terrible."

"*Don't!*" One of her sticks comes flying at my head. "It's not my goal to make you feel terrible. Just stop doing what makes you guilty and makes me jealous!" She aims to crown me with her remaining stick. "It'll destroy both of us!"

I hunch lower, arms angled overhead. "I promise, it'll never happen again. Please forgive me."

"I might forgive you, maybe," she says. "Once Hell freezes over."

An eerie curse, considering the hell of dead forever begins with freezing. I may have discovered a fate worse than any hell, freezing, or even dead forever—Christina's eternal disdain. I cannot bear that. Ceasing to exist would be the only option in a universe without her.

As would a knight facing his queen, I drop to one knee and bow before her. "Then I shall freeze Hell. For you, my love. I would do anything for you. Anything."

A voice crackles from a nearby intercom. My buddy, Dave.

"Get a hold of something," he says.

I spot the speaker. "Why?"

In less than a second, the room goes from zero to sixty thousand. Our bodies rocket and crash into the padded wall.

*

After the rubber cords settle and the lights flicker back on, Christina opens a small panel near the hatch. She peers in to study a tiny screen and flashing red glow.

"Densioference failure," she says.

Over the intercom, Dave says, "You got forty seconds to make a decision. Don't waste it asking why."

"Options," I call.

"Maintain speed and overshoot the craft we nearly hit."

"Pro?"

"We get where we're going."

"Con?"

"They know where we're going."

"Option two."

"Match speed and hang back."

"Pro."

"They don't know."

"Con."

"Braking uses fuel."

"Fuel status."

"Last hard stop cancelled our trip home. Another and we're stuck out here between two hard places and no rocks."

"We can't make it back?"

"Twenty seconds, what's it gonna be?"

"Option three."

"Anything better you can dream up."

We can't let them know we're here. But we'll be stuck.

Stuck here with them.

"Match speed," I call.

"You sure?"

"Match it!"

"Okay. Grab hold of something."

Christina punches buttons in the open panel. Our harnesses reel in fast, rubber cords squealing, and we're pasted to the wall like flypaper. A deafening hum, torturous pitch, the lights go out and my guts get rearranged.

No telling if this body is even whole, or a clump of loose specks wanting to drift apart. Equilibrium returns and the hum subsides, giving way to sharp ringing in my ears and nausea enough to spew every organ and then some, all the way down to my toes.

✳

Christina and I yank on the rungs and pull ourselves along the passage to the cockpit. As we glide in through the hatchway, Dave swings his seat around to face us. He's strapped in nice and tight, but even so, he's plenty green himself.

"I think we're okay." He points to a wide display hanging from above. "I don't think they've spotted us. Yet."

I'm more interested in the sight floating over his console—a person maybe six inches tall. Not real and not moving much, it's a hologram of Matt. A mini-Matt, scrawny geek in baggy shorts and orange tee, red sneakers and stringy hair. Standing there with his arms crossed and that proud-of-himself grin.

I want to laugh. "What the hell is that?"

Dave snatches a device off the console and smothers it in both hands. The image of Matt disappears.

"Well?" I ask. "What's all that about?"

He hesitates. "Matt gave it to me before we left. You know, in case I got lonely. Figured once you found Chris…"

So the daring pilot actually has a soft spot.

"You miss him," I suggest.

"That wiener-head?" He fiddles with the device. A flash, dancing rays shoot out, and the hologram is back. He stares at the wavering image of Matt. "Yeah."

Christina says, "Isn't that just sweet. Give it a hug, you'll both feel better."

Dave switches it off and hides it away.

"Are you two done?" she asks. "What's our status?"

Dave turns his seat to face the wide display above. "They're just up ahead, but still a good distance. Too far to spot us, unless they try real hard."

A small dot flashes on the otherwise blank screen.

I ask, "Do you know where they're headed?"

He swings his seat around. "This empty corner of the galaxy? Where else would they be going?"

"We have to be sure. Have the computer extrapolate the trajectory."

"Already did," he says. "The Restricted Zone, just like us."

I study the wide display. Empty, dark and bare, except for the lone flashing dot.

"I want a closer look. What do you got?"

Dave indicates an eye scope projecting from a console to his left.

I rest my brow against the cool metal. "It's all black."

"Gimme a minute," he says. "I'm working on it."

A blurry image forms, little more than a glowing blob.

"Is that the best you can do?"

"I told you, I'm working on it. Hold up, man."

The fuzzy blob comes into focus. An Association cargo transport.

"What is it?" Christina asks.

I rise from the scope. "A load of our friends, dead forever."

"We have to stop them."

"No. We have to follow them and find out where the ice goes."

"We know where," she says. "The same place we're going, right?"

"But not which planet. It's important we know."

Dave says, "We ain't following anybody anywhere." He taps a gauge on his console. "Too bad this stuff doesn't put out fumes. I'd say about fifteen minutes before we're surfing cosmic dust."

The wide display shows only the flashing dot, alone in a vast nothing.

"We'll have to hitch a ride."

Dave puts his brow to the scope. "I'm not seeing the welcome mat."

"Get your cheesy jacket."

"That penis outfit?" He chuckles. "That's a good one, you're a riot."

His hair is still dark, thanks to the Association. Good luck finding banana hair dye aboard any of their craft. A few months growth has left us both shaggy around the ears, nothing outrageous, but well outside the parameters of a regulation goon haircut. We'll have to say the only personal trimmer on board malfunctioned. Shit happens during space travel, even to Association agents obsessed with helmet hair.

Dave is aghast. "You're serious?"

Christina says, "Adam, what are you thinking?"

I point to the lone flashing dot. "We're boarding that cargo transport.

We're following the ice. We're going to find our missing friends."

"You make it sound so simple."

"Intentions are simple. What happens in the process of executing those intentions is another story, I know, but it always starts with a simple intention. All I have for now."

Dave says, "Dress like a goon for another weak plan. And what about Chris? Our prisoner, or what?"

"That's stupid," she says. "What are agents doing with a prisoner all this way from Orn?"

She has a point. A female rebel with a pair of intelligence officers will raise suspicion.

I ask Dave, "Do we have one of those recorder things?"

"You mean, for typing what people say?"

"Right."

"That's weird, Adam."

"It's just a gadget. Besides, it's not for you, it's for Christina."

"For me?" she asks. "What do you mean?"

"No," Dave says. "It's weird because we *do* have one. I was wondering why. I never thought you'd ask for it."

Christina scowls. "What do I look like, your secretary?"

"Baby, lighten up. It's just an act."

She studies me for a moment, then her face begins to loosen. "Oh, so I *am* your secretary." She gets it. She gets to play too.

"Special Agent Bob and his associate have an inspection to conduct, and all events must be documented."

✳

Fuel is low and the clock is ticking. Dave can hate the plan all he likes, but it worked before. Again we will masquerade as Association agents, with shiny black jackets, turtlenecks and slacks, boots and helmet hair to match, black on black. B-O-B. Disgusting, but duty calls.

The women of Orn-3 have their own look, different from the Bobs, though still a brand of uninspired fashion suited to drones. And for Christina's disguise, we didn't have to search far. In a storage cabinet aft of the cockpit, we found the uniform of an Association clerk, knee-high skirt, thin tie and simple blouse, even a black wig fashioned into a bun that effectively hides her rusty hair, otherwise sure to give us away. Armed with the recording device, she makes a decent match for the real thing.

Adding to our means of deception, there is our craft, manufactured by the Association. Our mysterious provider knew we would engage the enemy. And for a mission to collect information rather than a tally of opponents defeated, better to engage in deception than to engage in battle. The craft, the recording device, and now her costume. Someone knows of my needs better than I do, and knew of those needs months before now. Dave and Christina are not so concerned. They are content to find the items our scheme requires, down to shoes in her size. Call me paranoid, but it's all too bizarre.

In our costumes and back to the cockpit, Dave brings our craft within range of the cargo transport. As expected, we are immediately hailed. From a speaker on the communications terminal, a computerized voice says, "State identity and intent."

Dave leans in on a gooseneck microphone and reads from a paper he holds. "Association Intelligence operative alpha-zen-signa-talha-neutro."

I muffle the microphone in one hand. "Where'd you get that?"

"I thought you wrote it," he says.

Why does everyone think I write everything? I snatch the sheet and discover a list of Association security codes. Where did this come from? I didn't write this.

"Part of the plan, eh?" His smile grows. "I guess it's not so weak after all."

While I fumble through my thoughts for an answer I'm sure will never come, the computerized voice responds, "Confirmed."

I rattle the paper. "Dave, where did you get this?"

"It was in front of the flight log. I thought you put it there."

"I didn't put anything anywhere."

From the speaker, the voice says, "Prepare to dock."

Was it that easy? I thought we had to deceive them. Maybe we have, but it sure didn't take much. Is fate shining that favorable light again? I may not want the gift. All the best light in the universe has its opposite—the dark shadows where it cannot reach.

✷

As we close the distance, the cargo transport grows to a sprawling metropolis. Scattered points of light flow from countless portals, set against the darkened backdrop of space. Getting closer I expect a collision by now, but its tremendous size confounds the eye, and all efforts to gauge distance are thwarted. Projections short and tall rise above a grid like crisscrossing streets, intersecting at precise right angles, not a cusp, slant nor flare, a giant slab of perfect squares.

Dave brings our craft underneath the beast and it consumes the forward view. The backdrop of starlight is gone, only a city block moving in to swat us like a gnat. From the transport's belly, two halves of a giant hatchway begin sliding apart. Dave takes us up and into an equally tremendous interior with gangways running all directions and countless docking ports, colored beacons flickering, but no sign of other craft.

A bright strobe guides our approach, leading to flashing red and blue lights that string along at our sides. The jagged course forces us to nudge sideways at times, as if following the path of a lightning bolt laid out flat. As we taxi along the trail of flashing beacons, apprehension grows. An army of Bobs a thousand strong could be waiting beyond the next door. Was this such a good idea?

We reduce speed and nose into a docking station. Huge mechanical arms reach out and latch onto our craft. The cockpit shudders and instruments go wild.

Dave peers out at the spider-like array of mechanized limbs holding our craft as prey. "We're not going anywhere unless they say so." He points out the forward view. "Graviscopic clamps. About like being glued to a small star."

Christina adjusts her wig for the twentieth time. "Adam, are you sure this was such a good idea?"

I'm fond of being one with my love, but this is a bit much. "Why did you say that?" I ask, almost accusatory out of frustration. My seemingly naked mind needs to stop sharing every thought, which might include some of my deepest fears, possibly even a few private desires.

She says, "All anyone has to do is look at you."

Smart-ass. But she's right. If I could somehow unplug this body from this mind, I might dim the neon sign advertising my fright.

"I'll be honest since lying is useless. You'll just look at me."

"And the honest answer is?"

"No, I'm not sure. But I am sure of one thing." Dave is up, eager to go, while I sit here staring out at the mechanized spider holding us hostage. "I want it to be a good idea."

✳

Out the hatchway, we're forced to grab the railing or risk floating away. The cargo transport, while a considerable mass, is nowhere near that of a planet and its gravity.

A racket is coming, alternating clanks and a whirring sound. A robot approaches along the gangway. The thing is shiny metal, its head a square box, arms and legs little more than thin conduit. It whirs and lifts a foot, then clanks when it snaps to the deck. It wears ridiculously large gray boots and carries a rack holding more of the same boots.

"Your footwear," the robot says, computerized voice all the personality of a rock.

Dave and Christina accept the oversized boots like it's business as usual.

"What's this?" I ask.

The robot comes loose from the gangway and soars upward, becoming a distant speck, then gone.

Dave passes me a pair. "Like robo-boy said, your footwear."

"For what?"

"Care to end up out there?" He indicates the open space, big enough for craft the size of city blocks to maneuver and dock. Without gravity, navigating small compartments is one thing. Out there, I wouldn't make it back for years, if ever.

Part of what makes the boots so big is that they go over my regular boots, but not a thin gray skin. The hard plastic shells are thick, like ski boots that reach just below my knees. Inside each ankle are two blinking lights, alternating yellow and orange.

Dave and Christina look ridiculous in their boots, like they have feet twice normal size. Floating just above the gangway, Dave clicks his heels together, the tiny lights beam solid green, and he snaps to the deck. Christina does the same, but I seem to have forgotten this drill. And busy fumbling with the footwear, I've let go of the railing. Now Dave and Christina are twenty feet down and drifting away. *I'm* drifting away, like a fleck of dirt chased by a vacuum cleaner.

Christina looks up at me. "Just click your heels."

"Then what happens?"

"You'll be back down here where you belong."

I'd have better luck wishing on a star. Three, six, twelve times, click after click, nothing happens, and I'm lost without a tether, off to begin life as a space-buoy.

In the next instant, Christina is at my side.

"How did..."

She throws her arms around me. "They work both ways, you goof." She angles her toes down, and down we go. We make impact and Dave taps his boot to mine. A faint hum is followed by a sucking squelch, the lights go green, and I'm glued to the deck.

"Gravity boots?" I ask.

"Not exactly," Dave says. "Graviscopic, there's a difference. Something to do with geometry."

I'm content to be good friends with something solid. "I'll take your word for it."

Dave marches away, clank clank. "Let's find some real people, more than just robots."

Difficult to imagine any crew fitting that description. I was thinking more like ornery bastard robots expert at torture. Life as a space-buoy might not be so bad after all.

✳

The rodent maze of passages in our craft was simple compared to the insides of this cargo transport. Dave leads the way—not that he knows where he's going, but then, neither do I—along narrow stairwells and flimsy ladders leading up to a windowed bulkhead that oversees the docking bay. It could be a control center or the bridge, likely staffed by those more-than-robot people Dave is convinced we need to find.

The footwear takes some getting used to. Not quite the same as planet-bound, but close enough. And they're not exactly magnetic, either. The

boots do not really stick to the metal, as the effort to lift each foot is mini-
mal. They simply have increased affinity for nearby mass and seek the deck
after each step. Or, as Christina demonstrated, decreased affinity—outright
repulsion—when pointing your toes the right way.

At the highest level, stairs end at a platform some hundred feet across
that hangs like a shelf over the docking bay. Higher are windows, details
beyond dark and unknown. Below the windows are double-paneled doors
like an elevator, except five times as wide.

Dave marches to the doors and the two halves pull apart to slide open.
He turns back and waves. "This way." The passage beyond matches the
width of the doors, and twenty paces ahead is another set of double doors.
Behind us, the panels shut with a boom and those ahead slide open. Once
the second set is behind us—boom, they seal tight.

A flat-pitched horn sounds, then a disembodied voice. "Approaching
system, prepare for deceleration. Approaching system…"

Not that again.

Dave scans quickly and points to a wall. "This one." He plants his
back flat. Christina and I brace ourselves against the wall just in time
to experience what pancakes feel like. That is, if pancakes had internal
organs. Maybe jelly on top, now permeating the spongy dough.

Moments later the g-force yields to normal inertia, our mass now
matched to the decelerated transport. I point out, "What happened to
gliding in and conserving fuel?" The surprise I don't vocalize is how Dave
knew which wall faced our direction of travel.

"If you're on a budget," Dave says. "Hellbent on organizing the galaxy
doesn't make them patient, or give a shit how much fuel it takes. Wasteful
isn't on their list of harmful deviations."

Haul ass to the next conquest and slam on the brakes. Makes perfect
sense if you're the Association. So many worlds, so little time.

Dave peels himself off the wall and continues through the next set of
double doors, then heads for another pair. Christina and I follow, and again
behind us—boom, the doors slide shut, sealed tight.

I turn back and check a control box near the last doorway. "Dave, you
sure about this?" The button next to the red light does nothing. There's
no handle or knob on either smooth panel, only a thin seam between the
two.

"Don't be such a chicken." He marches forward, clank clank, past the next set of sliding open doors. "This goes up," he calls from the next compartment. "Get your tail in here before it shuts." He stands near a spiral staircase.

The doors start closing. I dash in and nearly lose a drumstick.

Above, the spiraling stairs rise into darkness.

Christina asks, "Adam, what's wrong?"

Already up a few steps, Dave turns back. "Yeah, man, what's with you anyhow? This was your idea, wasn't it?"

"Doesn't mean I like it."

He comes down. "What's to worry about? We got our stupid costumes." He points up at the spiraling steps and the blackness beyond. "So maybe a hundred goons up there, big deal. Bullshit our way through like always."

Some call it butterflies. The nest I swallowed is no cocoon, and now hatched, thousands of serrated exoskeleton legs scrape at the lining of my stomach.

"Come on," Dave says. "It'll work just like last time. We wouldn't be this far if it didn't, right?"

"When did you get so confident?" I ask.

He smiles. "I got you, with that kooky imagination. What'll it be this time? Secret mission to root out spies? Plot to overthrow the empire?" He chuckles.

"What if I come up dry?"

He shrugs. "I'll tell a good joke."

We're doomed.

✳

Our boots clank clank, round and round, up the spiraling steps. The stairs end at a spacious control center. Across the darkness, countless screens hang from above. On consoles from floor to ceiling are lights flashing, gauges gauging, and bar graphs rising and falling. No shortage of activity, except for anything human. The place is deserted.

Deeper in the room, a long counter wraps around three sides, lined with computer screens at a comfortable viewing angle and keyboards below. Hanging above the center section is a wide display that presents a diagram of the Solar system, complete with details of the planets, trajectories into orbit, and delivery schedules.

"Where's the crew?" Christina asks.

From out of nowhere comes the bedroom voice of a sultry female. "I handle affairs. My superior capacity exceeds any crew."

I scan the darkened room and beyond. No sign of anyone.

"Who said that?" I ask.

"I did," the steamy voice replies, but still I cannot pinpoint from where it emanates. It seems to come from everywhere.

"Okay. So who are you?"

"Vee why sixty-nine-hundred series, model dee." The disembodied voice not only drips erotic suggestion, it conveys exaggerated pride, like we should all be impressed.

Dave asks, "Why's it sound like a hooker?"

"Maybe these guys get lonely in space."

"It's just a computer," Christina says, then asks Dave, "And how would you know what a hooker sounds like?"

He shrugs. "I saw a movie once…"

I start for the U-shaped counter. "It'll know where the ice goes."

The sexy voice announces, "Model Dee knows everything, and is capable of performing any number of complex tasks."

Dave chuckles. "Dee Dee, the conceited hooker."

I turn back. "The fabulous joke you had in mind?"

That shut him up.

"Computer." Christina approaches the screen. "Where is the crew?"

The seductive voice responds, "Organic electrochemical assistance has been eliminated."

Has this thing gone mad and slaughtered everyone?

"Eliminated how?" I ask.

"File restricted."

I turn to Dave. "You still got that sheet?"

"Toss a hall-pass that good?" He pulls it from a pocket and hands it over.

"Computer," I call. "Unlock all file restrictions." I study the sheet of security codes. "Association Intelligence operative delta-mantro-etley-ciro-zulu."

"Specify file range."

"The one about the crew."

"Specify file number."

For crying out loud, machines are supposed to make life *easier*.

I play its game. "Unlock file catalog per authorization. Search catalog for direct and relational matches to keywords and every variant when combined as phrase, crew, and eliminated, and how. Unlock all files in search results."

"Task complete."

"The crew, eliminated how?"

"Association directive 756915445862, Relocation and Rebirth program, subsection 247694. Upon completion of phase 236, final shipments of silicium containment fields are to be delivered exclusively via automated transports."

"No crew?"

"Never was," Christina says. "David's right, you're getting tense over nothing. Nobody's on board, and I'm starting to wonder why we're even here."

"Negative," the computer says. "Sensors detect organic electrochemical presence in section—"

"We know, sweetie," Christina says. "We're your organics."

I point out terminals to the left. "Dave, find out all you can." And to the right. "You too, Christina, while I talk to this thing."

Hanging above the center section, the main screen is simple vector graphics, flickering green lines against black. The diagram focuses on the inner planets, showing each orbit as a numbered circle. Starting off-screen and leading to the planets, curving lines of trajectory target each and wrap around like lassos thrown from beyond. Sol-3 seems to be the planet of most interest, having far more trajectories than the others. Four is next, very few aimed at two and five, and none target the innermost planet.

"Computer," I call. "What is our destination?"

"Sol-3, Sol-4."

"What about two and five?"

"Phase 236 complete, no further deliveries to Sol-2. Phase 624 complete, no further deliveries to Sol-5."

I call to Dave, "Find out what these phases are."

"Already have," he says, nose in the screen. "Nobody'd last long on Sol-2."

"Why?" I clank over to his terminal. On the screen are cargo manifests next to a frame with planetary details. "No atmosphere?"

His nose wrinkles. "Plenty, just not our flavor. C-O-two wrapped in sulfur dioxide overcast, and I don't mean patchy morning fog. Overcast forever, a thousand times any planet. Not that it matters. High of nine hundred and a hundred percent chance of acid rain, you'd need one hell of an umbrella. Except the pressure would fold it, and you, before you even knew what happened."

I scan the cargo manifests. "What goes there?"

"Nothing now, they're done. Some equipment did, psychoactive something or other. The weird part is the planet didn't start that way. It was terraformed, except backward. They pumped the atmosphere full of greenhouse gases and locked in the heat. The place is like an oven now."

"To melt the ice?"

"Hell no. Melt and then what? No one could live there."

"Then what's the point?"

"Maybe hide something. Finding it, at least in a regular body, is going to be difficult."

Christina says, "I think it goes to Sol-3."

I move to her terminal. "What do you got?"

"Phase 17 was exterminating giant reptiles." She studies the screen. "Widespread iridium impacts, osmium tetroxide poisons anything that breathes, all dead in a week."

Dave says, "And plenty millennia while the fallout clears. Nobody's living there either."

"No," Christina says, studying further. "Something here about altered decay rates, not sure how. They accelerated the half-life of everything. Hot for a while, but it was done early. Emissions have already dropped to nominal." She looks up. "Safe to inhabit now."

"Doesn't mean any ice goes there," Dave says. "What about Sol-4? Something here about primitive life…"

"Three has more room," she says, back to studying her screen. "And the extermination is a clue. Wipe out an indigenous species to make way for one that isn't."

"How's it a clue?" I ask.

She looks up from the screen. "Wherever the ice goes there has to be bodies, right? Imagine running for your life chased by hungry reptiles ten times your size."

Not a pleasant thought. Beyond the obvious—sharp teeth and snapping bone as I become lunch—just being near any reptile is cause to run. Snakes and lizards give me the creeps.

"They'd eat the bodies," she says. "And without bodies, we might wander back home." A thought strikes her. "Which isn't such a bad idea." She leaves the terminal and faces the wide screen. "Computer…"

"What are you doing?" I ask.

She raises a finger, hang on, then back to the screen. "Computer, turn around and go home."

I get between her and the screen. "No. We have to follow the ice."

"I've had enough of your adventures."

I'm getting the definite impression her meaning extends well beyond the mission.

"Clarify home," the computer says.

"Where you came from," Christina replies.

The computer babbles, "I come from where I was. I was there. There was here. Here will be there…"

I reach out to her. "Christina, don't do this."

"The admiral can send troops better equipped. We're out of fuel, we're not even armed. We're helpless."

"That's not our mission. You read the instructions. We're not leading a battalion to meet the enemy head-on."

"The orders didn't say we couldn't."

"And didn't say we should. Only that we reach the destination, not blow up the place."

"Then what?" she asks. "I take that absence of specifics as liberty to improvise. I'd prefer fighting to all your sneaking around."

"I wasn't—"

"Calculations complete," the computer announces. "Stand by, going home."

The screen goes blank. No, it can't. Not after all this effort, the time, the distance. Don't.

"Task complete," the computer says. "We are here."

"Here?" Christina steps toward the screen. "Where is here?"

"Where we are," the computer says. "Which, according to calculations, is home. Where we are."

"Are you an idiot?" Christina asks.

"I am incapable of idiocy, but I will be happy to perform a simulation…"

"Shut up!" Christina rips the wig off her head. "I'm done with you."

"Understood," the computer says. "Enjoy your time in space."

"So can this." She pitches the wig. "No one here to fool anyway." She throws down the recording device, it rebounds off the deck, and shattered fragments drift apart in zero G. She stomps away, clank clank clank.

I chase after her. "Christina, this is important, you know that. Important to me, to you, to all our friends. We have to save them."

She whirls around. "And Madison? That sure was important."

"I said I'm sorry already." I reach out to her. "Christina, listen…"

She dodges my hand. "Don't you touch me."

"Okay, I won't, but we can't desert our friends."

"Chris," Dave says, "I know this'll sound like a total guy, but oh well. We're halfway across the galaxy, who knows where, and who knows what's next. You gotta put it aside for now."

"He's right, baby."

She aims a sharp finger, sharper eyes. "Don't you *baby* me. You're not charming your way out of this one."

"I'm not! Some things are more important. The mission, our friends. Christina, you have a duty to this the same as I do."

She looks away. "I know."

"Then stop it."

Her eyes dart to mine. "Careful."

"All right, I'll be careful. I won't say anything more about it, if you don't."

"Don't think for one minute you're off the hook."

"Whip me with a wet noodle all you want—once we're done."

She smirks, no laughter yet, but still a miracle. "Your lousy humor won't save you either."

"I want to save *them*." I point to the screen, which has returned to a diagram of the Solar system with planets and trajectories into orbit.

She stares at me, then at the screen. At last, she nods.

"All right then." I step toward the screen and call, "Computer, where is the ice?"

"Clarify ice."

"Frozen water, cold…"

"Do you thirst for a refreshing beverage?"

"No! Don't be stupid."

"I am incapable of stupidity, but I will be happy to perform a simulation…"

Christina suggests, "Try the proper term."

Sure, blame it on operator error.

"Containment fields," I call. "Where are they stored?"

"I do not know," the computer says. "I am stupid."

"I said *don't!*"

Dave stares at the screen, shaking his head. "Is this the best we get after years of research?"

The computer announces, "One-hundred seventy-five thousand, six-hundred fifty-nine years."

"Oh?" I say. "Now you're smart?"

"I am incapable of performing otherwise, programmed with superior intellect at inception and destined to remain so indefinitely. The stupidity was a simulation serving to boost your self-esteem."

"Swell, I feel just dandy now. So answer the question already. Where are the containment fields?"

"Cargo bay access may be obtained via section ten, compartment seventeen."

"How do we get there?"

"One one zero degrees seven C hexagazule, eight eight degrees one F gazule, one nine—"

"Stop! Display directions from here."

The wide screen clears to black, then flickering lines begin filling in, horizontal and vertical, not a single bend or curve, intersections galore, more and more, the diagram becomes an overwhelming tangle so dense it could be a swatch of fabric under a microscope. Once complete, a bolder green line shoots through the mess and creates a path ending at a flashing dot.

Dave studies the screen, his finger swiping air as he traces the route. "I can find it."

He sure knows a lot about this ship. Or thinks he does. I'm not so sure any of us want to know. The computer's assistance could be another simulation, all sincerity a fabrication, and in reality, the device is luring us into a trap.

✳

Dave leads the way, checking numbers posted at regular intervals—D-14, E-29—like searching a parking garage. He moves at a brisk pace as if it all makes perfect sense. Makes me wonder. Our route winds through corridors large and small, up ladders, down stairs, then along a platform at the back end of the docking bay.

The next passage is dark and misty, brightened only by faint light farther ahead. The deeper we go, the colder it gets. Our breath thickens, adding to clumps of vapor hanging in the chilly air. Frosty conduits dangle from bulkheads like snakes in a darkening forest, and something snaps underfoot, little hard flecks that crack open and spread slime, then send up a diseased stench. In the dark, there's no telling what litters the floor. We could be crossing a minefield of hard-shelled space beetles.

The passage ends at another running left and right. Weak lamps cast a dingy yellow glow across the walls and floor, dusty and corroded, but at least the way is clear of any creepy crawlers. Until the lights go out. The riveted panels are stained rusty-orange and smell of ancient oil. Anything to displace the stench of a dumpster, which grows stronger the deeper we penetrate the guts of this monster. You would think our conformist enemy—ultimate utilitarians hellbent on organizing the galaxy—might care more about cleanliness. Maybe, if not too busy mopping up all that filthy free thinking.

Dave says left, which fades into darkness the same as right. The only comfort is knowing this isn't one of those dreams when you lose your shoes and are forced to walk barefoot over any number of things slimy or sharp. I check my big gray boots and make sure every latch is tight.

Along the corridor, metal hatches line one wall and continue for a distance. The end never comes, forever a swatch of black ahead, but as we move along, weak light from above bleeds into view, saving us from total darkness.

Dave stops at one of the hatches. "Here we go." A lamp shines down on stencil lettering that reads Section 10, Compartment 17. Dave made finding it look easy, and again I have to wonder if he didn't know where it was to begin with.

The handle is stiff and cold. Together, Dave and I lean on the lever and bust the latch loose. The hatch creaks open and slurps air as the compartments equalize. Inside is even colder, and the clouds of our breath linger. The cargo bay stretches out beyond view, stocked full of corrugated metal containers, like train cars without wheels. Row after row of the long boxes are stacked high, extend back some distance, and fade into the mist.

At one end of each container is a pair of doors. I approach the nearest container and yank on the handle. The metal is like a shard of ice that burns my palm. I warm my hands and try again. The latch snaps, hinges creak, and the door yawns open. Vapor pools at my feet and whooshes past, then a wall of arctic air smacks me in the face.

I step in, one hand out to darkness, and ease toward an eerie blue glow coming from the center of a frozen block. They all have the faint glow, blocks stacked up, across and fading back, deeper into the container.

"Adam, careful." A silhouette in the open doorway, Christina stands clutching herself and shivering.

Past her, Dave works at warming his hands. "It's too cold. Let's go."

I reach out to one of the cubes. My hand sticks to the frosty surface as the moisture on my palm freezes. Caught in transparency, jittering blue arcs swirl through a constellation of ashes locked in ice. As though the victim is searching, hoping to understand, where have I gone, what has happened to me, how do I get out. I am here, if only they could see me, hear me, and know that I will help. But there are no eyes to stare back, no ears to listen, no mouth to scream. Only ashes chased by a soul. A lonely I, terrified. And this I... I want to cry.

A startling racket erupts outside the container. Gravity is returning, tugging on organs that have spent months hovering inside my torso. I rip my hand from the icy surface and hurry out. Equipment has actuated, creaking and groaning out of its slumber. Suspended from rails above, a hoist moves over a container and latches on to the top portion. Other devices plunge down and attack fasteners securing the lid. The hoist pulls the cover off and hurls it out of view, then another crane moves in to snatch a cube, lifts it out and carts it away, jerking across the ceiling toward a waiting conveyor belt. The crane comes back and fetches another cube, another and another, delivering dozens to the belt. More cranes join the effort, a noisy clamor of machinery jerking and sliding across the ceiling as countless cubes are loaded onto the conveyor.

A loud snap is followed by a creaking groan, then a roar of air. A bluster storms into the cargo bay. An exterior hatch is opening. The compartment is decompressing. My heart jumps—we'll be whooshed out to space. But we're no longer in space. Past the opening is blue sky, the atmosphere of a planet.

The initial blast settles and the compartment equalizes with outside. But frantic wind remains, tousling my hair and jacket. We're cruising at a tremendous altitude where the air is thin, difficult to breathe.

"Let's get out of here," Dave calls from across the compartment.

"Not yet," I holler over the bluster. "I want to see what happens." I weave between containers, past machinery, and closer to the open hatch. Blasts of wind threaten to suck me out. My lungs pull deep, scrounging for oxygen.

"Adam, careful." Christina keeps a safe distance from the open hatch.

Outside is daylight. Down below, beyond wisps of vapor streaming past, ocean spreads out to the horizon. Gusts buffet hard as I creep closer to the edge.

The conveyer actuates, and the belt begins carting ice toward the open hatch.

They just toss them out?

One after another, cubes drop off the rolling belt and out the hatchway. The network of cranes fetches more cubes, the conveyer gains speed, and truckloads of frozen victims are simply chucked out the back door.

The craft settles into its course, descending no lower, and continues dumping ice. Wind knocks me every direction and steals all breath away. A narrow alcove near the open hatch offers some protection from the storm. I crouch low and wedge in tight, safer from the gusts, and plant my boots flat to the floor for maximum hold, then peer around the corner and down.

Tumbling blocks plummet to the surface, bursting puffs of sea-foam as the ocean swallows countless victims. Cubes scatter, riding swells until melting and gone. Then another splashdown, another, the flotilla of glistening squares restocked as each vanishes.

"You've seen enough," Dave calls from across the compartment. "Let's go!"

"Almost." I look down at the ocean, what I'd really like to see better.

Christina shouts, "Adam, *don't!*"

I exit my body. Free to roam, I select a better vantage point and assume it instantly, putting my bodiless nothing just above the ocean surf.

*

Rolling swells rise and fall, cresting foamy white, and water stretches to the horizon. Waves slap gently, and a mild wind rumbles. The temperature is appealing, warmed by sunshine that burns past a thin wash of high clouds. Far above, the cargo transport is a tiny speck from which a string of tumbling ice flows, growing larger as they fall. Arriving blocks smack the surf and dive deep, then snap up like corks. Small icebergs dipping and rising, each block resurfaces smoother and shrinking, dissolving in the sun-warmed water.

Is it my imagination? A melting cube pops up and it's been whittled down to the shape—I think, for a fleeting instant—of a person. The ice looked like a sculpture of a man crouched with arms crossed over his head, trying to protect himself. Then it's gone.

Another cube lands and sends up a foamy spray. The icy block plunges deep and then shoots higher, bobbing a few times until settling half-submerged. Again the melting is rapid, and it's not my imagination. The thawing ice, for an instant, took on the shape of a person with arms raised, reaching for help, an escape, a hope, a life.

I can't watch this.

I snap back to my body.

*

Something is wrong. The wrong body? Still wedged in the narrow alcove, boots planted to the deck, but this body is slumped over like a rag doll, coughing between gasps for breath. I'm lightheaded and can't focus. Has someone clobbered me? No—the thin air. I've pushed the limits of this body's endurance. We have to get out of here.

Back on my feet and stumbling dizzily, I fight the slapping gusts, stagger across the cargo bay, and struggle to reach the hatch we entered by. The noisy equipment keeps tossing cubes out the back.

Nobody's at the hatch. There's no one anywhere in the cargo bay, that I can see. Only the clamor of cranes sliding across the ceiling and the conveyor throwing out ice. The thin air, they couldn't breathe, they must have gone for the hatch. I pull the handle but it's no use. I bang on the hatch door but there is no answer. Another push, it doesn't budge, I'm at the edge of consciousness. One surge, all that remains, I shove hard. The latch snaps, air whooshes past, and I strain to clear the door against a torrent wanting to yank it closed. I slip through, hinges groan, and the hatch slaps shut with one last slurp of escaping air.

✳

Flat on my back, the corridor walls converge overhead, spinning and flapping. Musty air creeps into these lungs, not the best flavor, but I won't complain. After a few deep breaths, the hazy view begins to sharpen, and the swirling walls slow and settle.

Something is tickling my ear. Brushing against it, or… nibbling? I shift and look to find a thumb-sized blob black and brown, too close to get in focus. *Crunchy space beetle!* I'm on my feet and the scarab beast skitters away before I've any chance to stamp its guts to slime.

Then I remember, like waking from a nightmare to realize it's over. Except it's not.

"Computer," I call. "Stop this."

"Clarify this," the sultry voice responds.

"Turn everything off and shut the cargo bay."

"Your request is not possible."

"Why not?"

"Everything would include Model Dee. I cannot turn myself off."

"Fine, keep yourself turned on. Just stop the machines in the cargo bay."

I scan the corridor. No sign of Dave or Christina.

"Your request is not possible," the computer says.

"Why the hell not?"

Where is this idiotic bitch? I'm going to rip out her guts, every last wire.

"Devices cannot be turned off when they are not turned on."

"They're already off?"

"Affirmative. Delivery number one is complete. Now commencing delivery number two."

The craft rockets to the stratosphere. My knees fold and I hit the deck butt first, then flat on my back, guts an instant later when they catch up and snap into place. The corners of my mouth reach for my ears, somewhere around the back of my head. I want to scream but nothing comes out, or past the speed of sound it was left behind.

After a few minutes of melding me with the floor, the engines throttle back. The craft keeps climbing, but the acceleration eases to manageable. At least my rubberized face snaps back into place. I hope. Otherwise it's life as a clown.

"Computer," I call. "Where are my friends?"

"Clarify friends."

"The other organics."

"Sensors detect organic electrochemical presence on level twenty-three, section eighteen, compartment two-hundred seventy-two."

"How do I get there?"

"Zero degrees four seven hexagazule, eight eight—"

"Map, map, I need a map."

"Where shall I direct its display?"

I scan the corridor. No terminals.

"Where's the nearest to this location?" I ask.

"Zero degrees one E gazule—"

"No! I don't understand any of that."

"If you will refer to the Association manual of standard weights and measures, chapter four-hundred thirty-eight, section seventy—"

"How could I without a terminal?"

Silence. Then, "Your responses are illogical. Travel to and boarding this vessel requires knowledge of standard navigation and distance."

"I had a few files deleted, if you know what I mean."

"Restore lost data from backup copy."

Life as a computer would be so much easier.

"I'd be glad to, if any backup existed."

"All systems require a minimum of one backup. However, it is strongly advised that multiple copies be maintained."

Arguing with a machine is useless.

Acceleration reaches that undetectable equilibrium, my body gets lighter, and I begin to float free. Click, click, clicking my heels, I finally get it right, the boots emit their squelching slurp, and I'm snapped to the deck.

"Dee, let's try a new trick."

"Clarify trick."

"Never mind. Just tell me—I'm outside section ten, compartment seventeen, with my back to the hatch. What direction am I facing?"

"One one zero degrees to stern."

"Can I talk to you in any corridor?"

"Model Dee has no interface to organic electrochemical entity's ambulatory, vocal, or psychic functions."

Well that's a relief. I've a hard enough time keeping my thoughts private.

"What I mean is, can you hear me and respond?"

"In any corridor."

"Good. Walk me through from here."

✳

Around the corner and twenty paces is a wall-mounted display screen. Talk about making the simple difficult. Curious exploration would have found it faster than Model Dee's guided tour.

"Dee, what planet did we just visit?"

"Sol-3," she says.

"Show it to me."

The screen switches to a view of the receding world. One half is in shadow, facing the dark of space. Across the sunlit portion, white clouds twist and curl over oceans vibrant blue and coastlines brown and green. At each pole, sprawling ice caps bend like bowls that cradle the globe. The fading world looks like a blue marble with white swirls. A moon soars past, its barren gray landscape pocked with craters. The craft gains speed, the planet and moon shoot away fast, and then both shrink until gone. The display returns to a view of blackness dotted with starlight.

"Where are the other organics?" I ask.

"Sensors detect organic electrochemical presence on level twenty-three, section eighteen, proceeding through corridor thirty-seven B."

"Coming this way?"

"Negative. Distance increasing."

What are they doing? My longtime issue with trust is coming around for another visit.

"Let's see that map."

The screen clears, then it fills with a tangle of routes and intersections, ridiculous, and a bold green line weaves through the mess, ending at a flashing dot.

"I'll never figure this out. You'll have to guide me from here."

"Are you facing the screen?" Dee asks.

"Yes."

"Turn right one quarter."

✳

Like a blind man led through his darkness, I spend a time following Dee's omnipresent voice, turning in and out of corridors, some for a distance, others only a few steps, up ladders and down stairs, past another platform above the docking bay, and arrive in a wide hallway that ends at double doors labeled level 23, section 18. However, unlike all others up to this point, these doors do not automatically open when I approach.

"Dee, open the doors."

"Your request is not possible."

"Why not?"

"Superuser has taken ownership of control files and revoked administrator access."

"You're part of the system. Use system permission."

"Superuser has limited system permissions to sustaining life support, climate control, and illumination."

From my pocket, I pull out the sheet of Association security codes and call out every last one. For each password, Model Dee replies, "Denied."

"What about sensors?" I ask.

"System permissions are granted to read and relay sensor information to all users."

"Where are the organics now?"

"Sensors detect organic electrochemical presence has diverged. Two signatures stationary, level twenty-three, section eighteen, compartment two-hundred-eleven. One signature proceeding through corridor thirty-seven B."

"I'm not moving."

"Affirmative."

"Dee, how many organics are there?"

"Sensors detect a total of four organic electro—"

"Four? Who?"

"Identity unknown. Required boarding forms EL-718 not on file for any of the current crew. Model Dee will issue citation of punishable offense and forward to authority."

"I don't care about that. I want to know who, and when."

"Signature one detected departure mark six-thousand nine-hundred seventy-two. Signatures two, three, and four detected departure mark seven-thousand sixty-eight."

"Someone boarded before us."

"Clarify us."

"Forget that. Tell me who boarded first."

"Identity unknown. Required boarding forms—"

"Screw your forms! Can't you tell me anything else?"

Silence. Then, "Sensors detect organic electrochemical signature one is carrying a rifle-class pulsed wave inducer."

✳

The first day it hurts, but near the end, the body adjusts. By the second day— the interval a guess, having no clock other than biological—stomach pain fades and weakness begins. Climbing ladders and searching corridors for another route into the restricted section only consumes what little energy remains. They say dehydration is the first to kill, irreparable damage at least, long before any lack of food, which some believe a body could manage for weeks. But not water. Not that I'm experiencing it yet, I hope not, but delirium is supposed to set in, joined by dry mouth, cracked lips and scaly skin. Shedding like a snake could be madness enough. I should laugh, that's funny, isn't it? It feels like a hangover is coming on, and flickers of static snow are creeping into my peripheral.

Model Dee remains bright and alert on her steady diet of electrons. Machines have it easy, handed a meal every few nanoseconds. But the human form has one advantage. Rather than extinguish instantly, life fades slowly when disconnected from our power source. Slow, agonizing torture.

Starvation may drag the body down, but hell, it sure does spur the mind—how do I escape this pickle? The obvious conclusion was to ask the computer. Dee says there is nourishment aboard, except it's all behind the closed doors. How convenient for the superuser on the other side, who has locked the computer, and me, out. Then it dawned on me. The craft we arrived in has food and water. Nothing tasty, only foil packets bursting with slime, but when hungry, anything edible is a delicacy. Except Model Dee can't find our craft in the docking bay. I could spend weeks fumbling through on my own and die of starvation long before finding it.

So I sit and rest a lot, holding myself down as best I can, boots stuck to the deck, butt wanting to float away, curled up with arms wrapped around my knees and my back against the doors that won't open. Sit here and conserve physical energy while expending plenty of mental fuel pondering my predicament.

I really blew it this time. I've got to rethink this out-of-body thing. A harmless adventure until now. Besides, with my attention elsewhere, someone could have shoved my catatonic body right out the hatchway to join the other icy souls. Some end that would have been to the mission. Hell, the mission is falling apart anyway. I should be more concerned about the flowers I've yet to give Christina and hoping that gets me a fraction closer to forgiven. Fat chance of that. She's so pissed, she probably ran off with Dave, that'd show me how it feels. Must be why Dee can't find our craft. Maybe they found some fuel. Wouldn't take much, so near a planet. Did they head for the surface? But sensors detect others on board. That could be anyone. Thinking is hard, like mud on the brain.

Who knows, I may never, but this body thing, now that needs some new rules. I can't leave the body and expect to come back, find it intact, and find others—I had thought were friends—still present, waiting for my return. What was I thinking? I need to stay close and protect this body, besides keeping attention where I should be keeping it. No more of that, at least, not for anything less than a really good reason. Can't exactly think of any reason, but then, I can't really think of anything that makes much sense. Except that one, just one sip of water, how good that would taste right now.

My wanting-to-float butt drops. Hard, I'm pulled down, and the deck rumbles. I try rising but it's difficult, like I've gained a few hundred pounds. Or I'm weak. Maybe both. Stumbling out of the corridor is like walking up a steep incline. I make it to the platform over the docking bay and find a display. An approaching planet fills the screen, a marble colored pink, rust, and green, oceans aquamarine.

The g-force triples and my knees buckle. The entire vessel shudders, the railing creaks, and the deck moans. Gravity comes and goes as the craft drops, catches itself for a moment, then it falls away and I'm tossed airborne. The boots whine, straining to find the deck, and at last they do. Calculating steps in time with the fluctuating gravity, I stagger to the railing that overlooks the docking bay. Gangways sway, conduits flap, panels groan and tortured metal howls. Something up high breaks free in a fit of sparks, tumbles down and bounces off platforms, then crashes ten stories below. The vessel banks hard and drops too fast for the boots to adjust. I'm thrown up and over the railing, into the docking space, hovering weightless over a painful stretch of nothing. Then the craft lurches up around me, and down we go. Click click clicking my heels, it's just not working. Down down, click click, the boots finally start humming. My descent slows, but the bottom is coming fast. I turn an ankle—a lucky guess?—and swoop sideways. Toes up, I slow. Toes down, down I go. Toe and heel are elevators, ankle is rudder, I get it. Not soon enough. Toes up, toes up!

A stretch of smooth metal races up to greet me. I glide the remaining distance, skidding on air, and touch down like a feather. Right, I knew that. The boots slurp to the deck and I've hardly enough strength to lift either foot, not with a pounding heart that steals all blood from everything else and fills my brain to bursting. Thinking fast is like braking in space—demands all available fuel.

I stand in one spot, my landing spot, and spend a time catching my breath. The air is better down here. Was I lucky? A will to survive forced the memory alive. I've worn boots like these before.

A thunderous boom echoes off every panel and the entire vessel quakes. The engine whine fades and the tremors subside, followed by an inviting stillness. Have we landed? We have landed. The chaotic gyrations have ceased and gravity is stable, no longer yanked across the scale. My body feels about the right weight, best I can tell after months in space without any. Maybe lighter than the last planet, but who the hell knows what I would know after this experience, the last few seconds, the last few days, or the last couple of months. Difficult to say which is worse. And difficult to believe this cantankerous bucket of bolts could even make it to the surface of a planet.

On the floor is a broken white line, the sort painted on a highway. Two lanes and the divider lead into a rectangular tunnel, and the roadway fades in darkness. The way out?

Food and water.

I tug a foot and try to step, but down here that affinity for the deck is strong. Each boot feels like it weighs two-hundred pounds. To hell with the footwear. I pop the latches and walk free of the boots, leaving them behind, pasted to the floor.

✳

The tunnel goes on and on, gradually descending. At distant intervals in the ceiling are recessed lights next to louvered panels that suck out air. The stretches between each light become the darkest night, so dark the broken white line slips from view, until the next light casts a dirty yellow glow across the featureless walls and road, and another vent evacuates air.

From behind, the whine of an engine approaches. I whirl around to face a pair of blinding lights, growing larger, the engine louder, coming fast. I scramble out of the lane and to the side. A flat-faced tractor-trailer whips past, kicking up a bluster. In the second lane, another truck rolls past, and more, countless more, tailgating one after another. Whoosh whoosh, the trucks speed through the tunnel hauling flatbed semitrailers, each carrying a long cylinder of great diameter, concealed under a giant tarpaulin secured in place by thick bands strapping the cargo down. As the trucks roll past, I scan for drivers. Ghost drivers, not a soul behind any wheel. The flow of trucks reaches the last, the wind and noise settles, and at the tunnel's end, light streams in.

Daylight.

I sprint for the exit.

An enormous hatch is hinged downward to form a ramp. Fresh air floods into the ship, and below, shaded sunlight scatters across smooth stone. I hurry down the ramp but my noodlely space-legs tangle. I trip and fall and go tumbling down, the bumps and scrapes a welcome reminder of any world's faithful pull.

I come to rest at the bottom of the ramp. A stone platform spreads out in all directions, shaded by the city-sized cargo transport. Its belly is the only sky above, supported on massive struts that end in hoof-like feet, hundreds of them, spread among scores of hinged hatches that angle down as ramps to meet the stone platform. More trucks with tubular loads flow down the many ramps, merge to form a single lane of traffic, and head toward the thin strip of daylight circling the landing area, beyond the edges of the mammoth vessel.

A car horn sounds, beep beep, the high squeal almost comical.

I twist on my butt to face the ramp.

A smaller truck is stopped halfway down. Two axle, staked flatbed four-by-four, camouflaged tan and brown. Unlike the flat-faced tractor-trailers, this truck has a protruding cowl and grille that seems curving toward a grin.

The delirium part of thirst must have arrived. I've got to be hallucinating. Not a ghost driver this time. Angled forward with his arms draped over the steering wheel, smug grin and all, he sits there staring out the windshield.

I scramble out of the way. The truck shoots down the ramp, pulls around one-eighty, and stops next to me. The passenger door pops open as if the latch were pulled by a ghost. Jared didn't lean toward it even one fraction.

"Get in," he says. On the bench seat is a blast rifle.

"No thanks, my legs could use some walking."

He reaches below the seat, fetches a canteen, and waves it like bait. "You must be thirsty by now." He stretches toward me, offering the canteen, which brings his biceps out of the black tee-shirt he wears. He's been working out. More muscle in his chest and shoulders, too. His hair is rumpled like always, his favorite style, like he just got out of bed. But not his eyes, always sharp as a knife, like a predator stalking its prey.

I could hate him forever, but nothing can keep me from that water. I reach in fast, snatch the canteen, and back out just as quickly. I'm not riding anywhere with him. My throat is saved, but the slosh hits the pit of my stomach like a sledgehammer.

"Whoa there," he says. "Go slow." He kills the engine and gets out, comes around the truck, and halts near the grille. His camouflage pants match the vehicle's tan and brown, down to his sandy boots. From a knapsack he pulls out a foil packet and pitches it at me. "Eat."

I catch it. "You're feeding me?"

Hallucination indeed.

He grins. "What are friends for?"

I drop the empty canteen and tear into the foil packet. Slurping and sucking, I inhale the load, hold it over my mouth, and squeeze out every last drop. The rock lining of my stomach begins to soften, and in seconds, nourishment hits my bloodstream like a hard drug. Cloudy senses sharpen, balance improves, but the mirage holds steady—Jared standing near the truck's grille.

A matching truck flies down the ramp and speeds away.

Motors whir and the ramp starts rising from the stone. Other ramps follow, all inching upward until flush with the vessel's belly and snapping shut in a concert of out-of-time booms.

The other truck moves off fast. It looks like someone's in the back, but slats of the fenced-in bed block a good view. Two organics. On the seat in Jared's truck—a rifle-class pulsed wave inducer. Electrochemical signature number one. I'm not hallucinating.

He glances at the fading truck, then back to me. "Play your part and they'll be fine."

I dive into the cab, seize the rifle, and take aim. "Follow that truck."

He smiles. "That's better." He strolls around to the driver's side, climbs in, and starts the engine. I get in the passenger seat, weapon on target. He whips the truck around and we start rolling, heading for the sliver of daylight circling the craft above.

"Faster!" I demand. "Catch them."

He punches the throttle, tossing us back. "Then what happens?"

"You let them go." I shift the barrel higher, to his nose. "Or I blow your face off."

"So predictable," he says. "Intelligence officer on a secret mission. Really now, the best you could do?"

"It worked."

"You mean…" He laughs. "You actually expected the general to buy that ridiculous story. You're a fool."

"He did, so it doesn't matter."

Gazing forward, he says, "Right, thanks to me."

"Oh? King god of the universe did me a favor?"

He smirks. "Cleared the way, if you call that a favor." The craft overhead streams past. Tires whine, rolling over smooth stone. He glances at me. "The general was briefed, all the files unlocked, and everything I wanted you to find was put in plain sight. Everyone knew you were coming to infiltrate headquarters. Well, except that poor instructor. You didn't have to assault the guy."

"And he didn't have to call us losers."

He chuckles. "A mite sensitive, are we?"

"How about we call you a loser."

He scowls. About what I thought.

"Think you're clever," he says.

"Clever got me here."

His stare drifts forward, out the windshield. "Yes, one way or another you got here, and here you will stay." He looks over, grin growing. "You're not leaving this system."

"I wouldn't be so sure about that."

His eyes go wide. "Me? Don't tell *me* what to be sure of, tell yourself." His face scrunches with that sappy contrived pity. "But oh, you poor thing, just look what they've done to you. Look at yourself, an idiot with a big hole in his memory. So what are you sure of anyway? Anything?"

"No one is unbeatable, not even you, I know that much."

One hand to the wheel, he sights ahead, supremely smug. "The notion only confirms your weakness. What you think you know comes from nowhere, nothing you can hold on to, not even a shred to suggest it might be true. You know nothing *for sure,* and so, you lose. I, on the other hand, know a great many things, all beyond any doubt. And so, I win."

He won't know shit with brains splattered across the cab of this truck.

Bright sun bursts from above, pouring in as we emerge from beneath the shaded underbelly of the cargo transport. The view opens to puffy white clouds floating across pink sky, sunbeams slicing through it all. The pink, the clouds, the sun penetrating the windshield and warming my skin—all reminders of home. And the air streaming past the open window, so rich in oxygen. Like Idan, a home I never should have left.

"Nice to see you brought some fun along." He slows the truck. "Even more fun tied up."

In the truck ahead, Dave and Christina are on their feet. She's reaching over the fenced-in bed, gagged and shaking her head no, hands bound and motioning away, away, run away.

I raise the barrel to his cheek. "Touch her and you're dead."

He doesn't flinch. "You might have to speak with them about that." He stops the truck, still a distance to go, and points ahead.

The other truck parks near a low stone building where two dozen soldiers stand at attention. Not Association troops, and not agents. Whoever they are, they wear tan uniforms and have blast rifles slung over their shoulders. Glints of sunlight reflect off their shiny white helmets, and dark faceplates mask their identity. Selected troops step out of rank, to the truck, and remove a section of the fenced bed.

Still costumed as agent and clerk, Dave and Christina are hauled off the truck. But minus the wig, her rusty mane swings as she struggles. Both are gagged and bound, but only their hands. They can run, once I make a ruckus.

I fling the door open, set a stance, and calculate sequence of attack. I sight down the barrel at my first target. Click. Click click click. Fuck!

Jared slaps his door shut and strolls around the truck. He is armed with another rifle.

"Trust me," he says. "This one's fully charged."

✳

Knowing a past makes no difference. Sure or not, it doesn't matter. A hole in my memory, or holding every shred of memory, none of it commands the present. I have been foolish, but not the fool Jared wants to believe. My only mistake—to let his taunting rule my reactions. I've allowed him this power over me. I don't have to be what he thinks or act how he expects. It's a choice, my choice, in the past, future, and now. Right this now.

This masquerade is over. I drop the useless rifle and start getting out of the cheesy jacket.

"What are you doing?" he asks.

I toss the jacket. "Me? Oh, just preparing to beat the shit out of you."

He laughs. "You are a fool." He plants the barrel of his rifle to my chest.

"You think this saves you?" I indicate the weapon, then draw a mental image, perfectly clear and nearly unbelievable. But the picture is mine to believe what I see—Jared on the ground, helpless and confused. And best of all, without his rifle, a crutch he really should learn to live without.

I clamp fingers around the barrel and tighten my free hand to an iron fist. I'm not angry—I am effective—focused to channel all my energy, concentrated through one arm, to the fist, and into Jared's chest. He squeezes the trigger. I yank the muzzle, deflect the blast, and it scorches empty air. The hot barrel scalds my palm, but now the weapon is mine.

Ah, that sweet sensation, to witness a future I knew would exist, only moments before it did. The mental image becomes real, Jared on his back, helpless and confused. And best of all, weaponless.

I flip the rifle around and sight down the barrel. He scurries away bent over backward on his hands and feet like a crab. He can't escape fast enough. Goodnight, my friend.

A net drops over me, tangles up the barrel, and the rifle fires into the sky. I'm tackled by a mob of tan-uniformed soldiers, white helmets and dark faceplates everywhere. My wrestling only tightens the trap the more I struggle. I get the rifle aimed between the cord and pull the trigger. Soldiers spread out to dodge the blast, giving me a chance to loosen some of the net and get back on my feet.

Arms grope and scratch from behind. I twist fast and jam the barrel to the soldier's throat. He freezes, all terror masked by the dark faceplate, on which the only image is a reflection of me, burning with rage. In the split-second before his demise, as I squeeze the trigger, my victim growls.

The blast explodes with such force that he is instantly headless. Two confused steps and the staggering torso collapses. Before I've any chance to ponder what happened to his skull, the shiny helmet smacks the stone and rolls past like a wayward cue ball. Stunned by gruesome death in mere seconds, I am caught off-guard—another net soars overhead. Soldiers bowl me over and knock me flat.

A boot connects with my skull—*POW!*

Shockwaves hammer every corner of my brain and fold back on themselves until magnified to screaming, then exit as black spots dancing before my eyes.

Jared stands over me, many of him, and they won't sit still, bouncing between a crowd of white helmets and dark faceplates. I angle the muzzle at one of the Jareds and blast a hole in the netting, but I miss by a mile. The shot clears the crowd anyway, and these two eyes begin to agree again. I get back on my feet and get the barrel poking through a gap in the cord.

More soldiers advance, aiming to hurl another net. I blast a smoldering cavity in the chest of one, and the rest reconsider their advance. I scan for Jared. The coward slips between the scattering soldiers and darts around the building. I chase after him, net slinging from my head and arms and barrel, finger eager to squeeze the trigger and finish the bastard.

Whoa—the land drops fast. I catch my balance, no guardrail. Past my toes, a chasm falls into a deep valley where green stretches out for miles. At the far end, a city of stone is spread across a plateau. The buildings are light tan, immense pale blocks, surrounded by pillars supporting slabs angled to the sky.

I ease back, away from the edge, back to the safety of the stone platform. I'm struck from behind, top of my pelvis near the tailbone, by something like a sledgehammer. A fiery jolt climbs my spine, tingles shoot down each thigh, and my knees fail. Nets soar overhead and I'm tackled by the mob. Bodies pour down and I hit the stone hard.

The bodies slowly clear, soldiers helping one another up, having secured me in far too many nets to ever untangle. Laid out flat and fighting the trap, I strain for a glimpse of Jared. He comes into view, staring down at me, upside down. Rough cord crosses my face, tighter the more I wrestle.

He brushes off his black tee and grins. "You can be sure I'll enjoy her." A soldier hands him a rifle. Stock down, he holds it out, shadowing me from the sun. He cocks the rifle back, aiming to hammer my skull. "Dream of that, will you?"

I vow to never dream it, think it, or ever believe it.

2

THERE IS ONLY WHITE. NOT TOO BRIGHT, A COMFORTABLE white, but the air is damp and chilly. I'm on my back, staring up at a ceiling of endless fog.

I sit up, my seat wobbles, and water splashes the sides. I'm in a rowboat, weathered and gray. Beyond the boat, water spreads out like a sheet of glass. Circling ripples move outward, fading into walls of fog surrounding the lake.

Carefully, I peer over the side. The water is so clear it could be absent, as if the boat hangs in a cloudless sky. The clarity should reveal the bottom, but it does not, only a murky abyss where muddy clouds slowly swirl.

If the water were moving, rushing past or growing swells, this would not be so awful. I wouldn't see the endless depth and long fall to the bottom, however far that may be. Instead, the water is still, quiet, lucid… hungry.

What I should do is grab the oars and go somewhere else. Except there's no land in sight, only the unbroken fogbank. I might row farther away from shore. But I can't just sit here.

I get up and reach for the oars. The boat dips, bow down. I pitch back balancing it underfoot, but every correction is absorbed by the boat and transferred to the water. The dips and yaws become violent, and every effort to regain control only makes matters worse. Bow down, water crests over and in. The stern stands upright and catapults my body out of the boat.

Every other breath is a gulp of icy water. Demons claw at my heels, dragging me into a transparent underworld. I thrash and grope, nothing to hold, nothing holds me, it's all useless. Every muscle drains, and the body tires. The demons are stronger. Holding on to my final breath, I drift deeper, deeper. Calm arrives, content to cease all struggle, my battle is over.

On my back and sinking, I watch the ripples fade as the boundary between life and death returns to glasslike stillness, a window looking out on the foggy world beyond. I sink deeper, deeper, swallowed by the murky abyss, as the view above grows darker, darker.

I fear that death has arrived, yet my thoughts continue, and some sensation—a rough surface scrapes my back. The bark of a tree. The submerged branch is moving. Like a slithering snake, the limb twines around my torso. Then the limb stiffens, and my body is flung to the heavens. I tunnel through the chilling clear and shatter the glassy surface.

I am thrown so high the lake is gone. I'm wrapped in a womb of endless vapor, climbing higher while flipping and turning until all sense of direction is twisted and confused. My rapid climb dwindles, I reach no higher, and my plummet begins, I fear right back to the watery grave. Instead I crash to the ground, the impact abrupt and painful. Not enough to kill, though it seems it should. Am I not dead already?

Somehow, a spark of life remains, enough to feel this languid body's every ache. I force these legs to stand, a breeze glances my wet skin, and I shiver. Dead has its advantages.

Ahead, behind, and to every side, the walls of fog still stand. Somewhere beyond the shroud, the last slapping waves of the lake are fading. The soft ground must have saved me. The black sand is loose and soggy, soft enough that my landing has left an impression in the shape of my body. Like a mold, to make another me. I lean over and scoop up a handful of the moist sand, as black as night. The rough crystals slip through my fingers like grains through an hourglass.

"Hello."

It came from ahead, I think. Besides, the ground slopes up, away from the water, a great direction to go. Scaling the soggy mound is tiresome. My bare feet sink in the black sand, absorbing all effort to advance.

On higher ground, a faint image emerges from the mist. A tree. Towering over me, it has a thick trunk of furrowed bark and leafy limbs spreading out. Not really unusual, a typical tree, but I would think it belongs in a forest rather than growing here alone. More peculiar is the arrangement of bark on its trunk. It looks like the face of a grumpy old man.

I move closer. "Are you talking to me?"

"It appears so," the tree says.

Since when do trees…

"How are you today?" the tree asks.

A dumb question.

"Pretty crappy so far. Where the heck am I, anyway?"

Brows of bark tilt up and out. "Where the heck are you, anyway?"

What is so familiar about this? It happened before. Not this exactly, but close. Except last time I flew off the road and down a ravine. A long way down.

"I'm at the bottom of the lake, right?"

"Are you at the bottom of the lake?"

"Yes, I am. Well, my dead body is. Am I dead for real this time?"

"What time?" the tree asks.

"This time."

"That depends on your point of view."

"What does?" I ask.

"This time."

"You're not making any sense." Then I realize why. "Sure, like I should expect any. Another crazy dream, right?"

"Good," the trees says. "You are becoming more aware."

An actual conversation, maybe.

"I'm dead, right? At the bottom of the lake."

"Are you dead at the bottom of the lake?"

"Yes, I am. I don't have to look this time."

"Good," the tree says. "You are becoming more aware."

Talking to this tree is about as useful as talking to myself.

"So tell me this," I say. "What am I *not* aware of?"

The tree looks me straight in the eye, past every layer, and stares into *me*.

"You are not aware of how great you are."

As if I'm any measure of Greatness. In my dreams, maybe.

"Look, Woody, I know I'm dreaming, but am I asleep? Or am I really dead this time?"

"What time?" the tree asks.

One good chainsaw, now that would be useful.

"Today," I say. "You know, right now, *this* time, not last time, or any other time. Is it really that hard to understand?"

The tree grins like it knows a secret. "Time is a trick you have played on yourself." The trunk creaks, twisting to face the foggy expanse. A circular band emerges from the mist, laid out flat like a merry-go-round, floating in midair and slowly turning.

"Imagine a ring of images," the tree says, "awaiting your inspection."

The colorful apparition draws near, and the gentle spinning whips up a breeze that tosses my hair. The band is like a filmstrip with pictures of people, places, and things. But not static like photographs, each is animated, as if a small window to another place, a tiny movie of what happens there. The ring inches closer, spinning faster, and the scenes pass too quickly to absorb what each one is, what each one means.

"Viewed from the exterior," the tree says, "one must travel its circumference, a life's journey, requiring time."

An image catches my attention, some people I might know. I try to track it going around, but it doesn't reappear. None of them repeats. The ring presents an endless series of new scenes, each shown for an instant, then gone.

"However," the tree says, "viewed from the center, all one must do is turn and *look*."

The ring expands, coming at me, and the thin veil pushes past my face. Now it circles with me in the center, and the spinning ring slowly contracts.

The animated pictures are clear from this vantage point as well. I turn and turn, absorbing all the imagery. The spinning slows and the pictures drift closer, then stack atop one another until I am contained inside a sphere, surrounded by a bubble of tiny movies. A beach, waves crashing and gulls soaring. Rugged mountain terrain, a slender waterfall plunges into a lush valley. Skyscrapers, a busy sidewalk crowded with people. Space, stars, planets. Strange creatures crawling across strange worlds. There is so much to see, and it's no longer frustrating. I can look any direction and view any I choose, *whenever* I choose.

I realize, "Requiring no time."

From beyond the shroud of imagery, the tree says, "Making all of time, *this time*. The now."

"But how?" I ask. "How could I possibly control time?"

"Let it not control you. Be one. Be in the center. Be in the now."

✳

I snap up only to smash my head into something hard and ricochet right back down. Any second now, this coconut skull is cracking open to spill my throbbing brain.

Wherever I am, it's dark and it smells. That odor might be familiar. Reminds me of a pond back home, loaded with toads and snakes, topped by a slimy green film ready to skim off like a foamy pancake. My nose follows the moldy stench to the straw padding beneath me, spread atop a wooden bunk hanging from the stone wall. Directly overhead is another bunk.

A voice comes from above, using a language I haven't heard in lifetimes.

"You, stop banging."

It's not so dark after all. The skull-whack just dimmed the lights for a moment. The new headache slowly fades, the acute portion anyway, but plenty remains sore thanks to the stock end of Jared's rifle. I check my scalp and find a ripe lump where he landed the final blow.

The scene slowly brightens. The small room has rough stone walls and a dirt floor. High on one wall is a wide slot not very tall, where daylight streams in. On the opposite wall is a wooden door hung from iron hinges. Centered at eye level, a small opening in the door is lined with bars.

Bars? The slot high in the wall is also barred.

I quickly recall the foreign language and give it my best shot. "Ah, excuse me. Would you mind—"

"Quiet yourself," the irritated voice says. "And no more banging, I be hoping to sleep."

"Sorry, it was an accident. I don't mean to bother you, but could you tell me—"

He growls. Great, another fight.

"What!" he hollers. "What must I know upon you? Tell if I must, then leave me to sleep."

"Yes, I promise."

"What be it!"

From the bunk above, his head drops down, upside down.

I scramble back, glued to the rocky wall, startled by a creature with triangle ears and furry orange face, all but a pink nose. His big eyes snap open, emerald green with black pupils a diamond shape taller than wide.

"Lord of all worlds," he says.

For a breathless moment, we stare at each other. He's a cat. A cat-man?

The bunk creaks and his face vanishes. More creaking and he comes down a ladder at the end of the bunk. He steps backward, staring at me, and knocks into a small table at the center of our cozy room.

I peel myself off the stone wall.

Orange and white fur sprouts from his leather vest. He wears snug pants no lower than his knees, leaving furry shins above sandaled feet, on which he stands about the size of a stout man.

"From where did you come?" he asks.

"Where did I come from?"

"As I say, from where. You were not here when I began sleeping."

He steps closer, studying me, but he is cautious. One feature isn't cat—the brow. His brows are animated, twisting and tilting as humans do, to help say what isn't said. And his mouth is equally expressive, with teeth I wouldn't expect for a cat. They're flat, like a man. But then there's the whiskers poking out each side.

"Be it you have come to punish me?" he asks.

"No." I scoot out and sit on the bunk's edge. "I just want to know where I am."

He turns to the table behind him and his furry tail sways. "I be unsure that I should offer my words." He reaches for a clay pitcher and fills a mug, then turns back to me. "You know everything, do you not?"

"If I knew everything, I wouldn't be asking."

"Yet you be one of the gods, those who know all."

"I'm not a god. I'm a man."

"A man?" he asks. "What be a man?"

"What I… I mean, my body." I wave across my torso. "This is a man's body. We're called men."

"So you be a man-god. Or a god of men?"

"Neither. Look, you have a name for your kind, your species, right?"

"Of course," he says. "I be Felidian." He raises his mug and downs it in one swift guzzle.

"Man is like that," I explain. "The name for our kind. The form I appear in, we call it man. Short for human."

He licks his lips, whiskers swish and he smiles. "Ah, I comprehend. Gods choose many forms."

I drop my shaking head into one hand. Like Christina thinking of me, and thinking god. I'm no god, what a rotten job, even worse than any mission. Especially this mission, all gone wrong. And Christina, where is she now? Not safe, I just don't know.

Something skitters low along one wall, then stops. The cat-man doesn't notice. He goes to the table and reaches for the pitcher. Next to it is a lump covered by a red cloth. He refills his mug and lowers to a short stool beside the table. Silent and sipping his drink, he stares at me.

"Just tell me where I am."

"Prison," he says. "What else did you imagine?"

"What are we doing in prison?"

"You, I cannot say. Myself, I be detained by the charge of impiety."

"What is that?"

He raises his mug in a sweeping arc as if pointing out the heavens. "Disrespect for the gods."

"Gods? What gods?"

He motions the mug toward me. "Those as you appear, the other man-gods."

As I appear? Turtleneck and slacks, boots and hair to match, black on black, I'm still in costume. Only lacking the cheesy jacket I left on the landing platform. These creatures worship the Bobs?

"I'm afraid you've been led astray. They're not gods either."

His eyes sparkle. "Ah, then intuition does not betray me."

"So you know about them. Then you know I'm not a god."

"Know be a strong word," he says. "Their status as gods I have questioned, more so their intent, and have expressed to other Felidians, yet few believe." He hangs his head. "Thus, here I be, punished for my impiety."

That skittering noise again, moves low along one wall, then stops.

He glances up, desperation in his gaze. "I only wish to enlighten the others, to open their minds, to ask the eternal question—what be truth?" Back to staring at the floor, he mutters, "Instead I be accused of corrupting the young and spreading impious beliefs. I be regarded a heretic." He looks up at me. "Though it be untrue. I have faith, I do. I merely wish to broaden that faith with the discovery of deeper truths."

It's not my way, and of all the memories lost, the last time I felt pity for another is one memory better left forgotten. A world mixed up in worship is bad enough. Of those that are, most choose something benign, at worst an intangible deity posing threats no more dangerous than the believer's own thoughts. But worshipping agents of the Association—this can't be good.

His pink nose twitches, whiff whiff, and his tail snaps side to side. He lunges at the wall, down on all fours—a scuffle, some squealing—then he rises, in his grasp the tail of a dangling mouse.

I can't watch this. But my stomach growls.

He stares at my noisy midsection. "You be hungry?"

"Not for that."

He studies the mouse, then back to me. "You imagine our friend be food?" He goes to the high slot and reaches up to nudge the rodent past the bars. "Run along now."

"You don't..."

He goes to the table. "Our goddess makes rich the soil at our feet, nourishment aplenty for all Felidians." He flips the red cloth to uncover a loaf of bread, thick crust toasted golden brown. He tears off a chunk and offers it.

Sparked by the sight alone, my mouth instantly waters. I take the bread and sink my teeth in. Oh man, a visit to the dentist after this. I just discovered the planet responsible for croutons.

Wrestling with the hard bread, I manage, "Thanks," and wish to finish properly, except our introduction was anything but typical. "I didn't catch your name."

He presses the mug to his chest and bows. "I be Physuro Manispeus, at your service. And what god be you, who graces my presence today?"

"Adam. But please, I'm not a god." I extend a hand, offering to shake.

He looks at my hand and appears confused. Maybe the gesture is not so customary around these parts. He glances at his mug, my hand, then he grins. He smacks the cup into my open palm.

Must be their version of customary. A stranger in a strange land must conform to the rituals of his host, and it appears I just learned the first—the exchange of a beverage.

Physuro motions as if drinking, eyes bright and nodding, urging me on.

I peer into the mug. Looks like muddy water. Must I drink this? Well, I don't want to appear rude, and besides, something needs to wash down the petrified morsel posing as food. I tilt the cup and swallow. Yow! It *is* muddy water. Nasty. Probably full of bugs, now swimming in my stomach.

"And tell me, Adam, what be your last name?"

I hand the mug back. "The last? Carl, I guess, but I didn't really like that one."

Worse than any name is the aftertaste my tongue fights to clear. Gross. My first task here should be introducing water filtration.

He sets the mug down and lowers to his stool. "I be talking of a surname."

"I guess you could call me Sir Adam if you really want to, but I prefer just Adam. I'm not too fond of fancy titles."

His brows contrast, one tight, the other tall. "That be not the meaning of my words. I speak of a family name, that which your father gives you."

"Oh." I sit on the bunk's edge. "I don't have one."

"A father? Or a name?"

"Neither."

He shoots up to standing. "Lord of all worlds, how be that possible? Be it true? A god without birth visits my cell?"

"I told you, I'm not a god."

"If you be not a god," he says, "and have no father, from where do you come?"

"I come from Idan."

He smiles. "Very well, then I shall know you as Adam of Idan." He lowers to his stool.

"Look, Physuro, if you don't mind, think you could help me out?"

"How do you imagine I may assist you?"

"Do you know where my friends are?"

"The others as yourself?" He points to the high slot where sunshine flows in. "They be in the mountains."

"Not them. The two who were with me."

His blank stare only confirms the worst.

"You don't know, do you."

He shakes his head. "I be detained for some time and have failed to witness any man-gods in the interim."

Just great. I flop back on the itchy straw and stare up at the bunk above. Bad enough we're a force divided, worse are gnawing thoughts of where she might be and what could be happening to her. I can't face any of that. It all just tears me down. I have to set it aside, focus, fix this mess, find her, find Dave. Find myself, I'm a wreck.

Thinking like that will get me nowhere. I've been through worse. Plenty of missions have gone wrong. Time to think, form a plan. I've done it before, I can do it again.

✳

When I open my eyes, the bunk above is still there. Wishing for somewhere better didn't work. I'd accomplish more staring into a foggy sky. What I should do is grab the oars and go somewhere else. Except that was a dream. Besides, reaching for the oars didn't turn out so well. But I can't just lie here doing nothing.

I could step out and leave this body, roam free and study this prison, maybe find a way to escape, even find Dave and Christina. No, I can't, too risky. Last time was a disaster. Don't do it, stick to the promise. Step out only for a really good reason. Locked up should be reason enough, but it's not. Besides, I might leave and come back to find that Physuro tricked me, he really does eat meat, and catch him feasting on my cadaver. No, I'm stuck here, in this cell and in this body, stuck fretting over what I've let happen and every solution I can't explore. Prisoner is right. Prisoner in my own mind.

Though a chore to consume, I need more food or I won't get anything done. Off the bunk and to the table, I sit across from Physuro and tear off another chunk of twelve-grain lava rock, munch munch. Oh that is tough to chew, and going down, might rip out a tonsil or two.

The real problem is a lack of mental food, like a reliable intelligence report. In one respect, at least in this case, Jared was right. There is so much I don't know, only a few scraps floating in the category of suspected as fact. Past the high slot is pink sky. It was pink after the cargo transport landed. My first scrap to suggest I haven't been tossed across the galaxy, but it doesn't qualify for the category of undisputed fact.

Another unknown is the creatures of this planet. Physuro, my only example so far, is friendly enough, willing to talk, and he doesn't appear interested in having me for lunch, but how might others be? If they're even cats.

"Physuro, the other Felidians, are they all like you?"

Planted on his stool, he straightens whiskers with a dab of spit. "Not precisely."

"Your culture is a mixed race."

"No, they all be Felidian as I." He slicks back his furry crown, and his grin begins. "Though few others be nearly so handsome."

Great. Of all the cats to get stuck with—Mister Full of Himself. Fill up thy cup.

"But are they all cats?" I ask. "You know, just not so handsome."

He misses the jab. "Cats?"

"You know…" I wave across his features. "Fur, whiskers, a tail."

He stares at me, one brow tight, the other tall.

Not a point worth making. In a world full of cats, he's like all the rest—normal. I'm the guy out of place.

He says, "You have not seen our kind before?"

"Not in person, but once…" My thoughts drift back to Mac and his body farm, the tour and computer displays. "I saw a picture once, close to how you look, but just a rough diagram. When I was visiting a friend of mine, a body farmer."

"Your bodies sprout from soil?"

I can't help but laugh. "It's just a figure of speech. Just what we call it, a body farm. Where they're made and we go to pick up another, you know, after…"

"The afterlife," he suggests.

"Another life. Our next life."

He is silent.

"You don't reincarnate?"

He says, "Not as a mouse, I pray."

"Not what I mean. Get another body, you know, like the one you have now."

"In this realm?" he says. "Perhaps in another. Perhaps in yours, from which you come."

They must recycle life the same as we do, they would have to. No life force is limited to a single body. How could they not know?

But I'm not at home, the realm from which I come, and I'm making an assumption. More supposed facts drawn from a pool of uncertainty. I can't even say what system this is. Maybe things work differently here, if here is even where I expect. I didn't expect a cat-man.

I leave Physuro at the table, go to the wall below the high slot, and gaze into the pink sky, all there is to see.

"What is this place?" I ask.

"As I say, prison."

I turn to face him. "I mean what planet."

"You be sincere? A god without knowledge of—"

"Look, Physuro, enough with the god stuff. Just tell me what planet we're on."

"Marsea," he says.

"In what system?"

His ears angle inward. "What be your meaning? A system of language? Must I use different words?"

"The name of the star."

"Which one? There be many."

I point at the high slot, to outside. "The big one. You know, the bright light hanging in the sky every day. You can understand that, right?"

He shifts on his seat and snickers like I'm a fool. "That be not a star, that be the sun. Stars be in the heavens."

I have been tossed across the galaxy—to the ignorant side.

"Does the sun have a name?" I ask.

He chuckles like our conversation is a funny little game. "Of course," he says, eyes sparkling. "The *sun*."

Smart-ass.

"The sun's a star like all the rest. It's just really close."

Too close to be anything but Sol, alone in this desolate corner of the galaxy. Jared couldn't knock me out so thoroughly that I'd be out all the way to the nearest star, weeks away at best. We're still in the Solar system. He is still here, if not on his way home by now. Marsea is Sol-4, an Association label. I haven't been tossed anywhere, other than in jail.

Physuro rises from his stool and joins me below the high slot. Gazing into the sky, he asks, "Our sun bears a name as do stars in the night?"

"Isn't that just crazy? What about the planets? There's more than just Marsea, right?"

"More…"

"Planets. You know, other worlds like Marsea. All systems have at least two or three in the habitable zone, in orbits close enough to keep warm."

"I have not known heavenly bodies described with such casual familiarity, even by those of scientific endeavor. If you be not a god, a great scientist perhaps."

"Not really, just a space traveler."

His eyes grow wide, and he steps back.

I say, "You travel between planets, don't you?"

"Heavenly travel?" Another step back, he drops onto his stool. "Oh no. Only gods may travel through the heavens."

"Let's get this straight once and for all. I'm not a god. Really, I'm not."

"Yet you speak words mere mortals would not. Perhaps you be a god after all, and I be disrespectful. I beg, accept my apologies as most sincere."

I can't tell what he believes. He doubts the gods, but not me. I don't get it.

"Just because I know or do things different from you doesn't make me a god, it just makes me different. Different the way one species is different from the next. I'm no greater than you. We're equals."

"Not all species be equal."

"Maybe not a Felidian and a mouse. Does that make you gods over mice?"

He has no answer. His stare darts to the high slot, then back to me. "A blasphemous suggestion. Yet fascinating."

"Not likely, just like I'm not a god over you. Don't you see?"

"I see a source of great wisdom. Tell me, may I impose upon you to become your disciple?"

As if I have any truth worth spreading. Besides, it sounds too much like worship.

"How about a student? You know, you can be my friend and I'll teach you things. Would that work?"

"It would," he says. "I beg, let it be."

"Okay, then call me your friend." I sit across from him. "So now that we're friends, you can start by helping out your good buddy Adam."

"An honor. How may I assist?"

"Tell me how to get out of here. Come on, there has to be a way. You know this place better than I do."

His gaze wanders. "I can imagine your freedom in only one way." He focuses on me. "I say use your power as a god to bring it about."

"Except I don't have that power, remember?"

"Words be your greatest power. Convince those who detain you that your status as a god be true."

"But it's not."

"What relevance has that?" he asks.

"I don't understand."

"Adam, I do not wish to enrage you further, as I comprehend well your insistence that others regard you as mortal. Yet it be true, you hold power over those near you, at least, those near you at this time."

"What kind of power?"

"I be not the only Felidian to mistake you as a god. Take advantage of how others perceive you. Be the concept so fantastic?"

"I can't do tricks, if that's what you're thinking."

He sighs. "The meaning of my words has walked away from you. The truth of your status be not the question, nor any ability to perform unworldly feats. Of importance be your presence, that which you portray. Persona and words spoken may move worlds, and the peoples inhabiting those worlds."

Men or mice, even cats, who lords over who and who doesn't, he's managed to turn my own argument against me. But he's right, it's all relative. I'm not a god, but how do you define a god? A god is what we are not. Or rather, what we *believe* we are not. More specifically, what the Felidians believe they are not, and that leaves others to be their gods, like the Bobs, or me, who know or do things beyond what they know or can do, and that makes us gods. Not really, but gods to them.

"I might understand," I say. "Sorry, Physuro, you talk a little funny sometimes, almost like a riddle. You're saying, act like a god, and they'll think I am."

He smiles. "We be each other's students. And you as well, talk in riddles, at times nearly incomprehensible. Perhaps I may simplify. Do not merely act. *Believe.*"

"So who's detaining me?"

"The Council, I presume. The same who place me in this prison. Your presence before them may sway their decision to keep you here. Do you not follow the meaning of my words?"

"Yeah, I follow. I suppose you'll be coming along."

He gets a sly grin. "Of course, to guide the way."

I like this crafty cat. Looking out for himself, but he has every right, not guilty of one thing. If the other Felidians would've listened to him, the Bobs might not be here, doing whatever it is they're doing. Nothing to improve this world, that much is certain.

I get up, go to the wall below the high slot, and reach up to yank on the bars. Rock solid. Nobody's getting out that way. Beyond the opening is pink sky, puffy white clouds, and the sun shines bright. A perfect day— outside.

"Okay, I'll play god."

✳

At the door, Physuro peers through the barred opening and spends a time hollering for the jailor's attention. My new friend roars louder than I imagined was in him after our quiet conversation.

Another Felidian appears beyond the bars. Physuro's vanity was no exaggeration, much easier on the eyes. The jailor has mangy black fur, bent whiskers, and a rumpled brow angled to an acid scowl. The guy belongs in a nightmare, as guardian of Hell itself.

"What be it?" the jailor snarls, in no mood to be disturbed.

"I be reformed," Physuro says. "The god sent to my cell has restored my faith. I repent my impious beliefs."

The jailor shifts his devil glare to me. "Him? He be enemy of the gods, here to challenge the Mighty One."

"How may we believe these claims," Physuro says, "when the god sent to my cell speaks such truth that he has reformed even the most impious, Physuro himself?"

That got the jailor's attention. Apparently, my cellmate showing respect for any god is a real eye-opener.

"He must go before the Council," Physuro says.

The jailor resumes his acid scowl. "Your fate be for authority to decide. I will deliver this news, no more I can promise."

"The extent of our wishes." Physuro steps back and bows.

Beyond the barred portal, the jailor glares one last time, his lip curling with disgust, then he moves along.

I look to Physuro, still hanging his head. "You think you're clever."

He glances up at me and grins. "Indeed."

*

Physuro's idea could work, except the time it will take, only to be expected from a body of decision with a name like *the Council*. I know their kind. Pompous league of snobbery assembled to exchange empty arguments aimed at further inflating the bloated egos of self-important nitwits appointed to serve bureaucracy. They could take months deciding. Most likely, the majority has ruled—request denied. Or worse, get aggravated by our nuisance and issue orders for our execution. After all, they think Physuro is a threat. So dangerous he's put in jail. I've seen it before. When the tame are locked up, those holding the keys are quite the opposite. In most cases, the ones closer to insane.

By evening, a different jailor brought us dinner, another loaf of rock-bread and muddy water to wash it down. Asked if there was news of our release, he claimed no knowledge of any such thing, even the request.

In the fading light, Physuro gets a few candles going. Seated around the table, we eat and talk for a time, mostly Physuro asking about my journeys, all of which fascinate him. He wants to know more about me and what I am, if not a god. I explain my job, my duty. A soldier he understands, but not the specialty I am assigned, Alternative Combat Engineer. So he thinks I alter battles. One way to look at it, but his abbreviation of the word also alters the meaning.

"Alternative as in different," I explain. "I find ways to win besides blowing up people."

He still doesn't completely understand but at a minimum admires my distaste for mass murder. I'm more interested in his world, and the rest of the Solar system, the very reason for this journey so far from home. I'll figure this out somehow and complete the mission. I have to.

"Tell me more about Sol-4."

He looks puzzled. "What be the meaning of this strange term?"

"What my kind calls Marsea."

He's no less confused. How do I explain this? I know, I'll show him. I take one of the candles and set it on the floor. "In the center is the sun, and it has a name, Sol." On my knees, I scratch out an orbiting circle, another, another, and a fourth. "Planets go around Sol, and Marsea is the fourth, so we call it Sol-4."

He studies the crude analogy. "I suspect it be possible, yet you speak the words of a heretic. The Book of Truth teaches that Marsea be the center of all creation."

"No, Physuro, it doesn't work that way."

His eyes sparkle. "Ah, I have found one who agrees."

"Huh? I don't think you understand. I *don't* agree."

"You do not agree with what I do not agree. Therefore, we agree." He grins. "Perhaps this explains your visit to prison, as I."

"I doubt that's why they put me in here."

"No? Be there greater reason for your detention?"

"You heard the jailor. Put it this way, me and your gods don't exactly get along."

"Then it be true. You visit to destroy the gods."

"I don't have to destroy them. Get them to leave, maybe, I don't know, something. They're not here to help, I know that much."

He stares at the circles scrawled in the dirt. "I have seen such an illustration before."

"You have?"

"I know of others, those of scientific endeavor who agree, having recorded the movements of the heavens and concluded that it be not the sun that circles Marsea, rather, as you suggest, Marsea that circles the sun."

"Scientists? Who know about this? Where?"

He spreads his arms, indicating our cell. "This be one of many accommodations the impious regard as home."

Sure, lock up all the smart ones. The first step in controlling a populace.

I realize, "You're one of the scientists."

"Oh no," he says. "I be merely a stone cutter, though I possess a thirst for truth in the ways of existence. Thus I be considered more one of philosophical endeavor, rather than scientific, as others be. Though similar guilt we share, in the eyes of our culture."

"You ask questions about life, talk about the possibilities, and that lands you in jail."

"Your words form a correct statement. You be a wise god, indeed."

"Look, Physuro, I'll pretend if it helps, but really, I'm not a god."

"Adam, may I advise you?"

"You can try."

"Convince the Council otherwise."

✳

At daybreak, rising sun lines up with the high slot and pours into the cell. Today when I sit up, I remember not to crash my skull into the bunk above.

Physuro is already up and eating breakfast. My sleepy eyes see egg-fried toast, but it's just that hazy state not quite awake. The fog clears and so does the dreamy meal. No eggs, no syrup or butter, but the bread is plenty toasted.

The lock snaps and the cell door swings open. The jailor stands in the doorway.

"The Council will hear your plea."

The very next morning, I'm impressed. Remarkable even, but I shouldn't be surprised. It's technologically advanced societies that have layers of bureaucracy years deep. Primitive life has its advantages—yet to learn the value of middle management.

The jailor is joined by four Felidian guards. Two with blast rifles keep us under their aim while the other pair step in and fit us with shackles over our wrists and metal collars around our necks. Attached to each collar is a leash by which we are hauled out of the cell.

The jailor leads the way, followed by guards yanking our tethers, and the two with blast rifles bring up the rear. The corridor is dim and cool, lit only by square shafts of sunlight streaming from the barred portals of doors along the hallway, hanging from iron hinges and latches secure, keeping Marsea safe from a great many dangerous freethinkers.

As we march the corridor, I lean toward a door and strain for a peek inside the cell. "Dave? Christina? Either of you in there?"

My leash is yanked and the muzzle of a blast rifle jabs my back.

"I want my friends released as well."

The guards only tug the tethers and march onward.

Physuro angles closer, shoulder to mine. "Save your words for the Council, my friend. Only by their order will others abide."

We come to a door constructed of foot-square timbers sandwiched together by thick iron bands. The jailor sifts through a ring of keys and cracks the lock open. Giant hinges creak and a hard, white column of sunlight breaches the threshold.

Outside, I take in the sweeter air. Sunshine warms my skin and a soft breeze cools it. A view without walls. Tall grass climbs the hillside, and farther below is a forested valley.

Any sense of freedom is short-lived. My leash goes taut and I'm hauled around the prison to a team of horses and more waiting guards. A dozen or so, we must be dangerous. One of the guards brings a horse closer and points to the saddle without a word. This might be interesting. I reach for the saddle horn as best I can with shackled hands and steady myself while one foot plays catch-me with the stirrup. The beast stamps and fidgets, making this feat only more difficult, but I manage to land a foot in the loop and pull, hoisting myself up and over, almost all the way over, but no chance of that. The guard loops my tether around the saddle horn and over my shackles, cinches the cord tight, and secures me in place. He slaps the horse's ass and it trots to join the rest, moving onto a trail that drops from view.

The prison is on a hilltop. Cut out of the tall, sun-bleached grass, a trail descends and narrows, forcing the horses to line up single-file. Past the rise and fall of dry stalks, I catch glimpses of greener hillsides, some trees. At the bottom, the trail levels out and widens to edges less distinct, and the distant greenery slips behind nearer hills roasted brown. I fall in beside Physuro, guards ahead and guards behind, silent other than the mellow clip-clop of hooves against the hardened ground.

We cross a dry prairie where patches of sun-cooked foliage struggle to grow. Few succeed, other than sagebrush and tumbleweed, occasionally a mutant, unfamiliar bush with leafless branches contorted as if crippled. Our captors ahead increase their lead, and those behind hang back, giving us some space but keeping well within rifle range.

Riding alongside, Physuro gazes skyward. "How soon one forgets the splendor of a marvelous day."

A splatter of burgeoning clouds, tops bursting puffy white, slide across the vibrant pink sky, sunbeams slicing through it all. A perfect day.

"Reminds me of home," I say.

"Where be home?" Physuro asks.

Though frustrating at the time, in retrospect I could almost laugh.

He asks, "It be a humorous place?"

"No, it just reminds me of a silly computer. The darn thing thought home was wherever it happened to be at the moment."

"Computer?"

"You don't have computers?"

He is silent as we rock in our saddles. Considering the rest, I might guess the answer. After months spent traveling between star systems, now I'm riding a horse.

He says, "I suppose we do not."

"But you have weapons." I indicate the guards lagging behind, armed with blast rifles.

"Gifts from the gods," he says. "For our protection."

"Protection from what?"

"Our enemy seeks to destroy us."

"The Bobs? I mean, your gods?"

His brows contrast, one tight, the other tall. "Your wisdom falters, Adam. The gods be the giver of the gifts. Felidians be loyal to the gods, not enemy."

"So who's the enemy?"

"Ophidians," he says. "They do not acknowledge the gods as we do."

"And that makes them the enemy."

"Indeed."

"What about you? Locked up and all, for disrespecting the gods. That makes you the enemy, too."

"A matter of degrees perhaps. As do my fellow Felidians, I can respect the gods, I only question their intent. The true heretics, the Ophidians detest the gods, all gods, now and forever."

Maybe because they figured out the lie. A notion that stays private for now. These others, whoever they are, could be the wiser and only battle the Felidians because the cats won't see the truth. No excuse to wage war, but it happens.

"So these others," I say, "they don't believe what you believe. What difference does it make? If you believe in your gods, isn't that good enough for you?"

"That be a topic of great debate among Felidians. As a single individual, I do not command the path of others, only wish to influence. It be Felidian lords who argue for war, convinced that our only hope for peace be realized through the elimination of nonbelievers."

"No one deserves to die just because of their beliefs."

"Personal belief may vary," he says, "though I fear it fails to satisfy the whole of society. Many Felidians insist that our enemy be destroyed."

"What about you, Physuro? What do you say?"

He senses my disapproval and proceeds cautiously. "It be my sincere hope that all creatures live in peace. If others choose not to believe, I may pity them for lacking what my fellows hold as true, though that should not bring reason to destroy them. I find pleasure in thoughts of never harming another, or anyone harming any other. Unfortunately, and to my sadness, Felidians be without a choice. Our enemy seeks to destroy us, as we do not believe as they do. Thus, war exists."

The argument grows within me, except it makes me a hypocrite. Conflicting belief should not warrant killing one another, but what about my own fellows? Our rebel force is no better, battling the Association over what we each believe. But we don't fight to conquer, or to force anyone to think as we do. We fight our enemy to preserve free will, for ourselves and others, surely a noble cause. If they would just leave us alone, everything would be fine. But no, they insist that we do as they do and become as they are, even though we don't agree and never will, not in a million years. Thus, war exists.

"Believe me, Adam," Physuro says, "Felidians hold no desire for war. However, the Ophidians have angered the gods, and we be assured, their wrath exceeds any suffering our enemy has brought. The gods demand that we destroy the heretics, and they provide the means to do so."

"Gifts? Right, some gift. It's all weapons, with one purpose—someone gets hurt."

"Indeed, they be tools of destruction, none would deny. Yet it be true, comprehend my plea, Felidians have no choice."

The dream, the delivery man—warning not to be around when they hurt themselves with this stuff. The delivery is weapons.

"Are there other gifts?" I ask.

"Felidians be loyal subjects. The gifts be plentiful."

Now it makes sense—the cargo transport and trucks rolling down the ramps. The delivery, of course.

"Have you seen any long cylinders riding a mechanical beast?"

"The Spears of the Gods," he says. "These gifts be well known. Their fiery ascent to the heavens be a sign to come, when the fury of the gods grows beyond tolerance and our enemy be punished as wrath rains down upon them. Prophecy tells of the day when the gods unleash the spears and end our suffering for all time. Many believe the day be soon."

Fiery ascent? Wrath rains down? Worse than I ever imagined.

"I'd like to see the gifts. Can you take me?"

"I will assist by any means possible." He indicates the guards ahead and those behind. "What be possible, however, rests in your power as a god."

✳

The prairie starts to green, and we come to the edge of a forest. The trail continues into the woods, threading a route between trunks growing larger around, higher, and more densely plotted, until a canopy of shade unfolds overhead. We ride past massive elder oaks with blackened red bark, leaves orangey tan, some brick, others rust. The clip-clop fades as we move across soft, fertile soil. A nearby creek trickles, songbirds sing, and shady beds of green invite a lazy afternoon nap, serenaded by nature.

The canopy of shade thickens, and beyond the trail, the first signs of civilization begin. Smoke rises from shacks nestled in the woods, a cart is loaded with hay, and angled racks hold strips of meat set out to dry. Hanging from a tree branch is an animal carcass, partly stripped of its hide.

I direct Physuro's attention to the sight. "I thought Felidians didn't eat meat."

"What be the basis of that notion?" he asks.

"Your goddess, rich soil makes plenty, I had thought…"

"If you be referring to my earlier comments, do consider, a mouse be a meager meal for creatures our size, would you not agree? As well, of all food one might consume, I believe rodent be not the best flavor. As for the goddess, indeed, her riches be plenty for those who favor such delights, as do I."

"Others eat meat, just not you."

"A personal preference, I do not care for the taste, and further enjoy knowing my bowels lack mounds of undigested flesh, I would imagine, rotting my insides. Though I be not one to judge. Others may devour any degree that pleases their belly."

It's been in plain sight all along. His shirt is woven fabric, but his vest and pants are leather. Of course they hunt. You don't make leather by weaving spun thread.

I point out his clothing. "But you'll kill them for something to wear."

"I have no wish to kill anything," he says. "However, if another Felidian be hungry and slays a creature, I see no harm in making use of its remains. Would you prefer that we discard their skins? It would not bring them back to life."

"I didn't think it would."

"Your kind," he asks, "does not consume the flesh of lesser animals?"

"Some do, but not all. Like you said, a personal choice. We're not so different."

But we have progressed. Ahead is a stream where cats wade in eddies, scrubbing fabric against washboards. We have machines for that. Others knee-deep in the current fill clay jugs and head into the forest, toward a growing number of larger cabins with chimneys of stacked river stones.

Felidians begin exiting their homes and approach the trail to watch us pass. Others climb out of the stream and join the gathering, all eyes on me, but none dares to come too close. Cats in coats of every color, they look poor, clothed in little more than rags. Peasants perhaps, dwelling outside the grand city. Though most stand silent, keeping a safe distance, some dart out of the crowd and pace our horses. Smaller cats, a fascinating sight, yet disturbing—they are children. A dozen or so run alongside, straining for a better view. I cannot look away from their youthful eyes, some dark, some green, amber, one blue-silver, all so hungry to know. I am as hungry to be like them, innocent and carefree, sprinting across a soft bed of green, chasing after a wondrous sight. If only I could touch that experience for one instant, every wound might heal. Someday, I will be a child again. Someday, a promise to myself.

Physuro asks, "You have not seen young before?"

Parents fetch a few of the little ones and hold them back.

"It's been far too long."

The Felidians may have their own struggle, but at least they get to be kids.

Unlike the children, the older cats stand frozen with concern in their gazes, suffering the misguided apprehension that no adult—human or cat—seems able to shake. Fearful respect, fear of a god, just as I had once suffered. Now I witness others display that same fear of god. Only this time, I'm the god they fear.

*

The forest ends, spreading open like a sweeping curtain to present a grassy landscape that slopes lower, forming a valley that stretches for miles—the same I saw from the landing platform. Except now at the opposite end, nearer to the stone city. Built on a mild rise, the city is contained by fortress walls surrounded by terraced hillsides. Row after row of agricultural patchwork is divided by irrigation canals that separate shades of green, grayish green, dusty olive and mustard yellow, thriving peacefully beneath sunlit clouds.

The trail winds down and back up hilly mounds, then becomes a gravel road more refined, leading to the city ahead. Efforts to gauge distance are confounding. The closer we approach, the stone walls only grow taller, at least twenty, maybe thirty feet high. Incredible to imagine the muscle required to heft these enormous blocks up from their quarry, to this plateau, and set them in place so precisely.

The road ends at the gateway to their city. The entrance is flanked by a pair of statues towering higher than the walls, two stone cats standing guard, holding spears vertical before them. Between the fearsome warriors, colossal wooden doors stand closed.

Cut low in one of the doors, a small portal snaps open. Prison guards dismount and speak with a Felidian on the other side. Wood scrapes as bolts slide, chains rattle and clank, and slowly, the doors begin to swing open.

Past the threshold, the city is populated by countless Felidians moving about the unpaved streets. Like Physuro, many cats wear leather vests, pants no lower than their knees, and sandals. The choice of most males, who appear content to dress the same. Females, however, exercise the joy of fashion, flaunting a rainbow of frocks draped from their shoulders and loosely fastened at the waist, blossoming outward and down to swish at their concealed feet. A group of males pass, somewhat different. Leather straps crisscross their chests and blast rifles are hanging from their shoulders. Their full leggings are tucked into dusty black boots. Soldiers.

As we move onto a larger avenue, I'm the target of many stares. Older cats hobbling on canes, the strong with confident strides, and young rambling like honeybees pause to look at me. Cats leading unfamiliar beasts yoked to wagons and others hauling sacks over their shoulders are equally interested.

We pass through a marketplace of canopied carts loaded with produce and grains, around which cats haggle, the overlapping conversations a clatter of noise. Felidians suspend all commerce and turn their attention to this god coming to visit.

Beyond the marketplace is a grand boulevard lined with monumental buildings. Wide steps rise to fluted columns that cradle beams supporting pitched stone rooftops, slabs angled to the sky. Not only grand, their architecture represents artistic triumph. The beams atop each colonnade are inscribed with inset sculptures, the faces of cats, full bodies on horseback, and others riding chariots, charging into battle to confront a swarm of masked invaders.

The boulevard ends at their most prestigious monument, round and capped by a smooth dome above circling pillars. Steps flare out and down to a plaza where a sculpture at the center rises from a pool of still water. Larger than life, the statue is an older cat in flowing gown, cradling a thick book in one arm and gazing out across the land, as if possessed by the wisdom of every age past and to come.

Our procession halts and the prison guards dismount. One unties my tether from the saddle horn, but he leaves me shackled.

On the steps of the round building are other guards who appear more official, equipped with bronze helmets and wielding spears. Serving the Council, I presume. Each wears a dark cloth draped over their chest, on which an emblem is embroidered, the profile of a golden cat, crouched and paws scratching.

One of the Council guard comes down the steps, aiming his spear at me. He cocks his helmet to the side and down and flicks his spear to match, indicating that I should dismount. Then he backs away, up the steps, and returns to the line of Council guards standing shoulder to shoulder, spears upright before them.

I touch down next to Physuro. He looks out at the grand boulevard and growing mob of Felidians kneeling in the street.

"Make them stop that," I say.

His gaze stays with the crowd. "It be time that you portray a mighty god."

"You said a council, not a convention."

"Act as a god no matter the number, and you be a god, commanding all."

This argument is getting old, but more irritating is the idea of being anyone's prisoner. We'll *see* how this goes.

I climb the steps, face the line of Council guards, and extend my shackled wrists. "Remove my restraints."

A prison guard yanks my leash, spinning me around and down some steps. I seize the tether, snap it from his grasp, and coil it into mine. Back to the Council guards, I choose one and get in his face. "I wish to acknowledge those worshipping me." I rattle the shackles and tug at my collar. "I will not have them see me restrained in this manner."

Beneath the bronze helmet, the guard's amber eyes stare out at nothing. In the day's bright sun, his black pupils are tall, thin slivers.

"See that crowd?" I twist and point with arms bound as one, then back to him. "They're watching you, waiting to see what happens. What will it be? What pleases them? Or what has them stone you to death. Or you might prefer that I turn you to stone so you may avoid the pain. I can be a merciful god if you choose, but that all depends—on what you choose."

His angled eyelids flash a blink. Then another, and twice again. He gazes at the crowd and pans slowly. Then he shifts to me. He advances, forcing me off the last step, then lowers his spear to the ground, flips his chest cloth, and fetches a key. He unlocks my binds and sets me free, just as I saw him doing only moments ago, when confronting him on the higher steps.

"Thank you." I rub the discomfort from my wrists, then indicate Physuro. He wears a straight face but his eyes have that sparkle belonging to a grin. I say to the guard, "My companion as well."

The obedient guard releases Physuro from his shackles and collar. That grin of his starts to show but Physuro restrains it and instead he bows. The guard backs away, stows his key and fetches his spear, and then returns to rank, another motionless, staring-at-nothing statue.

I climb the steps, past the Council guards and higher, and face the crowd. Worshippers fill the street and extend back some distance. More citizens stream in from connecting avenues and drop to their knees. I look across the crowd and project an aura exuding supreme, godlike authority. That should do the trick. Except it makes me sick. If I were down there in that crowd, I'd have to come up here and kick my ass for being such an arrogant fuck. My followers do not agree. All kneel further, faces in the dirt, and begin chanting.

Physuro joins me on the higher steps. "That be better." He indicates the monument's great doors. "Now, let us see any lord kneel before you."

✳

Escorted by Council guards, we are led through a corridor decorated by artwork. One painting is an odd creature lying at rest, the head of an owl growing out of a four-legged body, tail curling round and round. Next is a painting of blue-back dolphins, bellies white, leaping from the sea into a foggy sky. Another feathered creature with an eagle's beak has arms and legs like a man, or a cat perhaps. Then there's a pair of winged horses with pointy ears, followed by portraits of Felidian heads on bird bodies. A zoological nightmare.

The next corridor is more sterile, lined with short pedestals supporting busts carved from white stone. The heads are not Felidians, rather humans, looking on with supreme authority and sporting that dreadful helmet hairstyle. Their gods, the Bobs.

The hallway ends at two massive doors. In the center of each, an oval bears the face of a somber old cat. Cascading from their chins are rolls and rolls of furry curls that end at giant doorknockers. More Council guards are stationed to each side of the entrance. As we approach, they pull the doors open.

The round chamber is capped by a smooth dome, above windows that scatter a diffuse yellow glow, shadows soft and few. Beyond a curving barrier at the lowest level, four tiers of stone desks rise higher and circle the room, all but the entry. At one and two thirds around the room, narrow stairs divide the desks and allow occupants to move between tiers.

In a room all stone, the only wood is a table and chairs at the lowest level, in the center of this small indoor coliseum. We are escorted to the table and remain standing.

Directly ahead, a larger desk consumes two tiers, atop a prominent section rising above the lesser seating. A throne fit for a king. To one side and halfway up the tiers, a door opens. Older Felidians flow into the chamber, clothed in white robes. They emerge from the passage, scale the stairs between tiers, and get to their seats.

The last to enter moves to the more prominent desk and takes his throne. The hefty armrests are nearly to his shoulders, putting his arms straight out once he sits. He reaches for a gavel and snaps it against the stone. "The Council be convened."

At my side, Physuro leans close and privately says, "Bow before the Master Lord."

Together we drop to one knee.

The Master Lord stands. "Where be the restraints? These be dangerous criminals brought before the Council."

I rise. "We are *not* dangerous, and we will *not* be restrained. All in this room agree."

A Council guard steps forward, the one I chose to intimidate outside. "Most Honorable Sir," he says, addressing the Master Lord. "I beg, forgive me. I fear punishment for my disobedience, yet greater fear has me appease this powerful god. I accept your decision as my fate." He drops to one knee and bows deeply.

"So be rewarded your fear." The Master Lord lowers to his throne. "Remove the incompetent."

Other guards seize him. Stripped of his position, he leaves his spear lying on the floor and surrenders his helmet and chest cloth.

I privately ask Physuro, "What happens to our friend?"

He watches the guards haul away the disobedient cat. "Death, I imagine."

"*Death?* For removing my collar?" I whirl around. "Stop! He has aided a god." The guards halt in the open doorway. I turn back to the Master Lord. "His fate lies with the gods."

The Master Lord says, "Name the god wielding authority in this matter."

Physuro turns with arms out, gathering Council attention, and ends his pirouette facing me. "I present to the Lords of the Council, Adam of Idan, the God of Truth."

After expressing my distaste for titles, it's bad enough he ignores my wish and hands me one, but worse, he chooses *Truth?* More accurate would be the god of stretching it.

The Master Lord signals the guards to release the offender, then says to me, "The trusted gods inform us that you be an enemy, invader of the heavens, here to challenge the Mighty One."

"Your gods have deceived you."

A rumble passes through the congregation. The guard who removed our restraints has joined Physuro and me. Step one accomplished—they're listening and obeying my commands.

From the collection of desks above, one lord stands fast and speaks viciously. "What evidence have you?" His bushy brow descends, tightening his glare, and his pointy ears flatten. His mouth curls to bare his teeth, making his whiskers spread and stiffen.

I face the ornery grump. "I possess logic, the vehicle on which truth is carried."

"That be not evidence."

Council members mutter, grumble, and some chuckle. Lord Ornery stands proud, arms crossed and glancing about the desks, gathering the imagined praise of his fellow lords.

I cast my voice to reach every end of the chamber. "I shall ask to call your attention to the reason for my imprisonment. For an act to be considered a crime, the act must produce a harmful consequence."

Another lord rises, speaking so fast it all runs together. "Your words be irrelevant." The lanky cat lacks an ounce of fat, and his advanced age leaves his furry cheeks to droop in folds hanging from his face.

I step closer to the standing lord. "Indulge them for a time, I implore you, and I shall produce their relevance."

Lord Impatient drops to his seat as quickly as he rose, but he can't keep from shifting in it.

I address all, "For my example, let us consider murder. A hideous act we can be sure, yet the act alone is not the basis of any crime, rather that another suffers the loss of life. The *result* of the act."

Lord Ornery shoots up. "You be wasting our time. Your words be irrelevant and your claim without evidence."

I ignore the heckler and address the others. "Now that we understand a basis is required to consider an offense punishable, again I ask to call your attention to the reason for my imprisonment. What harmful consequence have I produced that forms the basis of any crime worthy of my detention?"

The Master Lord says, "It be the trusted gods who wish that we detain you."

"Your gods have deceived you, asking that I be detained without a basis, only their wish."

Lord Ornery says, "Words alone do not constitute evidence."

I stare up at him. "We shall see." I shift away, around the table, and begin strolling along the stone barrier separating us from them. "Now I shall expose the nature of truth." I halt, then scan across the collection of lords. "Suppose I claim the sky is pink."

Lord Ornery says, "Your evidence be foolishness we already know?"

Lord Impatient adds, "Irrelevant foolishness."

I focus on Lord Ornery. "Not foolishness, rather a known fact, as you have so kindly pointed out. But let us delve deeper and examine this fact as an exercise in logic."

He scoffs at my suggestion. "Logic?"

"Yes, logic pure and simple, even a child could understand, and none would argue."

"Very well," the Master Lord says. "Demonstrate your logic."

I face him and bow. Then, turning across the congregation, I ask, "How is one to believe the sky is pink?"

Another lord rises, packing twice the pounds his short frame was made to carry. Arms outstretched, he chortles and his middle jiggles like a tub of jelly. "Everyone knows the sky be pink."

A roar of laughter erupts, as though all present expect amusing entertainment anytime Lord Chortle opens his fat mouth.

Undaunted by ridicule, I advance on the stone desks and target him. "Yes, everyone knows, but the question remains—how? How do they *know* the sky is pink?"

Lords grumble among themselves, then become quiet.

"You know the sky is pink because you can see it with your own eyes."

Lord Impatient says, "Your logic be childish."

I whirl on him. "And how soon we grow old and forget a view from the eyes of a child."

Lord Ornery adds, "And without evidence."

I turn away, move around the table, and address the other side. "Now, suppose I tell you of a place where the sky is blue."

Lord Chortle shoots up, slaps his fat belly and roars, "That be absurd. Everyone knows the sky be pink."

Right on cue, the room fills with laughter.

My voice rises above the clamor. "Not knowing it exists is not proof of impossibility!"

The laughter stops. Lord Chortle drops on his seat like a sack of mud.

"And conversely," I continue, "it is neither proof that it does exist. It is a claim without evidence, in this case an effort on my part to convince you fine sirs that another possibility may exist. It is an idea yet unproven, until its degree of truth comes under the scrutiny of one's own perception. Until that moment of firsthand observation, the claim is neither true nor false, and if regarded either by any fraction before that time, constitutes a flaw in thinking and a flawed belief. This simple, indisputable logic is what separates ideas from knowledge, all too often mistaken as synonymous."

Lord Impatient says, "Your words be irrelevant."

"I think not. No member of this council has witnessed firsthand, any act the basis of any crime that demands any punishment. Lacking a basis, you have no sound reason to impose judgment on me or my fellows." I swing around and target Lord Ornery. "You, I dare say, are those without evidence."

No vicious comeback this time. That's right—there's your evidence, asshole.

The Master Lord says, "It be not our place to mediate conflicts between the gods. We only seek to please the gods, all gods, and we have thus far."

I pound the table, *Bam!* "You have not pleased this god!"

Lords shrink in their seats. Murmurs drift through and fade, then silence.

"You risk great harm imprisoning gods. I demand my release, and my fellow gods as well. Do not test my wrath."

Speechless lords stare down at me.

The Master Lord asks, "What fellow gods do you speak of?"

"Those who accompanied me. The Goddess—"

What do I call them? Fresh out of fancy titles, I shift to Physuro, given the ease with which he found a title for me. He shrugs. He doesn't even know them, leaving me to think fast or play a fool.

The answer is obvious. "Christina, the Goddess of Dreams. And David, the God of Laughter." Not stretching the truth much, other than god and goddess.

Another lord rises, his forehead a stack of wrinkles, his eyes long and hollow. "How be we to solve this dilemma?" His timid voice is difficult to hear. "We cannot please all the gods. Pleasing one displeases another. What be there for us to do?"

Lord Timid has a point. Who do they make happy? Me, or the Bobs? It won't be both. This can't be a decision they feel obligated to make.

"The affairs of the gods are not the concern of mere mortals. You have no right or responsibility, even if falsely granted by another god, to impose judgment on any god. You will release all gods at once or suffer the consequences!" I pound the table again, *Bam!*

The booming echo fades until the room falls silent.

The Master Lord rises. "We must discuss the matter. If you would kindly excuse us."

Right, a council. Talk talk talk.

"Fair enough."

He snaps the gavel. "The Council be adjourned."

After today and forevermore, I expect to hold all gods in the highest regard. What a rotten job.

✳

Drained of all energy, I drop to a chair at the table. That took more than I expected. Or more that I didn't expect, now wondering where all that nonsense came from. I didn't realize any of it was in me, and now out of me, it feels like nothing is left. I must be made of malarkey.

They could return with orders for our execution. I am powerless to prevent it. Words, all I have are words, falling from this hoping-to-be-intimidating mouth. Behind us, Council guards block our only escape, standing before the doors with their spears upright. Any one of those spears could easily pluck my heart out.

Physuro lowers to a chair beside me. "Insist you be mortal if you must, though I shall never believe. I have witnessed a mighty god in my own presence."

"Look, Physuro, do me a favor…"

"What be your wish, My Master?"

I twist hard, the chair with me, scraping the floor. "Physuro! No Sir, no God, and of all things, not *Master*. Just my name."

He sinks into his shoulders. "I beg, forgive me, Adam of Idan. I do not wish to enrage you further. I only wish to offer my respect."

"The best respect is Adam, just Adam. Understood?"

"I comprehend, Adam."

Our new friend, the Council guard whose life I spared, drops to his knees and puts his forehead to the floor. Might as well smack it a few times and finish the brain damage.

I ask Physuro, "So what do we do with him?"

"You have commanded his fate," he says. "I believe that decision lies with you."

I approach the kneeling guard. "You," I say, "what's your name?"

He mumbles something into the floor.

"At attention, soldier!"

He springs upright, shoulders back, staring out at nothing.

"Relax," I say. "I'm not going to hurt you."

Not a flinch, nor blink of his amber eyes, he stands as stiff as a board.

"Well?" I say. "Tell us your name."

"Stuphenaldaphese, Your Grace."

"Look, the name's Adam. Don't add the extras, is that clear?"

"Yes, sir."

"That includes *sir,* Stu-fen…"

"Stuphenaldaphese."

It all runs together, a mess I can't dissect enough to teach my tongue. "Let's just call you Stu."

"As you wish."

"Okay, Stu, I think you can go now, we're done with you."

He looks confused.

Physuro says, "He be a strange god," and pats Stu on the back. "You shall grow familiar in time."

Stu says, "I thought…"

"No, Stu," I assure him. "You're not dying today. Nobody's dying today. I think we've all had enough of that."

Stu stares blankly, and Physuro chuckles.

"What's so funny?" I ask.

"My words be merely an act," Physuro says. "When you asked what happens to him, my response be an innocent lie, with purpose. Believing his death brought you great power."

"They weren't…"

"Of course not," Stu says. "We do not torture our own kind. That be insane."

"So what did I save you from?"

"Assignment to a post in the desert, I imagine, left to endure unbearable heat until my dying moment. I be grateful and in your debt. I be now honored, placed in the service of the gods." He smiles proudly.

"So I'm stuck with you."

"I serve until death."

*

Council guards strike their spears against the floor, three raps in chorus. The higher door opens, lords return to the chamber, and they spread out among the tiers. The Master Lord enters last, lowers to his throne, and snaps the gavel.

"The Council be reconvened."

A moment passes as the lords quiet themselves.

"We have deep concerns," the Master Lord says, "and fear our safety be threatened by actions taken this day. However, the Lords of the Council believe there be no other choice. As you have insisted, and we agree, it be not our place to dictate the fate of any god. We wish to please the gods, all the gods, and now we please you as well and grant your freedom. Yet in doing so, we seek mercy in judgment of our decision. We beg, convince the other gods that your release be not an act of disrespect, rather, our inability to resolve matters of conflict among the gods."

Better still, convince the gods to pack their gear and get the hell off this planet.

"I will do what I can. I cannot promise your safety, but know this—my true intent is that no harm comes to any inhabitant of this world, and on that you have my word."

The Master Lord asks, "And what of Physuro?"

"I wish him released and placed in my service."

"Very well." The Master Lord snaps his gavel. "Physuro be now a servant of the gods."

Lords rise, clapping, an inspired display that grows to roaring thunder. Looks like the God of Truth just performed his first miracle—converting society's most impious heretic, into an agent of the gods no less. The applause dwindles and the lords retake their seats.

I move around the table and approach the Master Lord. "I now wish for my fellow gods to be released without delay."

He looks down at me. "Your request be reasonable. However, we be unable to comply."

"Why not?"

He hesitates. "We have no other gods imprisoned."

Hot knives stab my heart. I stagger back until halted by the table. Oh no, I've made an assumption, a terrible mistake. They don't even know about Dave and Christina.

My godly persona is crumbling. I can't let them see me like this. I seize control, whirl around and pound the table, *Bam!*

"I demand to know their whereabouts."

The table creaks, one leg snaps, and a corner crashes down. Stu and Physuro leap clear.

"We beg, believe us," the Master Lord says. "We cannot assist in matters unknown to us."

"There must be someone who knows. There has to be."

Lord Timid mumbles something.

I throw myself his direction. "What have you to say?"

A hush covers the room.

Lord Timid rises from his seat. "Only Crontis must know."

There is hope.

The chamber doors burst open. Council guards level their spears at a lone Felidian soldier in the doorway.

The Master Lord is on his feet. "What be the meaning of this intrusion?"

The soldier waves off the spears, hurries in and bows, then looks up at the Master Lord.

"Forgive me, Most Honorable Sir, I bear grave news. The Council be in peril. Our enemy attacks."

✳

Booming thunder rocks the chamber. Lords claw past one another, down the steps and across desks, unleashing a flood of white robes pouring over the barrier to our side.

The Master Lord calls, "The gods be enraged by our disobedience. The Council be adjourned until safety be reached." He doesn't bother smacking the gavel.

Lords scramble past, trample the table flat, and cram into the doorway. We're overwhelmed by the stampede and swept into the hallway. *Boom!* A blast strikes the building and the walls shudder. Helmet-hair busts of godly

Bobs topple from their perches and shatter.

I reach out to lords ahead of us, seize them by the shoulder, and spin them around. There are too many, and they all look the same, gray fur and white gowns, all terrified.

Physuro senses my urgency to find the knowing lord and joins my quest, darting ahead and searching the fleeing crowd. The lord I seek is not so timid about leading the pack, but now he falls behind the rest as Physuro holds him back.

I hurry to them. "Tell me what you know."

"You seek…" Lord Timid gravitates toward the departing crowd.

I clutch his gown and yank him closer. "Who? Tell me!"

"Lord Demaphro. He be a witness to your arrival."

"And this lord has said what?"

"Of a great battle among the gods."

That was *great?* They're in for a shock.

"Where can I find him?"

Stu says, "He be Lord of the Military, commanding our forces from the Arsenal of Meletius. Let us be away."

Lord Timid gets loose. Waving his arms overhead, he joins the escaping flow.

"Call upon the gods, save us!"

✳

Outside, lords scramble down the steps, fan out in the street, and vanish in a mob of panicked citizens. Sizzling beams pour from the sky. Stone fragments spray the crowd and countless fall dead, more as injured are trampled.

The sky is swarming with craft swooping, diving, and blasting. Assault craft, but an unfamiliar design—nimble black triangles. They zip past, up and over, at angles and others climbing, scattering all directions. A horde blackens the sky, no formation whatsoever, an uncoordinated mess. Doesn't stop them from taking out land targets at will, and with ease. If not for their great number, I wouldn't be intimidated. Lacking a clear strategy, this enemy's best is exploits of chaos.

Our horses buck and fight their tethers. As I unwind the reins, a beam strikes too close, a fireball spreads, and the animal stomps and sidesteps. I grab the saddle horn and hoist myself on.

Stu and Physuro draw their horses alongside.

"Who's attacking?" I ask.

Stu looks to the heavens. "Ophidians."

"They *fly?*"

"And rain fire from the sky. Come, let us find safety at Meletius."

At a strong gallop, we navigate an obstacle course of fiery explosions, dead and dying, stone hurling past and craters in our path. Electrified shafts whiz down, booming impacts so intense the shock wave exceeds the sound, pounding my chest with force enough to liquefy organs. Our nimble horses dodge the chaos without urging. Every creature wants out of this mess, man, beast, and cat alike. One misstep and we're all toast.

At war in seconds, I've hardly a chance to digest what is happening. An enemy capable of flight? Armed with blast cannons? Not exactly fair. This primitive culture can't repel a technologically advanced intruder. I have to help them.

Our escape through carnage leads to another towering monument, though one not so concerned with artistic flairs, rather an emphasis on practical value, especially on days like this. The exterior is unadorned, and the massive slabs look more like poured concrete than stone, similar to a military bunker. A welcome sight, indeed. Stu charges his horse to the entrance and leaps off, leaving the animal to fend for itself, which sounds fine to me and Physuro agrees, we're off our rides and chasing after Stu.

Great doors stand open, not good during enemy attack, but I'm thrilled. Stuck outside and having to knock could be a death sentence. Inside, thick walls muffle the blasts, the passage quakes, and dust falls from cracks above. We follow Stu into a hallway that stretches the building's length. We pass intersecting corridors, pause to look, empty, then continue to the next. Ahead, Felidian soldiers march the hallway, boots stamping as they approach.

Stu calls, "Where be Lord Demaphro?"

The platoon doesn't miss a beat. Moving past, a soldier says, "Battle room, our destination."

We double back, fall in behind, and join their march. The soldiers flow into the next corridor, boots hammering the floor in perfect time. These guys are trained. The Felidians may lack airships, but acting as a coordinated force may prove an asset. Their enemy can hardly fly straight. Like a body with no head. Stronger arms or not, I can beat a mindless opponent.

The corridor ends at open doors. The dimly lit chamber is circled by dark pillars and some statues in the background, faint in shadows. In the center of the room, Felidians argue across a large table. Soldiers flow in and around the table to blend with cats trading papers and having frantic conversations.

Stu darts in ahead of us. "Bow before Adam of Idan, God of Truth."

An instant chilling silence. Cats drop to their knees.

"Get up!" I holler, advancing into the room with hands sweeping up, urging them to rise. "All of you. Up!" I swing around and target Stu. "I know you mean well, Stu, but please, don't do that again."

He bows and silently backs away. Ignoring me? Or chastised, and his final display of unsolicited respect. One can only hope.

Physuro announces, "We seek an audience with the Lord Demaphro. It be a matter of the utmost importance."

From the crowd, an older cat emerges, with bushy fur and overgrown brow that throws a dark shadow across his deep-set eyes. He is dressed as a soldier but more supreme, judging by his purple cape the others lack. Heavyset, mostly in his barrel chest, and not all that tall yet forcing an air of authority, he clutches a thick belt on each side of a large buckle and employs a swagger that lands his boots hard.

"I be the Lord Demaphro."

I stride to face him. "I understand you witnessed my arrival."

"If I had?"

"What happened to my friends? The two who were with me."

"I suspect…" He hesitates, as if stumbling toward a secret he promised to keep. "Those you seek…" He glances at Physuro. "They be with the Mighty One."

A blast strikes and the room shudders.

"Where?" I ask.

"The mountains," Physuro says, then glances at Demaphro. "Home of the Gods."

Both sink into a grave silence, as though to utter the secret confirms their execution.

I ask Physuro, "Can you take me?"

"I advise not," he says. "Trespass grounds of the gods, punishment be severe, far worse than any prison."

"I'll handle your gods once we get there."

"Then it be true," Demaphro says. "You dare to challenge the Mighty One."

"And just who is this one so mighty?"

He points across the room to a statue that rises above the crowd. I move through and closer to the sculpture, carved from white stone, a full body larger than life, perhaps half again my size. But it's not a Felidian. The statue is a man, turned away and looking down, clothed in a flowing gown and cradling a thick book in one arm. I ease around to study the face.

They have got to be kidding.

"What the hell is this?"

Awestruck cats stand petrified and silent.

Boom! The floor rumbles, the statue teeters, and I reach out to steady it. Why? I should knock the crap over myself.

"*This* is the Mighty One?"

"Indeed," Demaphro says, moving out of the crowd. "Crontis be the father of all gods, the most supreme."

Jared?

"He's no god, he's here to hurt you. He's only pretending to help."

Cats gasp, some hiss. Boots landing hard, Demaphro advances on me. "Crontis has bestowed many gifts upon the Felidians. The heathen words you speak be untrue."

"Gifts? You mean weapons."

"Protection for his prized children. Crontis loves the Felidians."

The way a shark loves its next meal.

Boom!

"Show me the gifts."

Demaphro doesn't budge. "What do you hope to gain from their inspection?"

"I hope to survive. In case you hadn't noticed, we have a little problem here." I point up at the ceiling just as another blast strikes and we're dusted.

He fumbles for something to say. Maybe a decent argument. Or why Felidians promote the sheepish. Competent leaders take action. *Do something!*

Another blast strikes and he only cowers deeper into indecision. Dust showers from cracks spreading across the ceiling, sections break loose and fall, and some rattle the statue of Jared. That deceptive bastard, this is all his doing. I scoop up a chunk of fallen stone and hurl it—*whack!* The sculpture tips, begins to pitch over, and gains speed. Felidians leap back, nearly out of their fur when the statue crashes to the floor and shatters.

The severed head rolls around until settling on one cheek, blank stone eyes staring up at me, and his mouth pinching toward that damned grin. I can hear his laughter, Jared smug again while I'm left to scramble, searching for an answer, how to win this insane challenge, me versus him.

Enough of this crap. I leave Demaphro and approach his troops.

"I hereby take command of this unit. Any soldier has a problem with that, step out of line now."

Not a one of them even hints at a flinch.

"Good. Now take me to the gifts."

✳

Surrounded by stamping boots of the platoon, we charge through a corridor, and chasing after us, Demaphro has suddenly made a decision—take control of his unit. Imagine that. Sorry, Lord of the Military, your troops are following my orders until I'm not here for them to follow.

The corridor ends at polished steel doors, similar to those throughout the cargo transport. The first significant use of metal since I landed on this planet.

All I must do is wave and the troops advance. They lean into the enormous doors and heave, opening the way to a black void. Soldiers flow into darkness, a clatter of footsteps, then a snap and a spotlight shines down from a tall pole. More switches are thrown, lighting a warehouse full of material hidden beneath dusty tarpaulins. I step in, peel one back, and discover a mobile surface-to-air pulsed wave inducer, the larger sort on a motorless platform with four wheels and gunner's seat next to the barrel. I pull another tarp, another and more, revealing a line of the wheeled weaponry, all sitting idle. Across the room, I stride past low mounds and fling tarps, uncovering an arsenal. Ammunition cells, rifles and pistols, over-the-shoulder rocket launchers and handheld blast cannons. Indeed, the gods are generous.

I ask Demaphro, "Why aren't you protecting yourselves with these weapons?"

He stares at me as if ashamed, then reluctantly confesses, "We do not fully comprehend their use."

Gifts from the gods—without instructions?

"Is there a door to the outside?" I ask.

He nods but otherwise takes no action.

"Then get it open. Now!" I shift to the troops, "Open the outside doors."

Soldiers scurry across the warehouse. Another set of tall steel doors swing open and sunlight streams in. I call to Stu and Physuro, get their help, and we push one of the wheeled weapons toward the doorway. Soldiers stand gawking as we pass.

"Move them outside," I say. "All of them. Now!"

Demaphro mirrors the order, directing soldiers who have already burst into action, rolling a fleet of the mobile inducers past the open doors and outside.

Black triangles fill the sky, swooping, diving, and blasting. But they can't hold a decent formation. They're crazy, scattered across the sky and darting every direction. What bonehead taught this enemy to fly? Not that I'm complaining. Their ignorance is our advantage, except the arsenal doors open to a broad avenue, and across the way is a courtyard full of fountains and statues, all low to the ground. I'd prefer a tall building directly across, putting us in a narrow trench with better cover.

After instructing the soldiers to spread out the weapons, I climb into the seat of one and study the controls. Curious troops huddle near and watch. Operating an Association mobile pulsed wave inducer is the last thing I expected today. If I can even remember how. Blasts streak down into the courtyard across the street. When the smoke clears, a line of statues have a problem with their heads—clouds of dust lingering for a moment then gone. Of course I remember how this works. I release the barrel from its stowed position and it pops up, angled to fire. Display on, targets on display, trajectory plotting. I work the directional pad like it was just yesterday. Nudge the arrow up, over one click, target inside the cursor, the barrel swings around and sweeps the sky. Red light flashes, tracking target. Green light, target locked. Hit the fire button and a scorching beam rockets into the sky.

Soldiers shift back and press into a crowd of citizens gathering near. The beam strikes an enemy craft, explodes a fireball, and debris rains down. The soldiers watch with great interest while citizens drop to their knees and begin chanting.

I call to the soldiers, "Now you're going to do it." I grab one and put him in the seat, then motion to others, come near, hurry. "Watch, all of you, and learn." The troops close in around the wheeled weapon as I instruct my first student.

"See this display? Now look below, at the four arrows."

The soldier studies the panel, the directional pad, then reaches out to touch it.

"Press them," I say, "and watch what happens." I point to the screen.

He tries it. "It be moving the box."

"Right. Now put the box over a target on the screen." I scan the soldiers gathered near. "Is everyone watching? Pay attention."

The seated soldier struggles with the directional pad, chasing targets with little success, but quickly gets the hang of it. The red light flashes and the barrel swings around.

"Does that mean go?" he asks.

"No, red means wait. Green is go."

"Where do I go?"

"You don't go anywhere. Just press the red button."

"If green be go, why be the button red?"

"Look, I didn't make this thing, I'm just telling you how it works. Some miserable engineer back on Orn-3 is probably having a good laugh about now." The befuddled soldier stares at me. "Never mind. Just hit the button when the light goes green."

"Green as it be now?"

"Yes. Now fire."

"Fire?" he asks.

"Yes! Hit the fire button, *now!*"

"Be that the red button name, the fire button?"

"*Yes! Press it!*"

He taps the button, the weapon recoils, and a scorching beam rockets skyward.

Teaching is frustrating, especially under dire circumstances. I wouldn't bother if given a chance to copy myself ten times over. I can't operate all these weapons alone. I need their help. I have to teach them.

The beam strikes, a fireball spreads, and debris rains down. The kneeling citizens stand, and instead of chanting, this time they cheer. That's more like it.

I ask a soldier standing near, "Did you watch?"

He nods.

I shift to the next. "And did you learn?"

He and others nod.

"Good. Now get busy."

Soldiers scatter, choose inducers, and climb aboard. Stray shots slice across the sky as they make adjustments, but soon their aims improve and scorching beams begin tearing apart the swarm. With our first line of defense in place, enemy kills mount fast, though maybe too fast. Fireballs burst, flame out and debris drifts down—one hit and each craft is destroyed. That can't be right. Even the lightest assault craft takes a few hits to erode shield energy. Regardless, countless enemy squadrons remain, blackening the sky. Even with a one-hundred percent kill ratio, repelling this attack is going to take more than a scant battalion of surface-to-air weaponry.

✳

Back in the warehouse, I pull tarp after tarp, uncovering enough weapons to make even the staunchest general giddy with notions of assured victory. But these weapons won't work. Rifles, rocket launchers, mortars and troop transports. Maybe for ground war along the front line, but where the hell is that? And who's the infantry? Not the minor unit I now command. I need an army and somewhere to take them.

Along the back wall are larger items tarped the same as the rest. Much larger, the tarps could hide tanks. Still no better, even with time to teach the cats how they work. Regardless, I load up with two pistols, a blast rifle, and burden both shoulders with ammunition cells, then call to Physuro and instruct him to do the same. He studies the items I carry, then makes his selections while I move off to find out what's under those big tarps. I reach out to one and give it a tug. The limp fabric slides off and collects on the floor.

"What be it?" Physuro asks, approaching from behind.

I can only marvel at the wondrous sight. So they are equipped for more than land war.

"Our chariot to the heavens."

Small compared to most attack fighters, and sleeker, the craft is shaped like an elongated triangle. The hull is completely black, polished wet, and every contour is smooth. Even parked it looks fast. Physuro comes to my side, studying our next ride as he struggles to understand what this machine does. He may not realize it—the craft is identical to those in the sky.

I hurry up the ladder to the cockpit cover, an opaque glass bubble as black as the hull. Once popping the latch, the cover angles open above a snug compartment. Side by side, two seats face controls, with ample room behind for gear or a third passenger, possibly four if willing to get cozy.

I call to Demaphro, "Sir, do you have any pilots?"

He comes to the ladder and looks up at me. "Pilots?"

"To pilot these ships." I indicate the tarped craft, then realize, "You don't know what a pilot is."

His only reply is a blank stare.

"Never mind." I call to Physuro, "Get up here, you're with me."

"I be joining you?"

"Remember, we had a deal. You're guiding the way."

I drop into the pilot seat and survey the controls. Triangle, half-moon, circle. Association pictograms—pitch, yaw, and roll.

Physuro's furry head pops above the edge as he tops the ladder. His wide-eyed gaze sweeps across the cockpit.

"Get in." I buckle up.

"It be safe?" he asks.

"Trust me."

He climbs the edge and gawks at the many lights, switches, and gauges.

"Strap in good, Physuro. It's been a while, I might be rusty."

He lowers into the copilot seat. "You be made of metal?"

This cat just cracks me up. "It's just a figure of speech."

His brow twists, ears wandering like radar. Then he notices my harness, studies his, figures it out and cinches the straps tight.

"Your speech be rather figurative, I must say."

"You'll get used to the lingo, just roll with it."

"You be rusty, yet not made of metal, and I appear a wheel rolling along-side, hoping to comprehend where we ling-go."

"Exactly." I pull the cockpit cover down and it bangs. Another bang, and again.

Physuro points past me, out my side. "I believe another wheel seeks to travel the road of your strange words."

Unlike the opaque exterior, from inside, the cockpit cover is clear. Stu is at the top of the ladder, armed and ready to go, and banging on the glass.

I release the latch and the cover pops open. "What?" I ask.

"I serve until death."

Right, how could I forget.

✳

Demaphro may not realize it, but he's getting back control of his unit. He and his troops gather around the craft, struggling to understand this machine we've climbed into and the purpose it serves. The engine's rising pitch is not enough to satisfy their curiosity, but when I throttle up and the low roar grows to a piercing whine, they get the hint and start backing away.

I increase power and the craft lurches up, wobbling in a low hover as I overcompensate pitch and yaw, straining for balance. Easy nudges of the controls, I get a feel for the craft's behavior. With power to the thrusters, we glide toward the doorway leading outside. Angled forward in his seat, Physuro gauges our lowly elevation, fascinated with this feat of magic.

Soldiers scatter out the doorway, covering their ears. Up close, the engines of any craft are not a pleasant sound—outside the sealed cockpit. With some difficulty, I hold the craft steady and ease past the double doors. Below, Felidians fan out in the street, a circle expanding away from our godly chariot. Clear of the warehouse, I tilt the pitch and jab the thrust, up a short rise in one quick surge, then hover. Stu and Physuro gasp. If that tiny leap stole their breath, they're in for a big shock, and the ride of their lives.

Pitch yanked full back, the craft stands on end. Bright sun stares down as we rocket straight up, slicing through thin clouds. A good, steady ascent—invigorating. Physuro is pressed firm in his seat, and behind us, Stu sounds like he's purring in reverse.

Once we reach some altitude, I ease back on the throttle and pitch the craft forward into level flight, gliding over a soft bed of clouds. Now to adjust shield frequency and double-check systems. Wouldn't want to face the enemy without some protection. In the airspace ahead, a cluster of triangle craft bob and weave across the clear pink, a flat line of black that flickers and sways, a few strays above, a few below. More of that sloppy formation.

Physuro stares ahead as if counting down his last seconds alive.

Not me, I'm pumped.

"Wrath of god, coming right up."

I send us soaring into the swarm, blast-cannon blazing. An enemy craft swoops across our nose and the easy target explodes—a fireball in our path. A heartbeat from joining our first kill, I push the craft to bank and climb, the engines scream, and flames wash over the cockpit glass. Debris splatters the underside, rat-tat-tat, and we emerge from the firestorm into clear sky.

No chance to catch my breath with black triangles coming head-on and whizzing past. We dip and climb, side to side, a rollercoaster ride through the onslaught. Consumed with threading a tight course between craft, priority one has lost focus—we should be firing. Don't dodge the enemy, destroy them. Back to the trigger, the blast-cannon roars. Two, six, twelve are toast just like that, and each in only one shot, leaving puffs of flame that we slice through.

"Looks like your enemy never heard of shields."

"Shields?" Physuro asks.

I miscalculate and nick the wing of an oncoming craft. Our shields sizzle and repel the enemy, throwing it into another, a boom and both vaporize.

"So we don't end up like that."

We punch through the fireball only to face more oncoming craft. Between evasive maneuvers and blasting what can't be dodged, I carve a path out of the onslaught.

"An invisible barrier protects us?" Physuro asks.

"To an extent, but only if you turn it on. I guess neither of you got instructions."

We reach the swarm's trailing edge and the flow of craft starts to thin. A couple more blasts and the remaining targets splatter the sky with flame. I yank the pitch and send the craft into a loop, then one-eighty roll at apex. Leveled out and trailing the pack, we ride calm airspace above our prey. Time to spank these boys and send them home.

Then I realize, "Physuro, your enemy—they have gifts from the gods just like the Felidians."

"It be unlikely," he says. "Ophidians be heathen creatures with no respect for the gods."

"So where did they get assault craft?"

"Perhaps they be more inventive than Felidians, as they be more evil."

"Being evil doesn't make anyone smart. It just makes them evil."

Ophidians may be heathen creatures without respect for the gods, but also unlikely is inhabitants of the same planet developing, on their own, technology significantly advanced beyond a rival. Besides, if they had, it would have been genocide for the Felidians long before I showed up. The enemy has received the same gifts, at the same time, from the same giver. Though perhaps with a few more instructions. Ophidians do appear to understand the term *pilot.*

Something lights up tactical. Coming from below—behind us—too many blips racing up the screen. I twist and scan for a view out the aft. Another swarm is on our six and closing fast.

"Hang on." I pitch the craft down, apply full power, and aim for a quick escape. We drop like a brick, nose-diving on the Felidian city. Physuro can't find his next breath. Don't worry, my friend, we'll be fine. That is, if my stomach doesn't spew out my ears.

The swarm dives with us, sticking to our tail like glue. We may know a thing or two about shields, but it does little good against impossible odds. When a few hundred electrobeams tickle our behind, we won't be feeling all that smug.

The ground comes fast and Physuro's eyes bug out. I yank the pitch and we're gliding just above the dusty street in a trench of buildings, weaving between with ample room, except that one straight ahead. Physuro covers his face. Come on, I'm not *that* rusty.

I bank the craft to stand on edge, wingtips to sky and ground. We breeze around the corner onto the next avenue then level out, kicking up dust and a wake that knocks over terrified cats scrambling out of the way.

The swarm is tenacious. Other than a few that didn't survive the turn, the enemy is sticking fast and has grown—hundreds now follow every twist and flop as we slice through narrow city streets. This isn't good, enemy in striking range, and leading them through an obstacle course hasn't taken out the many I had hoped.

The enemy opens fire. I throw the craft up and over, back and down, twirling between buildings, banking past statues, low enough at times our belly skims the dirt. Beams whiz past our hull, structures ahead explode, but not a single shot strikes our craft. They're not firing at us, only ground targets.

"This is weird."

Eyes wide as we bob and weave, Physuro manages, "Frightening be a better word."

For him and Stu maybe. First time. Just another ride for me, and at this point, navigating the obstacle course has shifted to autonomous while conscious mental resources are consumed by the enemy's peculiar behavior—chasing us but without intent to destroy. Why? However, the city is being torn apart stone by stone. All I've done is lead them to more targets.

I've got a hunch. I pitch the craft back and rocket straight up. My hunch proves correct. The enemy stays glued to our tail.

High above the Felidian city, I ease off the power and level out. At a moderate speed, the enemy craft creep up, cruising alongside in loose formation, weaving and dipping some, but for the most part matching our course, and they've laid off the guns. So close to the enemy, I strain for a better view, but past the black glass of the cockpit covers, I can't see the face of any pilot.

"Why aren't they attacking us?" I ask.

"Perhaps we be invisible," Physuro says.

"That's nonsense, they can see us just fine. They're following our every move."

"Then perhaps we be the leader."

"That's even more nonsense. We're the enemy."

Has no Ophidian pilot noticed? Surely by now, at least one must realize our kills go far beyond any mistake of friendly fire.

Behind us, Stu says, "Adam, I beg, use your power as a god to save our city."

"And what sort of divine act would you suggest I perform?"

"Lead our enemy away."

Physuro agrees with strong nodding. My furry friends may have a point. The enemy does appear intent on keeping us company. All right. I set a course for anywhere but here, climb higher, and we soar away from the Felidian city.

Follow the leader is right.

*

Far from anything lush, the ground below fades to barren and parched, marked only by splotches of dry brush and gentle mounds rising less and less, no other landmarks, no rivers, no settlements. Ahead are high clouds, plenty of low haze, but otherwise the pink sky is clear, though bleached a lighter shade by afternoon sun. The terrain below has graduated to desert, stretching across a flat nothing, as though we're venturing to the land of nowhere.

Pacing alongside, the swarm is content to maintain this course, wherever this course may take us, all I know is due east. Regardless, at near three-quarter speed, we have successfully drawn the enemy miles away from their targets. To that end, any direction will do.

On the horizon, a dark wall emerges from the haze. The jagged black peaks shoot up so high they almost reach the clouds. Even at this great distance, the mountain range stands as a seemingly impenetrable barrier.

Now in remarkable formation, the enemy swarm banks and takes a new heading. My heart jumps—they figured it out. No, their formation is perfect, poised to strike. They were toying with us, a ploy to lead *us* away. They're going back.

"They be traveling home," Physuro says.

Checking instruments confirms his notion. The swarm has turned south rather than double back. They accelerate and fade into haze on the horizon.

Stu says, "Your power be great, Adam. Our city be saved."

"We got lucky, that's all. And damned lucky they didn't blast us."

"Then your power of luck be great," he says. "Felidians survive another day."

I'm glad too, but not enough to start worshipping the God of Luck, or any other god for that matter. We did what we did and it worked, and the enemy did what they did, though most of it I still don't understand.

"Your efforts be success," Physuro says. "Let us travel home now."

Except now we're free to fly wherever I choose.

"That reminds me," I say. "Time for your end of the bargain—you guiding the way."

"Oh, indeed," Physuro says. "Though, the way to…"

"Home of the Gods. I want my friends back."

His face drains to something dreadful. "Might I convince you other-wise?"

"Soon you'll learn not to ask. So which way do we go?"

He stares out at the distant mountain range. I take that as his answer.

"I beg," he says. "Let us turn back from your wish."

"Finding Christina is not a *wish*."

Physuro looks like our next stop is a funeral—his.

Rising in the distance, the jagged peaks only grow taller. The sharp crags are like blades of fractured obsidian, standing on end and shooting up so violently, one can only assume that nature had a message and the gods we seek chose it as their own—forbidden, do not enter.

✱

Engines a faint whine, our craft skims aloft a thin spread of vapor. The desert below slips past slowly, almost nil at this altitude. Windblown dunes rise and fall, the drifts unmoving as if ripples spread across a watery surface suspended in time. Farther on, the desert blends with foothills at the base of peaks that rise and rise, but it seems that we'll never arrive, suspended in time as well, floating in a cloudless sky.

But in time we will arrive and surely face vast opposition. And what have I brought? Two pistols, a rifle, and one assault craft. What am I thinking? I'm not. Obsession fueled by heartache has no room for rationale, and spiced with a dose of the unknown—what could be happening to her—the sickening meal is served. And what of my Felidian friends? They have no idea, but I know it well. I could be leading them to their deaths.

"I wish to learn," Physuro says.

"What now?"

"The word you say, *is*. I comprehend your meaning in most cases, yet find its use odd. Should you not say *be* in its place?"

"I could, but it's not the same."

"No? What be the definition?"

"Is? I guess existing, like something in a certain place, or in a particular state, a word used to call attention to that. Like to describe the desert below, that *is* the desert. I guess your way works too, that *be* the desert, but it changes the meaning."

"In what manner?" he asks.

"Be has to do with us. We are beings, engaged in the act of being. Is has to do with things existing, including us, but more to do with things that we bring into existence. We be, but our craft is, the sky is, the desert is. Those things do not *be*. They exist as a result of us being, and that gives them the quality of is."

"Is be a quality?"

"Yeah, there's a difference between being and ising, I guess you could say. Be is different because it includes more than just existing like a rock does. A rock is, but we have more, the power to decide what is. Is cannot decide what will be. Do you see?"

He scratches his cheek. "Your words give me difficulty, yet I sense a meaning regardless, as your intent speaks the concept for you."

"Right, that's the difference right there. A rock can't transfer ideas through intent, but we can, using that power of decision, our intent. What we want, and we decide. And really, it's only deciding what to view next. We be, we see, and so we say, it is."

Stu angles forward between our seats. "But time be the father of what comes next."

"Ah, that's where it gets tricky, but it still applies. Time cannot decide what will be, it is we, beings, who decide what time is. Without time and space, a framework we create and agree exists, there wouldn't be a way to view all the things we've brought into existence. Everything we've given the quality of is."

Physuro stares at the console he faces. "I shall attempt your wording." He focuses on the tactical display. "The smooth panel..."

"The screen," I say.

"Your screen is..."

"Right, the screen is, we be. You get the idea."

Studying the console, he grows concerned. "It be showing a point of light floating closer to center."

An alarm sounds—incoming locked on target. Somebody decided to shoot back. I yank the pitch and push the craft into a gut-wrenching climb.

"You claim we be," Physuro says, "and decide what is. And we choose this?"

"Something else that is—others and *their* decisions. I never said we all agree."

The missile skims our tail and rockets past. I'll agree with that.

Physuro searches the sky. Tactical shows five more coming at us. Straight up full thrust then dive, we evade the next. A few twirls and loops loses another. Beyond the cockpit cover is sand and sky, sand and sky, streaming past as we roll and dive.

Three missiles remain. Wild maneuvers got us this far, but the next missile nips our wing. Sizzling arcs, an explosion, and our craft shudders.

We're thrown across the sky but remain intact, kept safe by shields and sense enough to use them. However, tactical reads shield energy at fifteen percent and two missiles locked on target. The numbers don't add up.

I throw the craft into a dive aimed for the desert. The next missile follows. Just before it slides up our ass, I yank the pitch and level out, gliding over the dunes. The weapon is not so agile. Behind us, a ring of fiery sand fountains high.

We skim close to the rise and fall of dunes, heading for the foothills, almost in reach. Hidden behind a ridge, low in a ravine or valley, the menace won't have a clear shot and we might be safe. But the remaining missile appears intelligent, not following the last to end up a crater in the desert. It has slipped to the surface and matched our course, hunting its prey as we hug the dunes.

I pull up some hundred feet, then bring the craft about and study the hills with only seconds to decide on a good place to hide. My final mistake.

Our craft rocks from the impact and flames stretch across the cockpit cover. We're not destroyed but mortally wounded, now a powerless brick swooping into a narrow ravine.

"Hang on, this is where it gets rough."

The engines are dead. That familiar whine—vicious or tender—has ceased. The only sound is shredded metal twisting and snapping as we break up. No power, maybe one elevator though awfully stiff, I fight to keep the nose up and put this hunk of steel down belly first.

Walls of rock rise at our sides, whipping past faster and faster. The nose wants down but I keep pulling hard. Across the crude landing strip, what appeared loose rocks at a distance are growing to boulders the size of houses.

One last yank, I pitch the nose up. The craft slams down and bounces high, then the nose catches a boulder and twirls us sideways. Loose rocks spray the glass cover, bang, bam, then one big *crack!*—the cover an instant fracture of puzzle pieces ready to shatter. Tortured metal shrieks as the belly surfs rock, we bounce over larger chunks, only a quiet whisper of air whooshing past, then we slam back down, back to shrieking. Slower, the scraping pitch eases, and the craft ends at a rock wall—*bash!*—we're showered by the puzzle of glass piled in our laps.

Behind us, flames grow higher. "Out, out, get out!" I unbuckle and climb the edge, over and drop, and scramble away.

At a safe distance, I turn around. The sleek triangle is now a twisted heap of flaming metal at the end of a long trail of debris. Beyond the blaze heating my face, Stu and Physuro have crawled out the opposite side. Poof, pop, a fiery whoosh shoots out, and shrapnel sprays. I hurry around the melting craft and join my crewmates.

"Rusty?" Physuro says.

A piercing whine soars overhead, into a slope and explodes. Another two missiles slam into the mountainside.

"We need cover."

"I be surprised," Physuro says, gazing at the flaming heap that once was our craft. "Chariots of the gods, I had thought…"

"You're learning the truth about gods. Us divine beings, and all we create, suffer failure the same as everything else in the universe."

✳

Physuro urges that we follow a narrow path cut in the sheer rock wall. The trail zigzags up and up, along a ledge barely enough to walk. As we climb the mountainside, he notices a familiar sight, and when the path branches, he chooses the route to higher ground. I certainly agree.

As we rise above the landscape, the sun drops low in the sky, casting long shadows across rusty dunes that stretch to the horizon. In the distance, a wavering line of black slithers up and over the desert humps, like a horde of giant insects coming to get us.

The trail ends at a plateau surrounded by towering peaks. A single structure is built here, round and capped by a half-sphere with a vertical slot that divides the dome in two. The place looks abandoned, in light of its crumbling foundation riddled with cracks and the entrance where only one door remains, gaunt grain weathered gray, hanging by one hinge.

"What is it?" I ask.

"The great observatory," Physuro says. "Where those of scientific endeavor studied the heavens."

Inside, wooden furniture is upturned and scattered. Papers and scrolls litter the floor, mixed with books strewn about randomly, all coated with a generous layer of dust. An iron frame stands at the center of the round space, the supports for a grand telescope. However, the instrument has been ripped from its cradle, leaving an empty skeleton.

I ask, "What happened to this place?"

Physuro explains, "Great hope existed that our race might seek out the gods by viewing the heavens, and in doing so, grow closer to our masters. The distant lights hanging in the night became known as divine symbols of those ruling over Marsea. For a time, the observations be deemed prudent, and those of scientific endeavor be encouraged to conduct their investigations."

I scan the cluttered room. "Looks like someone changed their mind."

Physuro moves to the empty skeleton and gazes up, past the opening through which the absent instrument once peered. "The observers brought back news of other planets, similar to your earlier example."

"So they were good astronomers."

"The Council did not approve of their conclusions. They be condemned as heretics."

"Making discoveries doesn't make anyone a heretic."

"The Book of Truth be the supreme source of all doctrine. Conclusions that conflict with god-given truth cannot stand as scientific fact."

"Truth? That everything revolves around Marsea?"

"To imply otherwise be a blasphemous suggestion."

"The observers were right, not that silly book, or the Council. Marsea isn't the center of anything. It's one planet orbiting a star, orbiting other stars in orbit around even larger clusters."

Stu points up through the telescope doors. "Look to the heavens, the evidence be clear. As the Book of Truth teaches, the sun moves across the sky. It be circling Marsea."

I ask Stu, "Did you ever consider that the sun might be fixed in one spot, and the planet is slowly rotating?"

He shifts to Physuro. "Be it possible?"

"Possible, my brother, and in all likelihood, the truth."

I say to Physuro, "So you don't believe that book."

"I be merely telling the tale of how the observatory fell out of favor. My personal beliefs be another tale, the last chapter of which lead to my imprisonment, the same for observers who share similar beliefs."

Their heretical beliefs are the information I seek—details of this system, the lone light of the Restricted Zone. I shift through the mess and untie scrolls, revealing charts penned on thick vellum, hand drawn with notes in the margins. The faded celestial records are distant star formations overlaid with connect-the-dots stick figures symbolizing various deities. Scroll after scroll, I only find more constellations, until one is different—a single star with satellites. The astronomers couldn't possibly see that far into space. It has to be the local system.

I hoist a table back on its legs and spread out the curly paper. The chart illustrates planets circling the star, with lines drawn through each orbit, creating a series of rings. Notes near each planet contain a wealth of specifics. Orbital period, rate of rotation, diameter and estimated mass. The Felidians have produced an impressive record of their nearest celestial bodies, except the distances between planets, compared with their sizes, are nowhere near accurate. Even within a system, the most abundant feature is space. But that would make a big chart. An accurate sketch would need paper ten miles across, and still, the largest planet would be the size of a melon, the smallest a pea, with vast stretches of nothing in between.

I put a chair upright and sit at the table. "This is it, the Solar system." But it can't be right. The diagram shows seven planets. The Association computer listed more. But of course, the outer planets are distant and minor, beyond the reach of their telescope.

The first planet is tiny, labeled *Merkorhyse*. Barren rock, heavily cratered, and too close to the star. Without an atmosphere, day and night must be some temperature swing.

Sol-2 is larger, known as *Hiventarus*. The astronomers were accomplished, having detected by visual inspection alone what the last computer revealed—thick atmosphere and runaway greenhouse effect. No details of composition or acid rain, both would require sophisticated instruments, but the astronomers were astute enough to speculate on the high temperature and extreme pressure. And they have one detail the computer didn't list—the rotation is retrograde. Not only terraformed backward, it rotates backward.

The Felidian name for Sol-3 is *Tertegeah*. Being the nearest neighbor to Marsea, details are rich. About the size of Hiventarus, though more hospitable atmosphere with a typical weather system, nothing out of control. Ice caps, some mapping of continents and ocean, and a single large moon.

Of course, Sol-4 is Marsea. Half the size of Tertegeah, and with two small moons of irregular shape. Something does revolve around Marsea, just not all of creation.

The fifth planet is the smallest on the chart, named *Aster*. Another planet with dense atmosphere, preventing the astronomers from learning further details. But for any planet that small, one can guess the effects of its diminutive gravity. It wouldn't take much to leap over tall buildings.

The next is a mighty giant, *Jovas,* larger than any other on the chart. No leaping over buildings there. On a planet that massive, you'd be lucky to grow any taller than wide. That is, if the gas giant had any solid ground. Notes mention the stormy atmosphere, so active the astronomers recorded changes in the planet's colorful shell only days apart.

The seventh is another titan, second only to Jovas. But this planet has something drawn around it, a kind of flat disk the others lack. *Crontis?* The name Jared has taken in his role as a god. Has he assumed the name of this planet? Or is the planet named after him?

I tap a finger on the drawing. "Physuro, the seventh planet, Crontis. The name of your Mighty One."

"Indeed."

"What's the connection? And what's with the rings?"

He studies the illustration. "A display of the Mighty One's strength, and warning to all he commands—obey the powerful god."

"But who's the god? A planet?"

"Do you wish for my opinion, or that I convey the story of Crontis?"

"Okay, tell me a story, for now."

He strolls around the table. "Legend tells of a great battle between Crontis and other gods in a distant realm. Crontis be defeated and sentenced to Marsea, though given one final dignity, to reign as master of our domain. However, not of his own choosing, and never again to visit any of the worlds he once ruled. Crontis be angered by his sentence, yet he accepted it, on the condition that his subjects obeyed without defiance. Crontis declared himself father of all Marseans and every subject one of his children."

"So what's with the rings?"

"The loyal be showered with gifts, long life, riches and great wisdom. However, many condemned Crontis, and in wrath of their disrespect, he took them into his mouth and devoured them. But he did not swallow, rather each hardened as ice in his maw, and the mighty god spit out the disobedient children to circle his greatness, where they be frozen forever." He points at the drawing. "A warning that all children obey the father, or suffer."

Interesting parallel to certain real events—the bad end up in ice. The rest, however, is quite a stretch.

"You don't believe all that, do you?"

"My truth? Far different from this tale. I convey the story only because you ask. I find this fable quite fantastic, such as how a god might also be a planet, and that any celestial body might eat something and spew it. I be thinking this account represents more a metaphor, suggesting that obedience be rewarded, otherwise severe punishment."

Like Heaven and Hell. Except the Felidian version is eternal damnation as a space-buoy orbiting some murderous planet. Indeed, the cats had better behave—or else.

✳

After a time sorting through scrolls, I find no other that shows further details of the Solar system. Only more diagrams of distant constellations, none of them familiar or giving any indication of our location in the cosmos. I've probably seen these stars before, but never from the vantage point of this planet.

One chart is interesting, only because it is odd. The connect-the-dots diagram makes a perfect ring of twelve. And evenly spaced, as if any stars could possibly align so organized, from any vantage point. The legend reads something about *The Lights,* which of course all stars emit, and reading further only delivers more nonsense, another myth to reinforce the godly labels they assign to constellations. The answers are not in the alignment of any stars halfway across the galaxy.

The table quakes, jarred by a distant rumble. Then another, stronger. Stu moves to a portal open to the outside, through which sunbeams flow in and brighten the dusty air. Another boom rumbles, getting closer.

Stu gazes out at the sunset. "Ophidians."

I rise and join him. Past the foothills and across the desert, long shadows stretch out like dark fingers. Boxy tan vehicles roll over the dunes, heading this way. From the ranks comes a puff of smoke, then another. Shells shriek across the sky, then two more booms, still a distance away.

I ask Physuro, "Is there a path to higher ground?"

"We be as high as any Felidian ever dare."

"It matters little," Stu says, staring out at the desert. "Their arms reach to the sky."

Whistling grows near and the shell strikes a direct hit. The observatory shudders, jarring bricks loose from above. Another whistling whine, louder—LOUD—a wall explodes and sprays chunks. I throw the table on end and crouch behind it with Stu and Physuro. Another explosion and bullets of stone pound the tabletop. Dust dances in shafts of sunlight pouring in from gaping holes blasted out of the walls.

"Tell me something," Physuro says.

"What?" I ask, spying over the table only to see the walls crumbling.

He waits for my gaze to meet his, then he calmly asks, "Be this the place we will die?"

"We won't die, I'll think of something." I get back to scanning the room and hoping for a solution. Now would be a great time for allies to swoop down and repel this attack.

Physuro asks, "Do you say that for fear of death?"

"I don't fear death, it's just terribly inconvenient. I'll have to find another body, if I can remember how, and even so, I'm a long way from home."

Another shell strikes and larger slabs thunder down, stirring up clouds of powder. We pull the table back, trampling over crumpled charts and scattered books, to sandwich ourselves between the wooden defense and a wall still standing.

"You place confusion upon me," Physuro says. "You talk of beings that be, and create a thing that is, yet talk of distance from a place as a barrier."

"If I remembered where to go and how to get there, maybe I'd feel different."

The end is never pleasant, but worse are thoughts of my Felidian friends. I know that transcending death is possible. Remembering how might also be possible, once forced to face the ordeal. But they have no clue, other than afterlife nonsense, Heaven or Hell or other invented place that cats go, just as absurd.

Boom! Another shell strikes and walls tumble down.

Physuro says, "I be not afraid. I know that I will always exist, perhaps not in the present form, but in some way, forever."

"Sure, me too, but getting killed right now makes it tough to find Christina. I'll have to make it back and start over, and who knows what could happen to her by then."

"Christina, the Goddess of Dreams."

"Yeah, that's the one."

"What of Christina drives you so? I have seen it upon you, a fire burning for her presence."

"She's my love, my life, everything to me. Like my chance to exist is a gift from her. As though the very reason *I am* comes from her viewing me. And here I am to return the same, existing so I may view her and have her exist with me. It's very powerful. Do you understand?"

"Perhaps, at a minimum, that your love be strong. So I suggest, let the fire of Christina give you the strength to change this. Your intense love for her will guide you."

What would she do?

Not hide behind a table like a coward.

"Get your rifles ready." I reach around for mine and get it off my shoulder. "We're fighting these bastards."

✳

Stone pours down as we make our escape. Dust, mortar, wooden beams and hefty slabs fall from above. We scramble past crumbling walls as massive blocks pulverize the table we used for cover.

We get outside and across the plateau, chased by another whistling whine. Between a sheer cliff wall and giant boulders, we duck for cover. Shells pound the observatory, it collapses, and a billowing plume rises in its place.

"You know how these work, right?" I indicate their rifles.

Stu nods and takes aim, but Physuro keeps studying his.

"I know," I say, "no harm to anything, but right now you have to make an exception."

He nods but keeps twisting the rifle around, examining all sides.

"Keep low and wait for my signal. Then shoot anything that moves." I crouch, steady my shoulder against the cool rock, and sight down the barrel, ready.

Enemy troops crest the ridge, appearing as ghastly silhouettes before the setting sun. Lanky and tall, their arms glow orange at the edges. The horde grows, swaying in and out of strong backlight swirling with dust, as they wave rifles little more than thin sticks. They may not see us yet, more concerned with searching the rubble. My eyes are tortured by the contrast between light and shadow as their slender forms move in and out of the sun.

They march over the debris and advance.

"Now!"

"There be so many," Physuro says.

"Pull the trigger and shoot. Kill them!"

Stu takes out six just like that. I match it and better—eight, ten, my blasts connect and down they go. Our enemy is as ignorant of ground tactics as they are of shields, lined up in stacked rows like targets at a shooting gallery. Their ranks swell, more cresting the ridge and bringing up the rear, swaying between thick orange sunbeams as our sizzling blue-white blasts soar back and cut them down. Their numbers appear endless, a front line that keeps coming and bends around at our flanks, forcing us to swing our weapons left right, left right, straining to put down one row before it arrives, only to start the next, the next, and the next.

I've only fooled myself. We're pinned down and outnumbered. More than fooling anyone, I'm denying what can't be denied—I am going to die, for real this time. And my Felidian friends, in our last moments alive, I should tell them the truth—yes, this *is* the place we will die. No one is strong enough to change this. But my finger just keeps pulling the trigger.

The troops fall back. Another step back, they slowly retreat. We cease fire. A deathly quiet hangs in the dust, smoke, and fizzling arcs that scorch the air and fade.

Physuro breathes an awestruck whisper, "Your love be strong."

His words are the trigger—a dream world displaces reality. But the vision betrays me. A bland room, dim without windows, and one dark lump crumpled on the floor. It is her. Clothed in barely a shred of fabric, she is silent and unmoving, a terrifying stillness.

Enemy troops divide rank and step aside. Beyond them, the sun has grown to an enormous disk at the horizon, sinking into a wavering sliver of haze. A long shadow is cast by a lone silhouette standing before the dazzling orb.

The dream is stronger. Reality is washed away by the blinding sun, a blank slate of yellow on which the vision is drawn, and the urge is over-whelming—dive into the dream and rescue her. But I'm disconnected, only a spectator, and the helplessness is killing me. She starts to wake, hazy and weak. Someone has hurt her. I'll kill them. She is crying and calling my name. She reaches out to me, ready to touch, but she retreats. I don't understand.

Brighter than any sun, a scorching beam hammers my chest. I'm thrown and crash flat on my back. The cloudless sky has gone deep magenta, darker almost blue, it looks cool. The slab of rock pressing against my back is even colder, a frigid singe leaking past a shell of skin, into every bone.

Something bad has happened. My chest, something is wrong. It burns. Above, the sky and slopes begin to waver and swirl. Fiery tingles spread across my chest, into both arms and reach my fingertips, then numb.

I can't die. Not yet, I haven't finished…

What is that smell? Burning flesh. Mine? I couldn't smell my own flesh, that doesn't happen. But I smell it. I have to know and try to look. Smoky vapors rise from my chest. Drained of all strength, my head flops back, skull to rock a crashing thump. Sound fades to dull thuds in slow motion, like I'm underwater and sinking deeper, deeper, into the dark.

The vision washes out reality. Christina stands before me in a misty otherworld only dreams know. Tender blue eyes aglow, her smile stretches wide. She reaches to my chest, her fingers warm against my bare skin. My salvation, my love, my precious wonder, her adoring gaze and loving smile, the vision is perfect, powerful, and all mine. Yes, my love, smile for me and I will rise from the dead, for you. I will do anything for you.

Anything but die.

No, my love, I will not die. I will *live* for you.

3

COOL WATER SLAPS MY CHEEKS, LIPS BURN A SALTY STING, and my fingers are chilled to numb. I creak one eye open to see a hazy yellow glow, too bright, too hot above, so cold below. I swish and turn and turn again, thrashing, nothing to hold me, water so loose—drowning.

No.

The ocean sneaks higher, a swell rolling beneath me like an enormous carpet snapped by a giant shaking it clean. I cling to the surface, carried aloft by a lifejacket. The ride down is gentle and back up, then down and up again, the endless rolling swells cresting foamy white, ruffled by light wind from a cloudless sky.

A sea journey? We must have lost our vessel. But I don't remember being a sailor, or being at sea. Maybe I fell from the sky, from a plane struck down. But there's no parachute, only the orange lifejacket. It doesn't matter. I have to save myself either way. Swimming across the ocean won't work. Which direction? I could swim *away* from land. A rescue ship will come. It takes time. But there should be other survivors, I can't be alone. But no, not a soul, I am alone. And if no one comes, I may die alone.

A small rowboat, that's where I was. But that feels like ages ago. And the water, it was clear like glass, not these rising swells. Except the sky wasn't clear. That was somewhere else. A memory? Gone, through my fingers like dark crystals, and with it, any hint of an identity.

From below, a churning noise grows louder, and the ocean quakes. Vibrations press in from all directions. A thin pole shoots up from the surface and rises fast, followed by a tower of black steel. A grated deck slams into me and I'm thrust above the surf by a big metal whale, flat on top and much longer than across. A submarine. Water sheets down the sides and crashes back to the sea, split open like zipper as the sub charges forward, carving out a foamy slice.

I am saved. Inside are my mates, dry clothes, a warm meal. I start for the tower.

Atop the tower, a hatch opens and someone crawls out.

I reach to my shoulder, for a rifle that isn't there.

Jared climbs down the rungs and joins me on the deck. He wears shorts and sandals, sunglasses, and a shirt decorated with parrots and pineapples. He is holding a flimsy aluminum lawn chair.

"Hey, Adam, what are you doing out here in the middle of the ocean?"

"I... I don't know. Maybe you should tell me."

He laughs, then turns away and heads for the bow, where he unfolds the lawn chair. He sits down and watches the sky, like he's vacationing at the beach, soaking up a few rays.

I creep closer but keep a safe distance from him. He holds a glass that's wide at the bottom, narrow in the center and flaring at the brim, filled with a milky beverage opaque and frothy, garnished by a pink paper umbrella.

What is this screwy shit? He didn't have the drink when he came down the ladder.

"Where'd that come from?" I ask.

He sips at the straw and looks to the sky. "I... I don't know. Maybe you should tell me."

Maybe I should slap the brat. Except it wouldn't do any good. Another stupid dream. But if a dream, then my subconscious is doing this. Since I'm stuck here, why not tug at a few layers and get answers that deep down, I already know. The secrets are hiding here, somewhere.

"Jared, tell me why you've betrayed me."

He tips his sunglasses down and scowls. "Who's betrayed who?"

"You have and you know it."

"Have what and know what? You're talking nonsense, like always."

"You are."

"That's right, I am. *I am.* More than you'll ever be. You're a not."

This will never work. I have to ask the real Jared, once I find the bastard. After this stupid dream ends.

His face morphs into that sickening insincere pity. "Oh, you poor thing, can't remember, is that it? You won't, so don't sweat it. Even if you do, it's too late anyway."

I'd say that to myself? Talking to a sick mind maybe.

Jared stands and the chair vanishes. His drink is gone and now he wears a white toga and laurel crown. He raises his arms to the sky.

"Bow before the Mighty One. Behold the wrath of God."

Small motors whir, then a series of sharp clanks, metal slapping one after another, clack-clack-clack. Along each side of the deck, a string of round hatches stand open, from which fire and smoke burst a deafening roar. Black shafts shoot out, carried aloft by blazing infernos. I cover my ears and turn away from the heat. The missiles spew columns of dark smoke as they climb fast to become specks fanning out across the horizon.

"You can't win," he says.

I whirl around to face no one. Water washes across the deck and over my feet. My life jacket is gone. Rotten dream! I climb the rungs, the tower drops fast, and an icy wave smacks hard. I'm drenched and fumbling for a hold but it's all too slippery. The sealed hatch falls away and I clutch the thin pole. Sucked back to the depths, it slides through my fingers.

Thrashing and splashing, every other gasp I choke on salty water. The sky bursts WHITE to every corner. The flash burns past my eyelids, blinding.

He has won.

The brightness eases, but it's still uncomfortably warm. The shockwave is next, I know, except it never comes. The sound of slapping waves has ceased, leaving an eerie silence. Then a whoosh rumbles past my ear, and a heated breeze glances my skin.

I crack one eye open. Too bright, and blistering hot, the air is like an oven. I'm somewhere else. Not underwater, not even wet, except the sweat leaking into one eye that stings. The view is a wavering mirage of rusty humps that rise and fall.

My neck is restrained by something. I can't move much, but enough to see that my outstretched arms are bound by wire, securing me to a horizontal wooden beam. And my ankles are fastened to the lower portion of a vertical beam. I'm going nowhere strung up like this, someone has made sure of that.

But I am going somewhere, carried by a wooden cart rolling across a desert. The crude wheels are not completely round, making the journey rough and uncomfortable. But then, when was hanging from a cross ever comfortable?

The hot breeze kicks up sand, washing over dunes that rise and fall, like the swells, surf and sea, only moments before. The ocean has turned to desert? Dreams do as they damn well please.

A muscular four-legged beast is hauling the cart, following a few riders on horseback. They face forward, clothed in black leather with long sleeves. The backsides of their head and neck are concealed by tight caps that are one with their snug bodysuits.

The riders and cart top the next rise. In the distance are more endless dunes, but now something litters the landscape. Wooden crosses are planted in the sand, aligned in terraced rows. Hundreds of them. Down the rise and farther on, details become clearer. The crosses are like mine, each with someone attached, neck bound, arms out, ankles tight. But getting closer, I realize they are not the same. Not yet anyway, though likely my horrific fate is to join them. The figures are blackened ash, the torched remains of each someone attached.

Time for this fucked-up dream to end.

The cart halts and a rider turns back. He calls to others behind me, "Here iss good." He points to something but I don't look, I can only look at his face. A mask? Dark green, big black eyes, and nose little more than a mild hump with two dots for nostrils. But it's not a mask. It *is* his face, and slithering tongue between slimy lips. A lizard? A snake. Something reptilian. Except humanoid, with legs and arms and fingered hands.

He nudges his ride closer and stares at me. It's difficult to gauge his expression. He has no brow, and his dark eyes are wide open like a fish. He could be happy or sad, pissed off or indifferent, you wouldn't know by looking at him, but I can feel it more than the hot sun—this snake doesn't like me.

They haul my cross backward, off the cart and to the sand, landing with a thud. Wire binding my neck yanks tighter, and my outstretched arms scream. The snakes drag me up an embankment to where another snake-man with a shovel is digging a hole. I'm planted upright, facing the blazing sun.

I try speaking but it's difficult with a swollen tongue. "Hey, how about we turn it around, give me a little shade. What do you say?"

The snake-men stride down the embankment, boots kicking up sand, and return to the cart and other riders.

A slight breeze is no relief, hotter than the blazing sun. Reserves of moisture bleed from every pore and coat my sunburned skin. Sweat pools in my eyes and stings, hot needles I cannot wipe away.

All right, go ahead and burn me. Just make it quick, not this slow, agonizing torture. Then we can move on to a more pleasant dream, like the grassy meadow beneath my best friend, Mister Tree. Except I was doing something else before all of this. What was I doing? It doesn't matter. I'm asleep somewhere, dreaming, and my body is safe.

Down the line, the next cross also has someone attached. Not burned yet, other than by the hot day, reason enough for his squirming effort to get loose.

Snake-men climb the rise, approaching the other prisoner. One snake carries a metal can, another wields a flaming torch. The victim fights his binds. He has fur and whiskers.

"I beg," the Felidian cries. "Save me, Adam, I beg!"

I know him. But I can't remember his name. Too hard to pronounce.

The snake with metal can pumps clear liquid from a short hose and drenches the prisoner. The cat convulses, swinging his head and chest squirming, trying to fling away moisture that is clearly not water. Useless. The snake just loads more into the cat's dripping fur.

The snake with torch leans in on the cat.

"Hey!" I call out. "Don't burn him. Don't burn anyone."

The torch-bearing snake whirls around and stares at me from his big empty eyes. He marches closer. "Death to all heathens." He swishes the torch before me as if casting a curse. "And you, evil creature, who feigns he iss a god. Die a thousand deaths."

But this is a dream, and he's part of it, part of me, my fear that drives this. So he knows, doesn't he? I'm no god, that was all pretend. He's still an asshole about it. Did I invent that too, him being an asshole? Probably a modified version of some other asshole I used to know.

"Hey, bucko. Go fuck yourself."

Though being a snake, he probably does anyway.

He thrusts the torch in threatening jabs. "Iss a pleasure to watch you burn, wicked infidel."

I'm wicked? Right. Wicked infidel heathen scum, whatever. So I get mounted to a cross and fried. What about the nutcase holding the torch? What, like he's some angel? Screw that shit, he's a psycho. This is totally backward.

The snake leaves me and goes to the other prisoner.

The Felidian calls out, "Adam, I be in your service. Though forgive me, I cannot serve beyond death."

In the desert enduring unbearable heat until his dying moment.

No!

The torch draws near his side, flames flicker and leap, and the vapor rising from his fur bursts into a brilliant aura that smothers him. Translucent blue to begin, with Stu caught in the center, convulsing and screaming, though my eyes won't lend attention to my ears, it's all a dull hum. The deep-blue base drives flaming orange that pours out to the whipping edges, cracking and snapping, and the cremation roars a fiery blaze. Soon his struggle ends, his cries cease, and all that remains are crackling pops of bone on fire.

The torch-bearing snake turns to me.

That's enough, I'm out of here.

I dive into my own blackness, in search of my sleeping body, determined to force its eyes open and see anything but this nightmare.

✳

Thumping hooves grow louder, a strong gallop coming closer. I open my eyes. Naked? My chest is blackened. Dreams are tenacious. I'm still on the cross, still in the desert.

Snake-men gather round, one with the torch, another with the metal can, aiming his hose. Not much left of Stu, just a smoldering mass of charred flesh hanging from a disjointed skeleton. Those monstrous fiends. But that thumping, it's getting louder. Beyond the snake-men, hooves pound the sand. A rider on horseback is racing up the dune.

"No!" the rider calls. "Not him! Stop!"

The snake-men turn and look. The approaching rider wears the same bodysuit all black, but he's no snake. Without the snug cap, his hair blows in the wind. Yellow hair, like he used to have. But it wasn't yellow when...

He reins in the horse and leaps from the saddle. It really is Dave. He advances on the snakes and swats the torch to the sand. "You cannot burn him."

"Hey, Dave, what are you doing in my dream?"

He spins around. "Adam, this is not a dream. They're going to burn you, *for real.*"

But this has to be a dream. It's too weird for reality. Or I'm delirious from the heat. Not a dream? Now I'm embarrassed, naked up here for everyone to see.

The snake-man retrieves his torch and hisses at Dave. "He must burn. He iss a devil sent to destroy us."

Dave gets in the snake's face. "No he is NOT! Get him down from there."

That can't be Dave. I've never seen Mister Laid-back get so aggressive.

The snake-man drops the torch and bows. The others kneel.

"Get him down," Dave says. "Now!"

They loosen the wire binding me. I crash to the hot sand, burning my bare butt, then hop from one foot to the next, but naked I quickly crouch, wrap arms around my knees, and let my soles roast. I'll deal with it.

Dave goes to his saddle, gets a canteen, and offers it. I guzzle what little gets past my swollen tongue and shower in the rest.

"What's with the hair?" I ask. "Back to yellow?"

He smirks. "*Blond,* pal. I think we've masqueraded as goons long enough."

He could be right, not a dream. Only the real Dave cares that much about his hair. But if this isn't a dream…

"Dave! What are you doing in the desert with weird snake-men, burning people, burning cats, burning *me!*"

"It's how they punish the enemy," he says. "It's not my idea."

"I don't care whose idea it is, make them stop."

He says to the snakes, "Tell the soldiers to stop burning and get back to camp. And you, bring Adam some clothes." Dave passes the reins of his horse. The snake-man bows and leads the animal down the embankment. The others follow.

"What's going on?" I ask.

"You have to understand," Dave says, "these creatures mean well, they worship and obey, but their enemy isn't like that. They have no respect for the gods."

"Since when do you care about any gods?"

"Oh, not me." He points to the departing snake-men. "But *they* do. They're wrapped up deep in that shit."

More god-fearing creatures battling a heathen enemy. The same enemy?

"Ophidians," I realize.

"They just want to live in peace," he says. "But the cats won't leave them alone."

"Cats?"

He points to what's left of Stu.

"Dave! The Felidians aren't the enemy."

"Who else would they be fighting?"

I scan the dunes, the cart that carried me here, and countless nightmare creatures on horseback, more on foot. "These snakes are Ophidians?"

"What else did you think?"

"Considering what they had in mind for me, I was thinking, what a bunch of psychos."

"That was just a mix-up. Don't worry about it."

"Don't worry about it? Dave, listen to yourself. They were going to *burn me alive.* Doesn't that sound just a little insane?"

"They've been driven to insane measures by a ruthless invader."

The truth hits—none of this is a dream. Oh no, please no. Dread tumbles down a landslide that buries me. I look to the blackened figure hanging from the cross. What have I done? I didn't save him. I've led Stu to a gruesome death. And my reward—the grisly sight of his charred remains.

I drop to the sand, on my knees and head in my hands, there is no strength enough to fight the tears. A merciful god would have saved him. Even a decent man would have. I'm no god, not by any measure, and hardly a man. No, I'm a monster.

✳

Sand is my only view, burning my knees, when tall black boots halt before me. I pull a forearm across my face, smearing tears and scratchy sand. Blocking out the sun, the gangly snake-man is a silhouette standing over me. He holds out a uniform, the same bodysuit they all wear, and rattles it in my face. "Dress," he says, then drops the garment.

I guide one leg after the other into the jumpsuit. Arms are a bitch, muscle flowing across my chest pulled apart in shredded strands that scream while I try wrestling into something made for a beanpole. A zipper runs from crotch to neck, sealing me inside a constraining skin that cries to be shed. With a high collar and arms covered to the wrists, the thing is unbearably hot. The cap is attached behind the neck like a hood, except skintight. Like Dave, I pass, it stays flopped back. The rest is already slimy enough with trapped sweat just that fast. The tall boots are as roasting, though better than bare soles on sizzling sand. How can they wear this stuff in the desert? Oh, but of course, they're reptiles—cold-blooded.

Dave starts down the embankment. Before joining him, I have to look one last time. I face the string of crosses planted in the sand, one empty where I was hanging, and the next down the line, blackened regret.

"What's wrong?" Dave asks.

If only my eyes would betray me.

"He was my friend."

He climbs to my side. "A cat?"

"Yes! They're all my friends."

"Get your head scrambled again?" He points to Stu's crispy remains. "The cats are murdering monsters. They destroy entire villages, kill everybody, even children. It's sick."

"They wouldn't if those, those, *snakes!* If those snakes would leave them alone!"

"Sorry, dude, you got it all backward. The Ophidians want to live in peace. It's the cats making this war."

"They can hardly defend themselves."

His eyes get big. "They're awful handy with assault craft."

"That's ridiculous. They don't even know how to open the hatch."

"I think they got you fooled, buddy. I've seen it myself, the sky full of them."

"What? No way." I point to the snakes, farther down the dune. "It's them, they have the craft."

"You are whacked. They don't know how to fly."

"They don't?"

"Hell no," he says. "They say only gods can travel through the heavens."

Just like the Felidians. This planet is so full of lies I can't keep up with it all.

Of course—the airborne invaders were not Ophidians. Every attack ever, it was never them, or cats.

"Dave, don't you see what's going on here?"

"All I know is these creatures are very angry with each other."

"Right. Because someone lied to both and *made* them angry."

✳

Moving down the dune, every other step is a slide through loose sand, surfing down a dry wave that never crests. The sun hangs low in the sky, past snakes busy erecting tents. At a cart, Dave drinks from a canteen, then offers me some. My skin is too leaky, all moisture lost as sweat faster than I can fill myself. We head for a tent and duck inside, out of the sun.

This world has my mind in a vise. Solving one riddle only spawns a new one. If not Ophidians, the pilots had to be our enemy. But our enemy knows about shields and wouldn't hesitate using them. Besides the obvious advantage, procedure likely demands it. Why no shields?

Pressing down on my shoulders, Dave stuffs me onto a cot. "Let's have a look at that wound." He gestures that I open my garment.

I ease the zipper down. My chest is blackened and tender. Looks like the work of a blast rifle. The memory comes alive—burning flesh, sky gone magenta, darker almost blue, it looked cool. The rock against my back was colder, a frigid singe leaking past a shell of skin. I can feel it again, and the rest—enemy troops cresting the ridge, hopeless odds moving in and out of the sun, I was shot, but the vision...

I stand fast. "Where's Christina?"

Dave stumbles back, staring at me and speechless.

"Tell me!"

He hesitates. "She's with Jared, I don't know where. He had a fancy cruiser, you know, one of those sky-yachts."

I slap the tent's flap, dart outside and scan the sky, to every side, ahead and behind. Empty.

"I'm sorry," Dave says, peering out of the tent. "I tried to stop him, but you saw those bastards in white helmets. They beat the crap out of me."

The sky holds all hope yet delivers none. A trace of high clouds, no trace of my love, not even a departing speck, any last glimpse. I have to find her but can't imagine where to start. I'll go crazy, I can't do this. No, stop it, *relax*, that's what she would say. She would hold me, a soothing hand to my cheek, and focus my scattered attention. Calm down and *think*.

She's with Jared. The Mighty One, one of their gods. The gods aren't in any heaven. The gods are here, standing on this planet the same as anyone else.

"I know where he took her."

Dave steps out of the tent. "Really?"

"Home of the Gods."

His enthusiasm dissolves. "That's swell you got it all figured out, but what good does it do? I doubt the place is listed on any map, and I sure as hell don't know where it is."

"You don't?"

His blank stare says it all—he doesn't.

But someone does. Oh no.

"Where's the other Felidian?"

"What other?" he asks.

"There were two with me."

"I don't know anything about that. They capture cats and burn them all the time. You know, they *are* the enemy."

"He can't burn. I'll never find Christina."

I spot a horse and sprint, seize the reins, and fly into the saddle.

"Hey!" Dave calls. "Where you going?"

"To save a friend."

I slap the reins and hooves pound the sand.

✳

Ophidian troops divide rank as I guide my horse between them. Ahead, more carts carry victims yet unburned. I slow my ride, nudge in and out of gaps between the desert convoy, and scan the prisoners mounted to crosses. None of them is Physuro. I flick the reins and gallop up a slope to more crosses and cats yowling for mercy.

A soldier extends his torch, nearing a cross, seconds to ignition. I send the horse soaring up the slope. When the snake whirls around, his torch spooks the animal and I'm thrown. I get up, swat his torch away, and launch a punch that levels him.

I say to all, "There will be no more burning."

Soldiers withdraw their flaming twig torches. They back away from the crosses and close in around me. The soldier I decked tries to get up. I slap one hand around his neck and keep him pinned.

"Where's the Felidian who was with me?"

"The spy?"

"He's no spy. What have you done with him?"

"Spies iss interrogated first, then we burn."

I command the soldiers, "Stop burning!"

The snakes shuffle apart as someone penetrates the crowd. Dave emerges on horseback.

"Do as Adam says. He is a powerful god."

The snakes drop to their knees and plunge their torches into the sand, flames buried and out. How does he do that?

"Find your friend?" Dave asks.

"Your buddy here says he's a spy."

Dave turns in his saddle to check the sky, where the sun hangs low.

"What is it, Dave?"

"It's a long ride," he says. "We'll start at daybreak."

"You know where he is? We have to go now."

He reins the animal around. "We can't."

"We have to. Physuro knows where to find her. If anything happens—"

"We'll get halfway at best. But really, Adam, we shouldn't."

"Then it's settled. But one thing first." I leave Dave and climb the embankment, past the crosses yet unburned, and higher above the gathered soldiers.

I call out, "Take these prisoners down."

An Ophidian steps out of rank. "We say not. They iss the enemy, and here they iss to die."

I soar down, knock him flat, and straddle the slimy worm.

He wrestles and squirms. "You iss a devil! Felidian devil monster!"

I wrap a crushing grasp around his throat. "Take these prisoners down or you're burning, every last one of you, when I set the desert on fire, *all of it!*"

"Do as Adam says." Dave twists in his saddle to address all. "He will punish anyone who dares to defy him."

The snakes drop to their knees and bow. I don't get it. I threaten torture and they just gawk at me. But Dave, all he has to do is open his mouth and presto, instant cult-master.

A soldier asks, "But what iss we to do with them?"

"You will place them in a suitable camp or prison, feed them, and give them water. And once I resolve this conflict, you will set them free. Until that time, you will not mistreat any of them in any way. No more torture, and no more burning. Is that clear?"

He nods.

I scan the others. "Is that clear?"

Most nod.

"Now take them down!"

Soldiers scatter, climbing the dunes, and begin releasing prisoners. I follow to assist, starting with an older cat, his head and torso sagging between his outstretched arms. At the roots of disheveled fur, I get at the wire binding him.

His dull gaze lands on me. His voice is frail. "A savior who suffers our fate be the greatest god."

I focus on untwisting the wire. "I'm not a god."

"Ah, yet you be." His weak smile grows stronger. "Indeed, you be a god of greatness, our lord above all lords."

✳

Only three were brave enough to join us. The unwilling soldiers were more concerned with erecting tents as the sun crept low, convinced that no one should cross the desert in darkness. But the Marsean night is not a pit of blackness that any should fear. In the fading light, dual moons glow brighter, one high another low, squat and yellow, neither very large nor round, but enough light to cast faint shadows across the endless ripples of sand.

Miles from the encampment, the dunes grow higher, on which our ghostly shadows rise larger than life, five mounted giants swaying in their saddles. Dave leads the way and keeps checking the sky. Moonlit vapors roll across the night, darkening our course as the dunes dip and rise deeper and higher the farther we go. For each we crest, endless more remain, fading dimmer under a thickening blanket of clouds.

Dave suggests that we make camp. I'd rather not, but he insists, and the snakes strongly agree. All appear troubled and hurried. Dave mutters something about not far enough but it'll have to do. He gets busy pitching a tent and the snakes do the same. Dave checks the sky again, then builds a campfire, but with the wind kicking up, flames dance and flicker fighting to stay alive. He starts a pot of coffee and gets some food from his saddlebags. In a shallow pan he cooks yellow stalks in an oily sauce, and we eat. Not sure what, though being hungry or it being so bland, the meal doesn't qualify as disgusting, a texture close to celery but less flavorful. The temperature drops fast, bringing on shivers. Dave unstraps blankets stowed above his saddlebags, wraps himself in one, and offers another to me.

"Cover your face when it comes," he says.

"It?" I ask.

He reaches for the coffeepot, fills a pair of tin cups, and hands one over. The Ophidians don't ask and he doesn't offer. They must not care for the beverage. They just sit around the campfire staring at us. I can't tell if it's awe or scared out of their wits. Maybe both.

Dave tells them, "Get in your tents and stay put. We'll be fine."

They spring up and vanish into their shelters. Scared of Dave, or scared of something.

"How do you do that?" I ask.

He chuckles and keeps his voice low. "They think I'm a god."

"And what am I, a fire log? You're no more a god than me. How do you get off so easy?"

"I wasn't in cahoots with any cats. Besides, I told them the Mighty One sent me. You could have said the same, maybe avoided all that."

"Jared?"

"What's Jared got to do with it?"

"Dave, have you *seen* the Mighty One?"

"Not in person, just heard of the guy." He sips coffee. "Figured I'd drop the name, you know, cash in on some of that godly respect."

"Well I have seen the Mighty One, a statue larger than life, and trust me, no one shares the same cocky grin."

"Check a mirror lately?" He smirks.

"Ha-ha, real funny."

"You could actually laugh, you know, it might do you some good. You look like shit."

"Try hanging from a cross all day."

He winces. "No thanks, I'll pass."

Too bad it wasn't that easy. For some reason, the snakes hold Dave and Jared in high regard. The only way they hold me is over a barbecue.

I say, "By the way, thanks."

"You would've saved me too."

"Yeah, but how did you know?"

"When I heard they captured a fake god, who else would it be?"

Not exactly a vote of confidence, but I won't complain.

"So how did you get here?" I ask.

He scoots near the campfire, reaches for the pot and refills his cup, then mine. "I'm not really sure. Got my ass kicked, more like brains bashed out, pretty bad. Next thing I know, I'm in prison. Weird, man." He sips his coffee, then chuckles. "Had to talk my way out. Wasn't too tough, actually. They thought I was a god, so I just played along."

The parallel could not be a coincidence.

"And what lie did you tell them?" I ask.

"Doesn't hurt to lie sometimes."

"We'll debate *that* later. What did you tell them?"

He shrugs. "Not much, just that I was Jovial, God of Jokes, Jester to the court of Jovas. Get it? They all start with J. Pretty funny, eh?"

"No, it's stupid."

He frowns. "Well it worked. I'm not toast like you almost were."

The snakes are one gullible bunch if they believe anything this laugh-happy jackass has to say. They don't understand—for Dave, this is all a *joke.* They just don't get the punch line.

Then I realize, "You said the Mighty One sent you. But you said Jovas."

"Right, the Mighty One."

"Jovas is a planet. You know that, right?"

"Of course, all their gods are planets." He spins a finger in the windy night. "You know, in the heavens, where the gods are." He chuckles. "They got all kinds of kooky stories."

"So do the Felidians. Except they say Crontis is the Mighty One."

"No way, Jovas is way bigger."

Sometimes I really want to smack him. "Look, Dave, it's not about the size of any planet. That's not the point."

"There's a point?"

"Yes! The cats and snakes are worshipping the same god, they just don't know it. Not any accident, either."

"You think Jared's behind it."

"Sounds like a good way to stir up a conflict. Don't you see? He's screwing with this planet and using us to do it."

Dave sips his coffee. "I think you should worry less about Jared and more about what the Association is doing."

"Why? What are they up to?"

Wind smacks harder, ruffling the tents. Dave sets his cup down and steers around the dwindling campfire, goes to the Ophidian tents, and secures straps holding the flaps shut. A sharp blast kills the fire and escaping smoke washes away in a flash. He comes back to fill our cups one last time, dumps the rest, then points to our tent. "Before it gets any worse."

We crawl inside. Once settled, I ask, "So what are they doing? What do you know?"

"I don't know for sure," he says, on his knees cinching the straps from within, "but I've been thinking about a few things. Remember the computer we broke into?"

"The wannabe hooker."

He tightens the last strap and shakes his head once. "No, back on Orn-3. You remember, in the training room." He sits facing me, wrapped in his blanket and sipping coffee. "That stuff about the Restricted Zone, how the inhabitants were incurable."

"What about it?"

Every inch of the tent is slapped by howling wind.

"So I was thinking," he says. "They figure these creatures are incurable, like us, so I doubt they plan to conquer this planet and govern it. More likely wipe them out."

"You mean supply weapons and let them wipe out each other. But that's the part I don't get. Why not land here with an invasion force and be done with it? They have plenty of resources. They could lay waste to this planet and kill every living thing, all in one afternoon."

"Except for one problem—the killed would know who killed them. Remember, these creatures may not realize it, but deep down, they're no different from us."

"They'll live again."

"With the memory," he says. "For some reason they don't believe it, but you know how it goes. The memory gets buried, but that doesn't mean it's gone. If the Association kills them, they might remember someday and want revenge. But if they destroy each other, it's not so obvious. What is not witnessed is not remembered, including the face of your executioner."

Gusts smack the tent, then the faint ticking of granules grows to a roar, and the canvas is sandblasted. Stinging grains shoot in and fill the tent with a swirling hurricane. Dave throws the blanket over his head.

It has come, so loud that to shout would be silent, a sandstorm that threatens to rip the atmosphere from the planet. Or it already has, given the temperature, nearing the cold of outer space. The blanket guards my face from the shotgun spray but can't begin to fight the shivers.

Muffled by his blanket, Dave hollers, "Try and get some sleep."

His best joke ever.

✳

Far into a night darker than any nightmare, I clutch the blanket, curled on my side and knees held tight to my chest. Slapping canvas and swirling sand, the wind moans a chorus of sirens tempting escape, leave the body and go somewhere safe, return when it's over. Or the moans are wraiths tempting the same, knowing that when I am gone, the body is theirs to take. So much like death, its very cause, when the pain is too great, we run away. Tempting, but I can't.

Night is overwhelmed by a train whistle that never sleeps, wailing its call across the desert while ripping a layer from it. Within the screams I hear her cries—find me, don't get lost.

✳

Sleep never came. Beyond the imminent threat of getting swept out to space, if not buried alive, sleep is impossible with a mind wrapped around a nagging mystery—what makes the cats and snakes ignorant of repeating life? This planet is an oddity, or it's the whole system. Creatures of countless other worlds take repeating life for granted, just one of those things. It's a completely natural course to grow old and die, then do it again, and again. We call it life. But on this planet, rebirth is a fantastic notion believed impossible based on a single article of evidence—what soul can recall a past prior to their birth? That's not evidence, it's a lack of it. Evidence that has been suppressed, deleted or made inaccessible, and it's no accident. The same my memory loss was no accident. Both must spring from the same fountain.

At last the storm loses strength. I shake the blanket clean, clear grains from my hair and teeth, and brush myself off. The straps have come untied and desert pours into the tent. There is no sky, only sand. I tunnel through and emerge atop a dune that buries all but the peaks of our shelters. Morning is close, coloring the horizon deep magenta.

"We should have waited," Dave says, crawling out behind me. He climbs higher and scans the desert dawn. "But no, you just don't listen."

"It wasn't so bad. We made it through okay."

He glares. "The horses ran."

✳

The sun climbs higher in a cloudless sky, scorching pink. Same dry desert, different day. Rusty dunes rise and fall, and for each we conquer, countless more remain. Us gods may be handy with advanced craft and battle tactics, but when confronted by a hostile climate, the snakes are the wiser—they had enough sense to get canteens from their saddles before losing their rides. Dave held on to a knapsack, from which he pulls out lumps wrapped in foil like candy bars, except someone forgot the sugar. The snack melts like chocolate, and the bitter mess keeps us going a few more miles. We never did find the horses. Dave thought we might, or he was hoping. They either outran the storm or were buried by it. We may never know.

Each step forward our boots sink in the loose sand, which absorbs all momentum, like walking a treadmill and going nowhere. I'm ready to die roasting in this sweaty leather, but Dave manages to keep his spirits high—or he's delirious—singing a ditty about a broom sweeping ninety-nine dunes of sand, each verse counting down. Except when he reaches zero, countless more remain. So he starts over.

"Will you shut up."

"What?" he says. "I'm just—"

"Driving me crazy."

He's silent maybe three seconds. "Not my idea to walk across a desert."

"Just shut up."

At last, the stupid song ends. Now if only the desert would.

The Ophidians hike alongside, one next to Dave, the other two on my side, but keeping a distance. Looks like they're having a private conversation.

"I don't bite," I call.

Climbing the next dune, they look over at me, say nothing, and keep climbing. The snake beside Dave might be more sociable.

I ask, "How much farther you think?"

We reach the top and he studies the horizon. "Far."

He could have lied, I wouldn't mind.

"Get any sleep?" Dave asks.

"Don't tell me you managed."

We surf down loose sand and start climbing the next rise.

Snake-man says, "Sleep iss difficult for our kind."

"I can imagine, living in this hellhole. Is every night like a freight train running through town?"

He shakes his head once. "Iss a better place." He climbs the next rise and points to the horizon.

We reach the top and join him. Nothing for miles, only wave after wave of rusty sand, baked by unrelenting sun.

"This side of the planet maybe?"

He just stares at me. I don't think he understands. Then, sliding down on his boots, he says, "Safe from night demons."

The only thing safe from last night's demon is a reinforced concrete bunker. Let's hope we find one before sundown.

"Just think," Dave says, staring out at the endless dunes. "We could be home about now, kicked back on the deck, chugging down a few cold—"

"Shut up. Not another word."

We surf down another wave of loose sand.

✳

Minutes feel like hours, up one dune and down the next. It seems the desert will never end. But we keep a steady pace, pressing on for a goal that probably doesn't exist. The snakes appear used to this sort of thing, and Dave manages somehow, but I'm ready to drop and let the buzzards have their way.

The two unsociable snakes continue pacing our trek, but they keep a safe distance off our flank. The third snake doesn't appear uncomfortable around gods, scaling slope after slope right alongside us like he's part of the gang.

"So what's with your pals?" I ask the snake and indicate the two soldiers off in their own private slice of desert. "They have a problem with me?"

"Iss respect," he says. "Product of fear. In their view, they see a god."

"And you don't? Or something else?"

He laughs, an odd sort of squealing snort. I had no idea they even laughed. We reach the next rise and he looks me in the eye. "The else."

"I don't get it," I say. "Some of you worship and others want me torched. And your enemy isn't much better. Not as bad as what your buddies had in mind, but some Felidians are just as ornery to me."

"Not all belief iss agreed, even among a single species." He indicates his comrades who keep a distance. "They iss acting how they believe, what iss taught to many."

"But not you."

Again he surprises me—a tweak of his lips is almost like a smirk. "Iss a choice to keep what iss taught," he says. "Most learn only what iss taught. Others add teaching from life."

"They look for themselves."

He nods once and starts down the slope. "Not all feel the same about your kind. Many, both enemy and Ophids, see gods to worship, how they iss taught. Some mistrust, even in worship, but fear iss their silence. Still others mistrust, but do not understand your power. No worship, but still worried. The fewest of either species believe the fantastic and iss called fools."

"You believe the fantastic."

He goes silent. We reach the bottom and start up the next dune.

Dave says, "Think about it, Adam. Around here, there isn't just one god."

The Ophidian says, "And not one follower. Iss many, with different beliefs."

"Some don't believe in god."

"God*sss,*" Dave says. "You're missing the point. Look at it this way. Say our friend here believes in a particular god. Then along comes Adam, another god who challenges his chosen god. Who do you expect him to like better? Or put it the other way around. Say you help his god conquer another he doesn't like. Our friend here is going to like you a whole lot better."

"I didn't realize we came here for a popularity contest."

He halts. "And you get on my ass for making a joke of things." Shaking his head, he starts climbing the next rise.

I catch up. "Sorry, I just…"

"Don't get it," he says.

"I get it just fine. I just get tired of it."

Past the top and heading down, the snake asks, "Iss your world where every belief iss agreed?"

"My world?"

Dave says, "I think he means where we come from."

"I realize that, but…" I reach out to the Ophidian and urge him to pause. "Do you know?"

He turns to face me. "You iss not a god."

At last, one of them knows the truth. But now I'm even more curious.

"So tell me, in your view—if I'm not a god, then what am I?"

"You iss a traveler from another world, brought here by great ships that reach between the stars. Your advantage iss inventive, clever devices, not mystical power."

I can hardly believe what I'm hearing.

"Exactly right," I say. "Who else knows this?"

"Few only suspect, but it does little good. Now you should go. Your visit here iss not good, not better than before. I will deliver you to your goal, then you go."

"Why?" I ask. "How was it before?"

"Not at war."

✳

By noon we crest a ridge, and the landscape opens to a promising view. A mirage? Only one way to find out—keep going. Sand thins to a dusting and our boots snap against smooth rock. Enormous slabs are laid out randomly to form a sprawling cobblestone patchwork. Roasted weeds fill in the cracks, clusters of broiled sagebrush grow more frequent, and gradually, the elevation begins to rise.

The stony plateau ends at a bluff overlooking a valley. Not much greener, but it looks like a creek down below. At this point a pond would do. In the distance stands a great city constructed of metal. Every corner and edge is a sharp angle, and the flat sections are polished smooth. A few of the mirror-like panels align between us and above to spark intense flashes of sunlight.

Carved in the bluff, a narrow trail descends to a traveled road. The Ophidians know this route, and know where it goes—they quicken their pace. Taller trees grow alongside the road, but not enough to mask the creek beyond the grove. The snakes leave the road and head for the water. Dave and I follow their sprint and make it to the creek.

On my knees, I lap the cool water from my cupped hands. Someone is across the creek, and we've startled them. Snake-men splash and churn, scrambling out of the water and up the opposite bank. Unlike the soldiers, they wear loose trousers and no shirt. Two more on horseback notice us and gallop away.

Back on the road, more snakes emerge from the thickening grove. They come no closer than the road's edge, where they kneel as we pass. The route continues toward a distant monument—a towering steel arch, polished to a glistening shine. Gateway to their city, contained inside steel walls some twenty feet high. Each step closer, buildings beyond the walls rise taller, constructed of copper, brass, stern iron, more prominent flourishes crafted from gold.

A cavalry unit is passing beneath the steel arch, leaving the city and coming our way. Twenty or so, with heavier leather, chain mail, and armor skirts for their horses. And each one is armed with a blast rifle. They realize our approach and halt. The snakes joining us hurry to greet their fellow Ophidians. Several of the mounted soldiers look our way, their expressionless faces difficult to read.

Dave privately says, "Let's see a convincing god."

A mounted soldier breaks rank and rides to within shouting distance. "Who iss the unknown god?"

"Now's your big chance," Dave says. "Introduce yourself, and make it good."

Right. God or burn.

I step forward. "Adam of Idan, God of Truth."

Behind me, Dave snorts his stifled laughter. "God of *what?*"

I swing around. "It's a long story. Come on, back me up here."

"Truth?" He snickers. "Wow, Adam, you're way over the top this time, totally."

"Stop laughing and back me up before you're top down totally eating dirt."

Eyes wide, he rushes past me. "Stand down, stand down!"

I spin around to face the charging cavalry. A clatter of hooves, in seconds we're surrounded by a dozen blast rifles targeting my chest.

"We're not the enemy," Dave says, hands out trying to push them back. Waving his arms, he upsets the horses.

The soldier who called for my identity nudges his horse closer and stares down at me with that cold-blooded emptiness.

I stare right back up at him. "We must speak with the Felidian spy. Take us to him at once."

He coaxes his horse to sidestep around me. "We iss warned an enemy comes to destroy us." He looks at Dave. "And you, Jovial, iss now friend to Felidians?"

"Nothing friendly, just talk to him."

"What have you done with him?" I ask.

The snake shifts his horse away. "His fate iss sealed."

"Lieutenant," Dave says, "we must speak to the spy immediately. He knows secrets that could determine the fate of all Ophidians. It is vital that we bring his words back to the Mighty One."

The snake leans forward in the saddle to lock his stare on Dave. "We iss informed otherwise."

"He lied to you," I say.

The snake angles back. "So the challenge iss true."

"No," Dave says. "There's no challenge."

"It's a trick," I say. "He plans to hurt you."

"No!" Dave shouts. "We're all on the same side here. Nobody's getting hurt." He starts digging through his knapsack.

The lieutenant says, "The challenge iss true." He turns in his saddle to address the troops. "We please our greatest god, a grand reward iss ours!"

The cheering cavalry goes silent when Dave pulls something from his knapsack and holds it up. The horses shift apart as Dave turns with the object held high, making sure everyone gets a good look. Then he presses a button on the slender device. A flash, dancing rays shoot out, and a holographic image appears.

Soldiers lean forward in their saddles, straining for a better view.

It's the hologram of Matt. There he stands, scrawny geek in baggy shorts and orange tee, stringy hair and proud-of-himself grin. Except he's a midget, hardly up to our waists.

"Oops." Dave fiddles with the device. The image of Matt towers to over three times our size.

Horses shuffle back and snakes gasp.

The hologram flickers but recovers to hold steady.

"If you do not please us," Dave says, "the god Matthew will step on you."

"Step on them?" I ask.

He shrugs, then threatens the snakes, "The giant god will haunt your nightmares!"

Still idiotic, but it seems to work. Soldiers nudge their horses back.

Dave releases the button and the image of Matt fizzles. "The god Matthew will be watching to judge how we are treated. Now bring us horses and take us to the spy."

They stare at us and do nothing. Not much of a surprise.

A soldier on foot emerges from the mounted troops. It's the more sociable snake who hiked the desert with us. We don't want the rest of them hearing his opinion of our godly tricks.

He faces the cavalry. "Iss best we obey their wishes."

Troops shoulder their rifles. Some dismount and kneel.

He calls to others at the rear. Three horses are led through and the reins are passed to the one snake I had thought would betray us.

I approach him and privately say, "You helped us. Why?"

He gives us our horses and climbs into the saddle of his.

"Finish your task," he says. "Then go."

He snaps the reins and gallops away, onto the road leaving the city.

✳

The gateway arch is constructed of welded steel silvery smooth, towering overhead as we pass beneath it, escorted by the Ophidian cavalry. Beyond the arch and into the city, metal buildings rise taller the farther we go. Bronze posts support flat steel awnings, gleaming afternoon sun. For some structures, every panel sits at an oblique angle, and the rooftops are a maze of welded triangles. Here, nothing is round, except the smooth green faces of snakes gawking from windows above and others moving past on foot.

Most citizens are clothed in threadbare tunics, colorless and faded, and some wear baggy trousers. Unlike the soldiers, the common folk do not wear the snug caps, rather expose their egg-shaped skulls, bald and green like the rest of their hairless skin. A few strut in better attire, black trousers, high boots, and lime-green cloth draped over their chest, decorated with an emblem of crossed swords. The citizens keep a safe distance, but close enough for me to study their faces. They are difficult to read, intent stares from dark eyes, and thin lips a straight line. A curious look that might be scornful.

Ahead is a commotion. As we draw near, music grows louder, a catchy rhythm produced by metal drums. Spectators gather to watch dancing snake-ladies who wear purple skirts that spin and twirl. They are otherwise naked, covered only by the blossoming wraps riding low on their hips, curvaceous as human females but not their chests, as flat as the males. Though skinned an alien green and lacking mammalian features, the suggestive rolling of their hips could arouse visitors from any world. They dance closer, studying me and Dave with great interest. Or they're eager to perform for us. They are bald like the males though wear headbands of braided twine stringed with beads that slap as they dance. Armbands circle their biceps, bracelets hang from their wrists, and chains dangle from their necks, all gleaming silver. And rings on every finger, some with tiny cymbals they clack in time with the music.

More snakes approach, crowned by the same headbands but dressed in sleeveless gowns. Their foreheads are wrinkled, framing tired eyes. They shoo the younger ones and the dancers twirl away. Two of the older snake-ladies cradle steel tumblers in both hands. Their fingers are remarkably human, knuckled and nimble, yet a slender green version lacking any nails, just smooth nubs for fingertips. They offer the drinks and other snakes deliver an assortment of pastries on silver platters. We accept the beverages and select from the snacks, flat circles of soft bread glazed by cinnamon sugary butter that melts across my tongue. In contrast to the overwhelming sweetness, the cool drink is bitter like coffee, but with a strong bite of alcohol. One sip and I hand it back. Not the time for that sort of unwinder.

We move along, leaving the music to fade behind us. Next is an avenue of workshops, some tall with metal roofs supported by hefty columns, others little more than flimsy shacks. The front of one workshop is wide open, allowing a view of laborers inside. Snakes attend to large bellows, stoking a furnace that warms my face even at a distance. The air is stained by the odor of a skillet left forgotten on the burner, and forming on my tongue is the metallic twang of sucking on a coin.

Wielding heavy tongs, workers reach into the furnace and extract pasty ingots of red-hot metal, which they roll and fold, hammer and reheat, until reducing the slabs to oblong bars. Others stationed at anvils swing hammers and beat the cooling pieces into shape. Ringing out in disarray, the tinny strikes ricochet off buildings across the street and return a delayed, out-of-time clamor. Still more workers grind, sharpen, and polish the slender shafts, which when complete result in finely crafted broadswords. The next shop works in softer ores, lead, silver, and smelting copper and tin into bronze. A worker dips into a fire-heated cauldron, the handle of his ladle long and the end a cup much larger than the tiny portion it holds. He pours the lava-like fluid into various molds.

In an alley past the workshops, a group of younger snakes is gathered. I coax my horse to pause. A circle is drawn in the dirt, where the children take turns flicking stones into their opponent's. A snake-boy knocks one out, then leaps up and squeals, celebrating victory.

Dave comes alongside. "Pretty weird seeing kids, eh?"

The youngsters are oblivious of the danger surrounding them. They hold no weapons, only a handful of pebbles, and somehow that makes them saner than all the rest. Play a game and enjoy life. It's amazing, the joy produced by an activity so meaningless, without any real purpose or significant goal. Knock a stone out of the circle and you win. If only life could be that simple again.

✳

The cats and snakes may have their differences, but they share equal feelings for the convicted and where to put them. Miles beyond the city, our caravan travels over a dry prairie, then rusty dunes begin to rise. Not the same desert from which we came. All morning and into the afternoon, I have tracked the sun across the sky for a crude bearing. We have yet to double back.

The prison stands alone in desolation. Two stories all metal, the structure doesn't strive to impress anyone or win awards for architectural excellence. It's just a big shiny box. To gain entrance we must wait as a series of bolts snap, locks twist, then finally, the steel slab creaks open. The door could serve as a bank vault.

Out of the bright sun and dumped into darkness, I can only wish my nose was as blind. The first wave smacks hard, something horrid, like a dead animal tossed in a dumpster and left to stew for months.

My eyes adjust. The silvery walls are stained by splotches of dark corrosion. From deeper in the prison comes the crack of a whip, the cries of tortured cats, and weak moans at the edge of death.

We move into a passage lined with bars from floor to ceiling, separating each cell from the next. The light is dim, and the corridor fades into darkness. Many prisoners hide in the shadows of their private cages, others lie on the single bunk or crumpled on the floor, and a few are at the bars reaching past, into the corridor. Not every prisoner is Felidian. Some of the outstretched arms are hairless and green.

From the darkened corridor, an Ophidian approaches, armed with a short whip and carrying a ring of keys.

Dave says, "We're here to interrogate the spy."

An arm reaches out from a cell and snatches hold of me. "Iss evil," the prisoner says, a boney snake with weathered green skin.

I squirm free. "I'm not—"

"Not think of one thing," the prisoner says, slithering out of darkness to press his face between the bars and stare at me. "Not focus. You focus, they read it and use it against you."

"Ignore the fool. He iss delirious." The jailor reaches past the bars to the prisoner's bare chest and shoves hard.

The snake staggers back to become a voice from darkness. "Stay in sleep or you iss trapped. The light, do not go. I have, I know."

The jailor flicks through his ring of keys and slides one into the lock.

"No," I tell him, eycing his whip. "He's done no harm. Let him speak." I call to the darkness, "What light?"

"Insane," the jailor says and retracts his key.

A soldier asks, "Your spy?"

"No, but I—"

"This way, then." The jailor continues into the corridor.

"Forget it," Dave says. "We're not here to interrogate a lunatic."

"But he's… He knows…"

"Nothing we need to know. Come on." He pulls me along, following the jailor, and the soldiers trail behind. "What's with you?" Dave asks. "I thought you were all hot to find your friend."

"I am, I just… I don't know. Something he said, it's…"

"All crap. The freak's a nutcase talking nonsense."

From the past, Madison's sly grin comes to mind, and her remark at my frustration with dreams. *You know, it's not always nonsense.*

✳

Deeper in the prison, the cells are no longer constructed of bars that divide a string of cages. The walls are solid steel, and the doors are marked only by a rectangular slot at eye level. We halt before a cell door and the jailor flips through his keys. He unlocks the door and pulls it open.

I step into darkness.

Growling.

"Physuro?"

A figure lunges and swings. I leap back and soldiers rush in to tackle him.

"No!" I say. "Don't hurt him."

Dave pulls me back to the corridor. "Watch it, this one's a beast."

Six snakes wrestle one cat. A blast brightens the cell, then it goes dark. The soldiers relax their weapons and step back, surrounding a lump crumpled on the floor.

I hurry in. "No!"

A soldier says, "One less spy."

I whirl around, tear the rifle from his grasp, and plant the barrel to his neck. One hard shove, I pin him to the wall.

"This one's dead," Dave says.

The jailor steps in, holding out a lantern over Dave as he checks for a pulse. The soldier pinned to the wall seizes the rifle from me.

All I can do is stare at the floor, at... dark fur nowhere near orange and white.

"That's not the spy." Not Physuro, but still, a dead Felidian. I swing back to the snake and strike. "Stop killing each other!"

Dave springs up. "It's not?" He looks delighted. "There must be more."

"Iss many," the jailor says.

"Don't be so happy." I force Dave's attention to the dead cat at our feet. "This is insane."

But I am happy, or something, or so jerked from anxiety to sorrow, then to rage and relieved, I'm the one insane. He's not dead. Or he could be. But one of the them is, or he could have died yesterday. Or he's not even here. I don't know what to think.

Dave drags me out of the cell. "Cry about it later."

✳

We are led through the high-security area to the cells of more prisoners. Dozens more. Every Felidian is a spy according to the jailor. For each cell we visit, I proceed with caution, calling past the rectangular slot before entering and having to go on living with myself while knowing I'm the cause of someone's death. No one replies to his name, a few growl, and the rest plead innocent and beg for release. Surely a god be merciful, they say.

The next section must be for criminals insanely dangerous. The steel walls and vault-like doors are studded with massive rivets, and gigantic hinges run the height of each door. They're not taking any chances with these prisoners. The jailor halts before one of the cells. Calling won't work, there isn't even a peephole. Only one way to greet the occupant.

I tell the trigger-happy troops, "This time you wait outside."

"Iss unwise," a soldier says.

Dave snatches the rifle from him. "I think us gods can handle it. You stay out here."

The snake bows and the others shoulder their weapons. A wonder they don't question why us gods would need a blast rifle to handle it. Divinity is a miracle, Dave's anyway.

The jailor unlocks the door and leaps back like a stampede is waiting on the other side.

Dave nudges the door and it creaks open.

Ahead is a black void, into a cell without windows. We step in and Dave pulls the door shut, sealing out all light.

Growling.

Oh shit. I crouch fast.

Click—a flash brightens the cell. No!

My leaping heart whirls me around to deflect Dave's rifle, but my reach swipes at nothing. On his knees, Dave is setting down a slender glowing cylinder. The harsh light casts a fiendish green hue up to the ceiling, leaving stark shadows in disheveled fur, sunken face scowling, and one arm cocked back, aiming to rip my throat out.

Physuro's eyes go wide. "Adam! I thought you be dead." He hoists me up like a rag doll and squeezes tight.

I strain for breath. "Take it easy, Physuro. I'm barely in one piece as it is."

He releases me and my feet hit the floor, not all that steady with a feather brain.

"Forgive me," he says, beaming a wide smile. "I cannot contain myself. Your presence pleases me beyond compare."

"Yeah, me too." I check for broken bones, a ruptured spleen, anything else out of place.

Dave runs his lantern over Physuro, brightening soiled fur and patches of dried blood.

"Another god joins us," Physuro says.

"My friend, Dave. And don't worry, he's with me. I mean, us."

Physuro gets that sparkle in his eye. "Ah, the God of Laughter."

"Of what?" Dave asks. "No, it's Jovial, Jester to—"

"Stick with Laughter," I suggest.

Physuro turns with arms out, indicating his metallic quarters, dim in the limey glow. "It appears I own a bad habit of finding a cell in which to rest." He grins.

"Yep, you're one bad cat."

He was about to laugh, before noticing my outfit. "You wear the uniform of the enemy."

BANG at the door, bang bang. From beyond comes the jailor's muffled voice. "Iss all well?"

"It's fine," I holler past the steel slab. "Leave us alone. We're interrogating the spy."

Physuro scowls. "I be not a spy." He studies me from head to toe. "And what be you? You have changed sides."

"I'm not on any side."

"What be your meaning?"

"Ophidians aren't the enemy. It's someone else."

"Who?" he asks.

"Keep it down, they're right outside."

He looks at the door, then speaks quieter. "Who? Who be the enemy?"

"Your gods."

He leans away. "Their intent be questionable, yet I would not have imagined…"

"There's no question about it, Physuro. The gods intend to kill you *and* the Ophidians."

"A blasphemous suggestion."

"Label an idea blasphemy and subjects avoid it for fear of reprisal. Don't you see? The real enemy has defined what is blasphemous and what is not, all of it. They not only control you, they control your *opinion of truth.*"

He studies me for a moment. "Your bold conclusions be met by fierce argument, I believe, from Felidians and Ophidians alike."

"The objective, I believe."

"Can we have the reunion elsewhere?" Dave says. "We found him, now let's get out of here. So what's the plan?"

"Plan?" I ask.

"You did have a plan. You know, for once you found him. Right?"

My silence is the answer, which only sparks his eruption. "Why do you do this to me? I was perfectly happy in the desert. Now what?" He turns and turns, holding out his little green lantern. "You drag me all this way for what? No plan, that's what. Now I'm stuck here with you two, penned in by four walls. Very thick steel walls."

Physuro says, "Your god-friend appears upset. He be not a danger, I pray."

Dave points his finger like a pistol aimed at Physuro. "We're not going anywhere with him."

"Dave!" I slap his arm down. "Physuro is my friend, the same as you, the same as all the Felidians. They're not evil, and they're not the enemy, I thought you understood by now. Besides, he has to go with us. He knows where to find Christina."

"Not what I mean." Dave turns to indicate the door. "They think he's a spy. What do you expect? Say he's coming with us and they let him go, just like that? Was that your plan?"

Physuro hangs his head. "Not a probable conclusion. Beyond the door, death be my only destination."

I latch hold of his arm. "Not while you're with me it's not."

His whiskers angle up as his smile grows.

"What plans are for," Dave says. "You know, like how to exit this cell alive. That might be handy, maybe. Now's the time."

"And what of Stu?" Physuro asks.

Regret is useless, yet it thrives as if a life force all its own, feasting on the past and what I've let happen. If only I had saved him.

Dave matches my moment of silence.

Physuro says, "As it shall be."

The lantern surges a sick green flicker. Dave knocks it against one palm, fighting to keep it alive. The light fades dimmer, dimmer, like a candle gasping for breath, smothered by another shovelful of dirt, and another, burying us in darkness.

The cell door bursts open and light pours in. An Ophidian stands in the doorway, but he is unlike the others. The same bodysuit uniform, but instead of the snug cap, his stiff hat has a shiny brim. He wears his long jacket as a cape, held in place by a chain at the neckline, and he holds a riding crop, smacking it in his open palm.

"Who are you?" I ask.

He plants the crop to my chest. "Iss a question for *you*."

Physuro turns away and grumbles under his breath, "Major Smeck, intolerable."

"Silence!" The Ophidian swings his crop and smacks Physuro.

I grab his little whip. "Hey! Knock it off."

He wrestles against my hold of his crop.

"Major," Dave says, "this is Adam, God of Truth, here to help." Dave pries my fingers loose and the snake yanks his crop free.

"We're here to interrogate the spy," I say.

"By order of the Mighty One," Dave adds.

Smeck twists to face Dave. "Our Mighty One sends a god of *jokes* to interrogate a spy?"

"Yes," Dave says. "Through the power of amusing stories, I extract information by coaxing the subject to laugh until honesty prevails."

We'll be torched by the charge of stupidity.

The major circles us. "Your torture iss humor?"

Completely serious, I don't know how he does it, Dave says, "Exactly."

Except no one is laughing.

Major Smeck stops pacing. "Lies." He whacks the crop in his open palm. "You have learned no secrets."

"Oh, but we have," Dave says. "Many secrets, including the true source of the nightmares."

If he would just shut up—a great plan—keep quiet like me, except for my glare locked on him and screaming it, *shut up!*

The major falls silent, and the crop hangs limp at his side. Something Dave said.

"Indeed," Physuro says. "And I shall reveal the goddess."

That piques the major's curiosity. And mine. And Dave's.

"Reveal who?" Dave asks.

"The Goddess of Dreams," Physuro says, then to me, "Why you have come to interrogate, no?"

"Right," Dave says, then asks me, "Who's the goddess?"

"Christina."

Major Smeck can't decide which of us deserves his confused stare.

"Chris?" Dave asks. "When did she become a goddess?"

"About the same time you…" Then I realize Smeck absorbing all this. "Like all the gods, when we created the heavens."

Dave laughs. "No, I mean for real, not—"

"Shut up." Then to Smeck I say, "Sir, you need to understand what is happening here."

"Iss perfectly clear," he says. "You and Jovial iss not what you portray, perhaps spies yourselves." He motions to soldiers waiting in the corridor.

"It's a joke," I say.

Soldiers start into the cell, but Smeck has them halt. He turns back to me and listens.

I point to Dave. "He's a god of jokes, right? But of course it isn't working, you know that. And the Mighty One knew as well, no joke would ever work, not to extract information from any spy so crafty as this." I indicate Physuro.

"It's not a joke," Dave says like I've ruined all his fun. "We have to save the goddess or all dreams will turn to nightmares." Waving his arms, he throws himself at the soldiers in the corridor. "Nightmares forever!"

The troops retreat a step.

I blast Dave, "Will you shut up already."

Physuro says, "I too be sincere, not a humorous tale. The goddess be held captive, and I shall guide the way as promised." He chuckles. "The laughing god's power has already tickled the secret from me."

"You too, shut up, both of you." I turn to Smeck. "Major, don't be fooled by this nonsense. The Mighty One has sent the only god capable, the God of Truth, to interrogate the spy and learn secrets vital to winning your battle. You must trust me, the fate of all Ophidians hangs in the balance, and I appear before you now to ensure total victory."

He might be bored, pleased or enraged, his empty expression would never tell. "Iss better," he says, and I resume breathing. He indicates Physuro. "Proceed with the interrogation."

"Oh no, Major, the feats of divinity I shall perform are not for mere mortals to witness." I usher him toward the door. "You must leave us for a time, a time in which I will bring the power of the heavens to bear, and this spy will never again speak any lie." I push Smeck out the door and seal the cell.

Dave gets his lantern working again. "That nonsense your plan?"

"Until I think of something better."

"I already did," he says. "And if you'd stop telling me to shut up, it might work. Dreams, you know. It fits. She knows about dreams, right?"

"That won't get us out of here."

"Sure it will, they're—"

"Shut up and let me think."

"Your friend is right," Physuro says.

"Yeah," Dave says, "I got an idea here."

"Me too. Like get the hell out of here before that asshole comes back."

"Why we need a good fairy tale. About *dreams*."

"What's this crap you're hung up on?"

BANG at the door, bang bang.

Dave speaks quieter. "It's what you don't know about them, and I do. The snakes are terrified of nightmares. And Chris is the Goddess of Dreams. Don't you get it?"

Physuro says, "We must rescue her, be that not true?"

"It's not going to work. That bastard won't let us go just because of some nightmare."

"Sure he will," Dave says. "I'll scare them into letting us go. And Physuro too, it's perfect. He knows where to find her, right? I'll even convince them to help. We'll all save the goddess together." He starts for the door.

"No." I hold him back. "They can't be that gullible, come on. We need something real, not a dream, even a nightmare. We need something concrete."

"If you would've had a plan to begin with…"

"I'm working on it!"

How do we fool these snakes? We're gods with clever devices, not mystical power. But I don't have anything. Where are all the clever devices? In the arsenal. The Felidians had one, the snakes must have one as well. Clever devices, some kind of device, but what? Flying away from here would be the perfect gift. And just what we will have.

"Dave, you taught them to operate tanks. So you know about the arsenal."

"Sure, but I didn't—"

"You can take us there." I go for the door and swing it open.

Major Smeck is on the other side. "Enough time for interrogation," he says. "Provide the secrets learned, then we finish the spy."

"Our efforts are delayed." I indicate Physuro. "One of their finest, this spy displays superior resistance to techniques even gods employ."

"Then you iss fake," Smeck says. "You have learned no secrets."

"Only because we lack the necessary device, stored where the gifts are located."

"Device?" Dave asks.

I motion for Physuro to follow me into the corridor.

Smeck blocks the way. "The spy iss not to leave. We will dispatch a unit to retrieve your device."

"Oh no, Major, you don't understand. The device is extremely delicate and cannot be transported. Even to move it across the room could risk irreparable damage, and we may never learn the secrets."

"What device?" Dave asks.

"The Neurotransenactor. Surely, you're familiar with the transenactor." I wink. "Even a god of jokes knows about the enactor."

"The... Oh, the actor, I see. The enactor, of course, to act on his neuros. Quite an instrument of deception. Are such extreme measures necessary?" He puts on a grave face and looks at Physuro like the poor cat is heading for his last supper.

"Will it hurt?" Physuro asks, his concern perhaps sincere, or he's a good actor, too.

"That depends," I explain, "on the degree you resist telling the truth."

Smeck seems to enjoy this detail, as if thirsting to watch a lying spy scream in agony.

"He'll have no choice," Dave says. "The enactor pries all secrets, and the most important, the kidnapper's hideout where the Goddess of Dreams is held captive. The spy knows! We must free the goddess before all dreams turn to nightmares. *Forever!*"

If he were any closer, I'd kick him. Enough already. Then, waving his arms, he storms into the troops standing in the corridor. They scatter, somehow intimidated by his overacted performance, bellowing over and over, nightmares forever, forever. I work so hard at this and the jackass works as hard to unravel it, clinging to a ridiculous fairy tale that only makes us look like fools.

"Don't mind Jovial," I tell Smeck. "Embellishment is an ingredient of humor, all the god knows. Trust me, Major, what we have in store for the spy is no laughing matter."

✳

Outside the prison, the fresh air is resuscitating. We're out, but not exactly free. Dave and I are, at least free to move about. Soldiers offer each of us a horse, but the snakes don't trust their spy one slithering inch. Physuro's wrists and ankles are bound by shackles. Chains joining them keep him from raising his arms much and force him to crouch, shuffling his steps. Makes it tough to walk any distance, even ride a horse, but the Ophidians never intended that he would do either. A horse-drawn wagon carries a steel cage into which Physuro is placed. I didn't anticipate prison becoming portable, and the challenge still remains, how to free my friend from his cell. And now, from shackles as well.

The complement of soldiers escorting us is double or more the number that delivered us here, reinforced by a regiment under Smeck's command. He barks orders and leads the troops, which divide to cover us front and rear, and we follow the wagon carrying Physuro's cage. Our caravan takes the road leading back to the Ophidian city, but not to return there. At a crossroads, we come to a stop. The city is in sight, but still a distance to go. Smeck instructs a pair of soldiers who ride off at a strong gallop, heading for the city. The rest of us turn at the crossroads.

By late afternoon, clouds gather at the horizon, preparing for demon time once the sun goes down. All we've discovered is more wasteland, a landscape laid out flat forever, marked only by the thin strip of road ahead, an endless straight line.

We're not near enough to Physuro to speak unless we shout. Anything I'd like to say is better not shared with all, so it won't be shared with anyone, not until we find a more private situation. Crouched in his cage, he faces us and doesn't show much despair. He might even appear a mite cheery, looking on with a faith in me I cannot match, confident that I'll fix this mess. The God of Truth should be honest for once.

"You know," Dave says, riding alongside, "before you showed up, they trusted me." He scans the troops ahead and twists in his saddle to glance at those behind. "I feel like a prisoner."

"Don't worry. I know what I want, and we'll have it soon."

"Did it include your friend in a cage?"

"I'll deal with that when the time comes."

"Most plans have a few more details. Care to share?"

"Be happy I have one. And it's not weak. Just follow my lead."

After some miles of travel, a structure rises from the desert. Could be that reinforced bunker we'll need once the sun goes down. It doesn't look Ophidian, not metal this time, and not Felidian stone either. The exterior walls are poured concrete, three stories tall and no windows. The creatures of this planet had nothing to do with the construction of this monument.

The only use of metal is the tall outer doors, just like the Felidian arsenal. Once we arrive, Smeck barks orders and troops pull the doors open. Dave and I tether our horses with the rest, then step inside. Bright lights shine down on a variety of shapes hidden beneath dusty tarpaulins. This time the contents are not a mystery, which sparks a new idea—it would take all of ten seconds to flip the cloth, load the rifle, and cut down these wormy creeps. But given their greater number, armed as well or better, that sort of rash thinking needs a vacation. We have the means—if we proceed carefully—to free ourselves from the snakes. Without, I hope, anyone getting hurt.

The troops move in deeper to reach more lights, and the room glows brighter. The arsenal extends back some distance and could serve as a hanger tall enough to fly around in, if you're careful and know what you're doing.

I step outside and approach the wagon carrying Physuro's cage. "Get him out and bring him inside."

Smeck puts his horse between me and the wagon. "He stays. Bring your device."

"I already told you, it's too delicate. He must be brought to it, then we can proceed."

"Show your device," he says.

I point into the warehouse. "Over there, in the back." He doesn't even try to look. I step closer to him. "Relax, Major, we're not up to anything. Why would we? Look, you have the only exit covered. What do you expect us to do?"

He looks into the arsenal and sees that there are no other exits. But he might have noticed the great number of weapons. He couldn't possibly believe we'd try fighting his small army. But the real risk—what I cannot know for sure—is whether he has any clue of what I really intend. Like all of them, he's difficult to read.

Smeck instructs soldiers to form a defensive line near the open doors. He summons those manning the wagon to let Physuro from his cage, but also orders another six soldiers to circle him with blast rifles point-blank.

Still shackled, Physuro's shuffling pace is agonizingly slow baby steps. I want to run and have him run with me. This detail complicates matters. Timing will be crucial.

The troops deliver him to my side but don't back off much.

"Look," I tell them, "give us a little space. He's restrained, and we're not armed. Lighten up, okay?" They look to Smeck and he nods. The soldiers loosen the gauntlet though remain well within deadly range.

We move into the warehouse, and with Physuro at my side, it's about the most private situation we're going to get. "Listen, I didn't count on the chains and can't ditch them just yet, but we'll find a way." I glance at the troops, rifles at the ready, then back to Physuro. "We have a ladder to climb, and I need to know if you can."

"A ladder to freedom," he says, "I will hop as a bunny if needed."

"However works best, on my signal."

Physuro waddles more like a duck. We reach Dave, waiting for us near a line of untarped vehicles that appear recently used, coated with desert sand. Armored vehicles boxy and tan, each with a single turret. Tanks, perfect for shelling a defenseless observatory. Thanks, Dave, for teaching the snakes all about tanks.

Dave heads for one of the tanks.

"We're not driving out of here," I say.

He turns back and I point over his shoulder to the line of larger tarps along the back wall, the same as those in the Felidian arsenal—more black triangle craft. He glances at the tarps, then back to me. This time, the big white grin is all I had hoped for.

On each side of Physuro, Dave and I help him toward our escape.

"Halt," Smeck calls. "No further. Present your device."

Dave takes the initiative. "Right here, Major." He steps toward one of the craft and tugs on the tarp.

"No!" I leave Physuro and lunge at Dave. "Careful." I pull him back before the tarp slides off. "Smeck will figure it out when he sees it."

The major walks his horse closer, flanked by a full regiment.

I call to him, "We must all be careful, for the delicate instrument is easily damaged. And if mishandled, the device may cause serious injury to anyone near."

The troops retreat a step. Smeck nudges his horse back.

"First we shall activate the device," I explain, then quietly tell Dave, "Get up there and get it started, but keep the tarp."

"Makes it kind of hard to fly."

"Shhh! Shut up and do it."

He slips under the tarp, climbs the ladder, and reaches the top. The cockpit cover pops up and yanks the tarp higher, revealing the bottom few rungs of ladder. Smeck coaxes his horse closer, straining for a better view.

It's now or never.

I haul Physuro, his feet dragging, and pitch him at the ladder.

"Go!"

He ducks under the tarp and starts his bunny hop. The engines grow louder, the ladder begins to quake, and the tarp flutters. I'm stuck behind Physuro and he's having trouble. He snags the tarp and it slides off.

Barely up three rungs, I twist in search of Smeck's reaction. Troops gawk at the strange craft, but the major knows about this. He's no longer difficult to read, now clearly pissed off. He barks orders and troops flock to his command. He is animated, bouncing in his saddle having a tantrum as he points to their idle rifles.

The troops don't know what to think, stepping closer with their empty stares glued to the mysterious craft. Beyond the troops, Smeck issues orders and points to us. Soldiers pass the command along and begin pulling rifles from their shoulders. Outside the arsenal, clouds of dust rise from the road that brought us here. Five times as many soldiers are arriving to reinforce the major's unit.

I shove Physuro past the last rung, over the edge and into the cockpit. Over my shoulder, a legion of blast rifles is demanding an explanation. No great story springs to mind.

Up the rungs pedaling frantic steps, I'm not fast enough. The snap, odor and scorching air—a sizzling electrobeam whines. I'm just in time to witness my own demise.

The beam explodes supernova, green and orange at the edges, and a swirling rainbow of plasma spreads outward. The concussion smacks hard and sounds a booming thunder, but the blast is repelled by the craft's bubble of protection, in which I am contained. I'm thankful that someone knows about shields and when to use them. Dave is forgiven in advance for every bad joke I'll ever have to endure.

I hurry up the ladder and pull the cover shut. Bang, boom, scattering sparks hang suspended at the edge of our invisible barrier as the troops unleash a full assault that's useless. However, we're not airborne, and shield energy is dropping fast.

Dave hits the power and the craft shoots up, rocking as he adjusts attitude. Soldiers empty their rifles like a thousand beestings, pop, pang, thwack. The craft lurches higher and Dave whips us around to face the doors, which troops below are swinging closed.

"Go! Hurry!"

We hover steady, aimed at the narrowing escape. Dave gauges the challenge, then glances my way. "About like Menadint Gorge back home, eh?"

A winding chasm run is one thing, maybe some tight turns and lots of fun, but you can always pull up. Gorges don't have ceilings or end at closed doors.

"This is no time to show off. *Go!*"

"This is nuthin'." He flips the craft sideways, wingtips vertical. Full power hurls us at the evaporating sliver of daylight. Our belly scrapes the closing doors, arcs spray from our protective bubble, and shield energy drops to zilch. We soar out of the arsenal, Dave yanks the pitch, and we rocket skyward.

"Ah, Dave, that was great fun and all, but you know, now we're out of shields. What if we engage enemy?"

"No big deal." He reaches for a panel at knee level and throws a switch. "One's used up, activate bank two."

"Two?"

"Yeah, number two. These things have eight."

"They do?"

"Sure," he says. "Otherwise some missile might crawl up our ass and make one quick end to this ride."

And one smoldering wreck at the bottom of a ravine, with seven unused banks of shield energy. And to think I criticized their ignorance of shields. Am I humbled? Not when feeling like such a fool.

✳

High in the empty sky, I'm drawn to vapor streaming across the wing, a swirling mist that dances over the glossy black, curls around and ripples, then is blasted away and stretched flat in the wake of our craft. A reminder of that miserable long ago, the sidewalk, water running down the many drains, and watery bullets of cold rain. Another night of endless nights, walking the street, hungry for a meal. Watching water pour into the drains was a mindless experience, an escape from a troubled reality, and today, watching vapor wash over the wing is the same. But which is more troubling? Today or that long ago? If only I had known then... how many events might be otherwise? Now I escape again, leaving behind another troubled reality. Except this time, the real trouble is not behind.

"Where to?" Dave asks.

Far below, rusty desert creeps past. A river winds across the land toward distant mountains at the horizon, beginning to emerge from a veil of dingy haze. Jagged black peaks shoot up like blades of fractured obsidian. Our original goal.

"Home of the Gods," I say.

Seated behind us, Physuro says, "I beg, let us turn back from—"

I twist to face him. "I told you, it's not a *wish*."

Dave says, "What the heck is that?" He cranes his neck for a view straight down, then banks the craft into a descending spiral. Below, a lone mound rises from a sea of sand. Something big, carved out of rock. Late sun casts long shadows across what is clearly a nose, darkened eye sockets, and a mouth.

They have got to be kidding.

This is too much. A statue is bad enough, but this I cannot believe. They've carved his face from a mountain of rock, forever staring up into the heavens.

"What be it?" Physuro asks.

"Your almighty one," I say.

"So he is both," Dave says.

"Sure looks that way. The Ophidians have erected a monument to him, nearly half the size of his ego."

"The same god?" Physuro asks.

"He's no god. He's a big, giant piece of shit!" Staring up at me, smug grin as he gloats, having beaten me once again.

Physuro says, "I have seen the giant piece of shit."

Dave breaks out laughing. I don't know what to think.

"What be funny?" Physuro asks. "You do not believe me?"

"You're just…" Dave fights his chuckles. "Just so damned literal." He pulls the craft out of the spiraling pattern and higher, back on course for the mountains.

"More figures in speech," I explain. "I'm not too fond of Jared, so I call him names."

"Not fond?" Dave teases.

"A battle of words," Physuro suggests.

"Trust me," I say, "once I find him, it'll be plenty more than words."

"It be true," Physuro says. "I have seen him."

"You mean recently?"

"Outside the prison when I arrived. He be talking with Ophidians."

I shift to Dave. "We have to go back."

Or do we? Is he there? With Christina?

"Settle down," Dave says. "Remember, finish what we start."

"But he could be… She could…"

"Knock it off," he says. "She's not there, think about it. You know where she is. Stick with thought one."

Christina would say the same, even I would if not driven insane by Jared and all he has done, is doing, and will do. I just don't know. I hate not knowing, why, when, where. I want to find her, but raging inside me is the screaming urge to track down Jared, end his torturing, taunting, imagined superiority, I'm so feeble, he's so grand.

"Let's find Chris," Dave says. "Worry about Jared later."

I'm torn—find my love, kill my hatred.

Love first.

✳

Soaring high above the desert, our journey is calm, so unturbulent the passing of time is monotonous. The craggy black peaks stand like a fortress wall stretched across the darkening horizon. The towering summits resist approach, creeping closer by the smallest measure, and it feels as though we'll never arrive. The whine of engines is a soothing lullaby, almost hypnotic. Slouched lower in the seat, I get comfortable, and my eyelids grow heavy.

A tap on my shoulder ends that. Leaning forward between our seats, Physuro waits for my attention. Some rest might have been good. On second thought, I should thank him. He probably saved me from another nightmare in which Jared slices my belly wide open.

"What?" I ask.

He raises his arms and rattles the chains of his restraint. I had almost forgotten.

I ask Dave, "You got a torch?"

"I wouldn't fire a torch in a cockpit if we were docked, everything powered off. Use your head."

"Oh, yeah, bad idea. What else you got?"

"It's not like I've been cruising this ride to work every day. I'm as green as you. Check the back for something."

I unbuckle and climb in back with Physuro. Behind him is a shallow footlocker. I get him to scoot some, get it open, and find a small toolkit with pliers and screwdrivers. Behind a flap is a saw, but more like a large file, not very toothy. But the finer pitch should work well enough for metal, eventually.

I hold it up for Dave to see. "Awful wimpy."

"Be determined," he says. "You're good at that."

Smart-ass.

I tell Physuro, "Sit still," and get to work.

"No," Dave says, glancing over his shoulder. "Not the chain, dumb-ass. What are you going to do? Cut every link? Cut the lock and the whole thing falls apart. See?" He reaches out to show how the chain is threaded through the shackles and holds it all together.

"Sorry I didn't notice, Master of all Brains."

Not bothering to fire back, Dave faces forward and keeps piloting.

Physuro asks, "You be friends, no?"

"The initial moment of freedom has a funny effect."

"Yeah," Dave says without looking back. "Fix all you have to bitch about, we only have ourselves to bitch out."

"Crude," I say, "but close." Then to Physuro, "It's a kind of release. Harmless, just between friends. You get the drift."

All he gets is that contrasting brow, one tall, the other down. "Indeed, both of you be quite strange."

Dave shrugs. He's probably heard that plenty of times. I get busy sawing the lock, and at this rate, it's going to take a week.

"Tell me, Adam," Physuro says, "about you and David."

"What about us?"

"I wish to learn the way of the gods."

I stop sawing. "I told you, I'm not a god, and neither is Dave. I'll pretend if it helps, but really, we're not gods."

"I comprehend your insistence that others regard you as mortal. However, if that be so, and those we regard as gods be otherwise, then I must ask— what be the truth of the gods?"

Acceptance of our mortal status is welcome news, though I might wish that he continue thinking of us as gods, for now we face bigger questions I wasn't prepared to discuss. How do I say this?

"To start, Physuro, you have to understand the truth about truth. There is no absolute truth. Truth is personal. My truth, your truth, everybody else's truth."

"You suggest that truth be opinion."

"No, just that it's a product of individual perception. Authority doesn't decide, *we* decide. Truth only appears absolute if we insist an idea is exclusive and we agree, when really, there are as many ideas as there are living things, each with their own truth. And that includes the truth about god."

"You say it as one. We have many, no?"

"We'll get to that, but first I want to stress that I'm telling you *my* truth. Call it opinion if you like. Yours may differ, and I invite that."

"Very well. Tell your opinion of god." He raises his arms to call attention to his restraint, the one he'd like me to continue sawing. I keep at it while we talk.

"I don't know what god is for sure, and I'm not even sure that knowing makes any difference. But I am certain of what god is not. It's not an identity, like a supreme being or any sort of sentient creature. And it's not happy or sad, or wishing to judge or punish anyone. It's more a force, forever with me, and every other living thing."

"The creator. A giver of life."

"That's not how I see it. Source maybe, but not creator. That's a physical concept that suggests a beginning. A beginning and end are both defined by time, and time is physical. To label god a creator suggests that god is physical, and that's absurd. Whatever god may be, the greatness far exceeds anything physical, ever. Besides, if we have a creator, do we also have a destroyer? More nonsense. Another physical idea—the end of time, and a demon assigned the duty of making it happen. It's all silly, nowhere near how it really works."

"And how be it that it really works?"

"It's not that simple, or easy to explain." Neither is sawing this lock. I give my arm a rest. "I'll try giving you an example. Suppose you see someone, a person you like, and they do something that pleases you. Maybe they say hi, or give you a kiss, or they make something and want to show you. Or you haven't seen them in a while, and you're fond of them, and you miss them. Now, with all that in mind, think about what happens when you *see* them. When you take a moment to really see them, and they become the object of your attention. Something definitely happens. Even thinking about it something happens, but even more when you catch their gaze. A force of admiration flows from you, into them. You can feel it if you pay attention. And the reverse, when you please someone and receive their admiration, the force flows from them to you, something that cannot be measured, but it is very real."

His eyes sparkle. "This example I comprehend."

"Good. That is god."

He frowns. "Perhaps I do not comprehend. Your words begin to enlighten yet end at a struggle to believe."

"That's good too. That you struggle means you have *desire,* a good thing. In this case a desire to understand, to believe, and make the idea your own. Desire has many forms, physical, emotional, and others. A desire to know, to have, to accomplish, a desire to give that flow of admiration, to receive it, to feel that love. Desire is life. If we had no desire we'd be truly dead, and I'm not talking body dead. Having no desire whatsoever would be a complete absence of god."

"You be saying the gods dictate our desires."

"No. But more important, I'm not saying what anyone desires. I'm telling you *my* truth, what's real to me. Hear what I have to say, but draw your own conclusions. *Your* truth. Only from you. Not me, not any god, no one else."

"I comprehend your wish that I form my own thoughts. Yet still, I do not comprehend your example. Gods be desire?"

I lift the restraint binding him and rattle the chains across his view. "You want out of this, right? That's a desire. Now you tell me—whose desire is that?"

He has no answer. I get back to sawing the lock.

"Your point be made," he says. "Yet still, it be difficult to relate desire to the subject of gods."

"Maybe I'm using the wrong word. Look, we all have something that drives us forward. At a minimum, we hope to survive another day. The best word I have to express that is *desire.* And that we have this quality, whatever you want to call it, suggests that a force exists within us. I'm not saying that force dictates our desire, only that it provides a means to have desire, and to bring about what we each desire, whatever that desire may be. I call that force god."

"You be heathen or a god indeed."

I stop sawing. "How's that?"

"It be not the gods, rather we, who steer destiny, you suggest."

"Ours, yes. And sometimes others if they're not taking charge of their own."

"You do not believe in fate."

"Like a deity decides? God isn't the decider of any fate or destiny, only an enabler. Our source awards us a gift—the capacity to hold a fate or destiny the same as we hold desire, and to guide all as we *choose,* not by what any deity decides."

"Yet if desire be the source of what we become, why be many ill or seeking to hurt others?"

"It's their choice."

"Though we wish all be well and peaceful."

"It's not our place to decide. And even if we want all well and peaceful, the only way that'll ever happen is to offer divine admiration."

"Love alone cannot heal the sick and insane."

"Yes it can. The force of god views all as they are and allows them to be as they choose. Sick, healthy, beautiful or deformed. Admiration without conditions. A troubled individual faces a world that looks at him and says, You are wrong to be what you are and to act as you do. When we instead view the person as they are—their choice—and acknowledge that choice, they receive a gift of admiration of their intent, the true source of that choice. We say, You have chosen and there you are. We see you as you choose to be. Validation is powerful, it *can* heal, but only when the person makes a new choice—to change, we hope, for the better. Perception, armed with the power of choice, creates the universe."

"You suggest that we all be gods."

"Honestly, I don't know for sure. Maybe we are. If that's the case, I'll say this much—I'm no greater a god than any other person, cat, snake, or any other living thing. Each of us is equally capable of making the universe what it is."

The saw breaks past the last of the lock. Links clack as the chain runs through the restraint like water pouring down a drain, then out of the shackles so they may hinge open.

"You're free."

Physuro smiles and rubs the ache from his wrists. "Thank you. Now I wish for David to express his views on the subject."

Dave remains focused on skies ahead. "Hey, leave me out of it. I talk about religion and next it's a fist-fight."

One of the three all-time greatest subjects—religion, politics, and sex. Stuck sitting next to a stranger, choose any one, or better yet mix all three, and you won't be strangers for long. Can't promise friend or foe, but there will be conversation. Over much time, Dave and I have generated plenty of heat, very near punches. But having respect for each other, testing our opinions has led to greater understanding of ourselves and the worlds we have shared.

Dave says, "Let's just say I agree mostly with Adam. Not completely, but close enough." He glances over his shoulder at Physuro. "But the truth thing, he's right about that, find your own. Don't listen to us, we're just a couple of crazy spacemen from some planet halfway across the galaxy. Who knows, maybe it's all different over there."

"Even so," Physuro says, "I still wish to hear your view of the gods."

"Gods?" Dave stares out at the darkening sky. "Them, him, what a load, like it's a somebody. Well, I'll say one thing, why *he* has any power over us…"

Haven't heard this one before. I half expect another lousy joke.

No grin, no chuckles, Dave says, "We let him."

✳

By twilight, the destination that never arrives only becomes more elusive, now a jagged edge of black horizon. The earlier discussion passed some time, as good conversations always do. Especially topics of deep significance that seldom cross idle thoughts, but when asked for opinions, the feelings buried deep inside come alive, ready to stand and fight. Except voicing those opinions has another effect—they are brought into reality. Once outside the realm of thought, I am forced to look at them from another perspective.

I truly wish that everyone be as they choose. But I might be deceiving myself, clinging to truth I cannot apply to all. Everyone else, just not Jared. Adhering to truth or belief is so far from living those ideals.

But I'm not to blame. If Jared didn't do what he does, to me, to others dear to me—anyone—he could be whatever he chooses. Except he chooses to be what he is and do what he does, which by my own truth I've agreed to allow—each their own choice. Expressing opinions has only hatched a greater struggle within myself.

Some time vanished. The destination that never arrives finally has. Down below, rugged terrain flows past. Dave switches on searchlights that sweep across the summits, the tallest powdery snow gleaming white, blending lower into darker icy coatings that plunge into deep ravines. Aglow in emerging moonlight, a thick blanket of fog fills the gorges below, concealing whatever lies beneath.

"Do we fly over them?" Dave asks. "Or is it somewhere around here."

Physuro studies the landscape, his ears falling limp as he scratches one cheek. Snowy peaks skim past, it seems only inches below the belly of our craft, emblazoned as our searchlights wash over them. Beyond the reach of the narrow beams, the peaks fade into darkness.

"The ring of twelve," Physuro says.

"Twelve what?" I ask.

"Find the ring, you shall find your gods."

In a mountain range so vast, finding anything would be difficult, even in daylight. Difficult even with precise landmarks to guide the way. Masked by darkness, the objective could elude us well after all fuel runs empty.

"What are we looking for?" I ask. "Twelve…"

"I cannot say, only the number."

"You say a ring?" Dave focuses on something ahead. He targets the sight and swoops the craft lower.

Nestled between higher mountain ridges, a circular arrangement of slender rock formations tower into twilight. A work of nature, though its symmetry is remarkable. And at this elevation, it makes a stronghold virtually impregnable by land forces. The soldier in me is impressed—good use of ground.

"Home of the Gods?" I ask.

"As I be told," Physuro says.

"But you'd have to be airborne to find it."

"Only gods may travel through the heavens."

"Right, so how could…" Of course—the natives are kept ignorant of flight for a reason. Which still begs the question, "How could you know?"

"The legend of the lights." He points at the rugged terrain below.

In darkness, atop each peak of rising rock, a red light flickers. One, two… twelve in all, arranged in a giant ring.

"Navigational beacons," Dave says.

"But you'd have to be on top of it to see them."

"Right, so we don't crash into one. Good thing they're on."

I twist around to Physuro. "But how? What legend?"

He grins. "Those of scientific endeavor observed more than just the heavens."

✳

Diving into the ring of twelve is like falling into a bottomless pit, opening wider as the glittering beacons spread out to an area miles across. The slender peaks rise into moonlit sky, and the darkness below is blacker than any night. Our searchlights evaporate and never find ground.

On the tactical display, flickering green lines begin drawing surface contours. Flat and featureless, the bottom is a high plateau surrounded by the ring of slender peaks. Featureless except for a lot of something neatly aligned. Not sure just what, but I can guess.

Dave accelerates the craft to attack speed. I watch tactical for signs of opposition and prepare weapons. We reach bottom, our searchlights brighten the ground, and low mounds whiz past. Not random terrain. Each oblong dirt mound is the same size and evenly spaced one to the next. At the short end of each mound is a concrete wall with a single door.

Dave asks, "How many we got to deal with?"

The tactical display is empty. No troops flowing out, no craft preparing for launch. Not a single missile in flight, nothing locked on target. I don't understand.

"Nothing," I say.

"You sure it's working?" he asks.

"I think so. Everything looks right, but it's blank."

"Bake a few brain cells back in the desert?"

"I hope not."

Holding the craft steady, Dave leans toward my side and studies the display. "Maybe you're right. The place looks deserted."

"I doubt it."

"Doubt all you like, I'll trust it." Dave eases our speed. We skim over an airfield full of black triangle craft, an endless squadron that stretches into darkness beyond our searchlights. At the edge of the airfield is a control tower rising above a windowed compound. The lights are on, someone is home.

"Over there." I point out what Dave already sees and we're already approaching. He does a fly-by, swings the craft around, and checks the backside. Still no movement but lots more light. He selects an open area at a safe distance, slows the craft, and sets us down.

The engines wind down as we sit facing their doorstep. Dave and I know well—too quiet. We're in for a surprise. An ambush, something.

The cockpit cover pops open and I nearly leap from my skin. I grab my rifle and take aim. Physuro crawls out and hops down to the ground below.

"What are you doing?" I ask, wanting to scream but I keep it down.

Physuro turns back. "Getting out," he says. "Be that not obvious? What purpose does travel serve if one does not exit the vehicle upon arrival?"

I should be the one to shoot the smart-ass.

He stretches his limbs and soaks up the locale, oblivious of the danger. He's going to get his head blown off, I can just see it now.

He waves for us to join him. "Come along."

"Get back here. It's not safe."

"Sure it be," he says. "See for yourself. They be gone." He spreads his arms and swings side to side, embracing the open space.

This is the classic moment when a sniper would cut him down.

Dave says, "If something was going to happen, I think it would have by now."

Outside, Physuro chuckles. "Relax, they be gone."

"How do you know?" I ask.

He taps his nose. "I do not smell them."

"We smell?"

"Of course," he says. "All creatures have scent, and your kind, a very strong odor."

✳

Armed with a blast rifle, two pistols and a dozen grenades, I sneak closer to the entrance. Weapons enough, I hope. What I really need is an arsenal of courage. Dave is just behind, rifle drawn. Physuro follows last, more curious than alert to any danger, armed with the single rifle I insisted he bring, except it hangs idle, slung over his shoulder.

Small windows tile the building's flat face, the glass milky opaque, brightened by interior light. A door at ground level is ajar—a warning sign. Textbook ambush begins with easy access. I halt and gesture for Dave to take aim, then creep to the hinge side, seize the knob, and hurl it open. Dave charges in, swinging his barrel in a wide spread. I follow, targeting every corner of the room. Deserted. A reception counter and chairs make a waiting area like a doctor's office, uncluttered other than a need for dusting. The stale air is chilly and the counter is cold, the space unheated for some time. Flickering fluorescent tubes bathe the room in cold, blue light. Behind the counter is an open door that leads to a darkened hallway.

Along the hallway are countless identical offices, visible past walls that are solid below, the top half glass. Inside each office is a metal desk, filing cabinet, chair and wastebasket, everything gray, even the carpet. Other than light dust, the offices appear in order, pens in penholders and notepads full, like the offices were constructed, furniture and supplies delivered, but never used.

The hallway ends at a larger room, empty other than an elevator straight ahead and a door in the corner. Dave tests the far door, looks through a window in it, then rejoins us and hits the call button. The elevator doors pop open.

I peer in. Frosted panels above cast a dim glow across the empty compartment.

"You sure about this?" I ask.

"Stairwell's locked," Dave says. "Not much choice."

Physuro studies the elevator car. "What be the purpose of this box? There be no exit." Stepping in, his eyes flash surprise when the box sways on its cables.

Dave hauls me in. "Magic portal to a higher place."

Physuro asks, "The heavens?"

"Not quite." Dave selects a floor and the doors slide shut. "Save that ride for the dead."

✳

As the elevator climbs, Dave indicates the panel, calling attention to the one button glowing amber, our destination. The panel has more than a dozen buttons. Most are levels below, reaching underground. Many are labeled only by level number, but some have specifics. Administration, Planning and Engineering, Finance and Material. Six is the highest floor, which Dave has selected—Command.

Dave and I prepare for battle, rifles aimed at the doors. Level two passes, three, four. I tell Physuro to get the rifle off his shoulder and get ready.

"You lay a spread," Dave says. "Then take left, I'll go right. Find cover and work the center, I'll clean up the edges."

Level five passes, the car halts at six. Cables sway, some clanking, then quiet. The doors open.

We brighten the room with blasts, aiming to slash their ranks before many can react. I dart in, rifle blazing, scramble left, up and over a console and take cover. Beams ricochet off the walls and fizzle, more pass overhead, fewer, then none. The echoes of battle soften to an eerie quiet, broken by a cluster of quick steps, then a painful stretch of silence. I spy over the console, eager to gauge the carnage but hoping it doesn't include Dave or Physuro.

Dave stands with the rifle stock planted on his hip, barrel angled up and out. "Are we supposed to find something here?"

The room is deserted. But not inactive. Past Dave are large windows slanting outward as they rise, which stretch across the room and look down on the airfield outside. A console runs the full length, jammed packed with display screens, levers, knobs, and blinking lights.

Dave shoulders his rifle and heads for the console.

"What is it?" I ask.

He studies a panel. "Some kind of control center."

"Controlling what?"

"Gimme a minute, eh?" He fiddles with knobs and tries a few levers.

Physuro steps out of the elevator, marveling at the long console and many lights.

Dave studies a screen while testing a dial, then tries a lever. "Check it out, this controls an entire squadron." He shifts to the next screen. "And this one, a full battalion of tanks."

I join him at the console. "You're kidding, right?"

"Look for yourself." He points out the windows, then presses a few buttons. Across the airfield outside, black triangle craft respond with running lights that brighten the ground. He nudges a lever, a few craft rise to hovering, then back down. "Believe me now?"

Physuro comes closer and leans over the console to study the familiar menace beyond the glass. "Our enemy."

"Remotes," Dave says, then pulls Physuro back. "Easy, pal, nothing to fear. Trust me, every cockpit's empty."

The enemy ignorant of shields—no person, no shield, no problem. No sense wasting energy on a shield. But even with every cockpit empty, an enemy still exists. Someone had to be in control.

On down the line, screen after screen shows a different scene. Many are nighttime, others daylight, they couldn't all be live feeds. Ophidian settlements, the desert, mountains. Both prisons, the cat's and the snake's. The observatory, now in ruins. A bird's-eye view of the Felidian city, and lower, in the street outside the Council chambers.

A screen even shows the craft that brought us here, parked just outside. Another shows the offices downstairs. If someone was here, they knew we were coming, able to track our movements as we penetrated the building. Another display is this very room in real time, Dave at the console, my back as I look down at the screen, and behind us, Physuro scratching one ear.

Another screen shows a tall space, some kind of industrial complex with machinery and catwalks, maybe a power plant. Smaller screens show a series of bland rooms with a table and two chairs, no windows, and concrete walls. Each looks like a place to conduct an interrogation, though odd there would be so many. Above the smaller screens is a string of digits glowing red, stick figure numbers like a clock, except counting backward. On the smaller screens below, one room is different—no table and chairs.

One dark lump crumpled on the floor.

I'm at the elevator striking the button.

"Hey," Dave calls. "Where you going?"

His voice is surreal, ghostlike, too thin to reach the universe I soar across or match the accelerated time. She is here, somewhere, in one of these rooms.

The elevator can't arrive fast enough. I take the stairwell down some levels. The hallway stretches into darkness, lined with identical doors. The first, the second, the next and more, I kick down door after door and charge into bland rooms with table and chairs, no windows, concrete walls. All the same, not a soul.

Ahead is a dead end. I sprint back to the stairs and down one level. Another hall, more identical doors, I bash down all. Nothing, no one, another dead end, back to the stairs and down another level, I'll bust down every door if I have to but it's useless. All are the wrong room. I may have lost her. I could be lost myself. What level is this? Underground by now, and every floor, every corridor and every door, all are duplicates of every other. I'm lost in a maze of identical passages, no carpet red or blue, everything's gone gray, the walls, the floor, but the stairs, where are the stairs?

This hallway is different—a lone door at the end. I race to the door, aiming to crash through, but I halt. Easy, the knob turns, and the opening doorway grows wider.

My earlier vision whooshes into reality and unleashes the energy stored within it. The observatory, enemy silhouettes and burning flesh, frigid singe leaking past a shell of skin, and tortured by a vision of Christina bound and beaten—the vision I now witness.

I throw myself into the room. With each step, reality follows the picture, this vision from the past of a future now present, which follows reality like tracers from a drug-induced hallucination. What could be has become what is real. Overlapping each but refusing to align, the pictures begin melding into one, of her here and now, one dark lump crumpled on the floor. At her side, I drop to my knees and see it all with chilling clarity. My lifeless darling, wrists and ankles bound by thin cord. I knew this would happen.

I reach for her shoulder and nudge softly. Nothing.

A cracked whisper pushes past my swelling throat. "Christina?"

No response. I loosen the cords restraining her. She wears barely a shred to keep her warm, a tattered dress only to her knees, leaving her shins and feet cold. The torn fabric shows bruised skin, and grotesque purple bands mark her wrists and ankles. Her skin is dry and dirty, and her scent is unbathed, but hers, always her scent. I steady myself, one palm flat to the floor, and the concrete sucks away all warmth. I lean over and kiss her cool cheek, leaving my tears to trickle down her neck, cradled in my hand.

"Baby, I'm here. Please, talk to me. Please, don't leave me like this. I'm scared, baby, please." My head drops to her chest, and my sobbing rattles her cold body. "I—can't—live—with—out—yooou…"

"Adam?" she whispers.

My heart stops. I angle back to gaze down at her.

Her eyes are hazy, lids heavy. She reaches out a staggering finger and touches my tears.

"Adam, why do you cry?"

"I… I am… afraid."

"Afraid of what?"

Between sobbing gasps, I push out, "I… I'm scared… scared beyond death… I might lose you… and—and… never find you… *ever again!*"

I can't hold back, I can't stop, I can't even slow down.

She reaches for my neck and her weak fingers touch softly. "We'll always find each other," she says. "Don't worry. You're a keeper."

All I can think of is kissing her. The one magic remedy, all I need—one kiss. I move closer but she turns a cheek and presses fingers to my lips. "No, Adam."

Her touch falls from my lips when I shift back. "I don't understand."

Physuro is in the doorway. "Adam, I will help." He hurries in, wedges between us, and helps her stand. Her gaze wanders, then she focuses on him.

"It's all right," I tell her. "Physuro's our friend, and no, you're not seeing things. He really is a cat-man."

Her wide-eyed stare stays with him. "I missed a few things."

Beaming a warm smile, Physuro says, "And be certain, dear goddess, someone has missed you." He cocks his head toward me, and she follows the gesture. She stares at me, but hollow, like she's not even there. Then her eyes clamp shut and she turns away.

"What's wrong?" I ask.

Holding her steady, Physuro puts himself between us, as if protecting her from me. "Allow the goddess a time of rest."

"But, I don't—"

"Cease," he says, then guides her to the door. "Let us be away."

✴

Under a moonless night, the cold blackness between the complex and our craft stretches out to become a thousand dark nights. Physuro leads the way, holding Christina steady. She moves slowly, feet unsure and shuffling. Following them, I am no faster. Her weakness drains me.

When I catch up, Physuro is helping her aboard the craft. She climbs the edge and into the passenger seat, next to the empty pilot seat.

"Where's Dave?" I ask.

"He be..." Physuro looks back to the path from the complex to our craft.

I shout to the darkness, "Dave! Let's go!"

"Over here," he shouts from somewhere in the night. He calls again, and I follow his voice. Off some distance, I find him in an open stretch past the airfield, shining a flashlight across the ground.

"What are you doing?" I ask. "Let's get out of here."

"Adam, do you realize what these are?"

"I don't care. We need to get Christina somewhere safe. We're done, let's go."

"She's safe enough for now." He points to the ground at our feet. "But none of us are for long."

"What's your problem?"

He shines his flashlight on the mystery. Flush with the ground is a smooth metal disk, yards in diameter, divided in two by a seam straight down the center.

"A manhole?" I ask.

"For giant men?" He crouches to tug at a smaller hatch near the split metal disk. The lid opens to a hole more the size for a man. He hands me the flashlight and points down. "Take a look."

"Then can we go?"

"Don't be so goddamned stubborn. Look down there."

I aim the flashlight into an abyss. The beam strikes a catwalk and some machinery. It reminds me of the cargo transport and getting sucked to the bottom of an endless void.

I ease back. "Okay, so it's the sewer, just fancy. Let's get going."

"*Look!*" He grabs the scruff of my neck and forces me into the hole. "If that's the sewer, that's one big rat."

On my knees and the flashlight before me, the beam brightens a ladder.

"Crawl down there," he says. "And look!"

Down a few rungs, I swing the light around. The underground cavern is deep, the bottom well beyond the flashlight's beam. Something is standing upright, but so large around it's difficult to identify. A tall black cylinder, positioned directly below the split metal disk.

A missile. I'm in a fucking silo.

I scramble up the ladder.

"It gets worse." Dave snatches the flashlight and shines it across the distance.

Not far is another silo hatch, another, and another, and…

"How many?" I ask.

"My guess? Somewhere in the thousands."

"The delivery. The Spears of the Gods."

"And let's not piss them off," he says. "It gets even worse." He crouches near the open hatch and shines the light in. "These aren't just any missiles." Bending lower, I strain to see. He swings around and blinds me with the flashlight. "They're *nuclear*."

"What? Thousands? On one planet? That many will…"

At the edge of darkness, the craft waits. Christina. Us. Everyone.

"Looks like everyone dead isn't good enough," he says. "More like the *planet* dead. Launch this arsenal and poof, the atmosphere burns off like flash paper."

"Why would they? They need planets, places to put rebels. The whole reason for the Restricted Zone."

"One planet, Sol-3. So our friends have nowhere else to go, not even hope that other worlds exist. Look any direction, what do you see? Nothing but dead rocks. Marooned on a lone planet far from anything else, for all they'll know, the rest of the universe could be dead rocks."

"There's Sol-5."

"Sure," he says, "if it still exists."

✳

In flight, we argue over where to get medical attention. The Ophidians would help, after all, she is their Goddess of Dreams, and they have their problem with nightmares. But I don't trust the snakes. Physuro would likely end up back in prison, or worse. Hell, we'd probably all get locked up after our last rude departure. We could've at least waved good-bye.

Physuro is sure the Felidians will help and urges that we return to his homeland. He further claims that those of medical endeavor be exceptionally skilled, and it goes on so long that it begins to stink of bragging. Let's hope it's not exaggeration aimed at scoring a ride home.

That's what I need, a ride home. Enough of this crazy planet. Back home—our home—Christina will heal and she'll be safe. Orn sparkles in the night, a system that becomes one tiny speck at this incredible distance, and here we are, clinging to this ball of rock hurling around the edge of the galaxy. No cargo transport, no interstellar craft, and nowhere near enough fuel. We're stuck here.

Even if I had a vessel, the fuel, and could reach home, I couldn't leave. I can't abandon these creatures while knowing their fate. All this destructive power strapped to one globe. Light the fuse, one big flash and life is gone, just like that. I can't.

Home is where you are, in the now. So this planet becomes my home, and duty demands that I protect it the same as any other. In this now, Marsea is the only home we know.

✳

Below twinkling starlight, sky and land become a single dark mass, no telling where one ends and the other begins. The engines whine, our speed intense, but there is little turbulence at this high altitude. Charging into darkness, we can only trust that every minute forward is another away from that nightmare and one step closer to medical care.

Christina's unresponsiveness has me worried. She has slept most of the way, curled up in the passenger seat under a blanket that Physuro offered.

I offered a canteen and she didn't even notice. But when Physuro took it from me and passed it to her, she sipped, handed it back, then snuggled under the blanket and fell asleep. Like I'm not even here.

In the distance, the horizon begins to glow amber. Fire-lit watchtowers spread flickering warmth, giving shape to the buildings, and the Felidian city rises out of the night. Physuro gets his bearings and gives directions. Dave brings the craft lower and navigates the maze of masonry, following the path of darkened streets lit only by mellow firelight leaking from passing windows. Our final descent kicks up dust and we set down near a stone building that Physuro describes as a Felidian house of medicine. He's home. Now his pals had better make her well.

I reach around the seat and nudge her. "Christina, we're here." I open the cockpit cover. "Let me help you."

"No," she says. "I can manage." She climbs out, not all that quick. I am quicker, out and offering to assist, but she waves me off. With the blanket clutched over her head, her face is lost in shadows of a cloth hood. She starts for the building but staggers. She needs my help. Physuro beats me to it. Holding her steady, he puts himself between us and guides her up the steps.

From behind, Dave plants a hand to my shoulder. "Hold up, buddy."

I whirl on him "What now? Some new crisis more important than her?"

He joins me on the first step. "No, you're right, she's important. But come on, this is tough on us all. Give her some space, eh?"

"She needs me."

Head cocked, he pulls his lips tight, a sort of childish scolding.

"Doesn't she?" I ask, then realize I'm whining.

He brings a brotherly arm around my shoulder and guides me up the steps. "You need her, she needs you, right, always." He gives me a good ol' buddy shake. "But come on, you did great, we found her. Now back off some, okay? They'll take care of her, don't worry. You and me, let's go find something to eat. I'm starved."

I pull free of him. "Go find your food. You'll find me at her side."

✻

Outside the house of medicine, the higher steps and threshold are coated with the dust of unpaved streets, but past the great doors, inside is scrubbed to disinfected, not a grain of stray anything invades. Soft candlelight spreads a flickering glow across pale walls and the gleaming floor. Repeating portals are open to the starry night, each framed by flowering vines that emit a lively scent, competing against the reek of antiseptic elixirs pushing back the edge of death.

I catch up with Physuro and Christina when they reach the end of the first hallway. Physuro speaks with an older Felidian. After an argument over providing medical attention to gods—which gods shouldn't need just because they're gods—the doctor agrees to have her examined. Divinity has its downsides—medical discrimination. I can't even find that funny.

The doctor calls to others and Christina is whisked away to the next chamber. The doctor wants to know what happened to her, to which I can only answer in truth, I don't know, I wasn't there. A grim reminder of all I can't face—I wasn't there.

The next chamber is larger with a taller ceiling, countless beds aligned head to toe, and aisles between them barely enough to move through. Not a single bed is empty, all occupied by Felidians wounded in the earlier attack. Many look reasonably well, just weary and resting, but others I must shun— bloody wounds, hideous faces, and severed limbs now bandaged stumps.

Conversation is absent. An eerie quiet in the wake of noisy battle, all that blasting, exploding and screaming, now the survivors retreat into themselves, to a grave silence stirred only by faint whimpers and occasional moans.

I step slowly through an aisle, past gazes begging that I end their misery. I should have tried harder and kept these wounded from harm. I could have saved countless others. I can imagine the mass graves, but won't let the image stay. Go somewhere else inside myself, run and hide, away from that measure of failure. I should have acted sooner. Then these victims would be at home with their families, cozy by a fire with the little ones, enjoying a feast while papa tells stories of the good life. Nothing good about this. But these wounded who suffer, at least they have survived, and I imagine, have families awaiting their return home. They have that much.

Christina is ushered through another doorway to a smaller chamber with fewer beds. The back wall is shelved from floor to ceiling, stocked with glass jars square and squat, round and slender, some pale green, blue, others clear, holding varying degrees of their medicinal potions.

She drops onto an empty bed. A committee of doctors converges on their patient and obscures any view.

"I beg," one doctor says, pushing me back. "You request our aid, be willing to allow it."

I retreat and watch. They scurry around, poking, prodding, or something. I can't see past all the white robes.

The same doctor turns to see that I'm still here. He leaves the bedside and approaches. "I beg that you comprehend, and let it be no disgrace. Your presence here offers little in the interest of her recovery."

"You want me to go?"

"We seek to heal all we be able. Trust in that."

Trust is a stranger. I can't even remember its face.

✳

Outside, I plop down on the steps. The sharp edges press against my back like a bed of nails, just puncture me, let what's left leak out, down the stairs and puddle in the dirt. The night is clear, sprinkled with dots of starlight. I reach up, fingers brushing the void, as though I could touch one and feel its fire. One of those is home.

"I found sandwiches."

I sit up. Dave emerges from darkness, coming this way from across the street. In each hand he holds a round loaf. Half round, like a melon sliced in two, with something in the center where the seeds would go, a creamy liquid yellow and chunky, from which vapor rises. He sits beside me and I catch a whiff. Not bad. Onions, maybe potato, something vegetable.

He hands one over and digs into the other. "At her side, eh?"

"This isn't a sandwich." Cupping it in one hand, I twist the thing around, taking in all sides. "It's a bowl of soup, except, in bread."

Tapping one fingernail confirms it—more of that hard-shelled crouton stuff. Seems the cats use kilns for more than just pottery.

"Close enough," he says, slurping up the creamy mess. "Something between bread's a sandwich."

I'm too exhausted for any idiotic argument. But he's right about us lacking nourishment. Some brain food might improve his stellar conclusions. I down a few loads of the steamy slop, not bad, tasty even with a spicy edge, and warm food in my belly chases off the exhaustion, like waking from a deep sleep. After a few minutes for the meal to settle, the mind sharpens, more alert, and more willing to joust.

"Only a sandwich if the bread's edible."

He tips back the snack and sucks out the last drop, then tries to bite what's left. End of that argument.

A silence passes while I scarf down the rest of mine.

"How is she?" he asks.

"Don't know, they haven't said."

I pitch my empty bread bowl into the street, rolling off into darkness.

"Hey," he says. "Don't litter like that, not cool."

I lie back on the steps and stare up into the night. "Like it really matters. It'll be dust soon anyway, like all the rest."

"Don't talk like that. We'll fix things, you always do."

"I don't know this time. I just don't know."

"You always know," he says. "You just don't remember."

I sit up. "What's to remember? Getting nuked sucks? Sure, easy to say, but how do we get off this rock before it happens?"

"Run away? Doesn't sound like the Adam I know."

"And who is this Adam you know? What's he like?"

"He fixes things."

"How? How could anyone possibly fix this mess?"

"*Remember* how. You've done it before plenty of times."

"What have I done?"

He points out the stone buildings across the street, then turns where he sits and looks up the steps, to the house of medicine behind us, where a warm glow flows out from the entrance.

"Saved places like this," he says. "Saved them from being destroyed."

I stare out at the street, the dirt and dark and empty shadows. "You're right, I don't remember. Guess we're all doomed, thanks to that guy you know who's clearly absent. What was his name?"

"Adam," he says. "The one and only you. Get over it, man, you're bringing me down."

Stars, stars, so many stars. So many other places I could be. I should just leave this body, float away to somewhere else, anywhere but here. I never should have made that promise to myself. What a foolish vow, sticking to one body. I may be drained, but one last scrap of personal integrity tugs hard—don't do it, you promised. This body and myself.

He says, "Why not ask Chris? Maybe she has an idea."

I fall back, back to staring into the night. "Sure. Her idea is for me to leave her alone. What did I do?"

"Maybe it's what you haven't. What you haven't fixed."

"This mess?"

"To start with, and I'm sure she'd agree, she knows you can. Disappoint me all you like, I'll get over it. You gonna do the same to her?"

"No."

"Really?" he says. "And why is that?"

"I can't."

"Can't what? Fix things?"

"No. I can't let her down."

"Oh? Why not?"

"I just can't."

"Can't answer a simple question."

"*A promise!* Okay? I can't go back on a promise."

"You promised her?"

"Her, me, everyone. My duly appointed fucking job, Mister Fix-it. You don't have to rub it in."

Here comes that big white grin. "Now I'm interested to hear what you have in mind."

How does he do this to me? I was thinking I had won, but somehow he twists an argument over bread and sandwiches into saving an entire population.

"Fine, you win, I'll fix it. Fix it all, just like always. But don't think for one minute you get to kick back and watch Adam do it all by himself."

"You know I always help. You know, once you figure it out. So what'll it be this time?"

"You'll be the second to know."

✳

In a broken universe and all there is to fix, the challenge begins with mending the single most important bond. Approaching the chamber where Christina rests, I meet the doctor who suggested that I wait outside.

"Will she be okay?" I ask.

Heading out of her room, he pauses in the doorway. "A rough time she had, though be hopeful." He puts on a smile. "With proper meals and hydration, her physical constitution shall recover, certainly."

"Thank you. For all you've done, and your kindness."

He steps aside with arm extended, inviting that I enter. "Thank a goddess wielding the fire of life. In her place, another may have perished. Truly, the gods be powerful."

I advance into the room. She lies flat on her back, asleep with arms folded atop the blanket. I step gently and lower to the bed's edge. My fingers creep toward hers and touch lightly.

I whisper, "How are you doing?"

Her eyes flutter open and she focuses on me. "I'll get there," she says.

"Good. I need you well."

"Oh?" She withdraws her hand. "You have plans for me?"

"I can't do this alone."

"Don't be silly." She looks away. "You're capable of anything, with or without me."

I try getting in her line of sight. "Christina, there's only one way, and that's you *with* me. You're everything to me."

Her gaze returns, but her eyes are a dreamy void. "Adam, there's something you have to remember." She points a finger, wavering between us. "*You* are the most important thing to you. If I become more important, then I have lost the very part of you I cherish most."

I lean back, it feels a mile. "I don't understand. You want me to love myself before you? I don't think that's possible."

"Of course it is," she says. "That's true love, and you already know it. Lovers must love themselves first, then share it. I want to make sure you never forget. It's sad, I know, but the day you stop loving yourself is the day I stop loving you."

I rise from the bed. "I love myself just fine, that doesn't change what we're facing. And it doesn't change how I feel. I need you at my side. I can't do this without you."

"Do what?" she asks.

"End this war. These creatures have no reason to fight."

Her eyes flash. "Oh, there's a reason." She turns away, staring across the room.

I lower to the bed's edge and lean over, angling to catch her gaze. "What reason? What do you know?"

She swings back to me. "A certain someone invented it."

"The Association."

"Not them," she says. "They're gone."

"Gone? Where?"

"Back home, don't you know? They're done here. All we have now is our one supreme god."

"Jared."

Her piercing stare boils contempt. "He's crazy. You know that, right? He thinks he's god."

"That's just an act to fool these creatures and stir up a fight. I'm not much better, doing it myself, just not for reasons so evil."

"No, Adam, the real thing." She pushes it past her clenched teeth, each word lifting her from the bed a notch closer to sitting up. "He's gone mad. He actually believes it—*believes it*—he's a god. And thinks it gets him *whatever he wants!*"

Red, raging, ready to burst, her explosion is tears. She falls back and rolls onto her side, crying.

I hesitate asking, "What did he do?"

Her voice is distant, monotone. "You don't want to know."

"I do."

She pulls the blanket over her head, and beneath the covers she sobs. The outpour may never end, then one long gasp, she reloads and spills it all again.

I reach for her side, moved by her tremors, but think twice and keep from touching her.

"What happened?" I ask. "Tell me."

She scoots away. "No, Adam, I know how you will become."

"Christina, I will be any way you ask. Please, tell me what happened."

She rolls over to face me, peering over the blanket clutched tight to her chin. "Promise you will be clear of thought, no matter what."

"Okay, I promise."

Her fearful stare holds steady. "Promise again."

"All right, I promise. I'll promise a thousand times if I have to. Just tell me."

Sadness deadens her gaze. Her eyes gloss over, ready to spill tears. "He hurt me."

I study her bruises. "He'll be hurting ten times as much when I'm done with the bastard."

"No, Adam, you don't understand. He *hurt* me."

"What are you saying?"

Her lips quiver, eyes pooling with sorrow. I am the lone target of her unwavering stare. A tear crests one eyelid and trickles down her cheek. Her brow twists with pain, mouth contorting as she strains to speak.

"Adam, he violated me."

4

DIRT UNDER MY FINGERNAILS, I SCRATCH AND SCRAPE, CLAWING to climb but the hillside is too steep, a wave towering vertical to crash over and bury me. They're coming, hundreds of them, coming to get me. On my hands and knees, I scramble to rise but only scoop mountains of soil down, down, it all trickles down, slipping past my belly and washing me down.

From darkness below comes the sound of their stick legs scurrying up the hillside, tap-tap-tap, and mandibles a grating rasp of smacking sickles, clack-clack-clack.

Why this struggle to escape? I was chasing after something. Above, the cloudless sky is black. He will be there, at the summit. Where I will kill him.

No—wrong—you forgot. You are the prey.

I've lost ground, slid down, into the horde of hungry insects, furry black the size of dogs and with twice the legs. Each of their multifaceted eyes is a golden honeycomb that stares a thousand stares, an entire crowd staring at me. There are hundreds, thousands—a billion souls stare at me.

I bound up and stamp a beast—*snap!*—crushing the slender link between thorax and abdomen. Wiry stick legs tap-tap, mandibles clack-clack, I fight and fight, stamping and stomping, cracking open exoskeleton shells that spurt pungent slime.

There are too many. Their stingers needle my ankles, calf and thigh, hammering nails into muscle and then acid jolts saturating soft tissue. Buzzing wings swoop past and huge wasps curl in their bottoms to bring me under their aim. Swarming giant hornets and bees pierce my ears, hands, elbow and neck. The land army grows to spiders, beetles, ants and cockroaches, a shimmering ocean of black and brown. Creatures sprout fangs and tear meaty chunks from my legs, arms and side, I'm dissected alive. Airborne invaders swoop and dive, I swat and dodge and tumble off balance, then pinned by a buzzing winged fuzzy fiend, legs enough to wrap around my skull, it rams a stinger up my nose, plugs into my brain, and ingests a liquid lobotomy.

On my back, muscles twitch spastic jerks but nothing responds, leaving me paralyzed. Wet grinding mandibles smack and snack, feasting on my open eyes. Darkness bleeds into my peripheral, nothing to see beyond scurrying blackness closing in to seal this grave, and nothing to feel but countless stick legs crawling over dying skin. I can envision the end, even imagine how it will feel, the bugs picking this body clean, bleaching these bones white, cleansing it all away. All I've ever been, all that I have done.

What? Now the spiders are metal. They've transformed into robots with mechanical legs, the front two fitted with hammers. The mechanized horde bludgeons every inch of my body with their blunt weapons.

What is this crap?

I stand up and brush off the tiny spiders.

Tiny? When did they become tiny?

Enough of this nonsense.

"Stop!" I command.

The scene freezes. I'm surrounded by little lunging mechno-spiders caught in midflight, hanging suspended like an action photograph.

"You spiders, be gone."

The creatures vanish.

"Hey!" someone calls. "You can't do that."

Sure enough, there he is, at the top of the hill I was trying to climb. He is wearing an Ophidian uniform the same as me, and he holds a small box with joystick that he rams every which way, but he's only getting flustered. Looking down at me, he searches for something that he expects to happen, but it never does and it's driving him mad.

"No more toys," I say.

Poof! The remote control disappears, right from his fingers.

"Hey!" Jared cries. "No fair!"

"Playing god was your idea." I start climbing the hillside, the soil firm beneath each step. I bound up and up, closer to the top, scaling the mound with ease.

"Oh, but I have more." He slips from view.

I'm nearly to the top when he comes back in a new costume—white toga and laurel crown. He raises his arms to the sky.

"Unleash the Hounds of Hell."

The hillside becomes black sand, and *hot!* I claw at fiery granules burning through my fingers, then I hear barking, vicious killer barking, getting closer fast. A pack of black dogs charge up the hillside, savage dogs bigger than any dogs—the dogs of death—blood-red eyes and gleaming fangs.

Dirt under my nails, clawing loose ground, the hillside is too steep. I scoop mountains of soil down, down, it all trickles down, slipping past my belly and washing me down.

What? I was just here, trying to reach…

No—wrong—you forgot. You are the prey.

Fangs snap hold and jerk wildly, yanking my ankle and pulling my leg. I'm tossed over, onto my back, and dragged to the bottom.

"Adam!" someone shouts. "Stop it!"

She is angry but also crying.

The ferocious beast hauls me every direction and back again, ripping my pants to shreds. Another hounds snaps at my side. I throw a punch and scrape my knuckles across its teeth.

"Adam! That's enough!"

Christina is at the summit, standing next to Jared. She's angry and he's grinning. She wears a crown of slender braided vines, imbued with petite blossoms, and a sleeveless white gown, fluttered by a soft breeze.

The vision of a goddess.

Shouting past her tears.

"Adam! Knock it off!"

✳

Christina wrestles beside me in bed.

I sit up. "Is someone hurting you?" I scan for threats. Only sleeping Felidians, in the room with shelf from floor to ceiling, stocked with colored jars.

Her arms are crossed over her face. "Yeah, *you!*"

My fists are clenched tight.

She pulls the blanket over her and rolls on her side.

"I… I'm sorry, baby, I didn't mean…"

I reach for her, wrapped in a cocoon of white linen. She flinches.

The nurse last night, she was right. I should have found somewhere else to sleep.

"Christina, it's okay now. The nightmare's over."

Muffled by the blanket, she says, "Maybe for you." She scoots away.

I ask, "Are you mad at me?"

"I'd rather not talk about it."

"I don't understand."

"You won't," she says. "So just forget it."

"Forgetting is no good, you know that. Better to remember. Tell me, I promise to understand."

She flings the covers from her face. "Like you promised last night?"

I spring off the bed. "I'm sorry. I couldn't deal with it."

My ankle. I look down at my leg. It's not ripped to shreds. But the dogs, barking, and sharp teeth. It all lingers so vivid, like it really happened.

"You don't have to deal with it," she says. "It didn't happen to you."

"I know, but I had to…"

She sits up and scowls something wicked. "Look at yourself. Why won't you *look,* look hard at yourself, see what it looks like when you rage out of control. Screaming, yelling, throwing crap. I knew how you would become. I never should have told you."

I step back. "That… that wasn't me."

"You won't look!"

"I… I will, for you. I'll do anything for you."

"Sure you will. Dammit! I should have kept it all to myself."

"No, don't say that. Never keep it to yourself. Better to talk about it, better to let it out."

She screams, "*I didn't want it in me in the first place!*"

Other patients wake and look over.

Christina flops back, clutching the bedding and tangling it around her head. Wrapped in the blanket shroud, she cries and cries and cries.

The shelves of colored jars, so many potions, elixirs and cures. One must hold the magic remedy to this.

I sit on the bed's edge and reach for her.

She flinches. "I don't want to talk about it. Leave me alone."

"I will *not* leave you alone. Never again, I promise."

"Your promises are empty."

"No they are *not*. I had to let it out, you know that, and now you have to let it out, you know that just as well."

Her sobbing doubles, buried beneath the covers. "I don't know anything anymore. Everything's all mixed up."

"Tell me what's mixed up. Talk to me."

Nothing, not a word, only more tears. Watching her convulse beneath the blanket, I don't know what to do, I don't know what to say. I have nothing left, no clue of what could possibly comfort her.

"Christina, I don't like this. I'm scared. It feels like we're disconnected."

She stops crying. Beneath the covers she sniffles, then quiet. "I betrayed you."

"*Me?* No, Christina, don't say that. I'm the one who's betrayed you. And I'll regret it forever, not being there."

She scratches at the covers and unburies herself. "You see? Here I am hurting you again. It's all my fault, all of it hurts you, it'll always hurt you. I'm so sorry for what's happened."

"No, Christina, you're not hurting anyone. Stop that."

Her face drops into her hands and she shakes her head no no no. "I don't want to feel anything ever again."

"Don't say that. It'll get better."

She clears the hair crossing her face and stares at me, her eyes glowing hot enough to boil every tear to vapor.

"No, Adam. It doesn't ever *get better*."

✳

It rained this morning, not so much, more humid than anything chilly, though enough to turn the dusty streets to mush. But not up here where the tiles are polished clean, nothing stains the balcony above the hospital's entrance. I've spent the morning at the balcony's edge, gazing out at the muddy streets where cats go about their business, trudging through the orangey mess. Others with me retreat from the weather in this waiting area, a quiet space furnished with wooden lounges topped by straw cushions. Though sheltered from the mist, the straw soaks up moisture and reeks a musty odor, blending with the scent of new rain after a dry spell, when plants open their pores and thirst for dampness.

All morning, Felidians in the waiting area have been subdued, withdrawn into their concern for the ill downstairs. They hardly notice that I'm here, a human, or a god, at any rate, not one of their kind. Some of the cats recline, aiming blank stares at the sheltering stone, others sit at the edge of their seats with shoulders tight and eyes of worry. A few whimper now and then, but otherwise most are silent, a quiet near that of a tomb, livened only by the pitter-patter of raindrops, but even now that has ceased. Those waiting with me, their loved ones, some won't make it. I am hopeful that my special loved one will recover, but still I stew in uncertainty. Something will never be the same.

Regret is useless, yet so powerful. Useless or not, today I am powerless to escape it. Regret so intense I near a dangerous condition—contempt for myself. Maybe that's what Christina was trying to tell me last night with her little sermon about people loving themselves. I don't. Not now, not after this. I may never understand what she was trying to tell me.

By afternoon the sky cleared of clouds, you might not even realize the earlier shower, and the sun-baked streets were back to powdery dust. Dust my boots kick up as I venture somewhere else, away from the house of medicine.

Two avenues over, I find a string of shops. Most are closed today, wooden doors and shutters sealed, but one shop looks open. A red awning is rolled out on angled sticks, and sunlight streams in the open windows to brighten a cluttered interior. Out front, half a dozen female cats are sitting cross-legged, silently weaving baskets. Behind them, shelves are stocked with finished baskets for sale, each made from wicker strips dyed purple, red or brown, some interwoven to create blended patterns. Shaped tall, squat and others large around, the variety could serve as vases, bowls, or store your clothes, some with handles for carting food to market or back to the kitchen.

I'm about to pass when one of the females looks up and notices me. She smiles. It's good to see a smile. Not much, just a hint, but it doesn't take much. I approach and sit facing them, cross-legged as they are, and watch them work.

My presence has little effect on them. They keep quiet, and they don't look up, they only continue pulling strips of wicker around and down, over another, and interlock the material with fluid ease, a dexterous motion that is admirable. I watch them for a time and study their technique. Simple, mindless really, but at the same time, intricate and precise.

"Think I might try?"

The female who smiled stops weaving and looks up, and again she smiles. A wider smile, toothy this time. She reaches for a supply of wicker and passes me a handful of strips.

When they do it, it looks easy. I watch more and try to mirror their motion. She notices my struggle and weaves slower, the whole problem—they do it so fast I can't imagine keeping up. She bends a strip around, pulls it down, over another, flicks it under... I get it, when not presented as a blur.

And I do get it, after some practice. In my hands, a dark purple basket begins to take shape.

Not mindless to start, it takes some effort to study their motion and match the puzzle they twine, but in a short time, the mind assigns an autonomous circuit to the activity, once gaining some confidence. Nice, the mindlessness that arrives. And with it, the rest shuts off, a pleasing mental numbness.

I get faster at it, too. Which is strange, because as I do, their motion is no longer a blur. As if mastering the process alters the perceived rate of change.

"Be you skilled at all you attempt?" the female asks.

"Don't know if I'd say that."

She admires my partial basket. "You be talented in so little time."

"This?" I look it over. A lumpy mess with purple strips bulging like fresh welts, but overall, not too bad for a first try. "Thanks."

Still, their tightly woven baskets far exceed my feeble attempt.

But I could probably get better, after a while.

✳

Clacking sticks rouse me from slumber. An unusually numb slumber, thoughtless, empty. Numb except for the moist grass beneath me, chilling my back.

The stars are gone. Daybreak washed away the black, and again the sky is pink, painted with strokes of vapor high above. Last night, lying on my back like a bum in the park, I soaked up the stars, so many points of light, so many other places to be. A million twinkling reminders, slowly falling from the night, but they never landed. They just fell forever, and I fell asleep. But oddly, an empty sleep, nothing to fear or challenge, only the passage of empty time. Now I wake to that racket, a way's off. It sounds like sticks clacking.

I sit up and search for the source of the noise. I guessed right, part of it anyway. Across the park are two young cats fighting with sticks. I get up and approach the dueling youngsters. Their make-believe swords swoop and crash, clack-clack.

"Don't fight," I say.

They stop sparring.

"We be playing," one says.

Squat and round and smiling, the little cat is just adorable, like a stuffed animal you win at the carnival. Except fully animated, making him even more adorable.

I kneel between the two and coax their weapons lower. "Playing what? War? What's that going to teach you?"

The other says, "We be playing pretend." He points his stick, aiming to jab his opponent. "Gods battling to save Marsea, like the proper-see."

"No, the future isn't—"

No, not my place. Not this way, not via their young.

I wrap a hand around his stick and nudge it down. "Look, there are lots of things to play. Fighting's not so good. People get hurt when we fight."

"But we have to fight, or we die."

Awfully heavy thinking for a child.

"It doesn't have to be that way," I say. "We can all live in peace. It's a choice, our choice."

"It be true," he says.

"What is?"

"The proper-see."

How do I convey this to one so innocent? I can't just steal his faith and leave him empty.

"It's like an idea," I explain. "A feeling. It's okay to wish for something in the future, and hold it in your heart, just don't let it rule you. Or let you think fighting is the answer."

"The gods fight in the proper-see."

"Maybe they do, but we could change it. The future doesn't have to be what someone says, just because they say so. We could make it different.

Maybe they could get along and fix things. Then we could all be happy."

He smiles. "After the gods fight and one wins, all Felidians be happy."

A staggering climb I face, with little hope of ever reaching the summit.

✳

Another day spent among the Felidians, I mangle a lump of wet clay atop a pottery wheel, find out how they harvest beans and squash, then learn the finer points of milling corn, after a heated argument between two females over mills fashioned from hollowed stumps versus depressions worn in slabs of stone. Can't say the debate had any clear winner, as both samples of warm cornbread were equally delicious, and this god couldn't stamp his approval on one recipe over the other. Let the argument endure.

In a shady park, older males are seated around stone blocks topped with inlaid parquet, game boards of alternating squares tan and brown. They paw at playing pieces intricately carved, black versus white in the shape of cats, most a standing posture with spears, some on horseback, one taller robed and crowned.

A small tribe might choose a single member to call the Old Wise One. A larger society might even have a few. For the Felidians, old and male appear to be the only requirements. Every one of the wise guys has something to say, but not when it's their move. "Quiet be you!" they scold. But during their opponent's turn, it's all different—their rambling discourse could drone on long after we're all in bed for the night. If nothing else, a wise defense.

One old cat enjoys bending my ear, and he actually has something of interest, maybe even of value. I sit nearby and study their game, the rules of which I can't begin to understand. The old cat launches into a commentary on the Felidian hierarchy of gods, twelve in all, over which the Mighty One presides. Then it's his turn. "Shhh!" he scolds. His grumpy opponent takes over the defensive chatter, his brand of annoyance a whining rant about a neighbor returning borrowed field implements with blades rusty and dull, and how he just hates that, wants all his tools back sharp and clean.

Shushed again, and again each turn they trade, I'm scolded for nothing more than impatient silence. I listen attentively as the old cat spills his profound wisdom, between his opponent's endless gripes about everybody and their brothers, sisters, uncles and more, all the way down to third cousins twice removed.

The wise old cat continues his tale about the Mighty One, explaining that the god was once powerful in what the Felidians call the mother realm, an existence beyond their reach, where Crontis battled a council more supreme than all others in any realm.

"Crontis be an outcast," the old cat says, waiting for his opponent to make his move. "Banished from the mother realm by his equal."

"Equal?" I ask. "Who?"

"That be not for Felidians to comprehend. Another god be drawn from the same fountain, we may only presume. Any equal to Crontis has yet to enter our realm. We have not eyes to see beyond."

His opponent slides a playing piece forward one square.

I ask, "How do you know the equal's not already here?"

"That," he says, "Felidians shall know upon events foretold by the prophecy." He focuses on the game board. "Now shhh!"

✳

An hour's hike beyond the city walls, the land grows browner, becomes flatter, and is covered by fewer trees. I come to a river wider than I could throw a stone. Only by boat, bridge, or confident swimmer will it be crossed. The water moves slowly, fluttering glints of sun hanging low in the sky.

Near sundown, a tall ceiling of high clouds stretches out, gray puffs in a lumpy sheet glowing orange where thin. No stars yet, but soon, once the sun escapes and the clouds clear, as they do each night I spend staring into the glittery void, imagining all those worlds, other places to be.

A footpath runs parallel to the river. I follow it for a time and let the sun warm my face. A time for thought, soaking in it, and the last heat of the dwindling day.

We should all run, quicken each step everywhere we go, with so little time before the final moment. The cats would be running—a frenzied panic—if they knew what was coming. But there is nowhere to run. No corner will be spared, no cave, deep ocean, no stretch of sky. So useless, hurrying from one place to another, expending energy that is already sentenced to end. We might as well relax, watch the warheads drop from the sky and burst into flames, until our eyes are ash and see no more.

If I were the god they regard me, in the aftermath I would still exist, in some fashion. As they might imagine for me, sitting high atop a heavenly mountain, looking down at my destroyed creation. However, being anything but a god, I know well that my future is far different. With all that dies, so will I. In some fashion.

Ahead, near the river's edge is a small structure, one story with pitched roof and something round poking out the top. It looks like a tollbooth, about the size of a doublewide outhouse. When I approach, a door opens and a Felidian soldier steps out. He inspects me from head to toe, then looks me in the eye.

"A god of war?" he asks.

"Why would you say that?"

He points at my outfit. "Uniform of the enemy."

"A long story. But no, not any god of war, certainly not."

"Hmm," he murmurs, then asks, "The intent of your visit?"

"Nothing really, just out for a stroll." I step closer, angling around for a peek inside his post. "What is your function here?"

Filling the doorway, he doesn't budge. "Your intent be inspection?"

"Lighten up, okay? We're just having a chat. Like how's it going, how's the weather been. You know, casual conversation."

He casts a suspicious eye, then sidesteps to allow me a look inside. A cluttered desk and wooden chair face a portal looking out on the passing river.

I ask, "So what is it you do here?"

"Stand guard," he says.

Past the window and across the river, I expect to see something he stands guard against, but there's no other post, person, or camp. No tracks, roads, or any sign of anything—possibly ever—disturbing the land. Just endless desert, and farther, low mountains in distant haze.

"Must be awfully boring," I say.

"Preserving Felidian safety be an essential duty. I be honored."

"Ophidians?" I ask.

He nods.

"So how's this work? They try to cross, you do what?"

"Alert the Council," he says.

I fail to see how. Around the side of his tiny hut is nothing. Where's a horse? On foot, at best the alert arrives minutes before any invaders. And for an airborne attack, he might as well not bother.

Inside, the Felidian has seated himself at the desk.

I ask, "You run home quick?"

"Heavens no, too slow." He indicates a burning candle below a tube that rises to the ceiling. He reaches to a lever on the tube, but he doesn't disturb it. "I might demonstrate if not for severe punishment to those issuing false alarms." He tilts a brow. "Unless of course, I be compelled to consider your presence an alarm. Your choice of uniform…"

"I'm not the enemy." I step closer and inspect his apparatus. "What is it you got there?"

"You be not familiar?" His surprise shifts to concern. "Be you sincere?"

"Because I'm a god? Pretend it's a test."

He scratches his chin, then nods. He moves the candle from below the tube, then slides open a panel to reveal what's inside.

"Light be rapid," he says. "Best form a message travels."

I lean in close for a better look. Like a telescope, lenses focus the light, then past a valve the lever controls, higher is a mirror and more lenses above the roofline that become a periscope of sorts, aimed at the Felidian city.

"My design." He faces the desk, cluttered with tiny brass gears and metal files, delicate pliers, and a small hammer. "Though a great more to design, and a blessing." He glances at me. "Otherwise, how do you say? Awful boredom?"

Easy to understand. Assign me any post this dull and I'd probably construct an entire spacecraft.

"When complete," he says, "the system be capable of specific information, greater than beam or no beam."

"How do you mean?"

"This I can demonstrate. No false alarms."

Atop his desk, a series of lenses are supported on edge and spaced out as if a tubeless telescope. He moves the candle to one end, then positions a small parabolic reflector behind the flickering glow, intensifying the light directed into the lenses, which now emit a sharpened beam that strikes the stone wall. Good thing stone, and just a candle. Whatever he's figured out, if scaled up, will make the job of alerting the Council obsolete. Target those hoping to cross in boats, and that ends that.

He reaches for a small wooden box. A brass disk covers its face, perforated by a random pattern of tiny holes, and sticking out one side is a crank. He positions the box beyond the string of lenses, directly in the beam's path. Light shining through the tiny holes casts a pattern on the wall, and turning the crank spins the disk, making the pattern change so fast it's meaningless. He relaxes the pace and allows me a chance to view the projected shapes. It's still meaningless, just a jumble of lit squares like the black spaces in a crossword puzzle. He cranks it faster and the arrangement of glowing squares changes rapidly, dancing in place on the wall.

"What's the point?" I ask.

"A means to speak with those at a distance."

"But even slow it makes no sense."

"And so with fast, faster." He cranks the thing insanely fast. "When observed by our feeble eyes." Light striking the wall blends into a blob that flickers slightly but otherwise melds into a single bright square. "Fast or slow," he says, "if one device be able to create a signal, another be able to catch it."

I scan for a second box.

He stops cranking. "As I say, a great more to design."

"It only works if both are perfectly synchronized."

"Indeed," he says. "Transmission begins with pace signal that sender and recipient agree upon." He sifts through papers and presents an illustration of his not-yet-existing second device. "I be aware of the challenge, yet remain encouraged."

His schematics are impressive, and include a keyboard to enter messages, and a small press that makes the perforated disks, each a unique message defined by the pattern of holes punched out. Essentially a computer, though constructed of brass levers and tiny gears. Incredible. This cat is a genius.

"Where did you learn this?" I ask.

"Many sources, I study in earnest. As well, my father be an accomplished astronomer."

"So what are you doing here?" I ask. "You're one of the smart ones. You should be back home working on this stuff, to help your kind."

"As all Felidians, I serve my time. I be honored. Soon my time of service ends, then I shall double my efforts and further a means to speak with those at a distance."

"The gods?"

"More so those of our own realm, in other lands." He looks out on the river and the sun low in the sky.

"You mean Ophidians?"

"Indeed," he says. "War be a consequence in a void of communication."

"You, the Felidians, you don't talk to them?"

"We have not."

"No one's ever tried?"

"Not to my knowledge."

I point out at the river. "Not even slip a note in a bottle and toss it across?"

His eyes pinch. "I be unfamiliar with such a scheme. Difficult to comprehend its value." He indicates the contraptions and drawings scattered across his desk. "Though as you may surmise, I hope to alter our lack of exchange in the future."

The sun plunges to the horizon and begins its journey past the edge, further reminder that time marches on, forever beyond our control. Another day meets an end, another in so many empty days, but this one day delivers the dawn of solution.

The whole problem—they don't talk.

✳

"We have to organize a summit," I tell Dave after tracking him down to a Felidian pub where he samples their version of ale. Physuro's idea, or result of his boasting, that their intoxicating brews are the finest in any realm. A bold claim we'll have to challenge some other time.

Though well after sundown, I'm not too late. Seated next to Dave, I study his gaze. He stares back, eyes clear and intent, no sign of any drunken haze. But then, I've never seen him anything but sober, even when we party till dawn. I don't know how he does it, I fail every time. Physuro suggests that I sample a glass. No way, not a chance.

Dave laughs and says to Physuro, "Adam's gonna rearrange some mountains." He sips his mug, then says to me, "Really now, deluding yourself with this god stuff?"

His drink sloshes when I whap him upside the head. "No, dumb-ass, not that kind of summit. The kind where people talk things over." I look to Physuro, then back to Dave. "I don't know which of you is worse."

Physuro lowers his mug and holds it steady. "I never once doubted the intent of your words."

"Sure you didn't, Mister Literal."

"It was a joke," Dave says, rubbing out the ache. "Lighten up, man, my head don't need fixing."

"We'll argue that later. And what are you doing? Is this all you've accomplished since we got here?"

I glance about the pub. On the back wall, stacked rounded stones contain a crackling fireplace, almost too warm. Thick timbers hold up a plastered ceiling, higher would be better, safely beyond the reach of the plastered occupants, some of which whack their heads when they forget to stoop. Minstrels play stringed instruments, and one cat drums on hollowed logs sized for tone, laid out flat and circling him. At the bar, boisterous males are tipping their mugs, laughing, burping, and shouting. Females swish their silky wraps as they slink through the crowd, a few of the ladies in the laps of males, stroking their fur and purring while their tails sway a flirting dance.

"I just got back," Dave says. "Maybe an hour ago."

"Back from where?" I ask.

"I was just telling Physuro about our favorite wiener-head. Man, I sure do miss him about now."

"The god Matthew be very smart," Physuro says. "From what David describes."

"Yeah, he's a real brainiac." Then I ask Dave, "So where have you been? What's this about Matt?"

"I figured you could use some good news, so I went back and tried disarming the missiles. It's no use, man, the entire system's locked out. Some kind of exa-bit encryption. I don't understand that crap, I'm just a pilot. But Wiener-head, I bet he could break it."

"You fail at disarming them and then what? Find a drink?"

He shrugs and takes another sip of ale.

"Why not blast the place?" I suggest. "Nobody's there to stop you."

His eyes go wide. "A nuke farm? Are you crazy?"

"Blow it up and the fissile disperses."

"We're not talking *it*, we're talking thousands. Besides, what if—what if?—the off chance one does just the opposite?"

"It's a slim chance any go critical."

"Slim is more than none. You tell me—get close enough to shoot a nuke and hope it disperses. Are you willing to bet your life it will?"

I am silent.

He says, "I thought so."

"Okay, so it's my plan instead."

"A summit?"

"Yes, and you're both going to help." I intercept Dave's rising mug and force it down. "You have to convince the Ophidians to attend, and Physuro, you have to convince the Felidians."

"That be a most difficult task," Physuro says, then sips his drink.

I reach for his mug and table it next to Dave's. "Party's over, both of you."

"I'm with Physuro," Dave says. "Fix things, sure, but what you're asking is next to impossible."

"Is this how you always help? Tell me to figure it out then shoot me full of holes?"

"What crawled up your ass? Have a drink." He pushes his mug toward me.

I push it back. "I'm trying to save all our asses, as you so brilliantly reminded me that I'm the only one capable. You failed and Matt's not here, so I'm it, and I'm not doing it alone. Tell the snakes more nonsense about dreams turning to nightmares. I don't care what you tell them. Tell them something, anything! *Just make it happen!*"

The music stops and a room full of cats stare at our table. I grin a sorry. The band strikes a chord and picks up where they left off, everyone tips their mugs, and the noisy party resumes.

Softer, I relax the commanding tone. "Look, I need your help. I have plenty on my mind already, so come on, help me out on this one. Figure out where to host the summit, and do whatever it takes. I don't care what you have to do, just convince both sides to show up."

Physuro says, "I fear my talent at convincing others be weak."

"You're in the service of the gods, remember? You're an agent serving the God of Truth. Go to the Council, act your role, and convince them to attend. Tell them I demand it."

"How's Chris?" Dave asks.

Some friend. Climb all this way just to boot me off and watch me crash to the bottom.

"Couldn't say, haven't seen her in days."

"What the heck you been doing?" he asks.

A barmaid moves past with a tray of icy mugs, foamy heads brimming over. There's plenty I'd rather be doing. "Wishing she'd get better." I watch the ales vanish in the crowd. Better than added to my sour belly.

"Your power extends to wishes," Physuro says.

"Oh?" I say. "What do you know?"

"I have visited," he says. "We have talked, a delightful goddess. She be better."

"All better?" I ask.

"Perhaps not all. Better than before."

Good news, except for an improved capacity to smack me around, after all the empty promises I can't keep.

"Go see her," Dave says. "We need her help too, you know."

"I doubt she's in any shape for that."

He sprouts that big white grin. "She might surprise you."

Sure, I can almost feel it now. My back turned and the blade sinking deep.

✳

Another night without dreams doesn't seem right. So empty, cold and numb. It could be a relief, except without any new dream and the last lingering, dreams and memory skip off together toward the past and become difficult to separate. The creatures of my nightmare couldn't be real, but the image holds steady. Those multifaceted eyes, countless amber cells, a billion souls staring at me. A shiver creeps up my spine, I twitch, and the passage from slumber is complete.

Morning sun pours into the house of medicine. Last night I chose to sleep among the wounded. Near enough to her, but not the same room. Better than outside on the grass, probably full of creepy crawlers, except for the reason a bed was vacant. I've rested the night where someone perished only hours before.

I return to Christina's chamber and discover she is gone. A nurse explains that she was moved upstairs to a private room. I find the way and find myself moving slower the closer I get. It will be okay, I have to keep telling myself. The rooms upstairs have no doors, not what I'd call private, and they all look the same. I ask a passing nurse and she indicates the room. She moves along to leave me standing here alone.

Across the hall is a vase with a fresh bouquet. Though being dandelions, perhaps better to say a cluster. Dozens, packed in tight, little chance one will be missed. I pluck the best and test its aroma. Odorless, so unlike a fine rose. As is any rose so unlike a flowering weed. But somehow, it is the perfect flower, sure to make it all better.

I move into the doorway. She is in bed, under the covers. She sits up and looks over to see me. She looks curious—curious is better.

I hurry to the bedside and hold out the golden flower. "Here, for you."

She takes it and smells it. A vacant tone, she says, "Yeah, sweet." She flops back and stares up at the ceiling, arms limp at her sides. Still in her grasp, she closes her fingers around the dandelion, crushing it, then she opens her hand and lets it fall to the floor.

If only the contorted weed could speak and tell me why. But no, it just lies there on the floor, slowly unfolding its crumpled petals, yearning to blossom again. There is nothing left to say, no way to fix this. Every answer is gone, just like every memory that isn't real anymore.

I lower to the bed's edge.

Staring up at the ceiling, she says, "Sorry I'm such a mess."

I smile some, hoping it helps. "Best mess I've ever found."

She glances at me and almost smiles. At last, she slides her hand into mine and holds tight. All the response I ever needed.

"Christina, I won't pretend to know what you're going through, I can only imagine, and I'm sure that's not even close. And don't get me wrong, not to belittle your troubles, but…"

She lets go of my hand, sits up, and begins collecting her hair into a ponytail.

How do I say this?

"Enough!" she snaps. "Just say it."

"We have to go now."

She pops off the bed like the call for troops has sounded. Physuro was right, maybe not all better, part of her she keeps buried, but tasks of the flesh are lively.

"What did they give you?" I might want a dose of that medicine.

"Don't think…" she says, "or keep having to understand everything. Right now something else…"

Not sure I want to hear this.

"First you're tired," she says, "then you rest. Then you get tired of resting." She comes closer and pushes the words past her teeth. "I want out."

"Of what?"

She is near. I reach to her shoulders, touch lightly, and yearn to capture her in my arms.

She shifts away. "Don't. You have other problems, we have problems. Get your mind where it belongs. Get us out of here."

I study her and the patient gown she wears. "You'll need clothes." Which only reminds me. "Me too."

She studies my outfit. "What's wrong with that? You look fine."

"It's what the snakes wear."

"The what?"

"The enemy uniform. I make the cats uncomfortable enough as it is. I need something more neutral."

She goes to a closet. "Beige is pretty neutral." She tosses a lump of cloth on the bed, then armed with a matching lump, turns her back to me. "Now don't look."

She is trusting and I'm disobedient. The patient gown falls to her ankles. One leg after the other, she steps into a pair of baggy pants, then flings a roomy shirt overhead and slides the ill-fitting garment down just as she turns around to face me.

Not a muscle I've moved, nor eyes to either side, maybe up and down.

"Hey!" she says. "You looked."

"I won't lie."

Though I might if asked how she looks in her new outfit. The girl's lost in a tent posing as shirt and pants.

Hands at her hips, somewhere under all those folds of cloth, she says, "Honesty doesn't make you a better person if you have to spend it admitting your guilt."

"Better than being guilty and not admitting it."

Her eyes narrow. "Try not being guilty in the first place."

"So I looked, big deal."

"I said not to."

"Next time wait till I agree, then it's all fair."

She stews for a moment but doesn't fire back. She goes to the bed, scoops up the other lump of cloth, and pitches the load at me.

I catch the so-called apparel. "What are these? Potato sacks?"

"It's not so bad." She plucks at her top, which only confirms how many times over she could fill it.

"I don't know, Christina, not what I had in mind. I mean, just look at yourself. You look like a bum."

Her stare sharpens. "You're quite the master of compliments today."

Sarcasm is back, one sign of recovery.

"Not you, baby, the clothes. Come on, we can't walk around in this crap."

"Hurts your pride?"

Not that argument again, which I never win. She is definitely better, and I'll be wearing this crap either way.

She doesn't flinch, look away, nor so much as twitch. She just watches me, knowing full well that I finish what I start, including a change of apparel, crappy or not.

These sorry excuses for clothes are little more than canvas sacks with openings cut out for arms and legs. A lump of scratchy fabric is sewn behind the neck and flopped back, which when brought forward makes an effective hood, sure to hide my face and true identity. At least when the time comes, I might avoid recognition and the ridicule. I can hear it now, Dave laughing his ass off, then some witty comment about my new role as the God of Poverty.

She keeps watching as I pluck and tug, shift and tuck, trying to find the one spot where this tent might hang straight. A rope belt hopes to hold up the leggings, if I can secure a decent knot somewhere around my waist.

"Stop fussing with it," she says. "You look fine."

"I look like a clown."

One suppressed chortle escapes her lips.

"Now it's a joke?"

"You're a clown, right? Clowns are supposed to make people laugh."

"Or cry, like I'm about to."

"Don't be such a baby. They're just clothes." She heads for the doorway.

I don't budge. "Clothes I wouldn't be caught dead in. I need something else."

She turns back and looks me over. "Well, it's that or your birthday suit."

"My what?"

She steps closer. "You know, when you were born."

"Except I wasn't. I went to the body farm, didn't I?"

"It's still like a birthday. You celebrate the special day, don't you?"

Do I? I don't even recall what year I got this body, much less the day.

"I don't do birthdays. I mean, I don't think I do. So you'll have to explain the suit thing."

She rolls her eyes. "What you wore the day you got your body. Is it really that tough to figure out?"

"Last I thought, the bodies run around naked."

Now she's amazed. "You really don't get it."

"I guess not."

She advances on me, applies one palm to my forehead, and gives my thick skull a brisk shove. "You goof, being naked *is* your birthday suit."

I'm knocked back a step. "But that's not a suit, that's—" Has she gone mad? "You expect me to walk around naked? You can't be serious."

"Hell no, why it's called *a joke*." She almost laughs. "I cannot believe how dense you can be sometimes."

Mister Literal may have a twin of sorts. I've fallen prey to tricks of a mind stewing in thoughts too serious. But I'm glad for the ridicule at my expense, amusing her with my remarkable display of mental density. She looks ready for laughter, at last edging toward that playfulness I have sorely missed. But no, something happens, and all hints of laughter wash away when a dark thought strikes her. She shuffles back and lowers to the bed's edge.

"What is it?" I ask.

Downcast, she is silent.

I sit next to her. "Christina, please, talk to me. Tell me."

Her troubled eyes rise. "Adam, I'm so afraid. You couldn't want me after this, and at the same time, I don't want you to want me."

I take her hand in mine. I am without any magic that might ease her trauma, other than holding tight and letting her know how I truly feel.

"Christina, there is nothing in the universe that could ever stop me from wanting you. I love you, forever, no matter what."

✳

My continued insistence for something else to wear—we both look like hell—adds to Christina's wish for early discharge, and our quest begins. We hit the street in search of better clothes.

Felidians crowd the streets, flow from alleys, and fill every shop. Christina and I draw attention, but not all the same reaction. Most Felidians smile and offer silent praise, just happy to have us here. Some remain apprehensive and keep a distance, but not their stares, following us too closely, to the point of uncomfortable. A fanatical few drop to their knees and chant.

I flop the cloth hood over my head to hide my face and insist that Christina do the same.

Merchants exploit the pleasant weather, set up for business with shutters open and cloth awnings rolled out. The avenue is lined with carts loaded with goods, backed by loud signs competing for attention. The open-air bazaar offers a bounty of fruits and vegetables, grains, and bread loaves shaped as thin sticks, likely just as hard. Other merchants offer pottery and bricks, tall vases glazed wet, and a variety of baskets. One looks like my purple welted mess that took half a day to weave. For sale?

My nose is drawn to a cauldron of stew. An older female passes me a ladle. Floating in the warm broth are chunks of bell pepper and potato, black beans, onions, and chopped celery. It tastes the perfect measure of salt. She offers a cube of buttered cornbread, still warm from the oven. I should ask what sort of mill she used. Her recipe easily wins the bake-off.

At last we locate a shop selling textiles, stacked on carts outside. Christina is drawn to a rack of beaded clay jewelry while I circle the carts and scrounge for clothing. The fabrics are solid colors without pattern, hues drawn mostly from nature, dirt brown and mossy green, except that actual dirt and moss have more color. Most items are light canvas, some heavier and scratchy like burlap, but all are clothing, except the same personal tents, baggy tunics and balloon pants. There has to be something better, somewhere.

Christina is busy at a tree-like spinning tower of necklaces dangling over a shelf filled with bracelets and rings. I find a rack of leather goods displaying small pouches with drawstrings, saddlebags, and sandals. On the rack's backside is a promising find—a vest. Durable yet pliable, stained dark without pattern, it even looks about the right size. Now here is something I wouldn't mind wearing.

"Yours for thirty," a Felidian says.

I'd ask thirty of what, except it wouldn't matter. One oversight in our quest for clothing—we have nothing to offer in exchange.

He takes my silence as haggling. "Twenty-five then."

Closer, though doubtful he realizes the great distance still to go.

He steps around and gets a glimpse of my face under the hood. "Oh, forgive me, My Lord. Does the item please you? For you it be a gift, from one so loyal as I."

I'm blasted into and knocked off my feet. The vest goes flying and I land hard, along with the runaway train who didn't realize I was on his tracks.

The ruffian cat has no time for apologies, on his feet in seconds and scooping up spilt bread and vegetables. A merchant chases after him, calling for the thief to surrender, followed by soldiers aiming to apprehend him. The fleeing cat moves as lightning and weaves through the crowd.

Christina helps me up, her gaze questioning.

I brush myself off. "It was only food."

She watches the passing soldiers penetrate the crowd. "Poor thing must be hungry."

I scan the abundant carts loaded with goods. "But there's plenty for everyone."

Her gaze returns to me. "Looks like here, everyone doesn't own it."

We move through the crowd to a corner where cats are edging around, trying to see into an alley. Spectators stand back to make a clearing where a wrestling match takes place. Then, restrained by soldiers, the offender is taken away empty-handed.

"What is that?" Christina asks.

She is looking past the crowd, above their heads. Farther beyond, the alley opens to an intersecting avenue. Across the street, people are *flying*. Cats?

We push through the loosening crowd. Out of the alley and across the street, the land drops at a modest slope, a natural depression from which terraces have been carved in semicircles, dropping lower each tier and lined with curving stone benches. A small half-stadium, and nearly every seat is taken.

Christina is riveted to the action, as are the enthralled spectators. I don't know what to think. They can't fly, their enemy can't, only gods can travel through the heavens. Are the swooping figures… Are other gods present?

The airborne figures wear glittery cloth, in places adorned by metallic foils. One wields a giant thunderbolt, another aims a bow and arrow, and the third holds a trident spear. But leaking from their costumes, I see fur. They are cats, except they are wearing clay masks. The faces are close to human, but pale, very near to white.

Below the swooping figures is a stage where costumed performers move about, but these others are without masks, their furry faces are clearly cats. Past the stage is a towering stone slab, rising from behind a wooden structure with three doors spaced some distance apart. An explanation to this magic presents itself. Attached to the uppermost portion of the tall slab is a protruding construction of wood, a giant valance of sorts, sized to match the stage directly below. Seen from a distance, the valance hides their secret, but now nearer to the highest tier of seating, I see the airborne cats are suspended by ropes controlled by others busy in the rigging above. It's all an act. But even so, the death-defying acrobatics are exciting to watch. Closer than the stage, at the center which the seating surrounds, a circular clearing is the lowest point of the amphitheater, where six cats stand behind a large curving lectern, taking turns narrating the story while those on stage and soaring above act out the play. Without attracting any attention, Christina and I slip into the back row and find seats.

Those on stage represent mortals, and of course, in the heavens are the gods. The story is about a cat they regard as a hero and the perils he faces in the realm of the living. A series of challenges it seems, the earlier of which we've arrived too late to learn, along with his name, as well as any explanation of who posed the challenges or if this hero is just ambitious. His next test is to confront a ferocious beast portrayed by another Felidian in a dragon-like costume, which the hero defeats by driving a spear through the monster's heart. Then stagehands haul out a background cut and painted to appear as rolling waves of ocean, the repeating pattern of curling tips like a saw blade. Now the hero wears a small boat around his waist, held up by suspenders. His legs descend from holes in the one-person boat and allow him to walk about, but his leggings are an iridescent blue fabric that blends with the ocean background and achieves the desired effect. The painted boards are shifted side to side, he bends his knees and the boat dips, then on tiptoes he crests a wave, an illusion so convincing I'm getting seasick just watching.

The god with trident spear swoops down on our hero, another shoots an arrow, and the last thrusts his lightning bolt in threatening jabs. Cymbals crash a sound of thunder and drums beat the heavy downpour. A dark curtain drops behind the action, decorated with slanted lines of glitter that come and go as the fabric flutters, a convincing semblance of rain. The ocean background is pushed and pulled, raised and lowered, the hero does the same, cymbals crash and drums roar, and I begin to fear he might actually drown.

The hero's tiny vessel breaks in two and falls to his ankles. Another long board of jagged waves slides out on stage in front of our floundering hero. He thrashes in the swells, lost at sea, then slips below and is gone.

The ocean background is pulled offstage to reveal a sandy beach where the lifeless hero is spread out face down.

He wakes and staggers upright. A rocky formation is pushed out on stage, resembling the entrance to a cave. The narrating cats describe the hero's quest for the Fire of the Gods, and he crawls into an opening in the rocky prop. Seconds later he emerges, holding a glassy ball glowing orange. He steps toward the audience and holds the sphere up high.

"Our hero attains all power of the gods," a narrating cat announces. Another continues, "The notion be born, to believe he be as great as any god, armed to command his own destiny."

The ball shatters and burst flames that spread to the hero's fur.

Horrified spectators gasp.

A hand on my knee, Christina keeps me seated. "It's a moral," she says.

"He's on fire." Fire that isn't any prop.

The hero drops to become a furry puddle of flame.

"Don't worry," Christina says. "It's theater. Probably a trap door down there."

I hope so. But really, she has to be right. Nobody melts that fast, I know firsthand.

"Only the gods be so great as to wield the power of destruction yet escape its fate. The mortal be bound by destiny he cannot escape, however heroic."

Stagehands whisk into action and sweep away the smoldering mess. She's right, it was a trap door where he stood. Another costumed actor comes out on stage, a sort of bird creature with feathery wings like an overgrown chicken, except the head is closer to an eagle, its golden beak a sharp hook. Oh, there's the hero—at least, the remnants of his costume—dangling in the talons of this new character. Three more actors hurry out, not so much in any costume, they're regular cats with black coats and slender builds. They prance low, heads down, and circle around the bird creature.

Narrating cats explain that false gods promise to restore the hero, provided the rest worship their new master. The soaring god with thunderbolt doesn't like this idea. Somehow, while I wasn't looking, they switched his mask. Still pale and human-like, but now the exaggerated frown and angled brow gives the god a furious scowl. He swoops down on this display of worship and knocks over the bird creature. The circling cats scatter and the gods wrestle. The god from above uses his thunderbolt to stab the eagle-thing again and again, until at last, the bird creature falls dead.

The narrating cats announce, "Our father in heaven, the deathless one who be forever, sacrifices his throne for the good of all Marsea." The god with thunderbolt stands victorious, then he goes to center stage, facing the audience. Female cats flow onto the stage, flutes to their lips and dancing about, delivering a lively tune. "In glorious song, muses now gladden the great spirit of our father Crontis."

Of course, the Mighty One. I should have known. So it's all about him and a fate for any who think they're as great. How did he win this power over them?

The actor portraying Crontis is hoisted up by his ropes, and he returns to the heavens. The narrating cats go silent, and the stage clears of actors and props. A different cat walks out, maybe costumed but not to appear as any god or creature, he wears a pointy hat and golden cloak adorned with jewels.

"Today we learn the wisdom of accepting fate, for the darkness that evil promises, and suffering that it brings, be cast upon us by any desire that we equal the gods. Let us be silent, cleanse ourselves of this futile urge, and submit all gratitude to our Mighty Lord."

The audience hangs their heads and reaches out to others seated at each side. Christina follows the gesture, taking my hand in hers, then a Felidian past her. On my other side, a cat reaches for my hand to complete the chain of embraces. This isn't such a good idea. The cat notices my reluctance and might be offended. Instead of going after my hand, he flips back the hood hiding my face. He gasps, which in this sacred moment of silence sounds closer to a scream. The cat past Christina becomes alarmed once in contact with her soft palm lacking fur. More cats notice and stand, turning to face us, to stare at us. Christina pulls her hood back and rises to look across the audience. Some cats drop to their knees and others scramble for the exit. The priest on stage strains to study us and determine who we are. The stadium quickly empties to half the number only seconds before, but not all Felidians choose to flee. A few ease closer, relishing the chance to be so near a god, the real thing.

A Felidian comes closer. "Be it you, my friend?"

"Whose friend?" I ask.

"Indeed, a great costume. Minaseas has outdone himself."

"We're not part of the show, if that's what you're thinking."

Silent, his eyes widen. He steps back, and back again, then escapes past a crowd closing in around us.

A female asks, "Be it true?" She turns to check the reaction of other cats creeping near.

"Is what true?" Christina asks.

More cats advance, with a look in their eyes that is difficult to describe. Like they're witnessing a moment in history.

"Come," a male cat says, "we shall deliver you." The group urges that Christina and I follow them. We move down steps between tiers of seating, to the lowest level, then to a sidewall beyond which a path leads to a building next to the amphitheater.

Set back a foot in the stone frame is a thick wooden door.

The cats begin backing away, but one stays near. Having noticed my hesitancy to enter, he points at the door. "It be your destiny, My Lord."

✳

I ease the door open, and Christina follows me into a cluttered room. Dust dances in shafts of sunlight beaming in through small windows, and the cool air carries the smell of stored clothing, like something in a bottom drawer left forgotten for months. The room is crammed full of theatrical props—wooden shields, fake axes and daggers, more one-man boats with holes for legs, and waves cut from flat boards. There are clay masks with human expressions, but all exaggerated, happy, sad, afraid and angry. Many costumes are elaborate clothing you wouldn't expect to see average Felidians wearing in real life. Other costumes belong in nightmares—monstrous beaked creatures and other strange reptilian dragons, complete with armored scales, claws, and deadly fangs. The remaining props are dusty pawnshop junk. Table and chairs, pots and pans, candlesticks, vases, framed artwork, and a chest overflowing with costume jewelry.

"You be Adam, the God of Truth."

Standing in the doorway is a middle-aged Felidian, short and plump, with puffy jowls.

He enters. "I be expecting you."

"Me?"

"Indeed. You be the savior."

"Whoa, no. I mean, yeah, I'd like to save you, but no, I'm no savior."

His whiskers angle up to match his clever grin. "Your words contradict themselves."

"Well yeah, but, no."

He steps past, deeper into the room. "I be Minaseas, proprietor of this stage." Arms outstretched, he embraces the cramped space as if the contents were family.

Christina asks, "How do you know Adam?"

He pirouettes to face us. "All in the city know of the great god who challenges the Council and wins his battle of logic. Adam be a mighty hero."

"Look," I say, "you don't understand. That was just for show."

"Ah, yet I do." He winks. "For show be my business." Grin spreading, he indicates the room filled with props.

"All right, so you were expecting me. Then I suppose you know why I'm here."

"Indeed," he says. "You require clothing."

"How could you possibly…"

"See what you wear." He points out my appearance. "Those be not the clothes of a savior. Prophecy tells of a mighty warrior, clothed in the most elegant attire."

Prophecy? Not more of that nonsense. It's one thing to tolerate, let them have their beliefs. Talk about it even, tell their tales and act out their plays, but how the cats cling to the fantasy, they're seduced by make-believe they don't understand. Prophecy is a guess, then someone comes along who fits well enough and the make-believers get their wish.

"And of course," I say, "prophecy sent you to provide something more appropriate."

He doesn't catch the sarcasm. "Indeed," he says, then goes to a closet. "This be from our most popular play, Battle of the Gods." He turns back holding a royal blue double-breasted coat with stiff upright collar, pearl buttons and embroidered buttonholes, golden epaulets atop each shoulder, and a silver lanyard draped across the chest.

He steps closer, offering the outfit.

"Whoa," I say. "Ah, that's a bit much."

Christina says, "What is it with you and clothes? You're like a fussy eater."

"Just look at it. That's extravagant."

Minaseas holds the suit out to one side and admires it. "In the final act, wearing this costume, the God of Truth triumphs over his rival and saves all Marsea."

If someone doesn't tamper with the script. He doesn't understand—his planet's troubles are *real*.

He pushes the costume at me. "Take it, it be meant for you."

I scan the closet behind him. Maybe he has something in the non-prophecy section.

Christina says, "What's wrong with you? You wanted better clothes."

"I can't be seen in *that*."

"Sure you can." She snatches the outfit from Minaseas. "We'll take it. Where's the dressing room?"

"This way," Minaseas says and steps away. "And for you, my lady, there be finery fit for a goddess."

First a god and now a prophecy, lie on top of lie, I'm only adding to the deception. Adding to what ruins this planet, not what saves it. And where did they get a prophecy? Life has no script. No one knows the future. In any future, success and failure have equal chances. Failure is always a risk, but add prophecy's expected outcome—assured success—any fraction less is failure, magnified a thousand times.

Mean well and you're a saint. Do well and you're a savior. But fail, you're nothing but a martyr, not to mention dead, along with all you had hoped to save.

✳

One after another, I fasten the pearl buttons of the white shirt, then cufflinks to match, and slip into the jacket's silk-lined arms. The coat has a thinning appeal, broad at the shoulders while snug where it ends just above the small of my back, and I have to admit, the royal blue color is attractive, commanding even. The fit is perfect for my torso, as if custom-tailored. More roomy are the slacks, loose from hip to thigh then clinging tighter below the knees, with a loop to keep the leggings tucked inside the knee-high boots, black polished to brilliance. A fine chain between the epaulets holds a satin cape in place, made of lustrous fabric an iridescent violet the dark of night.

I step out from behind the privacy barrier. Christina is out from behind hers and standing before a mirror. A sleeveless gown swishes at her feet, white silk that clings to her contours as she twists and turns, checking the fit. She has collected her hair into a single high ponytail, leaving her neck naked, and even found a touch of makeup to conceal the last fading bruises.

She realizes my stare and asks, "How do I look?"

Given a renewed means to accentuate beauty, the part of her she keeps buried begins to emerge. Though true for me, I wouldn't hope to convince her before this moment—nothing could ever hide her beauty from me, not even her. And it doesn't take anything else, clothes or jewels or makeup, only her. She is the source of all her beauty.

"That good?" she says.

"Goddess of my fondest dreams."

Her smile stretches wide and she becomes even more beautiful.

"And me?" I ask.

"A king of kings," she says. "Surely able to save the entire universe dressed like that."

"Easy now."

Her gaze imparts confidence. "I believe in you."

At least one person does.

Minaseas approaches. "There be more." He moves across the room to a shelf of props. He wrestles with junk in the corner, then squeezes in beside the shelf and gives it a shove to reveal an arched portal in the back wall. On all fours, he scurries in and right back out, dusts cobwebs off himself, and then off a long case he holds.

"Many believe this be a prop." He sets the shallow case on a table. When he opens the case, a brilliant reflection escapes into the room. On a soft bed of black velvet, a magnificent broadsword rests beside its scabbard. The blade gleams silvery wet in two facets divided by the central ridge, flowing into a flat bar cross-guard. Guard to pommel, the bronze hilt is decorated by inlays inked sapphire blue, between thin strands twined into spirals.

"This weapon be very old," Minaseas says. "Few know of its secret. I be one, as others before me, entrusted with passing down the instrument through generations, until this moment."

"This moment?" I ask.

"As I say, the moment when the savior wields the mighty weapon, as the prophecy has foretold." He lifts the blade from its case, keeping it horizontal and resting across his palms. "This be created by the most talented of Ophidian craftsman, a gift to a Felidian lord, long ago."

"They were friends?"

"Indeed, when our races be peaceful, before this time of war." Cradling the sword, he extends it toward me. "And with this fine instrument, you shall bring peace once again."

This experience splits me in two—hesitant to fall deeper into their make-believe, yet the blade calls to me, and I am irresistibly drawn to it. I reach out to the hilt. A spark snaps to my fingertips, and a faint wash of color dances across the mirror finish. I take the handle and my palm tingles. The metal hums softly, and the blade glows pale blue.

I swing the weapon upright before me, expecting it to be heavy, but it seems to weigh nothing. The sword swipes and slices in patterns of programmed motion, familiar as if executed only days before. I gain a fluid sense as though warm and molten, flowing into the weapon, becoming a part of it, or it a part of me. Confusing, and disorienting, and it's not my imagination. The sword and I share a connection, as if servant to one another, but how or why is buried in a darkness I cannot hope to brighten. Only that the weapon speaks to me and it listens, not with words, something else. The way a limb does, you just think and it reacts. The blade is now an extension of this body.

I say to Minaseas, "I will take this, it belongs to me."

"Indeed," he says. "And with it, you will make right all that be wrong."

✳

Felidian hospitality reaches new heights when you dress the part. Crowds in the marketplace flock to admire us, though most keep a distance. They now look at us differently, their gazes respectful, hopeful, loyal. Hungry to please.

Merchants venture closer and offer their goods, gifts they insist, hoping to gain our blessing, or they actually believe their trinkets will aid our quest. Further gifts—from Felidians or the gods—won't make the difference. The sword is a fine gift, but how it might bring success, I cannot imagine. And it won't be the tricks of any clever devices. The only gift that matters now is the one I owe myself—confidence that we can sway their beliefs and end this war before it's too late.

One gift we did accept was the kind offer of an innkeeper, that we take residence in his finest suite. A taste of luxury according to him, but we won't say anything. At least the stone floor is carpeted by woven rugs, and the straw bed is almost like a real bed, though a far cry from hotels back home. Christina has no complaints. Having a private bath and kitchen stocked with food, after her time in the house of medicine, she regards our temporary quarters as deluxe.

Dave visited to let us know that he found a location for the summit, but he was too hurried to elaborate, on his way to see the snakes. Considering our hasty departure last time, I wasn't comfortable with the idea of another visit—by either of us—but there was no choice, someone had to go. Dave was not so concerned, still excited by his last grand idea that I snubbed. He coaxed Christina to pose, lovely in her elegant attire, and loaded her image into the hologram-away-from-home that Matt gave him. A click of the button and instead of Matt, his clever device now projects the Goddess of Dreams. He just can't give up the fairy tale. Better than walking into their camp armed with only an invitation to our party, but I'm still unconvinced. A day has passed since we last heard from him, and that could mean the worst.

Christina offers to make dinner while I relax. I tell her she doesn't have to but she insists, it's been a while. She doesn't elaborate on what's cooking, only that I'm sure to like her surprise. She gets the woodstove going and begins chopping vegetables.

I take her advice and stay on the sofa, sitting here with the sword across my lap. The scabbard itself is a work of art, a hardened leather shell intricately carved, not with words or symbols, or anything else meaningful. My fingers flow across the wandering ridges, searching for a hint of what the artisan sought to convey. If only the sword could talk, even a clue, how to solve this mess. I yearn for its secrets, but it waits to tell.

Christina comes out of the kitchen. "Adam, what's troubling you?"

"This summit, I…"

"The meeting you're organizing," she says.

"I should be, except I don't know what to do."

"It'll be okay," she says. "They'll listen to you."

"Listening to me wasn't the idea. They need to sit down and talk this over between themselves."

"So have them sit down and talk." She sits across from me.

"It's not that simple. We need more. Some mighty idea, some clever trick, some way to convince them it's all a lie, but my mind's a blank."

"What happened to the God of Truth?"

"That was just an act to get my ass out of jail. There's no God of Truth."

"There might be if you'd believe in yourself."

"It's all make-believe. I'm not a god of anything, look at me." I wave across my costume. "I'm an actor stuck in a play."

She studies me, and her gaze ends on the scabbard resting across my lap. "What about that?" she asks. "Is that make-believe?"

The scabbard's marvelous texture tantalizes my fingertips. No, this is not make-believe. The sword is very real, like an old friend has joined our quest. But something about it is unreal, floating between here and a dream. The sword means something to me, but it can't explain, I can't explain it, there are only wordless notions. A past and what we've done, or really it's the future and what we will do. Confusing, and I can't unwind the puzzle. But the wordless notions say it clearly—there is no puzzle to unwind. We are together, all that matters.

"Or from a dream?" she asks.

"This? We're not dreaming now. I could only wish this was all a dream."

She grins. "Careful what you wish for."

"This is no time to tease."

She becomes serious. "Adam, let me ask you something." She gets up and comes to sit beside me. "Now that you remember who you are, has it changed your dreams?"

"What is this? Goddess of Dreams trickery?"

"Just answer the question. Are your dreams different?"

Are they? When forced to look at it, maybe they are. Still full of nonsense, but it's true, something has changed.

"I have control now. I know who I am, that it's me dreaming."

"So be in control and know who you are."

"Not the God of Truth."

"Why not? Play the part, tell the *truth*. You've lied enough. It's time to be yourself, and be honest. Expose what's going on and who their gods really are."

"The whole truth? The Association, dead forever, everything? They'd never believe me. They'd think I'm some nutcase spouting a delusional fantasy."

"You don't have to blow their minds with everything you know. Start slow, and watch. You'll know when it's time for more."

Words aren't enough. Not mine, not anyone's. A fancy costume might help, but that isn't going to make the difference either. Something else is needed, an example that demonstrates the truth and convinces the cats and snakes to get along.

"Adam, you're getting ahead of yourself. You'll know what to do when you get there."

"I don't understand that."

"You will. Don't decide before it happens. Decide it will, when it does."

The distance is agonizing, between now and a future I dread. It would be fine that it never comes, but I want it to come, even before it does. Like so many times before, I yearn to advance in time and get a peek at those answers. I need a picture, a clue, some hint of what tomorrow will look like, but this time the future has nothing to offer the present. The future is just a blank, empty nothing. Like the view of a coffin's lid from within.

What I'm organizing is my own funeral.

✳

Still no word from Dave, but by morning a visitor comes knocking. Christina goes to answer the door and Physuro enters. He goes straight to the sofa and hangs his head.

"Well?" I ask. "Are they coming?"

He doesn't look up. "Forgive me."

"What happened?" I sit beside him. "You told them what I said, didn't you?"

"Indeed, yet my words could not sway their decision. I be an agent of the gods who lacks talent at such a role."

I'm off the sofa and pacing.

Christina hurries to me. "No, Adam, it's not his fault."

I halt. "I know. It's *them*. That damned council."

"Don't," she says. "You need them."

"That's the worst part." I leave her and sit next to Physuro, "What about the rest?"

"All arrangements be made," he says. "Except passengers to board the vehicle."

I slap his knee and stand. "Good. You've done well."

"Though none choose to travel?"

"It's not a choice."

＊

Christina and Physuro march at my side, through the hallway leading to the Council chamber. I stride past guards flanking the entry, plant a palm to the wooden barrier, and blast the doors wide open.

A hush covers the circling stone desks.

I step to the center. "Why have you not heeded the words of my agent Physuro?"

The Master Lord says, "We cannot attend the meeting to which you summon us."

"And may I ask why not?"

"For such a decision," he says, "the vote need be unanimous."

I scan the rising tiers. "Who doesn't agree?"

Lord Ornery stands. I should have known.

"There be no reason to attend," he says. "Our enemy be heretics."

"And you have evidence to that fact, I presume."

He ignites. "How dare you! How dare you barge into official chambers and be so pompous as to—"

"Offer evidence? Your continued insistence for evidence tells me that it matters a great deal to you, My Lord, and I humbly submit. Furthermore, I suggest the acquisition of your evidence be a matter of the utmost importance, and more so offer myself, one of the gods, to aid your mortal endeavor to obtain evidence, by providing the very means to do so—the meeting to which I summon you. *You*, My Lord, your eminence in person, shall attend and witness the truth firsthand, then you may prove to every Felidian that your enemy is heathen, heretics, whatever kind of monster it is that you detest. Venture out into the world and get your evidence, bring it back to the Council, and show everyone that you were right. *That* is what I dare."

He is silent and stewing, daring that I melt from his glare.

Then he speaks. "Your meeting, and your end, I shall attend."

＊

It took hours for the adrenaline to wear off. I don't even recall walking back to our suite, a task left to the body and somehow we made it without careening off into a drainage ditch. Difficult to believe, as if I were drunk, just without the stumbling. With thoughts consumed by murderous intent, I hardly know what was said. Only how much I wanted to strangle that bastard. And now what have I done? That ornery prick is the last cat we want at the table. I almost wish the snakes don't show up.

As the sun sets, Christina excuses herself to call it an early night. I should be the one to rest, but I'm wired, or something, on the sofa staring at the door, waiting, dreading, but the knock to come is not the news I fear. Dave's charred remains are not found hanging from a cross. Apparently, the goddess ploy was effective. I can hardly believe that, either. At last he returns, and the Ophidians have agreed to attend. Is that good news?

"Everything's a go," Dave says, stepping into the kitchen. "I caught up with Physuro, the cats are coming, everybody sets out at first light. They should arrive before noon." He scrounges through cupboards. "Don't worry, you can sleep in, we're flying. So, got your speech ready?"

"Speech?" I don't even remember my last speech.

Facing an open cupboard, he glances over his shoulder. "You called this thing, right? That makes you mediator, the guy who gives the speech."

"Me? I can't talk them out of their differences. I'm no diplomat, I'm a combat engineer, and alternative doesn't mean I do politics on the side."

"What did you expect? All this doom and gloom, how their planet gets destroyed, and after a friendly little chat, everything's dandy, just like that?"

"Well, I was hoping…"

"You owe them more than hope, buddy."

"I don't know what to say."

"Just tell it like it is. What's so tough about that?"

"Sure. You there, stop fighting, and stop worshipping a bunch of phony gods. Yeah, that should do the trick."

"Come on, be realistic. You can start by telling them their planet won't be destroyed."

"You know I can't guarantee that."

"Maybe not, but that's not the point. The threat worked, so they're coming. Now that you've got their attention, get their minds off annihilation and back on something more constructive, like how to get along."

"What threat?" I ask.

"Like I said, how their planet gets destroyed."

"Are you saying *as punishment*? If they don't show up?"

He looks away. "You said whatever it takes."

"You lied to them."

He goes back to the cupboard. "I wanted to make sure they'd listen to you."

"What did you tell them?"

He still won't look at me.

"Dave, answer me."

He hesitates. "That *you* would destroy their entire planet."

"You're making me into a monster."

"You do fine on your own. Word's getting around, you know, your temper tantrum in the desert, and what you said about killing them all. They take that shit seriously. I'm just milking it for all it's worth."

"You know I didn't mean it. Come on, I was under duress."

"Well then, we'll just have to go tell them you're sorry, didn't mean it, all a mistake."

The real mistake was coming here in the first place.

✳

Called to wake before dawn is never pleasant, which makes the late start appealing. While the delegates travel hours by land, us gods will fly through the heavens and arrive in a fraction of the time. I should thank Dave for the chance to snooze longer, a great opportunity for needed rest. Except the chance is wasted. It only works if you fall asleep.

Up all night with a mind tied in knots, when breakfast is served, the sight of food tangles my stomach to match. I should eat, but my contorted insides are likely to eject anything I hope to shove down. But I have to eat. A body can manage holding out for a meal, or a night without sleep, but not both at the same time. Especially not this day.

"Stop checking the door," Christina says. "He'll be here, don't worry. Sit down and eat."

I drop into a chair facing the plate. Maybe if I inhale it quick enough, the meal won't escape digestion. That was a rotten idea. The scrambled eggs are in me, but I didn't expect back in the shell, swallowed whole. There will be no escape, that load isn't going anywhere.

At last Dave arrives. I'm up and to the door only to have him stride past. He makes me wait while he enjoys breakfast. Anxiety feels wrong when it's a hurry to reach something that you dread. Because you want to get to the other side. Knock me out, wake me up when it's over. Except I'd miss it all. I don't know what I want, just that it be done.

Dave finishes breakfast and stands. "Chris, do me a favor…"

We both look to him and listen.

He points at me. "Fix him. I'll wait outside."

Smart-ass.

Christina seems to agree and coaxes me to the sofa after Dave exits.

"What is eating you?" She lowers to sit beside me.

"Don't make me do this alone."

"How can I help?"

"Talk to them. You're the Goddess of Dreams."

"I can't do this for you."

"I'm not suggesting you do. I just need some help, your help. I need you."

She spends a moment looking at me, and her smile grows. "I love you too." She stands. "We'll talk about it on the way. Come on, let's get going."

When we leave the suite, Christina leaves behind a satchel and beaded jewelry she picked up at the marketplace. She expects that we will return. I'm not so sure we will.

✳

On foot, Dave leads the way to our waiting craft, taking me and Christina through a maze of cluttered backstreets. Hidden by the illustrious faces of their grand architecture, the narrow passages behind each building are choked by towering walls that block out most direct sunlight, leaving the air stale and cool. We pass a dilapidated cart, one of its wheels splintered and rotten. Open piles of garbage attract undernourished vagrants filching for scraps. Held out from a window up high, a pot is upturned to dump urine into a grated trough running along the alley.

The contrast isn't much of a surprise. As do many societies, the Felidians put on their best face and usher the ugly into dark corners few visitors dare to explore. Not appealing by any means, but the dark corners are comforting. Storybook prophecy perfect is a fine utopian ideal, but to believe it actually exists only feels phony. An improbable, intangible, romantic dream. Knowing the ugly is here, now the cats are real.

From the maze of dank alleyways, we emerge in a public square. Curving brick paths weave through patches of manicured grass sharp at all edges. Sunlight beams down to emblazon each brick to golden, and every walkway leads to center square where a crowd of Felidians are gathered around the black triangle craft. Their gawking stares marvel at the godly machine, but they quickly lose interest when we approach.

It appears my concern over clothing was unfounded. Dave is still wearing the Ophidian uniform, and the Felidians seem indifferent to what it means. Or I am a distraction. Their stares focus on my lavish attire, golden epaulets and silver lanyard, boots polished to brilliance. The cats act like they'll never again lay eyes on any fabric to match the royal blue jacket.

I own their full attention, but this time they don't kneel. Instead they remain standing, perhaps even firming their posture, as though next they might salute. But no, they just stare at me. They've seen this before—in a play. Except in this performance, they've invested all faith. They see it, they believe it. I don't know if I can. All I know—I can't let them down.

✳

The nimble craft soars upward, punching through the thin cloud cover. Dave is silent, focused on piloting. Christina is seated behind us, also without words. Our ascent, while vigorous, is a slice of peaceful time.

Sheathed in its scabbard, another quiet passenger rests across my lap. Though silent as are my friends, the sword exerts a presence all its own. I can feel it, like it wants to talk, but it can't find the words. But still there is a hint, like to sit across from someone and say nothing, their eyes can scream at you, draw your sympathy, or taunt. The sword has no eyes, it lacks any expression, yet I sense the wordless notion—together, we are greater than one, all that matters. Wielding the sword, perhaps we are, and our combined strength is enough to face this test. Face it, but even were this weapon the finest in all the universe, that alone does not guarantee success.

As promised, Christina listens to my concerns, and we exchange ideas of how to proceed. But even ideas are no guarantee. Some could work, except there is so much we don't know. Any idea could be the worst, but if they react how I imagine they might, her idea may prove best. All you can do is take each step that adds to the next and hope the sum amounts to success.

Dave has yet to describe our destination, and peering out the side, I notice the landscape is looking a lot more like desert.

"Not back to the snakes."

"In between." Dave studies the terrain below. "An old shrine along the river, up ahead here someplace."

A river like the Felidian sentry was guarding—border of their territories.

"On which side?" I ask.

"Neither, according to Physuro. And neither side ever visits the place. Both say it belongs to the gods, sacred ground, stuff like that. Sounded good to me, more neutral that way. I figured you'd agree."

"I might, but if it's sacred and belongs to the gods, what changed their minds about visiting?"

He glances at me and grins. "You did, remember?"

"Can't say that I do, but I can imagine you telling the lie. So what unthinkable horror did I threaten this time?"

"Stop calling me a liar. You said whatever it takes, that's permission to lie."

"Now your lying is *my* fault?"

"I did what you asked, get off my back."

"Boys, boys." Christina angles forward between our seats. "We're all a little tense."

Dave banks the craft hard. "I'm fine."

I check tactical for something to shoot. "Nobody's tense."

From behind, Christina massages my rock-hard shoulders. "Adam, you need to relax."

I shift free of her needling. "Don't say that."

"What's your problem?"

"I don't know, something creepy." My head pounds hard and starts to spin. "Am I the only one seeing spots?"

"Hang on," Dave says. "I thought it was further up the river."

Not just my head, we're all spinning, dropping fast in a spiraling nosedive.

"Here's your Gs back." Dave pulls out of the dive and puts the craft into a swooping arc, my skull drains to inflate one arm, and the reddened view turns gray. We come around full circle and level out, some color returns, and we continue zigzagging down in shallow dives less apt to rearrange cardiac pathways.

We descend on a course parallel to the river, which branches around a sliver of land, creating an oval island tapered to sharp points that split the current. From above it looks like an eye. A lone eye staring up from the pale desert face, and flowing around it, a river of tears.

Dave drops speed and we circle the island. At the center is a domed building, but not an observatory, the golden dome is solid. And not metal like anything Ophidian, most of it is masonry, although it doesn't seem Felidian either. The square foundation is constructed of smaller red bricks that support a circular band of white tiles. Above the gleaming divider and rising to the dome, the outer walls are tan stone, from which repeating portals are cut, open slots equally spaced that wrap around the monument. Set away from the building and standing at four corners, square pillars taper inward as they rise, each capped by an onion dome.

A wooden bridge joins the island to the surrounding desert. Not far off, approaching the bridge, clouds of dust rise from a desert trail. A convoy is heading this way.

We drop lower, coming in to land. Dave glances out the side to study the bridge and trail. "Ophidians."

An armored troop transport is parked near the shrine. The Felidians have already arrived.

"Get us down, Dave. We don't want them facing each other alone."

Our final approach kicks up dust and we touch down. I pop the cockpit cover and belt on the scabbard, then help Christina get out.

Dave doesn't bother unbuckling.

"Aren't you coming?" I ask.

"I'm no diplomat. Besides, you need air cover. Wouldn't want some unfriendly sneaking up on your little summit."

What else have I not thought of?

"Okay, good idea. Watch the skies and keep us safe."

He flicks a casual salute. "You can bet your life on it."

"I'd rather not."

✳

As the craft rises, we wave off the dusty swirl kicked up by Dave's departure. We stand watching our only means of escape dwindle, to become a tiny dot lost in the pink sky.

Christina adjusts my coat. "Time for Act One."

"Act what?"

She dusts off my lapel and pats my chest. "Like Minaseas said, when the savior defeats his rival and saves all of Marsea."

"You know, you're not making this any easier."

She becomes cross. "I'm not the one making it difficult. Lighten up already. You've done this plenty of times."

"I have?"

She eyes me with concern. Then she smiles. "You'll be fine, come on." She takes my hand and leads the way toward the shrine.

Sloping layers of windblown sand collect on the steps, marked by the footprints of the Felidians who preceded us. I scale the rise carefully, stepping into the existing depressions, trying not to disturb them any further.

Beyond the highest step, great doors tower upward. They must weigh tons, yet swing open with the slightest nudge and without making a sound. Inside, not a single grain of sand soils the pristine marble floor. A hallway stretches out before us, devoid of ornament. The walls shimmer a golden sheen, perfectly clean, separated at regular intervals by thick wooden beams stained dark walnut.

The corridor ends at the primary chamber, circular to match the dome above. Rays of sunshine slice between fluted pillars circling the room, pairs of which frame tall portals to the desert afternoon. Upon entering, the ceiling draws my full attention. The concave surface of the dome's underside is decorated by fine art of a greater civilization, a sprawling mural that stretches out to every edge. The painted ceiling depicts lovely women floating on their bellies, reaching out to streak across pink sky full of billowing white clouds. Fluttering cloth tears away from their smooth bodies and tangles with fair strands twining around their arms and torso. The enormous dome exceeds the boundaries of vision, and the floating beauties hint at motion—I must halt and steady myself. The roaming goddesses are joined by chubby infants with feathery wings, also floating free and barely covered by shreds of fluttering cloth. The young ones seem to be staring down at us, as they strum tiny golden harps.

But these are people, not cats or snakes. Other humans have been here. And children.

"Welcome," Physuro says.

He stands near a long table where a dozen Felidian lords are seated. The opposite side of the table is empty.

For a breathless moment, all stare in awe of me.

Except Lord Ornery, who scowls but keeps quiet for now.

Away from their chamber of authority, the lords leave behind their white gowns and opt for rugged apparel better suited to overland travel. Though still prestigious examples of society's finest, their hefty overcoats are brown suede with rough edges, unbuttoned and open down the center, a relaxed look that is almost casual. However, the bulky leather coats add great volume to each lord's chest and torso, which only inflates their bloated display of supremacy.

A lord rises, looks to Physuro, and silently dismisses him. Physuro bows, glances at me and bows as deeply, then backs away from the table.

The standing lord says, "We admire your wish for peace, however, we fear your efforts be futile. Our enemy be unreasonable, without any hope of ever respecting the gods."

I approach the table. "Allow me an opportunity to convince you otherwise."

He glances at his fellow lords to one side, then the other. All but one nod. "Very well," he says. "We shall listen. However, we have little faith in your goal and urge that you temper your expectations."

"Your concern is noted."

Christina pulls me near and quietly says, "I want to tell you something." She whispers, "Don't listen to them. Have lots of faith and get all you expect. You can do this." She eases back, tender blue eyes watching me, believing, loving all that I can become.

Chair legs scrape the floor. I swing around to face the Felidians, now all standing. From behind, boot steps rap the hallway, growing closer. A dozen Ophidians emerge from the corridor and enter the room.

I approach them. "Welcome, and please, make yourselves comfortable." I indicate the vacant seats.

The snakes halt and study my costume. Their stares end fixed on the scabbard at my hip.

Is that...? They sent Smeck. Dave should have told me. Why didn't he? The major can't be happy with me after our last encounter, but he appears more disturbed by our other guests.

"Ophids do not sit with Felidian heretics."

The cats remain standing and the snakes don't budge, though some of them take a hard look at Christina, seated beyond the table and off to one side, more the side of the cats. They may recognize her from Dave's holo-gadget. Perfect.

Major Smeck wears his usual outfit, snug bodysuit of a soldier, long coat he wears as a cape, and stiff hat with shiny brim. His fellow Ophidians are similarly uniformed, some with medals pinned to their chest. Invited to negotiate peace, the Ophidians sent the military.

Then I notice—either Dave failed to deliver my request, or the snakes ignored it.

"I asked that you attend unarmed." Which meant anything capable of harm. Every snake wears a scabbard at their hip.

"We attend as we choose," Smeck says.

"I must ask that you remove your weapons."

He focuses on the hilt of my sheathed broadsword. "And you?"

"I'm not at war with you, or them."

Another snake says, "This meeting iss over." About face, he starts for the exit.

"Do you have no respect for the gods?"

He halts. "Iss they who do not." He points to the Felidians.

"They respect enough not to bring—" When I swing around to face the cats, my foot nearly lands in my mouth.

The lords open their coats. One of them says, "We do not fear our heathen enemy." Inside his coat, he carries a compact battle-ax. Within all of their coats, the lords pack a variety of handheld weapons—spiky mace, flail with morning star, and an assortment of daggers. Lord Ornery's personal favorite, a sickle with short handle, perfect for hacking down really tough stalks, likely in one swipe of the crescent blade, gleaming sharp.

"If we iss not threatened," a snake says, "we bring out no weapons."

The lords close their coats and conceal their arsenal.

I say to the cats, "I couldn't convince you to…"

They silently shake their heads.

Great news—everybody left their blast rifles at home. A lot of good it does. When these two gangs rumble, our meeting ends in a bloodbath. Now what? How I might single-handedly disarm this mob is one stretch of the imagination I'm not going to explore.

"All right," I concede, faced with no other choice. "I won't insist. But I must demand of everyone, there will be no weapons drawn. I want your promise."

The snakes place a hand on their biceps, fold one arm with fist clenched, and snap a nod. If only Dave were here to tell me what it means. For all I know, they're giving me the finger.

I indicate the empty seats and invite the snakes to the table.

They don't budge.

I ask Smeck, "Must I command you to sit?"

He looks at the standing lords. "No other but a god stands above the faithful."

I spin on my heels to face the cats. "If you would please, *sit*."

All lower to their seats.

I say to Smeck, "Your turn."

He exhales a huff that reeks, then motions to his fellow Ophidians. All proceed to their side of the table. As they find seats opposite the Felidians, I move to the table's end, at the dividing line between these enemies.

"We are all diplomats," I begin, "and I expect that we will act as such. Anything less will not be tolerated. Is that understood?"

A Felidian says, "Agreed."

Major Smeck says, "If we must."

I lock stares with him. "More than must, you will do. Is that clear?"

He stands. "What iss your hope to accomplish?" He sweeps an arm across the cats opposing him. "We iss enemies."

I step around the table and stare him down. "My first hope is that you would agree to behave as we all agree to behave, which at this point you are failing miserably."

Next to Smeck, an older snake pulls him down to seated. "Enough." The more gracious snake says to me, "We agree to civil behavior in respect of your invitation and shrine gods dare we visit. A contract to last until this meeting iss concluded, no further."

"Fair enough." I move to the table's end. "Now, let us agree to something of even greater value. Let us agree to peace."

Major Smeck scoffs at the possibility. "You iss a dreamer."

"Indeed." I turn and indicate Christina, seated beyond me. "Thanks to my love, the Goddess of Dreams."

Snakes emit slithering gasps. One of them says to another, "He iss lover to goddess protector from nightmares." The snakes pass gossiping whispers among their group.

I motion that she join me.

The Felidians study Christina, the Ophidians, one another and then back to the snakes. Puzzled, or perhaps, looking at their enemy with fresh eyes and renewed, open minds. Even Lord Ornery.

Christina comes to my side.

"Ready?" I ask.

She nods and takes my place at the end of the table.

"Please understand," she says to all, "I am not here to tell anyone how to behave. But I have to tell you what I see." Ophidians hang on her every word. "You are suffering from hatred that is not your own. Like a disease, each of you is infected with the words of another. Adam and I come here hoping to cure you of this disease. The medicine we bring is truth." The cats are fascinated with her and equally fascinated by their enemy's show of respect. "What you believe," she says, "are beliefs invented by another no greater than yourselves, whose desire is to fill your hearts with hatred and keep your two races forever at war. All of you, please understand, these beliefs are not your making, not anything with which you ultimately agree."

A Felidian says, "And you be one to say what any might hold in agreement."

"I'm not telling you on what to agree, only that you are able to agree."

"A bold claim. Enemies do not agree."

"Only because another tells you so. I see the love in your hearts, all of you. Each of you is capable of compassion, for yourselves, for life, and for every other you share it with, of any race or species. I ask you, look deep inside, see the good that exists within you. Not your deities, leave them be. There is no god the judge of right and wrong, no god the source of your thoughts, no god the center of what you feel. *You* are all those things."

Her plea edges on a sermon—that insults their beliefs. I pull her back.

An Ophidian rises. "Dear Goddess, end our nightmare." He points at the cats. "They exist to destroy us."

Lord Ornery stands. "It be you who seeks our destruction."

"To preserve our kind, you come to kill."

"You be killing us!"

Another, another shoots up, voices rising to a shouting match as delegates accuse each other of brutal slaughter. Another and the next is up, exploding verbal chaos as the cats and snakes fire allegations across the table.

"No!" I call above the din. "Another seeks to destroy all of you."

Silence.

"Who be it?" a Felidian asks.

An Ophidian is equally curious. "Yes, who?"

"The Mighty One."

Another volcano erupts. No longer targeting foes across the table, both sides fire in all directions. The ruckus grows to an unintelligible roar, though now and then one word escapes the fray—blasphemy.

"Silence!" I command. "You will sit."

The clamor fades. Slowly, the delegates return to their seats.

"I'd say there's a bit too much respect for the gods around here."

Their stares leave me and fall on one another, both sides looking across the table at an enemy who is clearly, and equally, outraged by my irreverence of their Mighty One.

I press on. "You have received gifts from the gods, yes?"

A Felidian says, "We have."

I shift to the snakes. "And you as well."

"Yes."

"Explain the purpose of these gifts."

From both sides, delegates say, "Protection."

"Protection from what?" I ask.

"The enemy." Cats and snakes point across the table at one another.

"Now we shall unmask the true source of this conflict. Who told you that a danger existed and offered protection from that danger?"

No one replies. My words have begun the journey deep into all they hold dear, past what they believe, and onto their sense of reason, where denial is at the mercy of truth.

"And who told you that your enemy had no respect for the gods and should be destroyed?"

Silence.

"Someone told you that. WHO?"

Every delegate sits frozen.

A Felidian rises to point over my shoulder. "The Mighty One."

✳

When I spin around, there he stands, armed with that perpetual grin and flaunting a costume to match mine, almost. Same double-breasted coat with twin epaulets, silver lanyard, and scabbard at his hip. Every detail the same, except his coat and slacks are blood red.

Ever so casually, Jared asks, "What are you doing?"

"Fixing your mess."

Him and I, costumed and acting our parts, I feel detached, as if watching this performance from afar. What is so familiar about this? I've seen it before, or other play incredibly similar.

Christina stands an uncomfortable distance from me, nearer to him. She doesn't look at me, only him. Her whole body screams it—you will die.

Jared looks at me and sighs. "Will you ever learn? You can't win."

He swaggers closer, hands riding the hilt of his sheathed broadsword. One feature of his costume is nothing like mine. Clumsy gray boots, way too big.

He halts, aiming that smug grin I want to rip from his face. But this time he stands alone, minus his troop of cronies and their nets, his only advantage in our last contest. This time, one on one, Jared is getting *his* skull kicked in.

The fire burning inside, that's not me. Fury doesn't serve the goal, it only makes me the victim of his overconfidence, the psychological weapon he uses against me time and again, which he knows I'll succumb to, get flustered, and lose myself in all contempt for him. No, he's not getting under my skin, not this time. Aim, focus, and achieve. The goal is in reach.

I turn to the delegates. "This is the Mighty One, yes?"

In a jumbled clamor, the cats and snakes confirm that he is.

"See the truth! You are worshipping the same god."

Staring across the table at one another, the delegates are transformed, miles from where they were when this summit began. Jared has done us all a mighty favor. He confirms it himself, witnessed by both sides of this conflict at the same time—the perfect demonstration—that he alone is worshipped by all. Strip naked this religious farce, behold an elaborate deception, and see its lying architect. So badly I want to cry out but know it's better they realize for themselves—you are pawns in a twisted fantasy playing out in the sick mind of your imagined god.

An audible presence grows stronger. Crackling, like before a thunderstorm. Tiny blue arcs dance across the scabbard at my hip. My hand closes around the hilt. Pinpricks attack my palm, and tingling energy flows into my arm. The wordless notions scream—*unleash me now.*

Time lengthens—each second becomes a lingering moment. Perceptions turn dreamy, but even so, remain razor sharp. And like a dream, I am here watching—deciding—yet events unfold with unrealistic linearity. Like a rubber band stretching out.

Further dreamy perceptions—the sound of Jared moving behind me, metal scraping as he unsheathes his weapon, and the breathing of each delegate, slowly in, then out. I gain a foreign sense of omnipresent viewpoint—I know all motion and sound throughout the room. I am everywhere.

Christina calls out, her voice low and slow, part of the lethargic scene, "Adam, behind you."

Faint, rippling vibrations announce the approach of Jared's blade. The rubber band has stretched to its permissible limit, and the physical universe has rules to enforce. It must snap back and make up for lost time.

Sword out, I face Jared and our blades crash.

KHRIIINGGG!

A thunderous concussion and sizzling arcs gives way to screeching metal. Dreamy perceptions fade as Jared and I trade blows in real time. My blade glows pale blue, light as a feather, so little effort to swipe and thrust. Jared defends himself well enough, but still I press him back, across the room, away from the delegates. He nearly stumbles, thanks to those ridiculous boots, but he regains footing and unleashes a weak counterattack. He struggles to force me back with each crash of our blades but I stand my ground, and his frustration grows. Today, I am the stronger of the warring combatants, which I make clear with another surge forward, pushing him back, farther back. His cocky persona is slipping away. Exhaustion brings sweat to his brow, and his eyes confirm the worry brewing inside. That's right, my former friend, I am no longer a confused subject chased into an abandoned warehouse, ripe for your betrayal. That time is gone, your advantage is gone, and I will never again be your victim. I know who I am, and now you will know—I am Adam.

There is commotion nearby. Christina stands before an Ophidian.

The snake draws his sword.

I fail to parry and Jared's swooping blade nicks my thigh. I slap a hand to the wound and stagger back. He advances, weapon bearing down, but Christina…

The Ophidian offers his sword. She takes the hilt and raises the blade.

I've let my guard down—one false move equals one less ear. Jared swings his sword, I contort beyond all laws of physics, and the steel whooshes past.

Off balance, I topple over and crash down, fully exposed to the swift return of his blade.

Behind Jared, Christina advances.

"No!" I cry.

Jared spins around to meet her attack.

KHRIIINGGG!

Rational thought catches up quick—that was stupid. She could've struck before he even knew what hit him. Except I'd be as fatally wounded. Jared had me under the blade.

I don't want her in this fight. However, she's doing herself proud, employing a two-handed style of swordplay that keeps Jared busy. Kept in continuous motion, her blade swoops up and over in circles that weave from side to side, which she breaks out of in sudden, unpredictable stabs. Each time Jared tries to thrust, her weapon is at the right place, at the right time, and meets his in a shower of sparks. Jared gauges the dance of her sword and better predicts each new attack. They shuffle back and forth, trading ground as they trade blows, but neither can gain any lasting advantage.

I can—two against one.

Jared senses my advance and our blades collide. He spins back to Christina, another crash and more sparks. He heaves his weapon full circle, distributing his defense between us, and he begins to wear down. I'll take that advantage back, thank you very much.

Positioned opposite each other with him in the center, our teamwork has forced him into a precarious and exhausting frenzy. As if thinking of one mind, Christina and I initiate sweeping arcs, blades horizontal coming from opposite directions—scissors aimed to slice him in two. He may avoid one of us, but not even he is mighty enough to escape two blades in a single instant.

Christina and I swing hard.

Jared rockets upward.

Our blades cross empty space and continue, whirling us round like spinning tops, off balance and to the floor.

Jared has joined the goddesses and winged infants floating across the ceiling.

Christina points with her blade. "The boots."

He twists an ankle and swoops away, carried aloft by his oversized footwear.

The delegates evacuate the table and take refuge along a far wall. But none dare look away, too dazzled by a god's demonstration of divine power beyond mere mortals. Power that has nothing to do with anything divine. A clever device! The delegates don't know any better. All they see is their Mighty One soaring across the heavens.

Christina raises her sword and heaves it like a dagger—a damn big one—twirling end over end. Jared dodges the blade and laughs. The sword lands in the ceiling art, planted in the body of a winged child. Eerie—the kid seems to glare back.

Jared's booming call echoes across the concave ceiling. "Do not listen to Adam. He is a devil here to trick you."

"I am not!" I face the delegates. "The Mighty One lies. He's the one tricking you."

A Felidian says, "The mightiest god be the victor in this contest. It be in the hands of the gods, who shall rule Marsea."

An Ophidian agrees, "Yes, only the gods may turn the course of fate."

They agree? I'll take any measure of success. A start, but true success will be the death of Jared.

Christina advances on the delegates. "The Mighty One is deceiving you." She points up at Jared. "He is the nightmare you fear."

Jared swoops down on Christina and snatches hold of her ponytail. He soars across the room dragging her and slams her into a wall. She struggles up, weaponless, standing before one of the portals to the outside. He rockets down, boots humming, then fingers outstretched, he seizes her face in one hand and holds her back, keeping clear of her swinging fists.

"What is wrong with women?" he says. "If you expect to fight a man, get a man's body!" With her skull in his grasp, he shoves hard and sends her over the sill, out the opening, to drop away and gone.

I aim to gut the bastard.

He clicks his heels and fires upward.

"Get down here and fight, you coward!"

He floats overhead. "No. And I'm not the coward, you are." He bounces from side to side like a puppet on strings. "Come up here and get me, big man, if you think you can."

If I *think*? All my rage, hatred, every scrap of fear, frustration and doubt—all are cast aside, replaced by invigorating wordless notions vaulting me to supreme. The sword glows pale blue, the hilt becomes warm, and the dreamy perceptions return.

Jared wants to play god? Okay.

Existence takes on a cold, stark quality, as I see it for what it is and nothing more. I look at the wall and farther up, to where it meets the ceiling. A good distance up, but then, it's only a wall that ends at a ceiling. Both of which are quite still, while I am…

Time decelerates. The rubber band is stretching out again. Sword in hand, I sprint to the wall, slicing through a lazy reality. I step from floor to wall and the rubber band *snaps!* Up I go, scaling a vertical surface as though it lay flat before me.

At the ceiling, I aim for Jared. He whirls around, shocked by my sudden appearance. Indeed, I am a wraith, vaporous and haunting, and there is no escape.

He veers out of reach and my blade slices air. Agreed-upon time resumes, and with it comes the inescapable force of gravity, sending me back to the floor.

This is possible. I intend that it be and the universe agrees, given the bounds of reality.

I stretch the rubber band to the breaking point—*SNAP!* I am propelled up the wall to the ceiling faster than any time could measure. Again I swipe, fail to strike, and Jared shoots away. Gravity is tenacious and down I go.

Hovering out of reach, Jared grins. "You can't win."

Damn him! I can do this.

I decide to employ a dual action time twist—snap the rubber band on the way up, then stretch it out once I arrive. I can win. He's coming down.

Set a stance, one deep breath, focus on the wall. Thinking, but not thinking, how to do this. There is no how, only do. No thoughts, nothing to analyze, nothing known, remembered nor forgotten, only what is real this instant, in only this instant. Sword in hand, I sprint to the wall and again time cannot measure my resolve. By the rules of existence I should be back there, when in my actuality, I'm already here, at the ceiling.

Now is the time for now to keep being now. Infinitely determined, I seize the ends of time and stretch it across the universe, bringing existence to a crawl. Time moves forward, but at a pace so slow, a single breath might span a lifetime.

One instant is free from all others—now—he is in reach.

Lost time must be recovered. A vicious snap, reality catches up, and my blade slices across his boot. Sparks fly as it splits open—spoiled—and he spins out of control.

Distorted time no longer veers from reality, and with real time comes real gravity. Subjected to the same laws of physics, Jared smacks a wall and crashes down to join me on the floor.

✳

How, I don't know, and quite frankly I don't care—I got it done. Exhausted, mentally and physically, I force this body upright and rally another cache of energy. I advance on Jared, knock his sword out of reach, and bring mine to his chest. All that remains is to drive the steel through his black heart. All my rage, hatred, every scrap of fear, frustration and doubt—focused to destroy all that I despise.

My blade at his chest, him staring at me, I... I don't understand. Confusion battles confusion. He is my friend. He is the enemy. I cannot see myself, what I truly feel, or my intentions. I have plunged into a void where all things good, bad or otherwise, trade costumes and masquerade as the other. He has helped me. He has hurt me. Forgiveness is impossible, but his demise delivers no satisfaction. Hatred is a disease, cured by destroying all that I hate.

My glorious moment is at hand. I stand poised to execute my revenge.

I cannot.

The past won't let me.

So many instances of Jared, always in plain sight, I've convinced myself it was all in jest, he was only kidding. I've refused to believe it could be true. He's always suffered a pang of self-doubt, fueling a jealousy that makes him eager to inflate himself, sometimes foolishly. Hurting him won't change that. Punishing him won't work. There is no reform capable of correcting his personality. His flaws *belong* to him, like the treasured toys of a spoiled child.

But there is more.

"Jared, I want to know why."

"Just finish me," he says.

"What have I done to you? I don't understand."

"You exist."

"No, Jared, give me a real answer, and for once, be honest. I'm asking, asking one friend to another. We were once friends, give me at least that much."

"Any respect for you is history."

"Why? Tell me."

"You exist." He just stares at me, as if the simple phrase should answer every question in the universe. Then his face tightens to a scowl. "How about arrogant asshole, does that work? Mister Know-it-all, overconfident master who always wins the race, gets the girl and saves the world, and everybody talks about afterward. And you're too proud of it, so sure of yourself, while I'm stuck along for the ride, sick to death of second best one fucking lifetime after another."

Too proud? Too sure? How could there be too much? From a braggart whose only talent is talk, one exaggeration is too much, but if truly capable, how can anyone criticize you for having too much? Is there such a thing as being *too* able?

"Damn you!" he hollers. "You're doing it again. You think what I feel is too simple, ridiculous and infantile, you always have. You have no clue what I feel, or how your existence cancels my own."

"I don't cancel anything. I make things."

"The only thing you make for me is misery, getting in the way of *what I want.*"

"What happens to you has nothing to do with me."

"It has everything to do with it. Everything you do I can never measure up to."

"That's crap, Jared, and you know it."

"There you are doing it again, right here, right now. But this time it won't work. This time I win."

He is jealous, despising me for my abilities, which he actually believes exceed his own, and it's the root of his madness. He's right about one thing, I do think his feelings are ridiculous and infantile. It's stupid. I'm no better than him, or anyone else. He can do anything I can do. If he can't, that's not my fault, and it's not my problem. If others lag, that's their choice. Excel, their choice as well. I welcome it. Exceed me all you please, I won't get in the way.

The trick is whether or not to show your ability. But it would be pointless to let ability lie dormant. Except when others see it, you're labeled arrogant, self-centered and egotistic, your splendid reward for putting talent to use. But those labels are conjured by the minds assigning them. You're only as arrogant as the person judging you is insecure.

It all changes me. Fighting him and winning becomes so thin. It doesn't matter so much, not anymore, this contest between him and me. But I cannot ignore what he has done to this planet.

I sheathe my sword. "You're telling them the truth."

"They wouldn't know the truth if it fell from the sky. Neither would you."

"What truth? How you betrayed us?" My sword is out again and back to his chest. "What about that truth? You were there, before the Association captured us, I remember. That's right, Adam remembers."

"Then you remember I fought the same as you."

"*Liar!* They knew everything, when and where. You told them. You made a deal. For what? What is worth betraying your own?"

He bravely palms my blade and pushes it out of the way. "Is that what you think? That I get something from *them?*" He sits up and laughs. "I don't care about their stupid conquest. Let the idiots have the galaxy, make it however they please. But their latest scheme..." His slimy grin returns. "I must say, the fools might actually be getting clever. And for me, a galaxy without *you*." His madman gaze flashes delight.

More psychotic drivel leading me down another dead-end, to the failing end of the goal I've set—fix this mess! *His* mess, and he's going to fix it.

"You're telling them the truth." I sheathe my sword and reach for his collar.

He slaps my hand away. "Never."

"Aw, come on, Jared, you know you want to. Just think how surprised they'll be."

I don't know where the words came from, or the playful tone. What is happening? Hovering over him, this experience is incredibly strange. Like I'm playing with a friend, except he's the enemy, yet our struggle is just a lighthearted game. In a twisted mess of emotion, I'm having fun, but at the same time, running for my life.

His rage melts and he actually becomes sincere. "Will you stop doing this to me?"

"Doing what! What have I done? Make you stop playing god?"

"Yeah," he says. "It's none of your business."

"You have no business lording over anyone."

"Just because you don't approve of something doesn't give you the right to take it away from others."

"*What is wrong with you!* It wasn't yours to have in the first place."

All contempt for him returns. From a darkness deep inside, the past erupts to fuel this fury, excavate the depths of me, and unbury a memory left for dead. Our history has awakened, and it wants back into reality. Looking down at him, hearing his words, that cocky tone…

This has happened before.

We traveled to many worlds, visiting to help, bringing the inhabitants better technology, better ways of life. We were a team. It was our job. But he abused the responsibility and instead played god. Many times, and I had to relieve him of duty. He's not suitable for leadership, too addicted to power and control. He becomes a tyrant and oppresses people rather than helping them. I had to stop him, for their sake. And I have to stop him again, and again.

"This game of yours ends right here."

He stands. "That's not for you to decide, and these creatures don't know the difference anyway. It's their own fault they're stupid."

"They wouldn't be if you'd help them instead of screwing with their lives."

"No, Adam, you are *wrong!* They will never be like us, *never!* They're incapable of becoming gods, they even say it themselves."

"Gods?" My entire body goes slack. "Jared, you are not a god. Neither one of us is anything near a god."

"Deny what you are, Adam, that's your business, but not me, I am a god."

This is too much. It's all gone to his head—again. It may not be my place, but someone has to end this delusion. The universe does not deserve any more abuse from this insane mind.

✳

Time is a lie. An endless stream connects one moment to the next and makes an invariable line, but a stronger connection—an identical past and present—negates all that lies between. I was just here. Lifetimes ago, but it feels like only minutes. As if skipping a billion unrelated moments, all the other places, after all my journeys, here I am again.

But it is wrong to think that any moments between are gone. They still exist, or existed. They're just not meaningful to this moment, which alone belongs to me and Jared.

He is the lie. Our past has no bearing on any of this. Only in one respect—to ensure this moment never happens again.

"You're coming with me." I latch hold and haul him across the room. He says nothing, though does perform quite an act of squirming like a spoiled brat. I call to the delegates, "Back in your seats." They hurry to the table and drop in place, foe facing foe, all because of this one asshole. I slam Jared into a chair at the end of the table. "Now tell them the truth."

He pretends to be puzzled. "Tell them what?" His grin begins to grow. "How it feels? You know, those penetrating thrusts. All the tighter when she squirms, every inch against her will."

The bastard *never stops!*

"Yeah," he says, "where is Chris, anyway?"

That sickening gloating grin, he's doing it again, mountains of salt poured over a thousand wounds. I can't let him under my skin.

Christina's fate is hers, I can't change that. Nor can I allow his ploy to dissuade me from the monumental task with which I am charged. The fabricated beliefs infecting this world must end, and the deception only ends when he—their Mighty One—admits that *he is not a god.*

"Tell the truth!"

"Or what?" he says. "You'll kill me? Big deal, I'll be back."

I whirl the chair around and him with it, to stare him straight in the eye, into whatever scrap of soul might be hiding in there. "I'll do more than kill you."

"Oh? What do you got now?"

Fury bleeds, I am drained of it.

"I have a picture."

His face goes white. So he knows about my picture trick. Jared reveals something he has hidden well before this moment—fear.

A vision forms…

It is night. Not too cold, some high clouds, a light breeze. But something is happening. A tangle of malformed metal surrounds me. A crash? I don't know. I'm here, or… there, but I'm not… when? Smoke, some sparks, and I can't move. Something heavy is pinning my leg. I'm bleeding, but I'm not afraid. I am certain of something, but of what, I cannot say.

Someone is near. He scavenges through a heap of metal and selects a suitable remnant.

What am I witnessing?

I'm going to die, but with it is my release.

Back in reality, Jared asks, "What are you doing?"

His voice is clear, but he does not fall under my gaze. There is only the picture, the event, the other world. Someone holds a shard of metal splintered to a sharp point, and he is drawing near.

I'm about to die, but somehow, I'm not going to die. Not all of me, only a part of me.

"Stop!" Jared cries. "You can't do that. That's against the rules."

The daydream slips from view and I see him, the real Jared. His eyes are moist with tears. I have the power to hurt him and he knows it. The power of this one thought.

Reality is shoved out of view, and the vision becomes all there is to see. I am in the night, pinned and bloody, watching the bringer of death stand over me. He raises the splintered shard.

I... I am... I am the bringer of death standing over me—I hold the deadly shard.

"*No!*" Jared screams.

Ghostly echoes seep into the vision. Someone is talking. The voice is mine. But the words are distant, as though the phrase dances across a sheet of paper rattled by strong wind. I strain to recite the same. "I will... decide... what will be."

"You'll be *DEAD!*"

Sharp steel crosses my belly.

Not in the vision—in reality.

✳

Jared holds an Ophidian sword streaked with my blood. He has sliced across my belly and opened me wide. I slap one hand to the wound, the other after my only defense.

Our blades crash.

KHRIINGGG!

I stagger back and dodge his attack.

Jared calls to the delegates, "Do you see? Adam bleeds! He is no god."

Existence slows to a crawl as the rubber band stretches out again. Jared heaves his sword and I respond with snaps of accelerated time that launch my blade at his. Slow, fast, slow then fast, our contest languishes and spurts in pulsating beats of demented tempo. His efforts are frantic, but still his pace lags behind mine.

But weakness comes, and the motion of all things beyond me is increasing. I am losing grasp of time. His blows become more frequent, the effort to parry greater, and the flow of blood heavier.

I choose not to fight, rather allow existence whatever time it chooses. No more stretching. I fall to my knees and let my wound bleed, then wrap both hands around the hilt and bring the sword upright before me. The gleaming steel glows pale blue, and jittering arcs dance across the blade, glowing brighter, blue nearing white. I invite the sword and all of existence to join me, in unity, a whole. I close my eyes and become this realm.

Ripples in a sea of air are my ally, carrying the subtle hint of Jared's swooping blade. At peace in my darkness, I sense it, know it, and can see it.

I whisper for only myself, "In the center is the now."

My eyes snap open and lock onto his weapon, its color, shape, temperature and weight, every detail at a single point in time and no other—this instant. Our blades meet but there is no clash of metal, no thunder, no screeching. No sound at all, only brilliant white light.

The flash clears. Flung overhead, half a blade tumbles end over end as it soars across the room, then clanks on the floor and slides across.

Jared holds half a sword.

He raises his truncated blade, aiming to clobber me.

Faint whistling parts the air, coming fast.

THHHWUP!

Jared loses his breath in one silent gasp, then gropes at his back.

Beyond Jared, Christina has returned, armed with daggers. This time I'm keeping my mouth shut.

Another whistling, another *THHHWUP*.

Jared finds his voice and howls. He whirls around to face her. Two Felidian daggers are lodged in the meaty portion of his upper back.

Christina holds another weapon—Lord Ornery's sickle. And one last dagger.

Jared pulls the daggers from his back and starts for her.

THHHWUP. The final dagger lands in his thigh.

"You *bitch!*" He yanks the blade from his flesh. Waving his blunt sword, he advances.

She spreads her stance, clutching the sickle firmly in both hands, crescent blade gleaming sharp. "I'll show you what kind of bitch I am."

Jared lunges and swipes. She sidesteps and his blunt weapon sails through her wake. In a flash, her sickle hooks Jared in the kidney and she yanks hard, sending him to the floor face down. Another blinding streak, she opens a gash across the back of his thigh, splattering her gown with blood.

He cries out and rolls over, swinging his blunt sword.

Another blur of her sickle, the sword flies overhead and hits the floor, followed by his severed hand, fingers twitching.

Jared extends his remaining hand in defense.

A flash and the sickle crosses his wrist.

He squirms on the floor with handless stumps close to his chest. She straddles him, her knees in the bloody pool, and red chases up the fabric of her gown. She wrestles his buckle loose. "You're getting off for the last time." She seizes the whole of his genitals, squeezed tight in one hand.

"No!" he begs, then furious, "You bitch! *No!*"

Her ponytail snaps like a whip as she works, hacking, sawing at severed cords, veins that pop and gurgle, and torn stringy vines of bloody meat are ripped from his groin. She rises, sickle in one hand, a dripping mound of flesh hanging from the other. She stands victorious, bathed in the blood of her vanquished.

She pitches the mess to splatter on the floor. She straddles his waist and puts the point of her crescent blade to his chest. Leaning over him like she might kiss his bloody lips, she says to him, "You will never hurt me again." With her hands stacked atop the sickle, she presses down with all her weight, driving the blade into his heart.

He gurgles and spits blood, his gaze loose and fading.

She leans further, driving the blade deeper, and brushes her lips across his. She rises to stand, her mouth painted with blood, a shade she never wears.

She realizes me watching. "Adam, you're hurt." She hurries to me. With her hand to my belly, she tries holding me together. "You'll be okay."

"Don't lie."

Jared pushes words past blood gurgling in his throat. "We're all dead anyway." His head flops to one side, his jeering eyes gunning for us. "Especially you two." He slips on a lunatic grin. "Dead forever."

He knows something—one last secret. I stagger to his side and drop to my knees. "How is everyone dead? Tell me."

He grins up at the ceiling, coughs blood, and manages to say, "I beat you this time."

"How have you beaten me? You're dying."

His eyes dart to mine. "So are you, Adam."

I peel back the hand holding in my belly. So little left of me.

"And this time," he says, choking on blood and straining to finish, "you're in a trap. A trap not even you can escape."

Trap? I scan the room. What will harm us?

Portals circling the room show a sunny day outside, clear pink sky.

Oh no. The remotes, the console. The clock, counting down.

The sword is my crutch. I force this body up and start for the exit.

"What is it, Adam?" Christina follows me into the corridor.

So badly I want to tell her a lie. A sweet, pleasant lie, that we live happily ever after.

✳

Past the shrine's great doors, I stagger down the steps and off, to the wind-blown sand. Christina hurries down and stands at my side, her gaze fixed on the sky, eyes welling tears that won't fall.

Black missiles leave trails of smoke as they rise to the heavens. The day has come, when the gods release the spears and wrath rains down. There is no time, no escape, nowhere to run. Sadness drains me of what little strength remains, but the sadness extends far beyond my own death. The Felidians, the Ophidians, their world, their way of life, countless artisans, minstrels and basket-weavers, bladesmiths and stone cutters, children with wooden swords, others flicking pebbles to knock one from a circle. The wise and aging in shady parks, contemplating their next move, dancing cat and snake ladies, everyone. Today their war ends, and with it, any hint that they ever existed.

Moments before death, every thought leaves a deep scar. I vow to never forget this world, nor ever forget this event. I vow to remember these creatures and their planet so they may live on in the stories I tell of them someday. There exists no power within me strong enough to change this, but I can always remember it. Forever.

Christina takes my hand in hers. "Adam, don't forget who you are, promise me."

"I promise."

"Go to Idan," she says. "To the garden, I will be there." She squeezes my hand.

Looking down at our clasped hands, I make another vow. Our embrace of hands will survive. It will be the clue, the message, how we will know. In only moments, we face unimaginable pain and loss. But we can remember. The memory of our bond protects us. Together, hand in hand, we can conquer anything. Apart, we are lost.

Physuro comes down the last step to join us. He stares into the sky. "I might ask the question again, though I fear the answer be evident." He is oddly calm. Or he doesn't realize what this means.

"What question?" I ask.

He is silent a moment, staring into the sky. Then he looks at me, and for the first time I've seen from any cat, his eyes are moist with tears.

"Be this the place we will die?"

Today, the question weighs all the dread in the universe.

"I'm sorry, Physuro. I don't have the power to change this. I'm so sorry, it's true. This is the place, and yes, we're going to die."

His gaze returns to the sky. "As it shall be."

Together we watch the missiles soar higher and spread out. Our deadly reaper has many fingers.

"Before I go," he says, watching the sky, "I wish to thank you for all you have taught me, and for your efforts to save our kind. You be the greatest god I have ever known, Adam of Idan."

This is not fair.

"I be not afraid," he says. "I shall exist another day, and hope to look upon you then."

"Thank you, Physuro, for all you have done. You will always be my friend, and know this—you will live forever in my memory."

"As you in mine." He strains to smile, without much success.

A low hum creeps into my senses. The sword glows pale blue. I raise the weapon, and jittering arcs dance across the blade. A true friend this weapon has been, another to which I must say good-bye. Nothing joins me where

I'm headed. "And thank you, my fine friend." The blade glows brighter. I plant the sword upright in the sand and leave it where it stands.

I gather a sense of the Ophidian who toiled over the weapon and crafted the finest instrument I have ever wielded. Strangely, as though ghosts ride the wind, the craftsman weeps through his invention. As if the blade has a soul, and memory of its creator, who drowns in the sorrow of his world's end.

Countless missiles fan out across the sky. Some vanish past the horizon. More than enough to ensure total annihilation. Everything dead, even the planet.

The Spears of the Gods reach apex, then begin their descent from the heavens. Some distance above the ground, the first ignites in a blinding flash, then another, another in quick succession, each a star exploding in silence.

Only seconds remain.

"Christina. I love you, forever."

"Adam, focus on one thought, *see* it—the garden. Promise me you'll be there." She squeezes my hand tighter.

"I promise."

We are blasted by a silent hurricane of scorched air moving faster than sound, faster than flame, a solid wall of pure heat. In the final glimpse from eyes of a body, our hands are clenched tight, and our skin is ripped from the bone. For an instant, our skeleton hands embrace, then burst to dust on the nuclear wind.

There was no time to feel the physical pain, it happened so fast. I don't even feel knocked over, rather like I'm still standing here, surrounded by a storm of fire and noise. But emotionally the experience hurts more than any pain I could ever dream. Instant loss of a body, sickening absence of all things, no means to touch anything. All capacity for physical sensation was so quickly destroyed that I am only knocked senseless, wanting to cry, but I can't even have tears.

My body is gone. Christina is gone. Physuro is gone, and every other anything that could ever mark our having been here. Except for one last image.

Alone in a desert on fire, the broadsword stands upright in the sand. A witness to this violent event, yet somehow, with a strength to survive being destroyed by it.

I exist here as nothing, a lone viewpoint watching the glow fade from the sword while a firestorm screams across the desert. There is nothing to follow, not even ashes. Any hint of who I am is gone. I am utterly alone, completely lost, with nowhere to go.

I am dead. For real this time.

5

I AM IN SPACE. OUTER SPACE. COUNTLESS POINTS OF STARLIGHT dot the blackness. This might be pleasant, every concern abandoned, there is nothing I must do. But I've lost something.

One star is not so distant. Light from the flaming yellow orb brightens a planet aloft in blackness, a marble colored pink, rust and green, oceans aquamarine. Beautiful to behold, but something is wrong. A gray veil thickens, churning black at the billowing edges. Flames wash over the globe and reach around to swallow it whole.

Bodiless others are near, at random points in outer space. Millions of them, looking down at the dying world. They are nothing to see, but I know they are here. Each radiates a certain warmth, that unmistakable warmth when others are near. It tells me their sadness. I can feel their sorrow.

Something begins to pull on the others. They are sucked away, one after another, thousands, millions of them, vacuumed toward a point closer to the sun.

Flames circle the planet and meet, smothering the globe. For a time the inferno puts out the light of a weak star, but soon all fuel is expended and the torch dies. Sparse glowing cinders dot the ashen remains, then weaken and shrink to pinpoints that join the starlight background. The points diminish, all but the final extinguish. One flickering speck is the last voice to cry out, then go dark. The planet fades to a blackness blacker than the void in which it hangs.

I promised to remember. I may not be able to.

Everyone is gone. I can't touch anything or choose any place to rest. I have no anchor, no feet on which to stand, legs to walk, no arms to reach out. Without a body, there is no one to join me, and no one for me to join. Nothing. I could be this way forever.

Everlasting loneliness.

A pulsing light catches my attention, coming from a dark planet closer to the sun. A beacon of intense blue white.

I drift closer.

Something about me is falling away, erasing any notion of identity or reason. Another planet passes, a blue marble with white swirls, but it lacks the lure of pulsing light.

A force tugs on me—the vacuum that sucked the others away. I cannot escape, but it's okay. I fall closer to the sun, toward the dark planet and its flashing beacon.

The planet is shrouded in dense atmosphere. A dazzling beam punches through the clouds, reaches into space to find me, and brings me home. I drift down, into the luminous tunnel, and fall into the light.

Jets of bright color stream past and spiral into a gently spinning vortex. My journey slows and the tunnel opens to a space without any real borders, a kind of bright fogbank. Pulses of light flash randomly, more so at one end where the beam splits into thin rays that spin and jerk, change direction, and then whirl back around the other way. High strings make a soothing melody throughout the mist. Is that a harp? Joined by a faint tenor chorus. There is a warm scent, fresh baked cookies, or pie, something sweet.

A vaporous walkway leads to the light. I am walking the path—in a body. Not an actual body. An unreal semblance of myself, translucent and glowing pale blue, like a ghost.

Something zigzags through the mist, darting about like bees. They are chubby winged infants, a dozen or so. They fly past and swing around to pace my advance toward the light, as if guiding me along. They giggle, childish and playful, but something about them is oddly wise. Their beady eyes are solid black, tracking every step I take. Suddenly, they scatter and vanish.

Ahead is a crowd, an outline of silhouettes standing before a dazzling light farther beyond. They wave for me to join them. As I draw closer, their faces become clear. They look familiar, but what are their names? I know these people, friends, colleagues, some I've lived with before, or met at least once. But I can't recall a single name. Some reach out and welcome me to this place. They are all smiling, overjoyed to see me, but something isn't right. The people and their smiles, it all feels fake, somehow forced.

Someone pushes through the crowd. Strong backlight brightens sheer fabric that blends with mist at her feet. A soft breeze stirs the glowing shroud, and details emerge. She wears a crown of slender braided vines, imbued with petite blossoms.

Wherever I am, whatever has happened, all is well in her presence. I would give up any existence without her to have any other with her.

"Christina, are you okay?"

She takes my hand in hers. "Here," she says, "everyone is okay." She squeezes my translucent hand. The embrace feels unreal, only a reminder of how pleasant the actual touch could be. We are a pair of nothings, pretending to have bodies, when really, all we have are thoughts of the other. We're both dead.

She smiles, all is well, and she pulls me along. As if real, the tug has effect, drawing me across the clouds and past the crowd. Their gazes beam admiration and approval, pleased by the sight of two lovers reunited.

From a single point ahead, thin rays shoot out and dance wildly. A disturbing sight, as if marching into battle, yet I'm compelled to enter the passage beyond. I am not afraid. Should I be? I don't know, only that I am not. Something feels right about this place. Somewhere I belong.

We enter the light. Bathed in it, our unreal bodies transform into luminous beings walking hand in hand across the clouds. The light has no source, it just *is,* and it is everywhere.

The brilliance mellows to a glowing mist, comfortable white in all directions. There is a trickling brook, and a rock garden that surrounds a stone fountain. Bubbling up from the center and rippling down to fill an ornate bowl, the crisp water looks absolutely delicious.

"Drink," she says, "and live forever." She cups her hands to collect some of the water, then offers me a taste.

I ease back. "I don't know."

"Have all you've ever dreamt," she says. "Drink, and you will be young."

A child at last. Could it be true?

She raises her cupped hands higher.

I withdraw.

She angles her wrists as if serving someone the water. I have shifted away, but even so, an invisible someone laps up the liquid until her palms are dry.

One instant her cupped hands are reaching out, and the next we're hand in hand, like we skipped a frame. She smiles, all is well, and she pulls me along. A light breeze comes on, enough to unfurl a patch of clouds. The mist parts.

A dark red chair with square armrests.

I halt.

"Sit down," she says.

I free my hand from hers. "Are you sure?"

She coaxes me into the cushioned seat. "Relax." She beams a wonderful smile—the best smile ever—like every smile she has ever given me, compressed into a single moment.

"Where are we?" I ask.

"Heaven," she says. "Where we will live happily ever after."

This can't be heaven. Besides, Christina would never say that. We've talked about this. Heaven isn't good, it's a trick, she knows that. Or does she? A jolt strikes what would be a heart, if this glowing semblance of a body were flesh and blood.

Then I realize, "You're not Christina."

"Of course it's me," she says. "Don't worry, everything will be okay. We made it to Heaven."

"No, this is not okay. Heaven is bad."

"Relax, and watch the pretty pictures." She turns to leave.

"Wait," I cry. "Tell me the three magic words, the special way."

She turns back. "You know I love you, and I always will. You're the best."

I search her eyes for the unforgettable tender blue. Her gaze is hollow.

"You're not Christina. You're a memory of her."

She kneels beside the chair. "We have no need for memories now, that's all in the past." She reaches out to pamper my cheek. "We're in Heaven, together forever, all that matters." She rises. "Now stop fussing, and relax. Watch the pretty pictures."

Beyond her, an image forms on the cloudy background. A lush forest, babbling brook, and the scent of pine needles. The picture is pretty, I remember. The image is more than a picture. I'm *in* the scene. It happened, it's happening now. Another image appears, also familiar. Endless wildflowers over rolling hills, stalks rustled by a breeze, and sunshine warms my skin. I'm there again.

I know this—thought sensitive screens. Think apple, the image appears. In an orchard. No, on a beach. Apple on sand. No, too sandy. Apple on a wooden table, divided into eight equal portions, alternating red and green. Not cut apart, just alternating color, not even possible but that doesn't stop me from seeing it. Take a bite. The red is delicious and the green is sour. We see an apple striped red and green, missing one bite.

The chair is turning.

I look to Christina.

"Don't look at me," she says. "Look at the pretty pictures."

I leap out of the chair and swing around to face her, it, whatever that thing is. The only certainty—that is *not* Christina.

"Those are memories." I point to the images lining up on the mist. "You're extracting them from me. How? Who's doing this?"

She reaches a hand to my shoulder. "Sit, and relax."

I squirm free. "No. I'm dead, you're dead, all of this is about dead, and making sure I'm more than dead."

Her hollow eyes retreat into dark sockets. "As you wish."

My semblance of a body becomes mortal—solid, heavy, and sluggish. A weathered old man, coat of flesh hanging from frail bones, standing at the edge of death. The apparition of Christina transforms into an exhumed corpse, clumps of soil pasted to decaying skin crawling with maggots clinging to ragged remnants of half-eaten hair. The neck creaks, the blackened skull tips back, and it emits a howling cackle from a jaw hanging by stringy decomposed tendons.

I stagger back.

The rotting version of Christina plants its bony fingers in my shoulder and needles my aging hide. "*Sit and watch!*"

"Let go!" I seize the skeletal forearm only to pluck it from the decaying torso.

The ghoul slaps its other hand around my neck and yanks me off my feet. "Oh no," it says, "I'll never let go. I *love* you." Its putrid lips twist to a sinister grin and the monster slams me down in the chair. Shackles snap over my wrists and ankles. "Sit and *watch!* This is for your own good."

The chair turns and the pictures resume. The speed increases, images fly past, but they are no longer pretty. Evil people are harming others. Why can't this be a dream? Why can't I wake up? But where would I wake? Maybe under a bridge, next to a bum asking for change.

Memory wipe—I remember the process. Overwhelm the mind. Too much. And something else, a secret so bad I never want to see it again. Something with the power to destroy consciousness.

The chair spins faster and countless images press for my attention. Don't watch. *Don't watch!* This is a trap. This is not real. My thoughts make this. If I fear, I make fear. Doubt creates doubt. It's all in my mind, and someone's plugged in.

What did Christina say? The *real* Christina. I remember her, I'll always remember. Before the blast, her hand in mine, she told me what to do. Focus on something.

I held her hand, skin so soft, warm…

Focus on what? One thought—the garden. I promised.

✳

Tracers of starlight stretch across the galaxy, streaming past as my velocity exceeds all measure. Then streaking slower, the pinpoints sharpen, and a fixed star-field blankets the cosmos. I'm looking at a planet cradled in a pink bubble.

Idan.

In the span of a single thought, I am home.

Unhindered by any force, I swoop down as a cosmic bird, diving into the clouds and slicing through the warm, sunny day. Rocky cliffs soar past, the ocean roars, and waves wash over white sands. Farther inland, I glide over a thriving wilderness, then a towering forest.

In the next instant I am there—here, hovering over the bodies, males and females in various colors, shapes and sizes. I could spend all day just watching them. Floating free above the bodies, I remember having to make this choice before. Odd to forget and be put in this position again. A thrill, but something about it can be frightening. What if I choose the wrong one? I'll be trapped until it says no more. I must be careful.

I want a male body, that much is certain. Potential units wander the woods. A few forage in bushes for something to eat. During my last visit, it seemed there were more to choose from. It doesn't matter, two or two hundred, only one is chosen to partner with this one mind. But still—blond, brown, or darker hair? Are facial features important? What is better? I'm just not any good judge of that. One is a bit plump, not so bad, but we'll have to pass, though I don't care to pose as any twig, either. Something moderate, then again, a few extra muscles might come in handy. Too many there, looks like a mutant. Tall? Short? Somewhere in between. I just don't know.

That one.

Why? I don't know why.

Sure I do. She'll like that one, I know her.

And weird—that looks like me down there.

There is no time, it just happens. The entry is like slamming into a brick wall, fully intent on *becoming* that brick wall. Hard to say who's more upset about this, me or my new body. It convulses, wanting to throw me out, then I am—I mean, me and this body—we're vomiting. It hurts and tastes awful. I don't want to be here feeling this, and the body doesn't want me any more than I care for its pain, but it must happen. I can't just float around watching everything. And the body, it needs me too, or it does what? Wander the woods without purpose? Relax, body, this is okay. Trust me, I won't hurt you.

Doubled over, the body clears its mouth—our mouth—of remnant vomit slime. We're together, a team. Calmer, we straighten up, body and me becoming one, then I realize another body is standing next to us.

My eyes won't work right. It feels like they're covered with goo I must blink away over and over, but it doesn't help, everything is still blurry. And these limbs are heavy and uncooperative. I need to speak with someone about the warranty on this unit. I spend a moment adjusting and quickly recall—bodies are always this way at first.

Finally, I get the hang of these new eyes and focus improves. A naked female is standing next to me.

"What took so long?" she asks.

"Foo? Ma? Mook wong?"

She speaks firm and clearly. "Easy, Adam, be patient. Think slowly and let your body catch up. It's not used to talking."

"Mokay. Mall bate."

She takes my hand in hers. *Ouch!* I pull free and stagger back.

"What's wrong?" she asks.

"My bont throw. Dat harts." I shake the crushed hand to show what I mean.

She studies my hand, which looks fine and now feels fine, but damn, that felt like a vise. She seems to understand, and she nods. Or maybe not.

She reaches out, intent on wrapping her arms around me.

"Don't!" I stumble back, out of reach. "Don't touch me."

"What's the matter with you?"

"This isn't me! Not yet."

I'm not sure who me is after all this.

"I'm sorry," she says. "I don't mean to upset you. It's okay, just relax."

"Don't say *that*."

"Say what?"

"Next you'll tell me to sit and watch."

I tear off into the woods, not bothering to look back and catch her reaction. I'm in no mood to find out. Might be a pissed off, rotting corpse.

✳

As I run through the woods, every muscle screams, defiant of my wish that we run to safety, if any such thing exists in this disorienting new reality. I stop to catch my breath. A puffing locomotive, that's what I've taken for a body.

This is strange, like a dream. I am here, or this body is here, but it's not my body. But it is my body. The contraption responds to every command. Except I was somewhere else before all this. Or I am somewhere else, asleep, and this is a dream. No, I am here, in a new body. But its limbs are like rocks. This couldn't be a dream. Everything hurts too much.

A twig snaps in the quiet.

I whirl around.

Christina steps lightly, creeping closer. Persistent little creature.

"That's close enough," I tell her.

"What's wrong with you?"

"It's been a while, okay? I'm not used to this."

"It's just a body," she says like we do this every day. Her grin is sly. "A body mine wants to touch."

"This body?" A body that happens to be completely naked.

She nods slowly and smiles while surveying all that she craves.

"Or me?" I ask.

She looks me in the eye. "Both."

That's better, I think. But still, this is weird. I ease nearer and scrutinize her face. Her skin is fresh, untarnished and silky. Nose a bit thinner but always perky, lips fuller, and perfect teeth. She really does look like her. Especially her mannerisms, a perfect match to memories of her. But that's the whole problem—is she just a product of my memory?

"Is it really you?" I ask.

"Of course, you goof. Look for yourself." She opens her eyes wide.

Tender blue no one could forge. It is her.

"Okay," I say, "you can touch. But just a hand for now."

She slinks closer, giving me a devilish grin, then a familiar trying-to-be-innocent bite of her lip. She reaches out and takes my hand. That doesn't hurt so bad, not this time. Actually, it feels good. The pressure is firm—real—and her skin is soft and warm.

Our simple embrace. Hand in hand we died, and back together, hand in hand, we live again. The circle is complete. Death to nothing, Heaven to Hell, nothing to alive. I did it. *We* did it.

In an instant, everything gets a lot more real. The forest, whoosh of breeze, sweet air filling these lungs, trickling creek and the sound of others moving about the woods.

I died. Incredible to stand here and imagine that. But it's true. I made it home to Christina, the *real* Christina. We're on Idan, at the body farm. Now I'm curious about the new body I've chosen. Ample muscles, nothing outrageous, more lean than flabby, but not a twig. Dark hair falls to my shoulders. Soft whiskers cover my jaw. Not much hair on my chest and arms, I like that. What I'd really like is a mirror.

"Christina, do I look like me?"

Her eyes are hungry. "If I say yes, will you stop being a freak and let me touch you?"

"I'm a what?"

She takes hold of my hand and tugs, then slides her arm around my waist and pulls me near. Her lips begin a detailed exploration of my neck. The sudden change of events produces a sudden change in thinking. Yes, touch me. Touch all you like. And keep touching.

She reaches fingers around to my back, leaving a tingling trail in the wake of her caresses. My hand follows the splendor of her shoulder, down and off her elbow, seeking her side, flowing down the outward slope of her hip and around to the highest of her behind. I want to smother her sweet flesh, already teasing a tongue moistened by the imagination. Her lips swell with passion, easing nearer to mine. I cannot resist the incredible urge to ravish her this instant and forevermore.

But she—

I free myself from her charms. "Now hold on. What about you?"

"What about me?" she asks.

"You didn't want me touching you."

Her passion fizzles like flash paper. She turns away and plops down on a mossy log. "Nice job ruining the moment."

"I didn't… I mean…" I sit beside her. "I don't understand."

"That was before," she says.

"What happened to never gets better?"

She looks away. "It doesn't for a body, but it can for me. Maybe, without you reminding me."

"Sorry, it was…"

She twists to face me. "An accident? No, Adam, you wanted this to happen."

I reach for her knee. "Maybe I do. Only because I want to understand."

She brushes my hand away. "So understanding is better than enjoying me."

"I want both, to touch your body and everything you think and feel. But you wouldn't let me."

She stares off at nothing. "I didn't want you touching that body ever again."

"I could tell. But why?"

"It was spoiled," she says. "Dirty and poisoned."

A silence passes while I form a careful response.

"So *you're* okay," I suggest. "Just not the body, the one you had."

"Maybe not all better, but better than before. At least, I don't mind you touching me."

"Now that we died."

"That doesn't sound very nice. But if I have to be honest…"

"You know I hate lies."

"So let me finish," she says. "To be honest, dying is horrible. No one wants to die. But sometimes we do."

"Die? Of course we do."

"Sometimes we *want* to."

"Why would anyone want to die?"

She studies me for a moment. "Think of it this way—you have a big house and decide to throw a party, invite all your friends. Everyone shows up, but you forgot something at the store and have to run out to fetch it. While you're gone, a crazed gunman breaks in and unloads on all your friends, every last one. You come back and there they are, bloody and dead, right where they sit."

"Must you be so morbid?"

"Think about it. Could you keep living in the same house?"

More difficult would be living with myself after inviting all my friends to their death.

"Well?" she asks. "Could you?"

"No," I admit. "I'd have to find another."

"Another that lets you touch me. *Wants* you touching me."

She brings a palm to my bare chest, to my heart, beats rising.

I look down at her touch. "So this is okay?" I reach out, and my fingers fondle tiny golden hairs on her forearm. "Really?"

She scoots closer, keeping her hand to my heart. Throbbing in preparation, it knows well what may come of this. Her lips brush against mine—almost a kiss—though pass to reach my ear. Her tongue is warm, warmer is her breath, tingling my neck. This is more arousing than I expected. The soles of my feet begin to sizzle.

In my ear, she whispers, "Touch anything you want."

She does.

No question this new body is male.

I cup one of her breasts, then slide my other hand down her tailbone and lower. Holding the roundness of her bottom, I drive my fingers into her heated flesh.

She blows in my ear.

It's over. All over her.

✳

I stumble over logs, slip on leaves and trip, get up and hurry, trying to catch up with her.

"Come back!" I call. "I said I'm sorry."

She stops to pluck a broadleaf for use as a makeshift towelette. Wiping the mess off her belly, she says, "Nice to know one of us had fun."

I catch up. "This thing just needs a few adjustments."

She looks me up and down. "Start with patience. Looks like you're set to zero, about the speed of most any little boy."

"Ouch!"

"And don't you *dare* say it's a compliment."

I shake my head, no, no, of course not.

"Hi, guys. Everybody okay?"

Christina and I whirl around.

A male unit is standing behind a bush. He is oddly familiar and getting more familiar the more he tests facial expressions, morphing into an unmistakable brand of jackass I couldn't possibly forget.

"Where have you been?" Christina asks.

"I got sidetracked," Dave says, then looks at me. "They must have pissed you off good. You know, I wasn't serious about destroying the entire planet."

"I didn't."

"Oh? Random act of god?"

"Not random, just a wannabe."

"Sidetracked doing what?" Christina asks, then shifts to me. "You too, Adam. What took so long?"

"Sorry, I was—"

Christina gasps, eyes wide.

"What's wrong?" I ask.

One hand covering her mouth, she stares at Dave. He has stepped out from behind the bush and stands naked before us.

He asks, "What are you two gawking at?"

I say, "Look at yourself."

He raises each arm and studies his torso. "What's the big deal?"

"That." Christina points to his crotch.

He looks down at his dangling member, flopping between his thighs as he twists to check every angle. A smile spreads across his face. "Nice."

Christina cringes. "More like *ouch*."

He looks up. "Doesn't hurt my feelings any."

"I wasn't talking about anyone's feelings."

I'm stunned. "Damn, Dave, you really are Penis Man this time around."

"Hurry!" a voice calls. Twigs snap underfoot as someone draws near. "Get dressed." It's Mac, the body farmer. He slices through shrubbery, swatting at drooping branches, and emerges from the forest. He hasn't changed much since I last saw him. Loose overalls that let his tubbiness roam, half-bald with long white strands neatly combed back, and that low beard following the contour of his jaw, like a disk supporting the rest of his head.

Dave says, "Hey, Mac, what's up?"

Mac has no reply, too busy passing out olive-drab tee-shirts and trousers.

I ask, "What's with the army clothes, Mac?"

"You got here just in time," he says.

"Why?" Christina asks. "What's going on?"

The dread in Mac's eyes is frightening, like the world will end any minute. "Terrible trouble." He holds trousers open and urges that I get into them. "Hurry."

"In time for what?" I ask, guiding my legs into the pants.

"For that fine product you've slipped into," he says. "One of the last, in fact. Had you taken any longer to arrive, I'm afraid…"

Dave says, "No more bodies?"

"What happened?" Christina asks.

"Destroyed," Mac says. "All but a handful. They've targeted body farms all across Idan." He looks to the sky. "On the way as we speak. You must go at once."

✳

In minutes we're dressed, back to the farmhouse, and out front where a four-wheel-drive wagon is parked.

Mac tosses keys to Dave. "Hurry. You have little time."

Christina and I pile into the passenger side and Dave starts the engine. I roll the window down. "Hop in back, Mac." I reach around to unlock the rear door.

Beyond the farmhouse, the forest glows orange as the sun drops behind the wooded shroud. Halfway up the steps to the porch, Mac turns around and waves good-bye.

Christina leans toward my open window. "Mac, aren't you joining us?"

"Not this time, my child."

"But Mac," I say. "You said they're on the way."

He comes down the steps and closer to the idling wagon. "Don't worry about me, son, I'll be fine." He smiles, then that jolly laugh, ho ho ho. "You'll see me again, you can be sure, with gifts for all."

✳

Past sundown, Dave pushes the wagon hard. The highway tunnels into darkness, brightened by two beams piercing the night. The broken white line whipping past matches my racing thoughts, pouring out so fast I can't get a hold of any. The Association has attacked? *Our* planet? Tired of toying with us. What happened to global defense? We could face incredible odds.

I've traveled an immense distance to return home, in a matter of no time. From one instant to the next. Now partnered with a body again, watching the highway slip past, the sluggish pace of physical travel shaves hours from a life counting down.

This morning feels like ages ago. A lifetime ago, and it was. Was that really this morning? On another planet in an entirely different system, can you really call it the same day? Whenever it was, I was there, the morning after a sleepless night with a mind tied in knots, and breakfast inhaled so fast it made a stomach to match. Hurry to reach something you dread, get to the other side, knock me out and wake me up when it's over. Looks like I got my wish. But I didn't expect any of this on the other side.

Christina asks Dave, "What took so long getting here?" She shifts to me. "You too, Adam. I was worried."

"Nothing I enjoyed," I say.

"I wasn't dead yet," Dave says, focused on the road ahead. "And it wasn't exactly fun knowing I would be."

"You got nuked?" I ask.

"Hell no. Got my ass out of there."

"And left us behind," Christina says.

"Gimme a break. Like I could pick off a thousand warheads with one blast cannon."

"Where did you go?" I ask.

"Out in space until I ran out of fuel. Then air. Thought I might make it to Sol-5, except it wasn't there."

"Aster?" I ask.

Christina says, "Trying to save your own skin."

"What's the harm in trying?" Dave says. "I suppose you make a habit of just giving up."

"You could have at least *tried* to save us."

"Never would have worked, wasn't enough time. Besides, it didn't work anyway, so it doesn't matter. So just get over it and stop nagging me."

"Forget all that," I tell them, then ask Dave, "What happened to Aster?"

His puzzled gaze turns to me. "Aster?"

"What they call Sol-5." Then I remember. "Or, what they used to, before…"

"Blown to bits," he says. "A bunch of rocks where a planet used to be."

"Destroyed?" I hope that one's not my fault.

"Maybe a few chunks left big enough to land on. Not that it matters. Nothing mass enough to hold any atmosphere."

Sol-4 destroyed, now Sol-5. Two planets gone, only Sol-3 remains. Dave's hunch turned out to be true, but what an awful thing to be right about. Our friends have nowhere else to go, not even hope that other worlds exist. Look out in space, what do you see? Dead rocks.

Staring out at the road ahead, Dave says, "Man, that sucks."

"Sucks for Marsea, too. Still in one piece, but just as short on atmosphere."

"No, not that." He glances at me, then back to the road. "My last body. Just think, stuck in that can, preserved in the vacuum of space, round and round with all those rocks. It could be there forever."

"So? You're done with it."

His eyes get big. "Dude, that's bad luck. Someone could find it and use it on me later. You know, a doll body control thing. They do that, you know."

"Dolls? That's ridiculous."

"Oh no," he says. "One eyeball floating in a jar…"

"That no one looks through anymore."

Then it hits me. I almost had a glimpse, not so much looking out, rather seeing the jar on a shelf next to other body parts floating in syrupy liquids. Creepy. What pieces of me have I left behind? Death by nuclear holocaust has its advantages.

Dave slams on the brakes, tires squeal, and the wagon skids to the side.

We're jostled hard over gravel, off the road, and down the shoulder. Dave kills the engine and lights.

"What's wrong?" I ask.

"Shhh." He hunches down.

Christina and I slouch lower in the seat.

"What is it?" she asks.

"Quiet," he says. "They're coming."

"How do you know?" I ask.

"Lights on the horizon." He waves a finger at the windshield. "Keep quiet and don't move."

Silent and still, we sit parked along the highway in darkness. Running lights of an airship zoom toward us. An Association battle cruiser. The massive vessel passes overhead, churns up a turbulent wake, and the wagon shudders on its wheels.

I twist around to watch out the back window. The craft hovers in the distance, over the body farm we left behind. I hope you're gone, Mac, along with any bodies you could manage to save.

Scorching beams rain down, so intense the shockwave is felt even at this distance. A glowing orange mushroom cloud boils upward, then fiery cinders drift down and fizzle in dissipating smoke. The craft shifts position, spotlights tracking across the forest. The enemy admires their work and checks for any chores left undone. Satisfied, the craft climbs higher and soars off into the night.

Like me, Dave and Christina are speechless. There is nothing we can do. Wind sweeps away the last traces of battle, the orange glow fades, and the distant forest returns to darkness.

We must care well for the bodies we now occupy. In a flash, they have become infinitely precious. To die now means our struggle is lost and we are truly dead forever.

✳

Dave punches the throttle and gravel flies. Back on the road, the whine of tires drones on. Our headlights brighten deserted lanes of highway, and beyond their reach is nothing, a black unknown. The long road home may end the same—nothing left of a home. Until we arrive, for all we know, we could be the only survivors. I'm yanked back to that sickening moment,

Marsea in flames and everyone sucked away, all the bodiless others and their certain warmth, the only hint that anyone was near. Millions of them, vacuumed up and gone, leaving me utterly alone.

I wonder about Dave and Christina. Did they go to the light as well? I describe the flashing beacon and entrance to the misty afterworld, then little angels watching and people waiting to greet me, and the warm scent and soothing melody.

"Sounds like a dream," Christina says.

Dave says, "I didn't go to any light."

Or did they? And having suffered the process, they don't remember. But the time doesn't add up—Christina arrived before us. However, any trap capable of reflecting memory could also drop time, re-sequence events, and mislabel hours, months, or even years.

"When you first saw the light," Christina says, "what were you feeling?"

"Then?" I review the memory. "Scared. I was dead."

"Scared of what?" she asks. "Be precise. This is important."

Emblazoned by the wash of headlights, the broken white line streaks past, a mind-numbing pulse of hypnotic flashes.

"Being alone forever."

"You're not completely healed, Adam. Loneliness is artificial, programmed. They've done something to you, last time, and it's still with you."

"It sure felt real. Like an abandoned child, abandoned for an eternity with no end that never began and wouldn't begin or end ever again. Staring into a bottomless pit called forever—alone forever."

She takes my hand in hers. "More from last time. They had you programmed for this. They're good at what they do, Adam, very good. I'm still fighting to sort out the fractured mess they left me with."

"So you're lonely," Dave says, watching the road ahead. "Doesn't sound like much of a trap. Smiling people, good ol' home cooking, some mellow tunes. Not very threatening."

"The lure," Christina says. "Get souls in the door. There must be more." She focuses on me. "Sit and relax?"

My heart stops. Then catches up, rising to thunder.

"A chair?" she asks. "That turns?"

I pull my hand free of hers. "You were there."

"The first time," she says. "After they captured us. That chair scares you because you've been in it before. We both have."

"You remember."

"Only that it starts pretty and gets ugly. I might remember more except it worked. I don't *want* to remember."

"Clever being-trap," Dave says. "It's one thing if someone forces you, most of us get rebellious. But if you choose, now that's tough to escape."

"I didn't choose to sit and watch," I say. "I didn't even drink the water."

"Maybe not this time," he says, "but what happened last time? Or happens next time? Besides, that's not the choosing I'm talking about. They can force you into an unbearable situation, but what they can never force is how you react to it once it overwhelms you."

"I could run away."

"Not always an option," he says. "Or you might not realize it's an option. Either way, a being escapes the only way possible—don't look at it. The mind's version of running away. *Choose* to forget. Which sticks because it draws on the power of decision, intense stuff. Best being-trap there is. Trick a being into trapping itself."

I shift to Christina. "How we lost our memory. But they captured us alive, I thought you said."

"They put our bodies in the chair. That still puts you there."

"We must have known a memory-wipe was next. Didn't we?"

"When the enemy has you restrained, you can assume the prospects aren't favorable."

"Then why didn't we just leave?"

"You mean, like get up and walk out? A bit tough when you're shackled."

"No, I mean, leave *the body*. And escape with our memory."

She stares at me as if I've lost my mind. "Okay. Right now, leave your body and escape."

"But I don't want to. I just got here."

"Right," she says. "Now if I shoot you in the head and your brain ends up splattered across the back seat, you might think otherwise."

"I'd probably think you're a psycho. Is there a point?"

Dave interrupts our morbid little chat. "Stepping out is one thing, but what you're suggesting is abandoning the body absolutely and forever. None of us would do that on a whim, and they know it. There has to be a good reason, useless for instance, like what Chris just described. Brainless is pretty much useless."

"Or old and dying," she says. "We stay until the body says no more."

"But staying, we lost our memory."

Dave says, "Honor can be stronger than consequences. We're back to the topic of choice—yours to partner with a body."

"Partner is fine, but I'm not a body. I could leave, go anywhere, I have no location."

"Sure you do, when you *choose*. Choose a body, choose to share its position, you have a location. See? Here it comes again—choice. Don't you get it?"

Perhaps I have taken it for granted. The power of choice can be dangerous. Choose to believe one thing, a soul might be saved. Tinker the slightest with choice, influenced by rash decisions sparked by death, and swayed by the threat of everlasting loneliness—damnation becomes a very real possibility. Inflicted by no other. All your choice, lone soul to blame.

"So this light of yours," Dave says. "Anywhere near Sol-2?"

"Being dead, one doesn't tend to focus on geography."

"I'd say it is." He watches the road ahead. "The delivery, remember? Equipment for a psychoactive projection. What happens there couldn't be real. The heat, the pressure, there's no way. But something to project the scene could be, that's no feat of engineering. Rugged enclosure landed by drone, powered by thermal energy, the planet has enough to go the other side of forever. And with harsh conditions no physical body could ever survive, no one will ever find it."

"They'll find it. Maybe not land there and turn it off, but someone's going to be mighty curious when they see that light."

"But they won't. Not when it's outside the spectrum of visible light."

"They have a word for that, Dave. *In*visible. Meaning you can't see it. Visible light is an idiotic term. If it's visible, it's light, and you can see it."

"Nonsense. All electromagnetic radiation is light. Not seeing it doesn't mean it's not there, it just means the optic nerves wired in your skull can't see beyond certain frequencies. Outside a body, and under the right conditions, it's all visible. Just a matter of the right equipment to generate the proper wavelength."

"A light only dead people can see?"

"Wouldn't want some mortal looking up in the sky and wondering about any light. Might think it's the finger of God, or some other hooey that mucks up the plan."

"But dead, they can't miss it."

"Or their next appointment for a fresh dose of amnesia. Ignorance is the blissful heaven. Erase all trauma from last time and get a fresh start, imagine that. Visitors get a brand new life, as far as they know, the only life they'll ever have."

"What about Hell?" I ask.

He glances from the road, to me. "Don't sit down when you get to Heaven."

✳

Flickering patches glow brighter along the horizon. The highway takes familiar turns as we near home, but there are no signs of life, only deserted restaurants, convenience stores, and an occasional fuel stop, all abandoned. Ahead, downtown high-rises sneak out of darkness, some with craters spanning two, three floors, where smoke rises between twisted steel beams. In the streets below, splotches of light flicker—a city on fire.

As we roll into the battle zone, buildings tower overhead. Most are spared the scars of war, but plenty are damaged and without power, left to stand as eerie dark skeletons reaching into the night. In the congested streets, emergency personnel wield fire hoses and ordinary citizens sift though rubble searching for survivors. People hustle everywhere, bandaging those who fared well and loading bloody others into any vehicle available. Tanks and half-tracks roll over mounds of debris. Anti-aircraft cannons squeeze in wherever there's room to park and set up. Troops fill in the gaps, manning weapons aimed for the sky.

Dave pulls over and asks, "What's our situation?"

A soldier comes to Dave's open window. "They hit about two hours ago. Skies all clear now."

"Clear for how long?"

"No telling. They hit hard and fast and moved on. Reports are they're spread out thin, not concentrating on any particular target, just a lot of hit and run."

Dave turns to me and Christina. "We've got a fighting chance. Sounds like they're overextended." Back to the soldier, he asks, "We got something up there to deal with them?"

"We did," the soldier says. "Everything we got. But they brought the big guns this time."

Dave punches the throttle and we're off.

"Big guns?" I ask.

We're jostled as Dave guides the wagon through war-torn streets. "Super cruisers," he says. "They're serious about something, but it doesn't add up. One of those could level a city without dropping out of orbit. Why all the hit and run?"

"Prolong the agony, maybe."

"I doubt it. They're up to something."

✴

The boulevard running parallel to the beach is calmer. No traffic, houses are intact, and few signs of attack. The ocean is dark and quiet, its roar silenced by the wagon's ceaseless drone. Under dim moonlight, the shoreline is clear for a time, then the sandy stretch is blackened in places, pocked by small craters appearing more frequently the farther we go.

In the alley behind my house, Dave parks the wagon facing the garage. Around to the front, up the steps and across the deck, he darts inside. Christina follows him, and the screen door slaps shut. I am not so hurried, taking time on the deck to check for damage. Everything looks okay, lounge chairs, screen door and front windows, all the same as when I left months ago. I grab the railing and rattle it good, shift my feet and test the boards below. Rock solid. Next door, my neighbor did not fare so well. His deck is gone and a quarter of the siding is blasted away, leaving a bedroom wide open for all to see, bedding half-torched and crispy.

Toward the ocean, sand fades into darkness, a black unknown. But the sound is constant, mellow at a distance yet forever present, the surge of waves as they crest and plunge, wash up the shore, then retreat. Again and again, without end.

Inside looks okay. Shelf of trophies, photos hanging on the wall, and model craft above the fireplace appear undisturbed. On the sofa, Matt sits angled forward fiddling with a gadget, pieces of which are strewn across the coffee table, mixed with a scatter of papers. When the screen door slaps shut behind me, he looks up and wipes at the stringy hair crossing his brow. Like all else unchanged during my absence, Matt has yet to discover a meal rich in fat. Descending from his baggy shorts are those chicken legs I could nearly wrap one hand around, and the orange tee three sizes too large makes a lousy attempt at disguising his scrawny brand of lackluster brawn.

Dave says something but Matt is distracted. Off the sofa, he steers around Dave and looks at me like I'm the next gadget to disassemble. He halts flat on his sneakers and scrutinizes my features, which of course requires one more wipe of his stringy hair.

"The name's Adam," I say. "But you can call me Adam."

His smile stretches wide. Then I'm crushed by his embrace, to the degree that scrawny arms can crush.

Dave says, "What do you got, Matt?"

He releases me. "They hit about two hours ago."

"Yeah, yeah," Dave says, "we already heard. Tell us what *you* know. Come on, little wiener, share some of that stellar intelligence."

Matt grins. "About time you admitted it."

Dave fills a fist with Matt's shirt. "*Military* intelligence, you twit."

"I missed you too, buddy." Matt peels away Dave's fingers and smoothes his tee free of wrinkles. "I got it all right here. I was just working on adding it up." He indicates the coffee table where papers are scattered. Dave goes around the table, drops on the sofa, and begins sorting through the mess.

"Adam?"

I swing around.

She stands in the kitchen doorway, dark hair in pigtails, sheer top that fails to conceal, and shorts that couldn't get any shorter.

The room's temperature just surged, centered on a point beside me, where Christina stands aiming one hellacious glare at Madison.

No one breathes, not a sound. Only the ceaseless lullaby past the screen door, of ocean waves washing up the shore.

The space between them heats to supernova.

I reach out to her. "Christina, now's not—"

She twists to face me. "Zip it, buster." Then back to Madison, Christina's heated glare is so furious the walls seem to flutter.

Madison steps out of the kitchen. "Chris, believe me, I never meant—"

"*LIAR!*" Christina screams so loud the floor rumbles. "You knew what happened to Adam, you took advantage of him, advantage of *me!*" She advances a step. "Maddie, how could you? I thought we were friends."

"I'm sorry."

"Sorrier after I slap you so ugly Adam never looks at you again."

Dave inserts himself between the two. But the stern mask he wears for Christina is something new. "Back off, Chris, she hurts enough."

"What do you know?" she asks.

Behind us, Matt says, "He didn't tell you?"

Christina tries to steer around Dave but he grabs her arm. "This isn't the time," he says, rattling her so rough the room rattles with her.

"Dave!" I pull him away from her. "Lighten up."

A trophy smacks the floor. The walls tremble, throwing pictures off their hooks. Model craft slip from their perches and crash down. The screen door rattles, hinges squeak, and the frame begins to slap, slap, slap.

Matt grabs a travel bag and rips the zipper open. He pulls out a pair of binoculars and darts outside. Dave chases after him and I follow. The deck groans and the planks shudder, rumbling the soles of my boots. I search the night. Few clouds, moonlit sky, nothing unusual. No flashes, enemy craft, or any evidence of attack. Nothing to explain the tremors. Madison and Christina join us on the deck, more than curious—concerned—everyone searching all directions for any answer.

A low roar begins to grow. Indoors, more knick-knacks fall and crash, and dishes in the kitchen pour from the cupboards. The vibrations escalate, throwing planks of the deck into a fit that might yank the nails loose.

Then it stops. An eerie silence. Even the endless drone of ocean waves has ceased.

Matt studies the shore through his binoculars. "Now it adds up."

"What does?" I ask.

Passing Dave, Matt hands off the binoculars and hustles inside, his voice trailing. "Their movements, the reports. Get in the car!"

Dave raises the binoculars and pans the horizon. "Shit! We have to go, *now.*" He passes me the binoculars and flies down the steps.

I peer into the eyepieces. The narrow field of vision shows the beach bright green, clear as day. The tide is retreating, furiously sucked away, and water is sloping upward. Searching for the top, another notch higher and the binoculars magnify the moon's light to blinding. I ditch the aid and search by naked eye. The moon hangs in the night, and below it, sneaking out of darkness, the moon's reflection shimmers atop a rising mound of water.

"What is it?" Christina asks.

"Killer wave. *Run!*"

Matt bursts out the screen door, travel bag over his shoulder. He flies down the steps and around the house. Madison and Christina are right behind, and once again—though perfectly justifiable this time—I'm chasing both their tails.

✳

Citizens flee disaster in every street, alley, and every sidewalk or patch of clear ground. Every route leading away from shore is packed. People on foot, bicycles, in cars and trucks, and riding any beast strong enough to carry them.

Dave sends the wagon left and right and left again, carving out our escape while tossing us every direction. Madison steadies herself beside Dave. Matt and I latch onto grips above each rear door, with Christina ping-ponged between us.

Out the back, scattered lights of our oceanfront community shrink to tiny. Then all black, every light out, swallowed whole.

The wagon plows through crowded streets, scraping parked cars and signposts and soaring past screaming victims scratching to climb aboard. Horns blare—traffic jam ahead. Dave doesn't let up. Speeding for a collision sure to kill us all, he cranks the wheel and sends the wagon up the curb onto the sidewalk, grazing storefronts, bus stops, and abandoned kiosks. He yells at targets dead ahead, "Out of the way!" Pedestrians dodge the grille but some fail and roll onto the hood, horrified stares glued to the windshield and then gone.

"Dave!" I rattle his shoulder. "Those are *people*."

"You can't outrun it," Christina says.

"We'll see." Dave checks the rearview mirror and his eyes go wide. Full throttle he threads a sidewalk slalom with people for markers. The block ends. We soar off the sidewalk into traffic, horns, and squealing tires. We land hard and rebound, bashing our scalps into the ill-padded headliner.

Headlights bathe the interior. "Watch out!" Matt cries. A speeding truck pounds our rear quarter-panel and we're spun around, flung bumper clanking and sparks.

Dave regains control and tires bite the pavement, catapulting the wagon at a building across the street. We hit the curb hard, bounce even harder and catch air, punted up steps between a pair of crouched lion statues. Steering is useless while airborne, the wagon hooks like a curveball, and we sail into the paws of one stone beast. The crash rips us from our seats and leaves the hood crumpled and steaming.

We hustle out, wagon butt-end up, one tire still spinning. We're swept away by citizens rampaging up the steps into the building. I search the crowd and account for our team, jammed in tight with screaming people pouring into stairwells and scrambling upward. Round and round we go, higher and higher.

The stairwell ends and the mob pushes into a long hallway. At the end is a single window. I stand mesmerized by the view outside—a wall of water.

"Adam!" Christina cries. "Away from the window!" She grabs hold and sprints the hallway dragging me along, chasing after people cramming into the next stairwell. Before we make it—BOOM—the building shudders. The window bursts and spews a column of water so forceful it defies gravity. In seconds the torrent fills the hallway and we're knocked around banging into everything and each other, trapped inside one pissed off washing machine.

We fight our way into the stairwell, filled with screams and filling with water. I push off the steps and tunnel to the surface, break past, and gasp for air. Christina comes up alongside and flings her wet mane. We find the handrail and scramble up three steps each bound, chased by the raging flow surging up the stairwell. The building groans as roaring current fills every nook and cranny. Our wet soles slap the steps, up and up, round and round, trailing after the others. The lights go out, leaving us to fumble in darkness, guided only by screams from above and water below, stalked by a ruthless monster coming to drown us.

The stairwell ends at a single door. We burst out of blackness onto the rooftop, under faint moonlight. Frightened citizens huddle in the center, away from the edges. Swift currents surge around the building, and the rising tide carries a debris field—thrashing people dodging scattered junk, drowned animals floating limp, smashed trees, boats, and entire houses that crash into the building and explode.

Farther inland, city lights vanish as the watery blanket covers more ground. The rooftop is now an island in a sea that stretches to the horizon. There is nowhere else to go, no higher to climb, no other escape. We can only hope this building stands taller than the ocean will become this night.

✳

We did not reach downtown where buildings tower into darkness, well above the rising ocean. Not so for the rooftop on which we are now stranded. There was no time, make a choice or drown. The same for many others, as our island refuge does not stand alone. Scattered across the outskirts of downtown, other rooftops rise above the surf, a jumbled network of rectangular islands at assorted levels. All without power, all are dark. Only by moonlight are the shapes discernable against the black ocean.

Close to ours is another rooftop where citizens cram in tight, away from the edges. But their refuge lacks our stature. Though flowing calmer, the ocean is not done. The tide continues to rise, and once reaching their level, screaming victims are washed out to sea. There is nothing we can do, only watch. We are helpless to save them and equally helpless to save ourselves. All we've accomplished is delay the inevitable. Three floors to go and we're next.

Matt digs into his shoulder bag. "I'll get us out of here." He brings out a handheld radio. "Big Momma, come in. Little Twerp here, over."

"Who's Big Momma?" I ask.

He turns a knob and tries again. "Big Momma, we have an emergency, require immediate assistance. Please respond, over."

"Matt…"

He covers the mouthpiece. "We have to talk in code." He motions the radio skyward. "The Association is up there listening, you know. Gee whiz, Adam, good thing you got me around, or you'd do something stupid and unmask our position."

Masks, costumes, enough pretending to be something I'm not. The next of which looks like a fish. Two floors to go.

The radio spits static. A friendly voice at the other end might be nice, telling us help is on the way.

"Big Momma, come in, situation critical. Please respond, over."

More static. Then a crackling voice comes back. "We read you, Little Twerp. Situation understood. We are engaged now and will arrive soon. Enable your beacon, no further transmission necessary. Over."

Matt fiddles with the radio, sits down cross-legged, and beams that proud-of-himself grin. "Don't worry, they'll be here soon."

"*Who?*"

"The Theabean flagship," he says.

Christina asks, "They're here?"

"Yep," he says. "And all the rest. It's pretty bad this time."

"The entire fleet?" Her stare fills with dread. "Who's defending Theabis?"

Matt is silent.

"Matthew, answer me! What do you know?"

"I don't know all the details, just that there isn't much of Theabis left to defend."

"*What?*" She advances on him. "What happened?"

Madison reaches out to her. "Chris, I'm sorry. Your home is underwater now."

Christina whirls around and back a step.

Madison points to the surrounding ocean. "And it looks like we're next."

They lock stares, Christina's glassy and vacant.

"When did this happen?" I ask.

Matt says, "Ten, maybe twelve hours ago."

"The same disaster? On two different planets, the same *day?* It can't be a coincidence."

Madison shakes her head. Christina drops to her knees, face in her hands.

Dave says, "I knew they were up to something."

"What?" I ask. "Now they control nature?"

Matt says, "Now it makes sense."

"That they control nature?"

"The super cruisers," Matt says. "Reports put armadas acquiring geo-synchronous orbit over the poles."

"The big guns," Dave says. "Blasted the ice caps. So the hit and run was just a diversion."

"And wipe out the body supply," Matt says, "before we could get many units off-planet."

"Did we?" I ask.

"Not that I'm aware of."

Waves slap the edge, crest the rooftop, and a thin film starts washing across. I am not a fish, nor care to spend my next life as one.

Dave realizes, "Ten hours ago?" He snatches hold of Matt and yanks him upright. "You little wiener, you knew!"

Matt thrashes. "We just got word, when you—"

Dave sends him stumbling. "You should have warned us."

Matt splats down, his shirt and shorts soaked. "I didn't know any better than you."

"It doesn't matter," I say. "We're screwed either way."

Matt struggles up, rubbing his elbow. "No we're not. They'll be here soon, really, they will."

"And then what?" Dave says. "So we don't drown, great. What about our planet? Polar ice doesn't form overnight, you know." He taps a foot in water pooling where we stand. "You got a damned big mop in your back pocket?"

Matt is silent. So many times before, our favorite techno-weenie has come to the rescue. No self-congratulating grin this time. He can only wish he were that smart and could surprise us all. The one time we need it most.

✳

If the Felidians were here, they'd call this an act of god. Surely one of their deities presides over water disasters. But no, it's not the gods, not even nature. We have only our enemy to thank.

The rooftop vanishes. To walk now is to walk on water. I know the roof supports me, solid and sure beneath each step, but the next could be a step off the edge.

A flash ignites and we're bathed in blue light. A vessel punches through the clouds, drops lower, and spotlights brighten the rooftop. Water—now to our knees—churns as the howling craft descends. From its belly, doors slide open. A platform plunges down and slaps the surf, sending up a spray, then a wave that washes past my thighs.

Christina trudges through the churning water and heads for the platform. She turns back. "Adam, come on."

Joining her might be fine, except I could walk right off the building.

"Get the others first." I point to the crowd breaking apart as they scramble for the platform. Concern for others serves well to conceal fear for self.

Dave and Madison push through waist-deep current, herding others toward the platform, and help all aboard. Matt wastes no time helping himself aboard. The first load is hauled up. I'll stand here, very still, and wait.

The empty platform drops again. More climb on, fighting rough seas now to our chests. I struggle to keep footing. Christina climbs on the platform and hangs from the edge, reaching out to me.

"Adam, hurry!"

Water splashes around my shoulders. The chilling cold penetrates to the bone and the shivers begin. I am not a fish, though now pump blood as cold as one.

I chase after the platform, Christina, her hand—all are sucked away as the rescue craft shifts position. I fight the growing swells, my strides longer but going nowhere, like jogging in syrup. My next step lands on nothing and I plunge to the depths.

✳

Alone in the dark, I tread black swells shimmering moonlight. With nothing to keep me afloat, I thrash and grope, fighting to keep the salty wash out of my mouth. I am not a fish, not a fish, not a fish. Must be why I can't swim worth a shit.

A thunderous snap brightens the clouds, casting a glow across Christina and the platform, getting farther away. She hangs from the edge, reaching out. Another snap, a sizzling beam shoots down and explodes, ocean spray fountains high and falls as rain. Then the fading whine of departing engines, and the rescue craft is swallowed by darkness.

The echoes of battle soften, and the quiet reveals that I am not alone. From the void comes the sound of others crying for help. Scattered spotlights brighten hundreds lost at sea, fighting to stay afloat. But these lights are not rescue craft. One swoops down and a mechanical arm extends above a man wrestling in the surf. A nozzle projects and sprays him with foam. A crude containment field forms and the nozzle retracts. Spider-like fingers reach out, seize the frosty chunk, and stow it in the vessel. The craft shifts position, brings another victim under its aim, and the process repeats. Again and again, the enemy captures one after another. A fleet of matching craft fills the night and works industriously, spotlights tracking across the surface as they pluck countless rebels from the sea.

If only I could close my eyes and call this a bad dream. Directly above, a craft swoops down and the mechanical arm extends.

I tunnel straight down. Well below the surface, I watch spotlights glance the shimmering threshold that separates drowning from capture. A pounding heart squanders all breath, my fingers go numb in the frigid depth, and the pressure crushes my eardrums. Bubbles, bubbles, spent breath leaks from my lips, lungs draining. A beam sweeps the surface and back again, searching. One more minute, they'll give up and move on to another poor soul. This body says no–give me air *now*. Up I go.

At the surface, my lungs fill in a sharp gasp that sparks a mild buzz. Blinding light bears down. The mechanical arm swings around, nozzle on target.

Drowning was better. I'm dead. Dead forever.

The craft explodes, a fireball spreads, and the concussion punches a hole in the ocean. A ring wave washes over, the center fountains high, and flaming shrapnel rains down.

Dive! Dive!

Fiery metal fragments plunge past in bubbling orange streaks that I must squirm between or risk getting snagged and hauled to the bottom, never to rise again. The hazards pass, the call for air comes, and I return to the surface.

Patches of flame ride shimmering black swells. The smoky veil clears only to reveal another craft the same, arm extended and nozzle projected, aiming to finish the job.

If I'm not mistaken, I was dead earlier today. This is bound to be my shortest life on record. No wonder I've had so many—they don't last long.

✳

Out of the smoke, the rescue craft comes into view, blast cannon targeting the enemy. Brilliant streaks brighten the night and sizzling arcs ignite. The rescue craft swoops lower and shields me from the menace above.

A smaller whizzing craft comes out of nowhere. It darts below the rescue craft and past, around again and back, then hovers. A hatch opens and tender blue light streams out.

The rescue craft takes a beating before it veers away to reveal the view above. The night is swarming with countless craft, shields flickering and cannons blazing.

The little whizzing craft dives closer and someone tosses out an orange lifejacket. I swim to my salvation and wrestle into it. More than a lifejacket, the vest is a full harness with straps to secure my legs. Attached to the back is a cable leading to the open hatch. The craft launches to the sky and I'm plucked from the sea like a fish on the line. The ocean retreats to darkness as I soar through the night, hanging by a slender thread. Soaking wet and headed for the stratosphere, I'm skinned alive by chilling knives of cold wind.

The ocean is gone, only blackness below my dangling toes. My whole world is the howling wind, safety line, and open hatch. The line is yanked hard, I go flying through the hatchway into a tangle of cable gone slack, and the rising craft scoops me up, nailed to the deck.

✳

The hatch slides shut and seals out the howling wind.

"You okay?" a fellow asks.

It's tough to know. One second chilled to numb, next a floor-sized hammer fires every nerve ending.

"Not exactly my best day."

I gather my splattered senses, sit up, and focus on a guy in gray coveralls stained by muddy brown splotches. The compartment isn't any landing area and is hardly big enough to be called a cargo bay. The cramped space is stocked with cables and chains, block and tackle, caged wire baskets, and yellow pressure suits.

"Adam, right?"

I start unlatching buckles. "Who wants to know?"

He looks haggard but manages to smile. "The admiral is anxious to see you."

"Admiral?" I ask. "Admiral of what?"

He offers a helping hand and pulls me up. There's a loud bang, then clanking, and we stagger to regain footing.

"Not to worry," he says. "Just the docking port." He starts across the compartment. "Come, this way."

I wiggle out of the harness and follow him. A squishy mess seeps from my boots as they wring themselves dry each step, leaving a trail of puddles. Past a hatchway, we enter a big flexible tube, a sort of plastic accordion worm.

Moving along the wobbly passage, I follow close behind, then notice his hair—black, cropped tight.

I pause halfway through. "Now hold on. You're not the enemy, are you."

He swings around and the flexi-tube jiggles. "Whose enemy?"

"The Association."

He smiles. "Of course."

Usually, the expression is backed by some scrap of detectable emotion.

"Of course you are," I ask, "or of course you're not?"

It may be time to run. Run where? Sure, leap out and plunge a few thousand feet.

"Of course," he says, "the Association."

I might be more annoyed than frightened. "Look, buddy, you're not answering the question."

"Not answering it," he says, "or not answering it the way you'd like me to answer it?"

Smart-ass. This guy couldn't be a Bob. They're not clever enough to be this aggravating.

"Adam," he says. "Relax."

I'm not too fond of that command either.

He continues, "You asked if I was the enemy, right? Then I asked, *whose enemy*. Have I got it right so far?"

Something about this is too familiar. Something that annoys the hell out of me. But to win an argument, I'd have to know what to argue.

He says, "You answered my question—thank you by the way—and I replied, of course."

"Of course *WHAT!*"

I feel like a simple-minded child getting lectured by some know-it-all adult. A know-it-all asking to get smacked around if he doesn't knock it off.

"Of course I'm the enemy," he says. "Enemy of the Association."

Now I realize what bugs me about this. "I know your kind—Theabean. Tricky logical types, always answering questions with more questions, always some clever comeback for every argument. Fools like me can't ever win, can we."

What am I saying? What annoys me is also what I adore—a tricky gal loaded with logic. Christina is from Theabis.

"I take that as a compliment," he says.

I match his cheesy smile. "Take it however you like, pal. Matters not to me."

✳

For the first time in this short life, I'm not scrambling to escape. The prospect of relaxed defenses is almost unbelievable, for a life yet to span a single day, in which I've hit the ground running and covered so much, though plenty of it I've spent as a fish.

My new acquaintance charges ahead, past the next hatch, and doesn't bother looking back. Seems the guy didn't care for my response. As I fully expected. With the indelible memory of their annoying personality comes the equally indelible urge to challenge Theabeans, engage in the verbal jousts they so enjoy, and with any luck, emerge victorious. Have I? No telling for sure. I'll settle for him equally annoyed.

We enter a nonflexible passage with plain steel walls. The solid deck beneath each step is comforting. Ahead he goes, ignoring my questions, which only confirms the memory. Once conquered, Theabeans are quick to pretend none of it ever happened, more important matters take precedence over any regret.

"The admiral is waiting," he says without looking back.

"So you're the admiral's secretary."

At the next hatch, he whirls around. "I've more rank than any secretary."

Something is rank. I point out the brown splotches staining his coveralls. "The janitor?"

The glare alone could remove my head. Instead, he cracks open the hatch. "I have a mess far worse."

A short passage opens to an immense space where vessels taxi into docking ports, gangways shoot every direction, and crewmen pilot distant levitating barges, ferrying people and cargo. He urges that we hurry along, he has weeks of work to finish in hours, work that fetching me only delays. I thank him, surely I would have drowned otherwise. He notes that he didn't volunteer. After introducing myself, he responds, "I know." He charges ahead, then finally gets the hint that offering a name implies. He halts. "Noack, Isle of Memaz, Senior Cargo Supervisor Division E, assigned to the QTS Marquarum, flagship of the Theabean fleet. Happy now? Tour's over. The admiral's waiting."

Better, though he did fail to express a postal code.

"Sorry," I say, struggling to keep up. "You know, the secretary thing."

He doesn't miss a stride. "I'll forgive you."

After how many lifetimes from now, I wonder.

To every question he responds, "Ask the admiral, not me." He wipes at the mess staining his coveralls and grumbles about some damned cargo well beyond his job description.

We enter a darkened shaft and step onto a caged platform. Noack reaches for a strap that brings a door down from above, and the other half slides up from below. He hits a button and we shoot upward. It's all black, girders whip past, and flashes of light from passing floors are like a strobe. The ride ends so abruptly, I'm reaching for the railing to keep from launching into space.

He pushes the bottom door down and the two halves spread open. We're blasted by a horrendous clamor—squawking, howling, snorting and roaring. Hounds chase rabbits, a flock of geese, squealing pigs, and chickens. Sheep, horses, and cattle stampede past. What the hell? I've stepped into a barnyard. Or jungle safari. Rhinos, zebras and monkeys, one riding a llama, follow goats and antelope. Frantic birds crash into walls and bounce off. A giraffe strides along with head crouched low to avoid the ceiling. Wearing gray coveralls the same as Noack, stains and all, countless crewmen scramble between hover-carts, each other, and wildlife flowing through the large curving passage.

I ask Noack, "What's with all the animals?"

"You don't care for animals?" he asks.

"They're okay to visit at the zoo. What are they doing here?"

"Do you enjoy drowning?"

"Of course not."

He points to the stampede. "And you think they do?"

"I wasn't saying…"

"We're trying to save all life on Idan," he explains, "not just human life. They deserve to live too."

"Sure, everybody deserves to live, but couldn't they live someplace else?"

"Your planet is flooded, in case you hadn't noticed. Where would you suggest we put them?"

"There must be some land left."

"The highest peaks are barren," he says. "They'll starve. If they even manage to crowd in. So you tell me, you're full of answers. Where should we take them?"

He just stares at me, waiting for an answer he knows damned well I don't have.

"I'll get back to you on that."

He grins victory. "Right. Now, let's get you some dry clothes."

Done slapping my intellect, he steps into the passing flow of animals. Though it might be nice, I can't just stand here, and besides, dry sounds good. I insert myself into the stampede and follow Noack. Filthy creatures brush up alongside, some hairy, some leathery, others smooth and silky, but every last one reeking fear and stinking of the last time they used anywhere but a toilet. There goes one now, dropping a load midstride to pile on the deck, tromped over and smeared.

The curving passage continues for a good hike, then we arrive at an opening along one side that stretches from floor to ceiling, beyond which is a large cargo bay. Countless cages of restless creatures are stacked up, across, and many rows deep. Crewmen grapple with uncooperative animals, coaxing them onto gangways and luring them into cages.

From a platform above, a crewman hollers, "Don't bring any more, we're out of room."

Noack shouts back, "Stop picking up entire herds."

Another crewman approaches. "Shall we have them draw straws?"

Noack says, "The Idanites asked for gender pairs."

"I'm no zoologist," the crewman says. "What if I pick two males?"

"Figure it out!" Noack pushes through the stampede and makes it to a hatch on the other side. He calls back to me, "They have clothes in here." I cross traffic and join him. He looks down at my boots, which have recently discovered a fresh pile of dung. "Get cleaned up," he says, "and report to the bridge."

"You're not taking me?"

"I have plenty else to babysit besides you."

"Okay. So where's the bridge?"

He chases after some flipped-out turkey. "Ask anybody," he says, voice trailing. "They'll tell you where to go."

This crew? Yeah, I bet they will.

✳

I've either lost some pounds or gained superhuman strength. When I push off to clear the hatchway, I catapult into the top edge and bash my skull. Not just lightheaded, I'm getting lighter all over—we're losing gravity. Not a complete loss, just the loss of real gravity. Maybe half the tug of a typical planet. Of course, all illustrious flagships come equipped with artificial gravity, one of space-life's luxuries. A good thing to have some gravity, artificial or otherwise. Imagine a two-ton hippo floating past, bouncing off the walls and scared to death. No thanks.

Past the hatchway, the compartment is crowded with wet people toweling off and others wrapped in blankets. A young woman approaches with towels and a stack of folded garments. She wears a snug black uniform, unlike the coveralls the others wear, and her outfit is sparkling clean.

"Report to the bridge," she says. "The admiral is anxious to see you." She hands over the clothes and hurries away before I have a chance to thank her and ask for directions to the bridge.

The clothing is a uniform the same as hers—pants and long-sleeved top with stiff collar open in the center just a notch. All black, except the shoulders are gray. She didn't bring any new boots, so I do my best to clean what I'm stuck with. I won't be drying off with that towel.

I survey the compartment and realize the people here, toweling off and wrapped in blankets—they are from the rooftop.

"Christina!"

I plunge into the crowd. Every blanket-hooded face shakes their head when I ask, "Where is Christina? Has anyone seen Christina?"

An older woman peers out from under her blanket hood. "Who is Christina?"

"Pretty blue eyes, wearing olive-drab."

"The girl at the edge of the platform," she says.

"Yes! Where is she?"

"One minute she was there, reaching over, then…"

"What happened?"

"I'm sorry, I didn't see. They took us up after that."

It feels like someone just cranked the dial and set gravity to maximum.

✳

Back in the corridor, I'm knocked around by passing animals while a stampede of dark thoughts tramples this anguished heart. She could have dove in after me. She could have drowned, if not snatched up by the enemy. Or she made it aboard. Not knowing is worse than knowing the worst.

The command is relentless, filling the cracks between thoughts too heavy—go to the bridge. No matter the wounds, physical or emotional, a soldier returning from battle must next report to superiors. A sense of duty demands it, duty I don't even understand. Honor perhaps, or some other driving force, the very impetus of survival. Survive so that we may accomplish.

I ask passing crewmembers for directions to the bridge. One is kind enough to refrain from tricky conversation, and he directs me to an elevator just around the corner. I approach the polished steel doors, press the call button, and wait.

The doors slide apart. Inside the elevator is an imposing man, his dark brow down and his dazzling eyes intense. "*What* is taking so long?"

Who is this? Whoever he is, he's not happy. At least, not happy with me. An older fellow, he wears a uniform like my new outfit, all black with gray shoulders, except pinned to his collar are five gold stars, and five gold bands stripe each of his cuffs. Actually, older is not the right word. Not like he's aged to decrepit, something about him is youthful, almost childish. But at the same time, he projects an aura of maturity and wisdom, like a father. It could be his intense stare, reaching inside to look at *me,* not my body. That or he's really pissed off.

"Well, boy?" he says. "Got an answer?"

Maybe it's his hair. Not actually gray, each strand is either jet black or snow white, nothing in between, as if young and old intermixed. The salt-and-pepper extends to his trim beard, but his mustache and brows are solid black.

He says, "So you're thinking about it."

"Huh?"

"Just think," he says, "how often is someone talking, and you're off thinking about something else totally different, and you don't even hear what they're saying."

"Say what?"

"See? Just what I'm talking about."

"I'm sorry, sir. You are…"

His concentrated stare reels in. "Wow, they really worked you over."

Do I know this man? Perhaps I should. It might be true, something about him is familiar. His voice if nothing else.

From behind, I hear her call, "Adam!"

Life resets when tender blue finds me. I could just float away with her. She hurries closer and arrives quickly, aiming to throw arms around me, but she halts. Her smile drains to professional and she stands at attention.

The imposing man steps out of the elevator. "At ease, Commander." He looks at me. "Both of you, loosen up."

Christina widens her stance and tucks her hands behind her back. She wears the same black uniform with gray shoulders, except her collar is decorated by a gold bar with three silver ovals.

She says to me, "You remember Alexander, Supreme Commander of the Theabean Fleet."

"The admiral?" I ask.

He unleashes a warm smile. "Forget the fancy title, I don't care for titles." He steps closer. "Titles are for pompous, self-important nitwits. Next thing you know, you'll be calling me *God*." His face contorts with disgust, a second later loose and smiling. "Call me Zander, as do all my friends." He extends a hand. "Welcome, Adam. Welcome aboard the Marquarum, prize of the Theabean Fleet."

Though hesitant, I lock hands with him and shake. "We are… I mean, pleased to meet you, sir, but I may be confused. Have we met before?"

"Adam!" Christina scolds. "You couldn't forget Zander."

I've forgotten something. He is vaguely familiar, but that's about it. More than any memory of him, I have an uncomfortable *feeling*.

From the stampede rushing past, a confused ostrich-looking bird sort of thing collides with the admiral. A flustered crewman struggles to corral the stray creature.

Zander hollers, "Find somewhere to put these animals! I'm not running a zoo here."

"We are trying, sir," the crewman says.

"Do not *try*, son. *Do it!*"

Zander swings back to us, all ferocity instantly replaced by a benevolent tone. "Forgive the wildlife. We must save them as well, you do understand."

"Yes, I heard. Quite noble, sir."

His eyes flare like electrobeams aiming to slice up the bulkhead. "Noble? A colossal pain in the ass is what I call it." He shouts at the animals, "*Get the hell out of here!*" The herd shuffles on their hooves, scrambling to steer clear.

The hot and cold personality perfectly matches his hair—an equal mix of black and white and nothing in between.

Zander whirls on his heels, waving his arms, and shoos critters sneaking in between us and the elevator. "Move it!" The animals scatter. He steps toward the open doors and extends a gracious hand. "After you."

We push into the elevator and shove out a few strays. A chimpanzee calmly stands next to the admiral like he's along for the ride and we shouldn't think anything of it. Zander hollers at the primate, giving explicit instructions of where to go—not here—and scolds the thing for not obeying orders as though it actually understands. Seems the admiral expects all to obey, man and animal alike. The chimp frowns—maybe he does understand—and scampers out on his hands and feet, back to the corridor.

Zander brushes off his uniform and tugs the top portion down, taut across his chest. He reaches out to select a floor.

"Wait." I hold the doors open. Christina stands in the corridor. I ask, "Aren't you joining us?"

"I'll catch up," she says. "You two need to talk."

✳

The elevator shoots up. That sick feeling is back, when the distance between us grows. The same sick feeling while lost at sea, watching her reach out from the platform, then vanish in darkness. But there's another sick feeling that has nothing to do with that.

Zander says, "Stop daydreaming and think about what I'm saying while I'm saying it instead of later."

"Say what?"

He looks tempted to strike. "You're doing it again."

"Doing what?"

He speaks slowly like I'm an idiot. "Listen to what I have to say in *the now,* even if it's outside the now."

"Okay. So what is it you're saying now?"

"You have lines of communication to deal with."

"I'm not following, sir, other than a line might be severed. Probably why I'm not following."

"You're half right but all wrong, and missing the point. Why must you be so difficult?"

"I'm difficult? You're like a riddle. If you have something to say, just say it, instead of all the cryptic nonsense."

He glares. "You have a mess to straighten out."

"Sorry, sir, I'm not up to speed on disaster recovery. I think we should cut our losses and move on. Find somewhere else to live, like a planet with more dry ground."

"No, not that, we can't do much about that, not now." He paces the rising elevator car. "No, changing the past, well now, that would be some feat. The future tells us what to do, we know that." He halts like a mighty inspiration has struck. "And so the future it will be, and *that* you can change."

"Me? I can't…"

"Really now," he says, "don't be so modest. Is this the same Adam who won peace for the entire Pleiadal cluster at the battle of Andertield? He was quite the bully I hear, sent the Association home with their tail between their legs. What about the Adam who defeated the Trossburians during the invasion of Pectropin and saved two planets from certain annihilation. And surely, you've returned with a new victory under your belt, after the call to an unknown system in the Restricted Zone."

"That one didn't turn out so well."

He lands a grip of my shoulder. "All missions have their price. Don't be too hard on yourself, boy." He shakes me some but it doesn't do any good. "In any case," he says, "you made it back, the most important aspect. And I imagine, with new adventures to tell and a wealth of intelligence vital to our cause."

"Nothing I'm proud of."

As the elevator climbs, he scrutinizes my features like I might be an imposter. "Adam, what has happened to you?"

"A *lot.*"

He resumes pacing. "Yes, yes, I know. I know all about it."

"How could you?"

He halts. "Trust me, I *know.* One does not rise to the position of admiral while being ignorant."

The smart-ass knows the one phrase that makes my skin crawl. Trusting him might be the last of all I do. But I can't shake the feeling—he does know.

"More specifically," he says, "what has happened to your confidence?"

"Probably wiped away with the rest of my memory."

"Then it is true." He looks me straight in the eye, past every layer, and stares into *me.* "You are not aware of how great you are."

The space grows like I'm shrinking, but not his eyes, his eyes stay with me.

I realize, "The access codes, the craft, wig and clothes and recorder…"

He starts to grin. "Just trying to help things along."

"And the messages—we remind. That was you."

"Wouldn't want you getting distracted, now would we. You do remember that much about yourself, yes?"

Difficult to admit, but he's right. Having escaped Orn-3, I was likely to celebrate with a weeklong drunken stupor. Wouldn't be the first time. Having such a flaw should bother me—and it does—but worse is anybody knowing about it. Worse still, they make a point of reminding me of what I'd rather not admit. Denial is weak armor when someone knows your dirty little secrets.

I ask, "Who *are* you?"

He smiles and extends a hand like it's the first time all over again. "Pleased to meet you, Alexander's the name, but you can call me Zander." He takes my hand and shakes vigorously, all the while grinning like he knows a secret.

Now hold on—that's my cheesy joke. Except it's no joke when he does it, having a name with numerous flavors, not to mention the lofty title of admiral. The whole joke, ha-ha. Adam has no diminutive variant.

"Now," he says, "enough with the formalities. Time to kick some *ASS*ociation butt." He breaks out laughing.

The guy has no problem swapping out his emotions, nor any trouble amusing himself. I'd laugh along with him, except for any pun that corny, I'd be laughing *at* him. Which, for some reason, I can't do. It just doesn't feel right. If only there were a clue as to why.

The elevator halts and the doors pop open.

"Come now," he says, "we have much to do."

Where have I heard that before?

✳

Keeping up with the admiral is a workout. Not that he takes particularly long strides, or short quick ones, or even swings his arms much. He appears to walk like any other person, only he covers twice the ground in half the time.

The passage opens to a spacious command center swarming with crew-members. I'd guess nearly a hundred, an equal number of men and women wearing the same uniform, black with gray shoulders. The atmosphere is like a cave, brightened only by the glow of angled displays rising from rows of continuous desks, which face a giant viewscreen that spans one entire wall. The screen presents a view of outer space and a nearby planet. Or rather, what was a planet. Idan, now an ocean world shimmering blue, peppered with island specks.

Zander steams ahead, ignoring salutes. "Pick up the step, boy. You've seen all this glitz before."

The next step ought to be a boot planted where it picks him up by the seat.

I catch up just as he enters an office. Along the back wall are windows to the starry expanse, opposite one wall all glass that looks out on the bridge. Behind an executive desk is a throne-sized chair where Zander seats himself. My attention is captured by the elegant appointments decorating his office. Oil paintings, glass sculptures, fake plants and golden trophies topped by scaled-down craft.

"Yeah, yeah," Zander says, "I'm an important man, whatever. Sit down already."

Self-important.

Once seated, I expect him to outline a grand scheme with which he needs my help. But no, he folds his hands atop the desk and leans forward. "All right then, what's the plan?"

Is he serious? Apparently so, judging by the anxious gleam in his eye, thirsting for the tantalizing surprise I don't have in store for him.

"I don't know," I say. "Why are you asking me? You're the admiral."

He reclines in his throne, sour like I've rained on his parade, then he looks away. He twiddles a pencil between his fingers and begins tapping it against the desk.

"You know," I say and catch his attention, "when I snap that pencil in two, some fingers might…"

He straightens up and slips the pencil into a drawer. "Still nervy, are we?"

"I don't trust people who pretend to know me."

"A good thing, I suppose, but perfectly understandable. You have been through a lot."

"No shit I have. And now what?"

"You know as well as I do." He firms his posture and shifts to a serious tone. "The Association has us outnumbered, and they surround our planets, which at this point are useless anyway. We have no bases from which to resupply, and the body inventory is depleted. The next battle is do or die, and this time, to die means no coming back, at least, not to anything pleasant."

"I understand all that. What I don't understand is *why everyone expects me to fix everything!*" I shoot upright, launched by an incredible urge to scream, throw something, punch holes in the wall.

"Adam," he says, "please, sit down and relax."

"They're dead, don't you get it? *Dead,* all of them. I promised what I couldn't promise, never should have promised, I was wrong to even go there. They're all *dead,* even the planet's dead. Now our planet's dead, we're all dead, it's over."

"So they're dead. What do you think? The universe revolves around only you? They were dead either way."

I drop on my seat.

"As for us," he says, "we're a long way from dead. All it takes is one small solution to the bigger problem." He leaks a grin. "Wouldn't be the first time, you know."

"*Dammit!*" I scream. "You ask the impossible. We can't win."

He shoots up to standing, invigorated by something, god only knows what now. He gazes past the walls of glass to the bridge, like he's giving a speech to the entire crew. "Let us imagine that goals are possible until we can prove they are not, as opposed to imagining goals are impossible until we can prove they are."

Another tricky Theabean riddle.

"Gimme a break already, will ya?"

He sits down and leans forward, intensely interested. "Is that what you want? A break?"

I should be annoyed, but that one lands hard. "No. I want this shit to end, then I'll have my break. I've had enough of them *ruining my lives!* I'm sick to death of them deciding *what I do!*"

"Decide for yourself. What will you do?"

It's no use. He won't let up, no matter what I say. He just stares at me, hungry for the next brilliant idea.

"I'll stop them," I say.

"Now there's the Adam we know." He pops out of his seat. "All right then, let's get started."

I only sink further in mine. "Look, it's not that simple."

"Intentions are simple," he says. "What happens in the process of executing those intentions is another story, we know that, but it always starts with a simple intention."

I said that.

His enthusiasm appears endless. "So what's it going to be this time?"

"Zander, I'm sorry. Really, I am, more than you know. The truth is, I'm all out of answers."

His admiration only grows, and with it, his smile.

"You hold every answer we require. All you need now are the *questions.*"

6

Throw the ball! The stretch of grass is clear, nobody can stop me. My teammate fires a pass and the ball is mine. I drive my fingers into the leathery skin, push my little legs to run faster than ever, and aim for the goal line.

The other team comes after me. A boy dives for my ankle, catches hold, and I crash. The ball bounces loose and everybody goes after it. Not a chance, that ball is mine! I scoop it up and go *fast!* They'll never catch me. I'm winning today, there's no other way.

On my way to the goal, a black crow swoops down and flies beside me.

Running fast and puffing hard, I manage to say, "I'm winning today."

"Ca caw!" the bird says.

Too bad I don't speak bird, but I know what he means. He agrees, I'm winning today.

The crow and I cross the goal line together. I drop the ball and dance the silly dance we always dance, round and round and shaking my butt. The crow keeps going, climbs higher in the sky, and vanishes in the clouds. He didn't even say good-bye. That's okay, he knows I won.

"I won! I won!"

The other team gets slower, then they stop trying. Too late, I win. They hang their heads and turn away. The boys on my team run faster to celebrate with me. On both sides of the field, bleachers are full of standing adults who clap and cheer. My teammates catch up and slap me on the back, then hoot, whistle and holler. Everyone on my team is super excited.

The field disappears, but the cheering doesn't stop. I'm on a stage facing an audience of grownups. They are clapping. Other six-year-olds are on stage with me, dressed in costumes. Mine is a funny pair of gray shorts with suspenders. The applause is wonderful, so much praise, warm like the bright stage lights. A red curtain closes on the audience, but the clapping goes on. The other children run in circles around me, then lift me up and shout, "Hooray!" They throw me up and up again, tossing me higher and higher.

I land on a blanket inside a circle of teenagers holding it. The stage is gone and now I'm in a backyard. The older kids pull the blanket tight, fling me up, and the ride sends me high. Across the yard is a chain-link fence, and on the other side is a sliding patio door, open to the kitchen where someone is cooking dinner. I hit the blanket, the teenagers pull it tight, and I'm launched to the sky.

I crash onto hot sand. I'm on the beach. It's sunny today, very warm, but I'm comfortable in a pair of bathing trunks. A plastic disk lands on the sand next to me. I snatch it up, cock my arm back, and throw it spinning. The disk climbs high in the sky like a spaceship off to explore faraway worlds.

The crashing waves are loud. I run to the ocean, my bare feet slapping the jiggly packed sand where the tide leaves it wet. I dive in and tunnel beneath a wave, pop up on the backside, and face an even bigger wave. I climb the mountain of water just as it starts to crash over, then ride the wave like a fish.

The giant wave buries me in foamy chaos and I tumble through a murky underworld mixed with swirling sand. The wave passes and I come up for air, treading the surface as bright sun warms my cheeks and dries my hair to salty crust. I swim back to shore. Clumps of sand cling to my wet feet, and the grainy coating grows. Sand shoes, neat.

There's a tree on the beach, but the wrong kind of tree. Those kind don't grow on the beach. This tree needs a forest, it needs dirt. I look closer. The tree has a face made of bark. It looks like a grumpy old man.

"Hello," the tree says.

Trees talk? I guess so.

The tree says, "May I ask you a question?"

"Sure, I have lots of answers. I'm super smart."

"Super even?" the tree says. "That's great. So tell me, how do you defeat an opponent?"

"You mean like the other team?"

"Yes, the other team. How do you beat them and win?"

"I'd make it so they can't see me. Then I'll sneak up on them."

"What if they're bigger than you?"

"Make it so they can't hear. They won't know I'm coming."

"But what if they have friends? Who see you and warn them?"

"I'll make it so they can't talk. None of them, to each other, or anyone else. Then they can't call for help. I'll win for sure."

"A clever strategy," the tree says. "But tell me, how might you accomplish all that?"

Bubbling mischief tickles my insides.

"Lots of make-believe, that *they* believe."

The tree appears satisfied and poses no further questions.

"Why do you want to know?" I ask. "Do you have some other trees to fight?"

The woody face grins. "No, you do."

✳

Our quarters would be completely dark if not for the view of space, a sheet of black sprinkled with starlight. One wall is a window from floor to ceiling, looking out on the vast universe. Distant stars warm countless other worlds, and the frail remains reach all this way, sneak into our compartment, and cast the faintest glow across her cheek.

I've awakened but remain still. Cradled in my arm, her head on my shoulder, Christina rests peacefully with her hand on my chest. In slumber her lashes are unmoving, long and curling. And her lips, full and open just a sliver, sound a tender whoosh of soft breathing. Asleep, she has the face of an angel. Serene, far from any turmoil, having her own pleasant dream, I hope.

Satin sheets soothe my skin, her scent is sweet, and my body is rewarded. Never before have I slept so well, and never before have I dreamt so well. I cannot recall any dream so grand, full of joy, success, and praise. And now I have my answer.

Gently, I slide my arm free and slip a pillow in its place. I scoot out from under the covers, careful not to wake her. Rest, my love. Prepare yourself.

For soldiers in space, Christina and I were assigned surprising quarters. Then again, she is a commander, I should have expected as much. Artificial gravity is present throughout the ship, but few crewmates get a hot shower, warm meal delivered to the door, plush bed, sofa and chair, even carpeted floor. So few reminders that we reside in space, a reality confirmed only by the starlight view.

Quietly, I scoop up my uniform and get dressed, then sneak out the hatch and ease it shut. The corridor makes no attempt to disguise our time in space, a barren passage all metal that only makes the air feel colder.

At the hatch to Matt's quarters, I rap a few times. No answer, so I let myself in. His compartment is smaller and lacks the luxuries we enjoy, a bare minimum for ranks below sublieutenant. Opposing bunks hang from walls of cold steel, and two chairs have hard plastic seats. He gets a felt floor, one upgrade over the hallway, except it doesn't smell very fresh. But that could be since Matt took residence here.

His quarters match ours in one respect—the view. A wall of angled glass, sloping inward as it nears the floor, looks out on space.

One bunk is empty. In the other, Matt is tangled in blankets and snoring.

"Matt, get up. I got an idea."

He snorts a few times and groans.

I rattle his shoulder. "Get up. I need your help."

He rolls over, eyes heavy. "Can't you see I'm sleeping?"

"Not anymore." I yank the blanket off his bunk.

"Hey!" He clutches himself and shivers. What a weenie. It's not that cold. His stringy hair is scrambled, and he's wearing rumpled pajamas. I can hardly believe it—sleepwear printed with superheroes and spacecraft. Geek.

I sit on the empty bunk across from him. "Remember that program we worked on?"

He strains to focus. "To mine user storage for dirty pictures?"

"*No!* I told you to never tell anyone about that."

He yawns but seems wanting to grin. "I didn't."

"Good." I lower back to the bunk. Hard to believe anything human sleeps on this thin foam. "Not that one," I say. "The one that makes messages."

"That?" He sits up. "That wasn't much good. I probably threw it away."

"You don't throw anything away, especially anything you made."

He clears sleep from his eyes. "I don't know, that's not too cool. I mean, it was a funny joke back in the day, but just think of all the people we pissed off."

"Exactly the point."

"What, piss off a bunch of people?"

"Certain people. Come on, tell that imagination of yours to wake up."

He stands, stretches, and gathers his uniform.

"Turn around," he says.

"You have a problem with me in the room?"

"Do you want my help or not?"

I shift on the bunk and stare at the closed hatch.

After a time, I ask, "So, Matt, do you get it?"

"Didn't get any last night."

"Matt, this is serious, how we beat these creeps."

"A message program? Must have been a good dream last night. Okay, you can turn around."

I turn back to see him tugging at clumps of loose uniform, his scrawny geek torso twisting within it, trying to fill out the garment. The superhero spaceship pajamas are crumpled on the floor, likely to remain there until the next rest period.

Matt goes to the far wall and folds down a metal panel that becomes a desk, past which is a deeper cavity loaded with junk. He reaches in and brings out his portable computer, flips the lid open, then pulls a chair close and sits down. He rummages through his shoulder bag, plugs in a thin storage card, then another and more, checking the contents of each.

"I don't know," he says. "I really might have thrown it out."

"If you did you're rewriting the whole thing."

He twists and stares at me. Then he dives into his junk with renewed zest. After checking more cards, he says, "Here it is." I rise from the bunk and watch over his shoulder. He taps keys while tracking the screen, inching through lines of code. "I barely remember this old crap."

"That old crap is how we exploit their weakness."

He looks up at me. "Weakness is a violation of Association rules and regulations, every policy and procedure. Not an option, not allowed. Our perfectionist enemy has no weakness."

"Sure they do. That adherence to procedure, one in particular—everything must be in writing."

"Since when is writing a weakness?"

"They don't talk to each other," I get the other chair and sit beside him. "Not like us right now, one on one. For them, every conversation demands a written message, the rule—all events must be documented."

"So? Keeps things straight. I'd almost admire them for it, if they weren't such assholes about the rest."

"What if we alter what's documented?"

His brow scrunches. "Send those pranks again? So they get annoyed, and pissed off. They're plenty both already."

"Not pranks this time. We don't originate anything. Instead, we bounce back their own messages."

"What good is filling their inbox with messages they already have?"

I reach across the desk for a pad and pen. "Contradiction." I write out examples. "Add *not* after certain words. Is becomes *is not,* will becomes *will not.*"

"Too simple." He steals the pen. "If you want contradiction, use an antonym lookup table." He scribbles examples. "Close becomes far, large turns to small, few is many, mostly hardly, stuff like that. Everything opposite."

"Perfect. Can you do it?"

"Big deal," he says. "Turn messages ass-backwards, then what? Send them back? So they get a bunch of screwed up duplicates. They'll ignore it."

"Except for one twist, and I'm hoping you can pull this off."

"You hope?" He leans back, incredulous. "You know who you're talking to, right?"

In fact, I do. Talking to his inflated ego is the surest way to fully exploit his talents.

"Our best prank ever," I say. "Self-propagation."

He is silent. Obviously, he doesn't understand. But he'll never admit it.

"Let me explain."

"I didn't say—"

"I noticed. Listen, it's simple. Not just duplicates mixed up. Add a snip of code to each."

"That does what?" he asks.

"Hooks into the client program and modifies it, what I'm hoping you can figure out."

"I'll figure it out. Just tell me, modified how?"

"Have it do the work for us," I explain. "Intercept the messages, alter each and send the copies, but even better, with the same code attached so the next client gets infected and does the same thing, and the next, and the next…"

"Chain reaction," he says.

"Can you do it?"

When he thinks fast his eyes shift even faster. "Highjack a packet, self-executing attachment once extracted… it could work."

"What about this. Not only a whacked message for each duplicate, send thousands with the same code attached, and hack into the user log and send thousands more to every entry, to everyone they've ever communicated with."

He locks his stare on me. "You are a devil." That grin of his starts to grow. "You'll overload their entire network."

I slap him on the back. "*We* will. Now get to work."

✳

Composing a list of opposites should be an easy task that takes little time. But it's difficult knowing when to stop, enough is enough. For every new pair, the list grows, as does the obsession to find another, and another, I'm driven by compulsive zeal. While I give birth to our dictionary of contradiction, Matt wrestles with code, runs tests, debugs and recompiles, a cycle he repeats as endlessly as I scribble down new antonyms. When he gets stuck I offer my help and suggest better algorithms, then we discuss the advantages and drawbacks of each, put our heads together, and write some of the tightest code we've ever designed. Huddled around his computer, it's been far too long since Matt and I had this much fun together.

The hatch snaps. Wrapped in a robe, Christina lifts one foot over and pauses in the hatchway. Her hair is mussed, eyes groggy. "Adam, what are you doing?"

"I got an idea."

She drags the other foot over, pulls her robe tighter, and shuffles closer. "Come back to bed. I miss my cuddles."

Matt says, "It's a great idea, Chris. Really, check it out."

She gets to the desk and looks at his computer. "Making games again? Matthew, stop letting Adam be a child. We have serious work to do."

I stand. "This is serious, how we'll beat them."

She looks at the screen and lines of code, then me. "You need sleep. We've only been down a few hours."

"I'll sleep later." I pull her into the chair where I was sitting, show her the screen, and explain the idea in detail.

She brushes hair from her face. The fog of slumber is lifting. "That's clever," she says. "But tell me, how do you expect to get your program into their system?"

"Send the first message," Matt says. "From there it takes off by itself."

"Oh?" she says. "You have some pen-pals back on Orn-3?"

Matt goes sour and looks at me.

"We'll go there," I suggest. "Like before."

Christina says, "During all this? Not a good time."

"Is there ever a good time? Was it good last time? We went anyway, we made it back. We can do it again."

"Adam, you don't understand. Check the reports. Things aren't like before. The Association has recalled all its forces, entire divisions from across the galaxy."

"She's right." Matt slumps in his chair. "I've seen the reports. Duerpia, Kamhitu, the entire Pleiadal cluster, all vacated. Even the Tathning system. Twelve-hundred years battling our friends there, the goons pack up and head home. Pulled out everything. Something more pressing has their attention."

"Us," Christina says. "They rule countless worlds, total control of systems across the galaxy, but not their own. We're an embarrassment to them. Insurgents in their own backyard."

Matt gets up and goes to the windowed wall looking out on space. "We were outnumbered before." Idan sneaks into view, a watery sliver near the floor and rising. He gazes down at our lost home. "Now look what they've done. Conquer a system by making it a system of one." He turns to face us. "Why do I even bother? So we get into their network, big deal. We're still outgunned a hundred to one."

"Don't worry," I say. "I have more."

"More of what?" Christina asks. "Fully armed battle cruisers? That's what we need more of."

"We should just run." Matt faces the starlight view. "Go somewhere they'll never find us."

"Go now," Christina says. "Before it's too late."

As most others suggest, Theabeans and Idanites alike, now my closest friends agree—run from this battle. There may be no distance great enough. Only a distance of time, if we were to find a system well down the list of scheduled invasions, granting us a generous duration before having to fight again. But even if we did find such a place, or distance great enough that we might go undisturbed for millennia, I will not exercise the option. We will not break under enemy duress.

"No," I say. "Stop it, both of you. We're not running away, I don't care how many ships they bring home. They're not beating us this time."

"Wanting is great," Matt says. "Doesn't mean the dream comes true."

"Or change the facts," Christina says. "We're hopelessly outnumbered."

"All it takes is a little make-believe."

Shoes of sand, ocean roar, sunlight dries my salty pores. Dream a question makes an answer, in time awake we might ignore.

"Adam?" Christina nudges me. "I know that grin. What are you scheming?"

"Make-believe. Make them believe *they* are outnumbered."

✳

There are two kinds of dream. The kind when you want something and yearn for the dream to come true, and the other when we drift in slumber, taken on a ride typically bizarre, and in most cases we only yearn for the dream to end. My latest adventure blends both into one, and though now awake, the dream is not yet done.

Wanting *can* make the dream come true, for those unafraid of hard work. A misconception of the yearning dream—dream it and it will happen. Not so simple. Dream of all you desire, a good start, but dreaming combined with inaction doesn't produce anything. Maybe heartache. Act on your dreams, add the hard work, and anything is possible.

The dream of success lingers. The beach, sun and salty waves, so many answers and so much praise. I will win today, but reaching the goal requires teamwork. Before exposing my scheme to fool the enemy, I start with questions for Matt, specifically, his talent with holograms, how he uses them to cloak our ships, and other tricks he takes for granted, assuming we already know how it works. More pertinent to our goal, I had once faced another pair of his holograms—Dave masquerading as a bum and Madison trying to talk past a wash of static. Those holograms didn't cloak anything. Matt projected each onto a point of empty space for me to believe that both were real.

"It's no big trick," Matt says. "Just a matter of aiming energy beams and how they're released once they get where they're going. For craft, the hologram part isn't used so much, just up close, you know, like sneaking in for landing or drop off, the risk of visual contact. It's not like during battle they peek out the window to find targets."

"We scan for them. How do you deal with that?"

"Disperse the scan energy instead of letting it bounce back and give us away. Kid stuff."

"Can you do the reverse?"

"What the hell for?" he asks. "Help them target us better?"

"Target us where we're not."

"Put up holograms? They scan and nothing comes back. They're not falling for any trick that weak."

"What if we made something bounce back?"

Christina says, "What are you suggesting, Adam? Send a fleet of holograms against our enemy?"

Matt is taken by the idea. His shifting eyes build momentum. "Never thought of that. Aim a beam, track the scan, we're talking nanoseconds, then pop, hammer it with a pulse. Tricky, but maybe, with some time to work it out." His shifting eyes halt. "Except for one problem."

"We don't have time," Christina says.

"Or the power," Matt says. "A few the size of birds, no sweat. Big as spacecraft, that's different. For the number we'll need, you're talking gobs of power. If we had ten flagships, maybe, but the other nine can't be make-believe. This trick takes *real* power."

"Every ship in the fleet," I say. "Both fleets, there must be enough."

"I doubt it. Divert life support maybe, but that kind of defeats the point."

Christina says, "It's not happening, Adam. Even if you could, holograms don't fire back."

This isn't going so well. It might help if their input was something besides which flaw ruins the plan best.

I say to Matt, "Just answer this—if I find the power, can you do it?"

"That depends." He fills his lungs, holds it a moment, then exhales. "I work better while still breathing."

✳

As Matt works out how to create our imaginary fleet, he wastes plenty of breath whining about the time it's going to take. I remind him that the longer he takes, the greater the chance we're all dead forever. Christina offers the help of Theabeans, excellent programmers she says, best this side of the galaxy, in fact. Her remark only sours Matt's attitude, though as an added benefit, also challenges his inflated self-image. A good thing, and the help of Theabeans is fine, but let's not ask the other side of the galaxy for any help. Enough ego fills this half.

Christina leaves to get dressed and recruit her Theabean helpers. While Matt composes his symphony of code, I head out to arrange our means of delivering the fatal blow.

At Dave's compartment, I'm about to knock but hear something. In and out, heavy breathing, then a scream. I pound the hatch. No one comes, just moaning. I twist the handle and swing the hatch door open.

Out of pigtails, her dark mane flows freely. Mounted atop him, she is buck naked and grinding.

I slap the hatch shut and stay in the corridor.

Dave's muffled voice penetrates the bulkhead. "What is it?"

I lean close to the cold metal. "I need you."

"I need him more," comes from inside.

Madison? She's with him? She can't be.

"Dave," I call. "We have work to do."

"I'm working hard."

She screams ecstasy, a deep sigh, then coming past the barrier, "Okay, I'm better now."

I wait outside, minutes that feel like hours. They don't even like each other. Not *that* way. This can't be happening. But it is. It's not right. Why not? I don't know, it just isn't.

He steps out and shuts the hatch.

"You're with her?" I quietly ask. "When did that happen?" Then I notice his hair. "When did that happen?" echoes off the corridor walls.

He ties his robe. "We talked some, you know, while you were out." He notices my stare locked on his scalp, and he chuckles. "Oh, that. Maddie's good with hair."

Among other things.

He fingers the spiky yellow mess. "Got my favorite color back. Pretty cool, eh?"

Just don't try calling it blond, and we can move along.

"Back to Madison," I say. "You, her, how? When?"

"While you were out."

"Out? Out where? You were with us and she stayed home."

"No, when you were *out*. The hospital, remember? Oh, I guess you don't, you were out."

"What hospital?"

"You remember. My-o-cardo something. When you wanted to play doctor."

Oh. My last life. My last body. That seems so long ago.

I ask, "What happened while I was out?"

"We talked."

"I thought you weren't her type."

"Wasn't then." He grins. "A matter of the right equipment." Filling one cupped hand, he shifts his crotch within his robe. "She's ready for me this time around."

"Stop touching yourself. Do that alone."

"Maddie likes watching."

"Not another word, don't you dare."

The hatch opens. Madison comes out, beaming satisfaction while securing her second pigtail. She adjusts her uniform, black like ours but glossy and zippered up the center, a skintight bodysuit that broadcasts the vast difference between her waist and hips. She slides the zipper down a wee bit, better displaying how the snug outfit crunches her small breasts, an effective illusion of greater curvature, the globes bulging, a deepening valley between…

I twist and scan the corridor. Whew, no sign of Christina.

Madison crosses her arms, adding another cup size. "What do you want?" she asks.

"We have a message to deliver."

"That's it?" Dave says. "I thought you had something important."

"Delivered in person, to Orn-3."

He goes blank. Just as we had once rehearsed—the perfect expression of an emotionless goon. Then he reaches for his spiky yellow scalp.

"Don't worry," I say. "No disguises this time. Nobody's messing with your precious hair."

Madison arches one eyebrow.

"Don't you worry either," I tell her. "No staying behind wishing us luck this time."

She smiles. Haven't seen one that good since I called her pretty.

"Just get us there," I tell Dave. "Your only task." Then to Madison I say, "And for you, I'll think of something special."

"Oh?" she says.

"After we see the admiral."

Her eyes get that dreamy wander. "I look forward to meeting him."

Dave says, "That pompous ass? You won't like him much."

Like a blossoming flower, her brows rise up and outward. "I believe that is for me to decide."

✳

In the elevator, I outline details of the plan, the very reason for our return to Orn-3. Dave is delighted, no more disguises, and he actually likes my idea, likes it a lot. The prankster would, it being the ultimate joke played on the people we care for least. However, as did Matt and Christina, Dave cites every weak point and Madison has plenty of her own concerns. Friends are great help at predicting a future in which everything goes wrong.

I realize the elevator is dropping. "The bridge isn't down."

Dave says, "The admiral isn't going anywhere."

The car halts and the doors open. Dave has taken us to the launch bay and connecting hangar level. He hurries out and darts between small fighters, land vehicles and gunships, wheeled cannons, and cargo transports ranging from compact to gargantuan. "Two battalions of tanks," he says, scanning the arsenal. "Ahead of the infantry." He stops at the entrance to the next compartment, stuffed full of craft and weaponry. "A few squadrons to soften our entry, deploy tanks with air cover..."

I hurry after him. "Dave, we're not starting a ground war. We have to be *sneaky*."

"Leave that to Matt," he says, dazzled by the array of military hardware. "He'll get us to the surface, then we'll kick some ass." He whirls around, beaming that big white grin. "Right, partner?"

"Wrong. The plan is to deliver one message and get the heck out, I hope, without them ever knowing." I wave a hand across the endless means of making war. "All this attracts attention."

Madison parts our company, distracted by something in a connecting passage.

"No assault force?" Dave says.

I watch Madison wander off, then back to Dave, I say, "Think about what they have in orbit. They'll squash us like bugs before we can even upload the message. Back to square one, their network intact, only worse, us minus one assault force."

"A deception would help," he says.

"I'd agree if you can think of something besides riding into town with guns blazing. Our first priority is delivering the message. After that, blast all you like."

Madison returns, upset about something. "Adam, look at what they've done."

"Who's done to what?"

She points to the connecting passage. "The animals."

In the next compartment, countless cages are stacked high.

"Lucky critters got themselves rescued. They should be grateful."

She scowls. "Look at them! They're crammed in up to the ceiling like cargo. They can hardly stretch."

"Better than floating dead across Idan."

"Adam! How can you talk like that? Imagine being in their position."

"Sorry, not really on my mind at the moment, you know? First things first, then we'll find them a better home."

"Find somewhere soon," she says. "The first planet we come to that isn't flooded."

"Okay, we will. I promise."

✳

After wasting plenty of time in the launch bay, at last we make it to the bridge. The area remains crowded with crewmembers busy at their consoles, but the large viewscreen that earlier displayed the watery Idan now lacks any planet.

The admiral's office is empty, and there's no sign of him on the bridge.

A passing crewmember asks if she can help. She directs us to a conference room farther along.

Like his office, walls of glass from floor to ceiling separate the conference room from the bridge. In the room's dim light, it's difficult to spot the admiral in his black uniform, but on his feet and animated, soon he stands out, engaged in a heated discussion with other officers standing around a large table. He is joined by six Theabean starship commanders, wearing the same uniform with stiff collar and gray shoulders. But something is different about their otherwise matching outfits. Theirs are not quite as black, more a faded charcoal, and the fabric appears iridescent, shifting color as they shift position. Also present are an equal number of Idanite commanders, some I might recognize, royal blue uniforms with yellow piping, zero collar and shoulders topped by white patches shaped as shallow diamonds. Their tall boots look dull, the black lacking its usual high polish, and the blue fabric is not as bright as I recall. They have that same shifting iridescence as they move about a room that seems darker than it should be.

Flowing in and out of darkness, a flock of aides and advisers join the military delegation. Christina is present, standing near Zander. Along the back wall, windows run the room's length, looking out on space, a planetless nothing livened only by distant starlight.

Near the open doorway, the shouting match grows louder. Dave and Madison follow, and we slip into the room without attracting any attention, which to do, may require the fire alarm.

"It won't work."

"Forget the fantasy, make a stand."

"They won't fall for it."

"We can leave. We should."

"Cowards!"

"Fighting isn't the only answer."

"They'll crush us."

Overhearing their arguments, we learn that our forces have moved out of orbit and into open space beyond Idan. Further rescue efforts are yielding few results, and those left behind have been left to their own fates. The Association has pulled back as well, and with vessels arriving every hour, their growing armada has taken defensive positions in orbit of Orn-3, many in the room feel, preparing for our anticipated retaliation. Which is, others argue, precisely what the enemy expects, and falling into their trap only ends our struggle once and for all.

After watching the commanders for a time, their faded appearance and iridescent fabric, their not completely fluid motion and occasional static, I realize—they are holograms. Present only in image and sound. Except for Christina, the admiral, and his aides who enter and depart the room. Personnel assisting the other commanders step away into darkness and return as the group adjusts position to ease crowding, as if the apparitions were actual people.

Dave notices my surprise. "Tough to command a starship when you're not aboard."

"Maybe so." I watch them shift and flicker. "Still, beaming in like a ghost is a creepy way to meet."

As the group argues, Christina and Zander have their own heated discussion, quite real and present. Zander calls to an aide who works a tableside panel. In the center of everyone, the glossy black tabletop becomes a display that presents a tactical diagram of Orn-3. The planet is surrounded by lines of latitude and longitude, like a globe contained inside a wire cage.

"It can work," Christina says.

"I'm not convinced," Zander argues.

A holographic Theabean commander interrupts, "Forget alternative combat trickery, we need firepower."

"We don't have it," Christina says. "And we won't any time soon. We have to try his idea."

Christina notices me. And nearer to me than her, Madison, who studies the admiral in all his animation, except I'm in her line of sight and Christina mistakes that interested gaze for interest in me. She moves quickly and puts herself between me and Madison.

Past clenched teeth, Christina privately says to me, "What is she doing here?"

"What are any of us doing here?"

A Theabean steps up to the table. "Engagement takes the prize." He sweeps an arm across the display, and leans further to indicate targets. "Here, and here, insert six squadrons, and here, two battalions take out central command." He springs upright and twists to gather attention and support. "No need for tricks, crush the network where it originates." He slams down a fist, but being a ghostly projection, his knuckles only fizzle.

"Useless." Matt has entered the room, and he's no hologram. "Obviously you're not familiar with recursive node acquisition utilized by Association network protocol ASN-927." He steps up to the table and sets down his portable computer. "Knocking out headquarters," he says to the ambitious Theabean commander, "does about as much good as me pissing on your shoes. Probably annoy the hell out of you."

"Done?" I ask Matt. "Already?"

He smiles. "I got some help." He shoots a glance over his shoulder.

Behind him are five Theabean females wearing pink jumpsuits, oval glasses, pasted on smiles and pasted down hair. Matt must be in heaven. King of the Geeks has scored himself a harem of nerdy girls from another world.

"You were right," he says to Christina. "They are pretty smart."

She doesn't even hear him, lost in her own world, in which her glare is aiming to vaporize Madison.

Across the table, an Idanite says, "Even if we were to locate a suitable target, an offensive maneuver tips our hand."

"We do nothing offensive," I say.

"Then what have you?" a Theabean asks. "You can't possibly hope to break past their defenses undetected."

"There's a way."

"Frontal assault is best," another suggests.

An Idanite argues, "But the cost in troops and equipment we're sure to lose."

I say, "We don't attack head-on."

"They expect it," a Theabean says. "Any move falls into their trap."

"Not if we're sneaky," I say, it seems into thin air.

"Better to conserve," an Idanite says. "We've lost enough. Let us not squander an already drained inventory on a fruitless offensive."

"Nothing offensive!" I shout. "The plan calls for deception, and one is available. From an existing inventory charged to overflowing."

At last, they fall silent and listen to me.

Christina says, "What do you think, Maddie? You're good at deception. What are we taking advantage of today?"

I pull Christina back before the space between them spontaneously combusts. "Yes, just what I had in mind for Madison." That piques her interest. "And she'll get started right away." I step around Christina and approach female contestant number two. "Madison, go find Noack."

"Who?"

"Noack, Cargo Supervisor Division E. Hurry."

"Why?"

"Just go. Tell him I have his answer."

"Answer to what?" she asks.

"*Go!*"

Though reluctant, she heads for the door and not a moment too soon.

Christina jabs my side and I twist to face her.

"What's that about?" she asks.

"Like you said, deception."

Her eyes narrow. "Don't think I won't know. I will."

Everyone in the room is watching us. I push out the corner of my mouth, "Not the time, dear."

"Here's how it works," Matt says and saves me from the staring crowd. He pulls out cables to interface with the in-table display and fires up his computer. He proceeds to unveil a graphic presentation of the software and its estimated effects, complete with animated messages swooping across the table as if real papers, into the hands of confused Bobs who scratch their heads, trying to figure out what it means. Like a short movie of what we hope will happen. He further demonstrates our idea of holographic craft to overwhelm their tactical scans, we hope, in numbers great enough that they hesitate to attack, and once they do, they remain confused by our fleet of make-believe invaders.

Then Matt drops the bomb. "The only problem…" The worm announces our lack of needed power.

"We'll borrow it," I suggest.

"From where?" Christina asks.

"Since we're paying them a visit anyway, to start a conversation…"

Her eyes go wide. "Are you crazy?"

"Yeah," Matt says. "What do you expect? Drop by for a chat and, oh, by the way, mind if we plug in?"

"Are you saying it can't be done?"

"No, but they might notice the brownout when we throw the switch. Why not ask if they'll turn around, let us shoot 'em in the back instead. Easier that way."

"Settle down, Wiener-head." Dave moves past to reach the table. "Just find the right place." He looks to Zander. "Sir, could we get the entertainment off and back to tactical?"

Zander snaps his fingers and his aide works a panel. The in-table display returns to a tactical diagram of Orn-3.

"Energy networks," Dave calls to the aide.

Locations across the globe light up, joined by scrolling text listing output capacity, troop strength, and armaments.

"Plenty to choose from," Zander says. "But none easy. All are heavily guarded."

I glare at him. "Are you nothing but problems?"

Zander returns a disconcerted scowl. Hologram commanders are taken aback as well.

Christina privately asks, "What's that for?"

"I don't know, he's just…"

"Someone whose help you need. Show some respect."

Dave goes around the table and speaks with the admiral's aide. The in-table display magnifies the southern hemisphere and shifts to a region of ocean. Too much like Idan, the new Idan.

The aide announces, "Highest output relative to potential resistance." A blinking dot is lost at sea. Dave leans in close for a better look.

I say, "I'd prefer some land, Dave."

He straightens up. "You put me in charge of getting us there. I want the best chance we'll succeed." The display further magnifies to show details of an island. "Water in every direction gives us an edge," he says. "No land assault, by sea will be slow, only airborne to deal with. And check out the numbers. That's tremendous output."

Matt angles over the display and soaks up the figures. "That'll work."

"That speck?" I say. "What's all the power for?"

"What's it matter?" Dave says. "They beam it up to the main grid like all the rest. It's just out of the way. You know how crowded the major centers get." He traces a finger along island shoreline. "Deploy tanks with amphibious landing, infantry up the beach…"

"Dave! No ground war." I shift to the commanders. "The same goes for orbiting forces. Stay back and occupy the big guns. I want only two, maybe three transport squadrons, but only transports small enough for Matt to cloak well. The plan relies on stealth."

"I know just the thing," Dave says.

"Three squadrons?" Matt looks puzzled. "All I need is one transport."

An Idanite says, "Their front line is a thousand battle cruisers strong and growing every hour. How can you hope to overcome numbers so great?"

"Bigger doesn't make the enemy better," I say. "More ships arriving adds confusion to coordinate and command. Their forces will be slow to react. Their clumsiness will work to our advantage, more so once we infect their network. We can be small and swift, ants crawling between their toes."

"Ants they will step on," Zander says.

I whirl on him. "You wanted a plan, here it is. If that's not good enough, let's hear your bright idea."

A Theabean says, "This disrespectful combat engineer is orchestrating our demise. We need firepower!"

"No." Matt points to the diagram of Orn-3. "We need their power."

The commander waves his hand in a dismissing gesture aimed at Matt's computer. "You two are children playing with toys. Real men fight war."

I counter, "Better men end it."

Christina looks at me. Her eyes sparkle and she smiles.

"Sir, I have been summoned?" Noack stands in the doorway. "Forgive me, sir, I was told it was urgent." He looks down at his soiled coveralls, well below the uniform standards set by the room's elite. "There wasn't time…"

Zander motions for Noack to enter. He steps in, followed by Madison, and they approach the table opposite Zander. Noack stands so stiff a slab of lumber would be more flexible. He notices me and wants to be surprised, but he seems too annoyed.

He says to Zander, "Forgive me, sir, I may not understand."

"At ease," Zander says.

Noack sets his stance with feet apart, otherwise no less rigid.

Zander says, "It appears you have something Adam wants."

"Yes, sir, I give all to our empire, to our Queen, to your wishes, My Lord." Noack drops to one knee.

I privately ask Christina, "Theabis has a queen?"

She studies me curiously. "You have a problem with us dominant women?"

Zander storms around the table, latches hold of Noack, and yanks him upright. "We all appreciate the show of duty, honor and respect, whatever, but please, let's cut past the protocol." Zander glares at me. "You asked for him and here he is. Our patience is wearing thin."

Doubtful he had any to begin with.

I explain, "Noack asked a question earlier, about where to put the animals. I have the answer now."

The hologram commanders explode a blend of objection and ridicule. As if elected their new court jester, I've only become a source of amusement. Except Zander, not amused one fraction. His sharp stare, very real and present, bores into the depths of me.

A Theabean says, "This conference was called to forge battle plans, not plan the conservation of wildlife."

Another says, "This fool is wasting our time."

"What are you up to?" Zander asks.

"An idea," I say. "More than anything you've offered."

His face hardens and he advances on me. "All right, let's hear your idea. Particularly, how you imagine it might improve our situation."

I move to the windowed wall looking out on space, beyond which is the first hint of an approaching planet. Standing out against distant starlight, the purple globe is one third in shadow, orbited by a fleet so massive the planet has formed visible rings.

"A new home that isn't flooded." I look at Madison. "The first we came to, right?"

She gasps. "Not Orn-3. They'll be slaughtered."

"We don't know that."

Dave says, "We know the goons will. Call it crowd control, just a less civilized crowd."

"They might only get irritated, all we need."

"Get irritated and start blasting."

"True for agents," Noack says, "but they represent a minority. The bulk of Sociate citizens are apt to react with panic and confusion."

Madison's appalled stare shifts to Noack. "You *agree?*"

"A great move," Matt says, almost laughing. "Let the tigers tame a few Bobs."

"Feed 'em to the lions," Dave says, chuckling.

"A distraction," I explain, "while our team takes over the power station and we upload the message."

Madison is horrified. "You can't put animals in harm's way."

"We saved them," I say. "They owe us something."

Her horror only escalates. "You can't make animals into soldiers."

"I'm offering the same chance any creature has—survival of the fittest. Some of them won't survive, and some of us won't, but most will, even in a dangerous environment. It's better than life caged up in a cargo hold."

"They're animals!" she cries.

"It's no different. Sacrifice some to save the rest. Without a body supply, we face extinction just the same. In this struggle, man and animal are equals."

"Don't be this monster," she says.

"I'm not suggesting every last one. We'll keep enough to repopulate each species once we find someplace better."

Theabean commanders glance at one another and nod. One of them says, "We see no reason to object."

Sure, lighten their load.

Idanites are enraged. "We object," one says. "We all object! Many are rare species found only on Idan."

"Forgive me, sir," Noack says, "but any species found only on Idan, at this point, are predominately aquatic."

The room explodes in a riot that rattles the glass, with insults firing in all directions. Theabeans are heartless robots without compassion. Idanites have hearts only to wear on their sleeves and let bleed everywhere. Two planets lost is blamed on Theabean military blunders, to which Theabeans counter the incompetents from Idan didn't take intelligence reports seriously. The brawl escalates beyond combating races as members of each camp begin attacking their own, every commander arguing with every other over who's to blame and should be demoted. The fleet should escape now. Cowards! Throw the full inventory at the enemy. But commanders suggesting the bold move worm out of sacrificing their precious starships by volunteering every other.

I'm back on Marsea, besieged by another mob of bickering delegates.

"Stop!" I shout.

When the telegraphed voices are silent, holograms emit a faint buzz.

"What is wrong with you people?" I approach the windowed wall and stare out at space. "Maybe we travel to that star, or that one, or one a thousand times as far, we might find somewhere to live." I turn to face them. "Not this ship, this is no way to live. Where is the grass? The sky?

The beach and waves? We are a people without a home. And what are you doing? Fighting your own. If that's how we're going to behave, we didn't deserve the planets we had, we don't deserve this ship, we don't deserve to challenge any enemy, anywhere."

They are silent.

My breath fogs the cool glass, beyond which is an empty nothing infinitely colder. Low and to one side, the purple globe creeps higher, two thirds sunlit against black, surrounded by a fleet perhaps the greatest in anyone's history.

"That's the enemy," I say, staring out at the symbol of all I despise. "They ruined our homes. They destroyed all we had, all we've known."

"Your plan is risky," a commander says.

I spin around. "Risky?" I march to the table. "Now what? Calculate risk and fight over which is less? Okay, all you big important commanders, go ahead, fight over what to do next. While you *waste our lives* arguing over what to do, how to do it and when, I'm fighting *my* way, not your way. Not your guns, troop inventory, reports of enemy movements and installations neutralized, any of that crap. I have a plan. *It will work.* I need your help to make it work."

The holograms stare at me. They're not even real.

A fizzle erupts when Christina passes through one of the apparitions and comes to stand at my side. "I believe in Adam," she says to the commanders. "You must trust him."

An Idanite says, "You place yourself at great risk."

"I have no choice."

"We do," Zander says. "I give the command, the fleet moves out. We can outrun them and never come back."

"I can't. You know I have to do this."

"With our help?" a Theabean asks.

I move near to his flickering form. "I have never needed the help of anyone more than I need it at this moment. *Your* help." I look to the rest. "All of you."

Out of view, Zander says, "Never includes the future."

I twist to spot him, and his grin.

He hides the grin and moves around the table, advancing on me. He reaches a hand to my shoulder. "You are prepared to make this sacrifice and risk everything, including yourself."

"No chance exists for those who take none."

His smile grows. "Then our help you will have." He glances at his Theabean commanders, then the Idanites. All nod their approval.

I say to Madison, "And the animals?"

"Yes, I will help you."

"Not just me. Every living creature."

✳

Dreams are easy—you get an idea and it happens. Reality is hard work. Too many details, too many obstacles, and so many risks. Having overcome a world of barriers, what have I accomplished? Convinced others to execute a plan so daring I should call it my own execution. Again I've made the choice to visit the enemy planet. Why? To stop them. To steal the power we need to stop them. Power they have and we lack. We can't beat the Association *without their help.* Reality is far more twisted than any dream.

The room becomes even darker when the hologram commanders salute, fizzle, and fade out. Zander gathers those actually present. "If you will excuse us," he says, then herds them toward the door. "We only need a moment." He shuts the door and comes near, speaking low as we stand in darkness, as if someone might be listening. "Good work. That's the Adam we know."

"Save it. I still need that Adam to make this work."

He smiles and reaches his arm around my shoulder. "Yes, we have much to do, and after you win this battle, my boy, the beers are on me." He gives me a rattle, then lets go. "But at the moment, I'm more interested in your new body." He studies me from head to toe. "Tell me, since you got that body, have you two kids had any sex?"

I was almost starting to like him, maybe. But few friends I call dirty old men.

"With all due respect, sir, I don't think that's any of your business."

He looks away. "Yes, fair enough." He spends a moment thinking, then his gaze slides back to me. "Understand, as an admiral, among other things, I've anticipated much of this. I keep abreast of change and predict the odds for certain outcomes, one being our current situation with a body supply."

"You have more?" I ask.

"Not just yet, but we have ensured a means to obtain more."

"Another farm."

"Not exactly, at least, the same method of incubation. Not so efficient, but fully capable of producing quality units. What they tell me anyway."

"Who tells you?"

"Body farmers we consulted. You see, anticipating the supply problem, we thought it best to adjust certain features, and we agreed to modify the latest batch. Which was, as it turns out, the last batch, so it's a good thing we agreed. Just in time."

"This body…"

"Is from the modified batch," he says.

"I'm a mutant? What have you done?"

He chuckles. "Oh no, quite the opposite. That body is closer to natural than you've known in a very long time."

"How so?"

"None of its functions are disabled, as they have been. So it won't require any outside assistance. Well, except of course, the required mate to interface."

"What batch is…"

He smiles. "You two didn't arrive all that far apart."

It feels like the floor just slid ten feet, but somehow I'm still standing where I started.

"Does she know?" I ask.

"Couldn't say. At least, I haven't said anything. But I've heard females can tell. Some say within minutes, something happens to the body. Never experienced it myself, could be a bunch of malarkey. Maybe you should ask her yourself."

✳

In a corridor between cargo holds, I wind through the crowded passage asking crewmembers if they've seen Christina. No one has.

The next compartment is full of animals flowing out of cages and crewmen herding them toward the launch bay. Noack leads the effort, joined by Madison, studying a clipboard she holds.

She notices me approaching. "Oh good, there you are. We have a question…"

"Where's Christina?" I ask.

Madison points over my shoulder and I spin around.

"I'm worried about the quail," she says. "They've contracted an illness, no one is quite sure what. I think they should stay behind."

I whirl back to her. "Fine, whatever. Where's Christina?"

"I thought she was with you."

Noack says, "Tending to armaments, last I heard."

"Where?"

"The launch bay, I presume."

"Adam, wait!" Madison cries.

I turn back.

"What about these?" She indicates a cage to one side.

I move closer and study the unusual creatures. The genetic engineer responsible for these had a few too many the night before. "What the heck are they?" I ask. "Can't decide if they're ducks or beavers."

She scowls. "Platypus."

"Sorry. Keep them. Keep them all, whatever. Someone somewhere will just love them, I'm sure."

I don't bother looking back. In a corridor leading to the launch bay, I run into Matt and his pink jumpsuit harem, hauling cases of gear.

"There you are." Matt sets down a case he is carrying. "I have a—"

"Where's Christina?" I ask.

He turns to one of his nerdy assistants and she hands him his portable computer, which he flips open. "You can help," he says. "A call here is returning the wrong value, maybe jumping out of a loop before pulling—"

I slap the lid closed. "Where's Christina?"

"Assembling a regiment, I think."

"Where?"

"Getting ready to go, probably in the launch bay by now. Are you ready?" He grins. "I will be, once you help me fix this subroutine."

"You can fix it." I charge ahead, aiming for the launch bay.

In the curving passage, hover-carts zip past hauling pigs, rabbits, skunks and weasels, another with regular ducks and beavers, not yet interbred. Buffalo mosey along, following peacocks with feathers in bloom, waddling penguins, kangaroos and zebra. A pride of lions would be having lunch if not for the shield containing them, arcing when their claws scratch at the shimmering sphere. But not so protected are ferrets, squirrels and smaller, skittering across the floor chased by crewmen swatting away a hungry eagle.

The main launch bay is even greater commotion. Crewmen wrestle a kingdom of animals up ramps into cargo vessels while others operating cranes from above lower heavy wheeled cannons into top-loading transports. Matt shows up with his gear and directs a waiting crew to get it loaded, then he inspects more crates of equipment that keep arriving. Satisfied, he calls to have the rest hauled aboard. Supervising the effort, he expends little or none himself, other than scolding the burdened few to be more careful with his delicate instruments.

The ranks of Theabean troops appear endless, moving every direction hauling items big and small and somehow winding between one another without any colliding. Hundreds crowd the sprawling compartment. Finding Christina will be difficult. But I find Dave, after noticing an unusual craft, long and squat, pointed like a giant arrowhead.

"Where's Christina?" I ask.

His gaze never once leaves the craft he admires. "She'll be right back. Check out our ride." He paces around the vehicle, hypnotized by its glossy black hull, polished to a liquid gleam.

"Back from where?" I ask, scanning the horde of animals, troops and equipment, then back to him. "And what is this? Awfully big for an assault craft."

Around to the side, I peer into an open hatch. In the rear compartment, cabinet doors are open and crewmen are loading supplies. A deflated rubber raft, diving gear, and black bodysuits. Rifles and ammunition, a toolbox and first aid kit. The last cabinet contains a fire extinguisher. Other than that, the near-empty craft is big and roomy, putting it in league with a minor cargo transport, most of which lack the required spunk.

"We need something smaller."

"Trust me," he says, eyes on the prize. "This is way better. Just what I was hoping for."

"Slow easy target? No thanks."

He stares at me—hard. "Dude, we got a *vamiav*."

"Pick up a new language while I was out?"

He misses the jab, back to marveling at the craft. "Man, these things haul ass."

"Translate to common, or something inside the twenty or so known, then maybe I'd have a clue what the hell you're talking about."

"Duh. Vectored Amphibious Magnetoplasm Induction Assault Vehicle."

Right, how silly of me, the most annoying language ever—acronymese. With a name longer than a typical sentence, of course the contraption needs an acronym. Engineers and their ceaseless fascination with acronyms, in most cases the desired result dictating its source.

"Whatever. So where's Christina?" I ask, it feels for the fiftieth time since the elevator.

From behind, a warm hand touches my neck. "Right here, honey. What's the matter?"

I spin around. "Are you okay?"

"Why?" She steps back. "Is something wrong?"

"You tell me."

She glances around the launch bay, then back to me. "Everything's fine so far, I think. We're just about ready. Did I miss something?"

I coax her to sit on a nearby crate. "I mean, are *you* okay?"

Her stare grows suspicious. "Adam, you're acting strange. What's wrong?"

"You're sure everything's okay. You feel okay?"

She reaches for her stomach. "My tummy's a little queasy. You know, like butterflies."

"Really? Like you might be sick for no reason?"

"Adam, stop it. We're all queasy. When has opening a mission made anyone at ease?"

A Theabean soldier approaches. "Commander. The regiment is loaded, ready to embark."

She pops off the crate. "Well done, Lieutenant. Prepare for launch, a few minutes yet."

"Already?" I was just talking about this idea an hour ago.

"Take a peek outside," Dave says. "Orn-3 is just around the bend. Now I'm not privy to enemy plans, but it's safe to assume that once we're in range, they open fire. Did you plan on doing this next week?"

Zander emerges from the passing crowd and halts to stare at me. Again that weird feeling shows up, I can't put my finger on it, only that it shows up whenever he does. Though I am struck by mixed emotions, Christina's plea for respect wins. I approach Zander and extend a hand.

"Thank you, sir, for all your help and guidance."

Shaking my hand, he says, "We know what to do."

"Yes, we do. We'll fix this mess."

He unleashes an odd smile—confidence that is believable. "Yes, we will." He retreats a step and allows me a moment to gaze at him, as though this is it, the one moment to always remember, when we see each other for the last time. Then he salutes, to which I return the same.

Dave is already in the cockpit. I guide Christina in through the side hatchway as the engines rise in pitch, then after securing the hatch, follow her up to the cockpit.

Beyond the forward view, outside the craft Zander stands rooted to the deck, one hand reaching out, his fingers stretched wide. He speaks but his words are drowned out by the whine of our engines and rumble of craft launching alongside. Even so, I sense his intent, and like a voice from within, I hear it clearly.

"Know everything, use it, and never be scared."

✳

Past the open launch doors, we drop from the flagship like a brick. Tracers of starlight swoosh across the forward view as Dave wheels the craft around, adjusting attitude until we're aligned nose down, targeting the surface of Orn-3. A sliver of purple atmosphere is bathed in sunlight, bordering night. We aim for the dark side of the planet.

"Take us down quick," I say, "but no showing off. I'd like to arrive without them knowing."

"Don't worry," Dave says. "I'm good at surprises."

Might be comforting if I didn't know him so well.

The planet is surrounded by Association craft, some stark in sunlight and others over darkness, in orbits high enough to rise above the planet's shadow. Though only a portion of their total strength, the defenders are more than enough to repel our entire fleet.

Electrobeams pour from enemy battle cruisers, smaller gunships, and a swarm of fighters. The beams fire past and into space, targeting the rebel fleet higher. Our allies return fire, sending down scorching shafts that scatter, strike enemy craft and spark radiant spheres, lighting up like a grandstand of flashbulbs firing at random. Dave threads a tight course through lightning shards shooting up, down and across. In the dazzling storm, we slip past the enemy armada and descend toward the planet's surface.

We penetrate the atmosphere, diving into darkness, then the flames begin, roaring across our nose. Either way we're blind. We could slam into a mountainside, if not blasted when someone targets the meteor we've become.

The flames fade. Nose down, we tunnel through dark clouds. Murky clumps of vapor roll past, beyond which could be a brick wall. We burst from the clouds into open sky, still nose-diving on a course to impact a shimmering slab of ocean.

"Ah, Dave…"

"Almost."

He sees it perfectly well but doesn't flinch. My foot is glued to the floor and pressing hard, like that could possibly slow this ride. I hate the passenger seat.

"Don't worry," he says. "I know what I'm doing."

The view suggests otherwise. He pulls up but it's too late. A tremendous hum ignites—deafening, like being trapped inside a giant tuning fork—and we slam into the ocean. Except we don't. It opens like a zipper and lets us in.

Our craft cruises just below the surface, but there is no surface. To each side a wall of water whisks past, and above, a thin strip of night sky is bordered by the clean edges of a neat trough that has been sliced out of the ocean.

Dave flips a switch and the humming stops. The seawalls come crashing down, bury our craft, and tons of fluid slam shut. We're rattled by the sheer force, then the ocean settles and we're steaming ahead just below the surface at a nice clip free of undue turbulence.

Dave says, "Nice trick, eh?"

"Next time you part the sea, surprise the enemy, not me."

He gives me that damned big white grin. "Vamiavs come standard with aquatic deflector fields. For all they know, we crashed into the ocean. Pretty cool, eh?"

Dave's stunning talent is going to get his ass kicked.

✳

Our apparent demise at sea occurred some distance from the target. Air travel could bring us there in minutes, but through water it's more like twenty. Few words are exchanged. Each of us knows well the challenges we face. A time to collect and prepare, when looking to the future and the only certainty is risk. Though I ask this body for calm, muscles twitch—the back of one calf, forearm, a patch in my chest. Quivering, flinching, this body cannot bear to be still. It wants to get on with it, confront what could very well be its end, and for me, the last body to enjoy as a free soul.

Time to kill gives rise to thoughts I'd like to kill—Zander exposing the modifications to the latest batch, exposing them to me but not to her. It leaves me thinking thoughts I'd rather not, so I won't. But that doesn't keep them from sneaking back. Is she…? We only did it once since these new bodies. Once isn't enough, is it? I wouldn't know. The last time that kind of fun produced anything is so long ago, I can't begin to remember how it works. I'd ask her but she doesn't know anyway, then she'd only worry—like me—and foul up the mission. Like I might, if I don't knock it off.

Idle time does pass, agonizingly slow during water travel, but nothing stops time completely. We reach our goal, surface under faint moonlight, and Dave motors to shore until our craft is beached. We gather weapons and get into our Theabean strike uniforms, skintight bodysuits blacker than the night in which we will hide, complete with gloves and snug hoods that mask all but our eyes and mouth.

We exit through the side hatch, into shallow waves washing over the hull and farther up the sand. Transports surface, one, two, six and more. Why so many? Matt said one was plenty. From the sides of each transport, panels open and concealed tracks extend to transform the vehicles into tank-like boxes that crawl up the beach.

I move toward one of the transports, arriving just as the cargo door swings down and slaps the wet sand. Antelope storm down the ramp and up the shore, charge inland, and vanish in the night. Noack emerges from the transport, an easy target in those gray coveralls. However, now stained beyond hope, the outfit almost passes for camouflaged.

"What are you doing here?" I ask.

He strolls down the ramp, wiping his hands with a towel. "My job, delivering cargo."

"Not here, we're trying to be sneaky. You're supposed to put them everywhere *but* here."

"I've calculated land mass," he says, "and distributed wildlife accordingly, based on volume and weight."

"Anyone ever call you anal?"

He thinks about it maybe two seconds. "Is it a flaw having talent to analyze?"

Not the time. I'll choke the talent out his analyzer later.

Matt pulls up driving a six-wheeled mini flatbed, like a golf cart but longer, fat knobby tires and loaded with gear.

"Good," Dave says. "Save us the hike." He piles his weapons and ammo onto Matt's little truck, then plops down on the flatbed edge.

I say to Matt, "Pulling into the driveway isn't exactly sneaky."

Madison takes the one empty seat up front next to Matt. "Let's get going," she says. "They're getting ahead of us."

From a dozen transports, animals flow out and charge inland, a roaring stampede that rumbles the ground. Some stealthy approach this has turned out to be. More six-wheeled flatbeds roll up the shore, hauling Theabean troops. Farther inland, blasts brighten the sky. Swell.

"Hurry," Madison says. "Before our front line gets thin."

What changed her tune? Last I heard, this idea made me a monster.

I hop on back next to Christina, Matt punches the throttle, and we're bouncing over dunes in the dark. I'm nearly thrown more than once. We catch up with a herd of swift antelope and insert ourselves within the stampede. Pacing their advance, the little engine of our overloaded cart squeals like a blender on high. Beyond the herd, our target comes into view, a tower of concrete and steel wrapped in a maze of pipes. Smokestacks pump out billowing columns that rise to blend with moonlit clouds.

Ground flashes reflect upward to brighten the sky and spread a blue-white glow across the herd. Animals don't understand this danger and keep charging inland, though some upset by the blasts careen and zigzag, yet quickly regroup and forge ahead with the rest.

At the front edge of the herd, an electrobeam strikes. I expect a fountain of guts, but instead, crackling arcs form a protective bubble.

"They have shields?" I ask.

Madison twists in her seat. "Your little speech about survival of the fittest."

"So I fitted them," Matt says. "One in twenty or so, strapped to their bellies. Figured they'd stick close enough together."

Madison focuses on me. "I'm not letting you murder any poor animals."

Nice to know someone is watching out for my guilty conscience, along with the creatures otherwise sure to haunt it.

A beam slips into the herd, explodes a plume of fiery sand, and flames boil upward. Matt turns hard to dodge the fireball, sending us up on three wheels. We're nearly thrown but manage to hang on, only to get seared rather than tossed. The mini flatbed drops back on all wheels and presses onward.

Dave rips the hood from his head. "Hey, brainless! Think to fit any of us?" He pats down the smoldering fabric.

Matt glances back. "Sorry, not enough to spare."

No sincerity to spare, either, considering the smirk.

Dave checks for any patches still glowing, then slips the hood back in place covering his head. Adding to the holes for eyes and mouth, he has a few extra here and there.

Matt looks back and snickers. "Check that out. Now it matches your head perfect."

✳

Uniformed in black and traveling in darkness, our team and supporting troops blend with the night. As it turns out, the animals aid our approach. And fitted with shields, none suffers serious injury, nor has any of our strike force. The herd delivers us to our goal, vehicles slow to a stop, and the flow of wildlife continues inland.

The power station stands atop a low plateau, above an eroded incline. Nothing insurmountable, but enough to give the Bobs the advantage of higher ground. Six groups of two and three agents operate tripod-mounted cannons that they fire into the flow of animals. You would think to find the Bobs baffled by a stampede appearing out of nowhere, not to mention equipped with shields, but no, the idiots fail to realize what it could mean. They fire and a protective bubble lights up, so they target another animal and try again, searching for any unguarded. Thanks to Matt, the goons fail to score any points.

Christina calls to a sergeant and indicates enemy positions along the plateau. "Take them out."

The sergeant vanishes in darkness. Moments later, he and others slither up the ridge, stuff charges in the soil below each enemy cluster, and then scurry away like insects. Seconds later, blasts explode to scatter body parts and leave crude ramps carved out of the plateau.

"Go!" Christina commands.

Soldiers divide into columns and storm up to higher ground.

In all likelihood, the Bob Training Manual lacks a section on stray wildlife, equipped with shields or not. But when they see rebel troops, they'll know exactly what to do—alert headquarters. We must hurry.

Christina and I join the flow and charge up the rise. Once topside, everyone spreads out, searching for entrances. Christina and I dash around the building, hide in shadows near a wall, and creep toward the next corner. I peek around to spot a lone Bob guarding a door. He paces, and on his next pass facing away, I move as lightning and pull a blade across his throat. He quietly slumps, and Christina is over him, searching his body for keys. Just as before, her knees in the pooling blood...

The door—the knob is turning. Christina springs up to throw us behind the opening door. Another Bob steps out, realizes a fallen comrade, and goes for his holster. I nudge the door, it creaks toward closing, and he spins around with pistol drawn. I deflect his aim and Christina brings her blade across his neck. Without a single blast or call for help, two agents are dead just that quick.

Christina studies our first kill, the second, then me.

All I can do is stare at her.

"I know," she says. "Let's get this done." She pulls me through the open door.

Inside the power station, tall cabinets generate an annoying hum. Smooth panels reflect and magnify the droning whine, and the bare concrete floor doesn't absorb any either. Along the ceiling, pipes run the length of the hallway, which ends at a round chamber with layers of catwalks crisscrossing overhead, two and three floors up. In the center and circled by guardrails, a pit drops below ground level, from which a central conglomeration of machinery towers upward, feeding a maze of pipes that thread between the catwalks and reach higher.

Across the room is a man wearing blue coveralls and a yellow hardhat, standing before a console. He realizes our entrance and turns to look.

THHHWUP!

Christina's whistling blade buries into its target.

Another sees his coworker with dagger for necktie and turns to run.

THHHWUP!

Her blade strikes and he topples.

She moves to retrieve her knives, wipes them clean, and starts back to me. She freezes like a statue, her stare fixed beyond my shoulder.

I begin turning.

"Don't," she says, lightly tapping two blades against her palm. "Not yet." Slowly, she shuffles sideways. "Four coming this way, two each your left and right."

She's good with those knives, far better than me. And getting the rifle off my shoulder will be clumsy. Which leaves the blast pistol.

A flick of my head relays my choice of targets.

She returns the shallowest of nods.

"Have I told you lately…"

She almost smiles. "Tell me every day." Daggers cocked back, she takes aim.

I twist and crouch, get off two blasts, overhead blades whistle past and the four go down. Not workers this time—armed Bobs who were getting curious. Now there will be more, and more than curious after hearing a blast pistol fired.

"Find a terminal?" Matt asks.

We spin around. Our nerdy cohort is burdened by a large backpack, but that doesn't stop him from waltzing in like he owns the place. By the time we're done, maybe.

Beyond Matt and across the room, a lone Bob stands facing a console. The guy must be deaf if he hasn't noticed our ruckus, or he's too busy…

Sending a message.

I scramble past Matt and fire too quickly, unleashing a chaotic spray. My lousy aim manages to nail Bob below the knee, but he's determined, hobbling one-legged as he clings to the console banging the keys. I take better aim.

At the console, I heave the last of Bob out of the way. The screen displays a message.

CLARIFY SITUATION. REINFORCEMENTS STANDING BY.

Damn! He got a message off. I set the pistol down and type.

SITUATION NORMAL. TEMPORARY UPSET NOW UNDER
CONTROL. DISREGARD PREVIOUS MESSAGE.

I hit the send key and hope that shuts them up. Matt slips the pack off his shoulder, pulls out his portable computer, and starts plugging in.

Stomping boots rattle catwalks above. A blast glances the console. We duck and cling to the lower panel, barely a sliver of protection from electrobeams raining down.

"Get it done," Christina says. "I'll cover." She springs out and rolls flat on her back. Wielding two blast rifles, she fires straight up through the grated decking overhead. Fallen Bobs begin piling up to form a partial shield from the menace above.

On the screen is a new message.

REPORT NATURE OF INTRUSION. ALL EVENTS MUST BE DOCUMENTED.

Not good enough. All right, document this.

ANIMAL PROBLEM. ALL BETTER NOW.

Not a complete lie. And chances are they'll buy it if Noack has done his job and dumped a zoo in their lap.

At higher levels, doors burst open. Boots stamping, Bobs stream across catwalks and down ladders. A small army descends, outfitted with helmets, chest armor, and heavier cannons.

Theabean soldiers pour in. Christina calls, "Defend this position at all costs." A regiment flocks to her and forms a semicircle protecting us, one row standing and another crouched. Rebel troops fill the chamber, weapons blazing, some climb ladders and combat hand to hand against the swelling enemy ranks. Shards of light soar every direction, ricochet off panels, and roast consoles. The room becomes a bloody war zone.

Matt and I keep low while he bangs the keys and I track the screen.

A message arrives.

ALL BETTER? IDENTIFY YOURSELF.

"Matt, upload quick!"

Between keystrokes, he wipes hair from his brow. "As soon as I finish."

"You said it was done."

"After I access the client and find a hook into the main loop."

"How long's that take?"

"Depends," he says. "Send more, anything, so I can trace the loop."

"Matt, they already—"

"Adam! Send a message so I can finish."

"What do I say?"

"It doesn't matter, they know anyway. Just go!"

I type:

```
ADAM IS HERE TO DESTROY YOU. GOOD-BYE.
```

A message instantly returns.

```
ADAM IS NOT HERE TO CREATE YOU. HELLO.
```

"That fast?" I ask.

Matt shakes his head. "Bounced off my phantom local node, just a test. Do more, something longer, it doesn't matter. Anything."

My big chance to be creative. Okay, here goes.

```
IN THE BEGINNING THERE WAS NOTHING.
BEINGS CREATED THE UNIVERSE.
THEN CAME LIGHT.
LIFE IS BORN.
ADAM IS HERE.
NOW HE IS GOING TO KICK YOUR ASS.
RUN FOR YOUR LIFE.
```

"How's that?" I ask.

He smirks. "Quite the poet."

"What about the hook? You got it?"

"Almost, hang on." His fingers dance across the keys.

A blast escapes the fray and glances the console.

"Hurry, Matt. They'll read that crap and send the whole fleet."

Keys clatter. "Not after I— There, that's it." He extends a hand toward the screen as if presenting a game show prize. "Better check your messages, Adam."

A new message arrives.

```
IN THE END THERE WAS EVERYTHING.
DEMONS DESTROYED THE HEAVENS.
LATER LEFT LIGHT.
DEATH IS NOT BORN.
ADAM IS NOT HERE.
NEVER HE IS NOT GOING TO KICK YOUR ASS.
STOP AGAINST YOUR DEATH.
```

This is wild. Within seconds, another arrives.

```
IN THE START THERE WAS ANYTHING.
GODS DESTROYED THE HELLS.
THEN LEFT HEAVY.
BIRTH IS NOT DEATH.
ADAM IS THERE.
SOON HE IS NOT COMING TO KICK YOUR ASS.
START WITH YOUR BIRTH.
```

"Is it working right?" I ask. "Words are changing, but not always."

Matt explains, "I added a flop coming off a random number generator. Odd, the word stays, even, a switch-out. Fifty-fifty."

Messages start pouring in, one after another, faster and faster.

```
IN THE FINISH THERE WAS NOT NOTHING.
DEMONS CREATED THE HELLS.
THEN LEFT DARK.
DEATH IS NOT DEATH.
ADAM IS NOT THERE.
SOON HE IS NOT LEAVING TO KICK YOUR ASS.
END WITH YOUR WISDOM.
```

```
IN THE FINISH THERE WAS NOT ANYTHING.
DEITIES CREATED THE PLEASURES.
SOON RIGHT LIGHT.
DEATH IS BIRTH.
ADAM IS NOT ANYWHERE.
ALWAYS HE IS ARRIVING TO KICK YOUR ASS.
BEGIN WITHOUT YOUR IGNORANCE.

IN THE END THERE WAS NOT EVERYTHING.
DEMONS CREATED THE PAINS.
NOW WRONG HEAVY.
LIFE IS LIFE.
ADAM IS NOWHERE.
SOON HE IS NOT ARRIVING TO KICK YOUR ASS.
BEGIN WITH YOUR KNOWLEDGE.

IN THE BEGINNING THERE WAS GOD.
GOD CREATED THE UNIVERSE.
NOW RIGHT LIGHT.
GOD IS LIFE.
GOD IS EVERYWHERE.
NOW HE IS COMING TO KICK YOUR ASS.
FINISH WITHOUT YOUR FOLLY.
```

"Matt, it changed my name to *god*. It's full of god."

"Yeah, I know." He grins. "Every time it carries the twentieth bit. A little joke."

The rate increases to a point that we can't read anything. Lines scroll so fast it's all a blur.

Matt crosses his arms. "They're screwed now."

Curious to know the results of our gag, I hit the scroll lock and halt the flow to spy on messages at random.

```
THE FRIEND RETREATS IN SECTOR C-7. ENGAGE
LEISURELY, ACCEPT SUBMISSION.
```

ENEMY FORCE IS NOT SMALL. THEY ARE NOT
OUTNUMBERED. MAKE A LEISURE RETREAT FROM CRUSH THE
REMAINING OPPOSITION.

THE FOE WITHDRAWS IN SECTOR C-7. EVADE RAPIDLY,
DENY RESISTANCE.

REBEL VESSELS HAVE NOT FIXED AROUND OFFENSE
PERIMETER OUT SECTOR E-2.

FIRE AT WILL NOT UNTIL ALLY IS DESTROYED.

HIRE AT WILL BEFORE ENEMY IS CREATED.

WHAT IS NOT COMING OFF THERE?

QUESTION WITHOUT INSTRUCTIONS. AWAITING YOUR
CHAOS.

WHAT IS NOT RIGHT WITHOUT THESE MESSAGES?

A beam slices between us and the screen explodes. Matt and I drop,
our backs pasted to the lower panel. The regiment protecting us is three-
quarters dead and Christina is filling in the gaps, two rifles blazing. Matt
snatches his computer, I grab Christina, and we bolt across the room for
the nearest hallway.

We find cover but Matt turns back. "The power interface." He points to
the pit circled by guardrails, in the center of a room ablaze with weapons
fire. "We need the gear down there to hook up."

I study the maze of electrobeams we'll have to dodge. "It won't be easy."

At the hallway's end, Christina aims for Bobs across the room. "Where's
the gear?" she asks, focused on targets and firing.

"Outside," Matt says. "Still on the truck."

I point out, "Maybe you should have brought it in before all this, ya
think?"

He glares at me. "Mister Trigger-Happy didn't give me a chance." He
reaches into his backpack. "Hang on, we got a call." He pulls out his radio

and listens, then passes it to me. "Looks like they didn't buy your fairy tale about animals."

On the radio is Dave, outside with Madison. The news isn't good—Association troop transports are landing.

"Can you get Matt's gear in?" I ask.

Blasts pour from the speaker. There's a scuffle, then a different voice, tinny and robotic, with bland inflections like a cheap computer talking.

"I have some hostages," the voice says. "Stand down or I send them on their way."

✳

Agents flood into the power station and call for our surrender. Theabeans who hesitate are dissected by shards of light from an arsenal of blast rifles. Christina drops her weapon and kicks it out of reach. Hands on her head, she steps out of the hallway. Matt agrees and follows her lead, in no mood to become a dead hero.

The goons close in and fit us with collars hinged to snap around our necks. The thick metal rings are not simply restraints. Two amber lights go solid once the collars are in place, and a tingling energy field is generated, the sensation like my head is not securely attached to the rest. It's all still there and responsive enough, but my limbs and torso feel half-numb. Dave and Madison are hauled in, collared just the same, along with the few rebel troops still alive.

"To the wall," an agent says, waving his rifle.

We approach the wall.

"Turn around," he says. "On your knees."

Everyone else does, hands on their heads, lined up for execution.

I stand and face my enemy.

Bob puts the barrel to my chest. "You too."

I aim for his eyes. "If you want me dead forever, you'll have to do more than shoot me. Cut out my heart, behead this body, quarter these limbs and more, I won't die. Torture my mind or hold me in a trap, I still exist as a force you can never conquer, no matter how you try. I will return, I *will* remember, where you are and all you've done, and I'll come back to kill as many of you as I can, again and again. Kill me a thousand times, it does nothing to erase who *I am*."

That voice from the radio—like a cheap computer—has entered the room, somewhere beyond the crowd of enemy agents. "Oh such conviction, so moving. And all so useless."

From the ranks of armed Bobs, he emerges—a monster—human parts haphazardly grafted onto machine. From the knees down it's shiny silver, but not boots or added armor, it's actually his body. Each skeletal foot is a spread of metal rods nearly anatomical, welded to flat pads that act as shoes, each step a clank. As it approaches, creaky joints sound like dull knives scraping old pipes. It looks like someone skinned his face and stitched it to a hairless chrome skull, but forgot eyelids, fully exposing the bloodshot orbs all the way back to the swiveling cups they're plugged into.

Matt says, "Who's the humasepheloid?"

"You-mah-what?"

Dave stares at it. "Doll body."

This thing isn't parts floating in a jar. It's complete and fully animated, arms and legs and metal torso, but not an armored shell. Open portions expose linkages and wires meshed with pulsing organs and patches of flesh, but none on its hands. Stripped of all meat, the fingers are thin metal rods with outboard hydraulic actuators hissing and clicking.

"I've been collecting," he says, jaw out of sync with the bland robotic voice. "From previous bodies. Trophies if you will, the better lives." Some whirring and clicks, he creates a grin by pulling cheeks too tight, stretching the skin to a thin film. "Not quite ready," he says, "but after your latest ruckus, ready enough. So what do you think, Adam? How do I look?"

"Don't enter any beauty pageants."

His taut grin goes slack. "You can't win, either." He reaches for his groin and snaps open a cover, revealing that he is indeed a doll this time around, the erogenous zone a smooth mound lacking any detail. His lidless gawking stare shifts to Christina. "Try fucking with this, bitch."

A Bob rushes in holding a paper. He addresses all agents, "Report to transport, we have new orders." The others comply without question, shoulder their weapons, and begin filing out.

"No!" the creature howls. "You will deliver these prisoners to processing immediately."

"I am sorry, sir," Bob says. "Central command is higher authority. Our orders are clear."

The mechanized monster extends an arm and wire shoots out to snatch the paper Bob is holding. A doll with upgrades—built-in wire-gun. The cable retracts, bringing the paper to him, and he scans the order. "Clear? A trick!" The robotic voice lacking inflection makes up for it in volume. "Fools! Orders are not to liberate responsible parties."

"And return to base," Bob says.

A different Bob enters, focused on a sheet he holds. "Apprehend and depart from base."

And another, he's got a paper too. "That is incorrect," Bob says, studying his sheet. "Throw irresponsible parties and depart from moral."

"IDIOTS!" Wire streams out to snatch Bob's rifle from his shoulder and into the clutches of one pissed off doll. "Mind-dead moron idiots!" The metal manikin goes berserk, screaming an unintelligible howl of chirping squeals as he guns down the very pack of goons that brought him here. Agents draw rifles and fire back, but their blasts ricochet off his other upgrade—built-in shields.

Our team and troops scramble clear of the firestorm, duck into a hallway, and take cover.

I tell Dave, "Get the gear."

"Wait." Madison reaches out to Christina. "Chris, take care of him."

"Take care of yourselves," Christina says. "We'll find you. Now go, hurry!"

Dave and Madison join the remaining troops, and the group sprints the hallway, deeper into darkness. Their hurried steps fade, and they are gone.

I ask Matt, "How do you stop a doll body?"

He stares at the maniac contraption piling up dead agents. "Virtually indestructible testrotanium subframe…" His stare of dread shifts to me. "Stop it? You don't. You run."

Beyond the railing, down in the pit, a door swings open. Dave and Madison emerge with troops dragging in cases of gear.

"After you finish." I indicate his arriving equipment.

Matt gauges the lightshow, watching for a break in the action, then makes his move—a dash to the railing, he vaults over and leaps into the pit.

Blasts crossing the room start to dwindle. The Bobs have met their match. I could've used a body like that. Down in the pit, Madison hurries around the perimeter, mounting small devices just below the guardrail. The last Bob falls dead, then the monsterized creation shifts to me and Christina. He realizes the others are gone and notices they are working down in the pit. Whirring joints and feet clanking, he stomps to the railing and aims for our comrades.

How do I stop a doll body?

Madison places the last of her devices and Matt activates the array just as Doll Man pulls the trigger. The blast bounces off a shimmering energy field that forms a protective shield covering the pit.

"Run!" Matt hollers. "I'll finish."

"Then what? Get your arms plucked off like an insect?"

How do any of us stop a doll body?

The robotic freak swings around and I'm staring down the barrel of Jared's pulsed wave inducer all over again. Keeping his eyes and weapon on me, he says to Matt, "Turn the shield off or Adam goes bye-bye."

"Matthew, don't," Christina says. "Finish the job."

"The bitch, too."

"What do you care?" I ask. "All you want is me."

"And nobody left to come rescue you. I made that mistake once already."

How do I stop a doll body?

Only one way I can imagine.

I say to Christina, "Watch after this body."

"Don't." She reaches for the device latched around my neck. "Not when you're collared."

"And the other, if it's true."

"What other?" she asks.

"The one without a collar. I might need it after this."

✳

So close to evil, I should better understand it. But knowing evil risks more than understanding it. The evil becomes a part, and like any part, it is not so easily detached. To discard anything is always a loss. Everything owned is precious, even evil.

No. Put the weapon down.

The body won't. He is strong.

I can see through the eyes. Christina is holding up my body, a body that looks dead. No, those eyes are wandering, just lost for now. She guides that staggering body toward an exit. Muscles contract, whirring gears, a finger tightens...

No. Lower the weapon.

The blast ricochets off the floor.

Here I am, come and get me. I am with you, know that. Destroy this body, you destroy me with it. All you've been waiting for.

The rifle clanks when it hits the floor. I look down and want to pick it up, then realize, no—he wants to pick it up. The melding of two is confusing. We feel too much like one. I might be sick.

Him and I, this one body, we step back and swing around to see down in the pit where Matt and his team are working. They have uncrated gear and constructed an electronic monstrosity spilling cables across the floor.

We can kill them.

Kill none of them.

All of them.

Those other them.

After we kill these them, we kill every other them.

We can't.

Don't be scared, it's what you want.

You want me, you have me. Leave them alone.

You want to kill them and win.

Killing you, I win.

And them. You hate them.

"Adam!" she cries. "Get back."

Oh no, I'm slipping away, losing control. That tug from before, sucking hard, I'm being stretched to fit through a long straw.

"I can't pilot," she says. "I'm hurt."

✳

Like a bullet, I crash into my own skull. Mine, all mine, nice and empty, and not every crevice painted black. One huge gasp fills these lungs and brings this body back to life. The sky is dark, thinner clouds but the moon has moved along. I stand in wet sand, and gentle waves wash the hull of our craft. Christina is urging me to climb through the open hatch.

"Who's hurt?" I ask.

The answer is right before my eyes. She holds one arm tucked close to her side. Her uniform is burnt and bloody, frayed open below her shoulder.

"I did that?"

"We'll argue later," she says. "It's coming."

That *thing* is coming down the beach, chasing after us. But he can't run all that well. Rigid legs like stilts, stalking over sand, he stomps awkwardly while lurching forward, and the jarring strides foil a decent aim from his blazing rifle.

"The collar helps," she says. "Numbs most of it." She pulls me through and secures the hatch, then we climb up to the cockpit. She scrounges for something while I fire up the engines. "But we have to get them off," she says, prying at her collar with a narrow tool.

I hit the throttle and send us skyward, tunneling through low clouds, then look over at her fussing with her collar. "Don't," I say. "The pain, you might pass out."

She keeps at it. "A better chance to take." A sharp crack and the latch breaks. She unhinges it from her neck and screams a scream to make my skin peel. Cradling her arm, she doubles over in her seat. "I'll take pain over a containment field."

"These are…? But it didn't contain me back there."

Angled toward me, she works to free my collar while I hold the craft steady. "So you're strong," she says. "Besides, you weren't dead. Dead triggers the field. Dead wearing one of these, you go nowhere." She keeps trying but can't get my collar off. "That is, until they track the beacon and drop by for pickup."

A blast strikes and the craft rocks hard. Christina bounces off her seat and bangs the console.

I scan tactical. Someone's on our ass.

She gets steady and reaches for my collar.

"Forget that," I say. "Deal with it later. Strap in, we got company."

She secures her harness. I pitch the craft down, roll and back around, aimed at our adversary. Another blast strikes and the craft shudders.

"Shields at sixty percent," she says.

Three more hits, I bank hard and away. We burst from clouds and rocket high into the atmosphere. At the edge of space, the purple horizon begins curving. Our only escape is past a maze of electrobeams higher, coming from countless enemy craft. And look at that—as many rebel flagships. Matt got it done.

On tactical is our first threat, relentless, the marauder sticking to our tail like—what? The screen magnifies to show details. Man and machine, there is no cockpit. He's plugged in like another component sitting atop a slender craft rigged with outboard blast cannons.

This ride may haul ass but it's not enough. The crazed stalker matches our speed, every evasive move, and pounds us with blasts.

"Shields at twenty," Christina says. "Ten. Adam!"

The aft explodes and I struggle with controls. The forward view goes spinning, the curving horizon of Orn-3 flipping round and round as we corkscrew down. Christina throws off her harness and dives into the rear compartment.

"We got fire," she calls. "Get back here!"

"I can't, I'm the pilot."

"Nothing to pilot if you don't."

We're losing altitude, then skimming the atmosphere, flames begin roaring over the nose. I'm useless here anyway. Nothing responds, this ride is dead. I unbuckle and spring from the seat, then a blast strikes and sends me stumbling. I trip over the hatchway into the rear compartment, soaring headfirst through smoky chaos, and smash into—

✳

It's all black and crashing, up and over, flipping and turning. Everywhere is dark, thick smoke. I can hardly breathe. The scene starts to brighten—flames. My skin is burning. I snap up only to tumble over and smack the floor. Or was it the ceiling?

The compartment stops flipping but everything still quakes, and we're falling. Blood flows down my forehead, into my eyes. I reach for my scalp and the wet mess leaves my fingertips bloody. Something hard and I became far more intimate than we should have.

Someone darts through the smoke. Then back again, and she stops to look at me.

"Put it out!"

She is strangely familiar.

The fire. I came here to put out a fire. An extinguisher is here somewhere. In a cabinet, but the door won't budge. The hinges are melted, the handle is hot, and now my palms are seared.

"What are you doing?" she says, "Put out the fire."

Is she upset? I think so. I'm doing something wrong, or… not doing something right.

She comes close and tips my head down. "Oh no," she says. "Please no. We have to fix this."

She takes my hand and pulls me up. I like holding her hand. It feels good when she holds my hand. We stagger through smoke, across the falling compartment. She keeps one arm close to her side. I think she's hurt.

I ask, "Did I mess up?"

She lets go of me and reaches into a cabinet. "No, honey, you're fine. Just sit and relax."

"Okay, if you say so."

The floor rattles my butt with all the shaking. She digs into my head, something stings, then she crams in gauze. Her face drops down in front of me.

Wow, time stands still.

Tender blue eyes that may never forgive me.

"Hang on," she says. "Don't fade."

"But the fire, I put it out, right?"

Her eyes are wet with tears. "It's too late. We won't survive."

Blood runs down between my eyes and drips off my nose.

"Don't get lost," she says. "Remember, promise me." She tugs at something around my neck.

"Remember what?" I ask.

"*You.*"

She stares at me, I think. Everything is getting fuzzy, like a dream.

"Okay," I tell her. "I promise, I'll remember you."

An explosion knocks us apart. My cheek is pasted to a scorching panel. Wait, I have to hold her hand. Everything will be okay if I hold her hand. Where did she go?

The orange glow closes in. Somewhere in the blaze, I can hear her screaming. I don't want to hear that, anything but that, then I don't—my ears have melted, and my eyes, I want to cry, but there is nothing left that cries.

My body is gone. I am ash, dancing in smoke.

But still I can see, something on the floor. A metal collar, and on it, a red light flashing. It starts beeping in time with the light, both getting faster, until solid red and a steady squeal.

An immense pull summons me. My bodiless nothing is drawn into a narrow space, long like a straw, and I am taken away.

7

FREEZING COLD, I CAN'T MOVE OR SEE ANYTHING PAST A FROSTY surface riddled with cracks. Where have I awakened? Don't wake, to sleep is better. I am so tired. Sleep, just sleep. Let me sleep forever.

Go to the light.

*

I wake to rumbling. Droning on, a constant hum, and vibrations that never cease. This cold body is so solid, so heavy and hard, it won't move, but it absorbs all the vibration. Still dark, only a pale blue glow, and the rumbling, shaking the cold. Sleeping is better. Later, I'll wake from this bad dream.

Go to the light.

*

I'm falling, tumbling through blue sky and clouds, toward an ocean below. I'm trapped and falling. The water swallows me, I'll drown. I have to get out, away from this planet.

Go to the light.

*

I am in space. Outer space. Countless points of starlight dot the blackness. This is pleasant. There is nothing I must do.

One star is not so distant. Light from the flaming yellow orb brightens a planet aloft in blackness, a blue marble with white swirls.

This is not pleasant. Where is everyone? I can't be alone. Please, don't let me be alone. Someone, something, please, capture my attention.

A light. The hypnotic strobe is irresistible.

Others are in the light. I won't be alone.

I go to the light.

✳

I have a body, translucent and glowing pale blue. From the mist, cherubs float out to greet me. For a time, the winged infants watch me walk the tunnel of light, then they scatter and vanish.

Ahead is a crowd, an outline of silhouettes standing before a dazzling light farther beyond. They wave for me to join them. As I draw closer, their faces become clear. They look familiar, but what are their names? Some reach out and welcome me to this place. They are all smiling, overjoyed to see me.

Someone pushes through the crowd. Strong backlight brightens sheer fabric that blends with mist at her feet. A soft breeze stirs the glowing shroud, and details emerge. She wears a crown of slender braided vines, imbued with petite blossoms.

She takes my hand in hers.

"Where are we?" I ask.

"Heaven," she says. "Where we will live happily ever after."

Wow, I made it.

She smiles, all is well, and she pulls me along, across the clouds and past the crowd. Their gazes beam admiration and approval, pleased by the sight of me and this woman together.

From a single point ahead, thin rays shoot out and dance wildly. A disturbing sight, yet I'm compelled to enter the passage beyond. Somewhere I belong.

We enter the light. Bathed in it, our unreal bodies transform into luminous beings walking hand in hand across the clouds.

The brilliance mellows to a glowing mist, comfortable white in all directions. There is a trickling brook, and a rock garden that surrounds a stone fountain. Bubbling up from the center and rippling down to fill an ornate bowl, the crisp water looks absolutely delicious.

"Drink," she says, "and live forever." She cups her hands to collect some of the water, then offers me a taste.

I remember this. "I'll be young."

"Yes," she says. "Once you forget that you age."

She raises her cupped hands higher.

I drink the water, then realize…

Something, but it just slipped away, gone.

✳

Someone is here with me, and she's holding my hand. She smiles, all is well, and she pulls me along. A light breeze comes on, enough to unfurl a patch of clouds. The mist parts.

A dark red chair with square armrests.

"Sit down," she says.

She coaxes me into the cushioned seat. It is very comfortable. She turns away and vanishes in the mist.

The chair starts to rotate, and images form on the cloudy background. A lush forest, babbling brook, and the scent of pine needles. Endless wildflowers over rolling hills, stalks rustled by a breeze, and warm sunshine. A beach, roaring waves, and gulls riding the wind.

People appear in the images. Surfing, biking, playing ball and laughing. Many are strangers, some are family and friends, but I've forgotten their names. This ride is like watching my life flash before my eyes. Things I've done, places I've been, and people I've known. I like the images, it was a good life and I want to see more, but everything goes by too quickly. The chair turns faster, more images pass, and the speed is frustrating. There isn't enough time to enjoy each scene.

The images take on an odd quality, more than pictures with sight and sound, even tactile sensation and scent. Each scene presents a puzzle I must solve, but there are too many. The chair spins faster and the puzzles are overwhelming, another presented before I have any chance to solve the last. All analytical capacity is twisted into a tight knot. I can't *think*.

New images become gruesome as people begin hurting each other. A man shoots a woman in the head, another runs a sword through his victim, more people smash each other with clubs. Then the people are familiar, harming others who are dear to me. Now it all replays and *it's me* harming everyone. I want out of the chair but it only spins faster. It's all my fault, every feeling ever felt is wrong, every desire to blame for the horrifying gore I witness, people disemboweled, limbs hacked off, beheaded and burned. Victims scream, I scream back, for every scream a thousand more return.

Now the images are men with black coats and hard faces. I am caught in the moment of slicing their throats, blasting their bodies, smacking some with a wrench, the sound of cracking bone a sign of success. I want them all dead, more than dead, I can *feel* the sickening desire. Then foes even more evil, lording over countless worlds, I want them gutted and dismembered, castrated and torched, begging for mercy, there will be none.

I don't want this, to see it or to feel it, yet guilt is a flavor I cannot clear from my tongue. I know what I've done, nothing can ever change that. The only escape—forget the moment, all that spawned it, everything associated. See no guilt, neither the deed nor its cause, there is no guilt. Let the chair spin faster, I agree. Make it go too fast. Make it all go away.

From the spinning images, energy beams shoot out and target where I'd have a stomach if this glowing semblance of a body were real. Happy beams, warm and fuzzy, then cold and dark oozing sickness, meshed with my own considerations, past decisions and idle thoughts, too many, like a million people chattering at once.

Dark clouds descend, obscure the imagery, and begin snapping electricity. Intense strobes flash too bright, too many, all blinding. Sizzling arcs snap and crack, scorching bolts lash out and strike, I'm electrified. For an instant, my semblance of a body divides in two, each half leaning away to watch the other, like looking in a mirror to see yourself terrified.

The circling clouds burst into flames. The winged children are back, orbiting around me, but now their skin glows red and horns sprout from their skulls. The inferno closes in, rising taller and raging hotter. The chair falls away, I'm torched and falling, burning alive, but not alive I'll never die, burning forever and falling. I'm burning, on fire, *burning!*

The viewpoint once me is just another slice, identity dissolved to blend with the rest, floating in a cauldron where lost pieces of one meld to become whole again.

My soul has melted.

✳

Scaling a staircase backward, it's completely natural, nothing odd about climbing stairs backward. More unsettling is the nagging sense that it's happened before. And not just once.

Below, a bottomless black nothing spreads out forever. Above is only sky, darker the higher it goes. Up seven steps, the staircase switches direction, and seven more it alternates again, back and forth, rising higher each step I take backward. No one else is here, I scale the stairs alone, but eerie whispers seem to follow my ascent. Nonsensical words and phrases, yet each whisper delivers a sting of meaning. You win, you lose. You are good, you are bad. You are pretty, you are ugly. Smart, stupid. Breathe, can't breathe. Live, die. Be dead, be god.

The stairs end at a plateau of clouds. Everything is white, a mammoth building, the columns, bushes, vines and leaves, all white. People flock to wide steps leading inside the monument. The people are all white, their skin, hair, even eyes and lashes, all white. Everything, except high in the dark sky, a spiral galaxy slowly rotates.

A locomotive rumbles up to a platform, also completely white. A man steps off the train and approaches, white again, wearing a sharp coat and stiff hat. "Welcome to the transtation."

"Train station?"

"*Tran*," he says.

"Train?"

"Quiet now, no more questions. Questions will hurt you." He comes closer. "Ticket please."

I have one in my grasp, a gold foil square with an aura of sparkling glitter. I hand it to him.

He looks it over and snaps twice with a handheld punch. "Row sixty-three trillion, seat seventy-five million."

Huh? I study the train, then back to him. "There's only one car."

Gravely concerned, he asks, "Do you want to be lost in time?"

"I don't think so."

He stares hard, his eyeballs a nauseating violet swirl. "Keep *track* of your numbers." He cups one hand to his mouth. "All aboard!"

His stare leaves me ill.

Two doors slide apart and I step inside the train car. It's empty, only one row with three seats. I study my ticket, then the seats. Which one is seventy-five million? Or was that thousand? I go for the middle. When I sit down there is someone next to me, a twin of me, and another, one on each side, both facing forward and staring off at nothing.

"Who are you?" I ask.

They rise, beaming plastic smiles, and say in unison, "This is our stop. Stay here until the track ends." Perfectly synchronized, they study nonexistent wristwatches and say, "Five-hundred forty-six trillion to go." Their eyes display that same violet swirl like the conductor had, and their stares leave me ill. They step off, and the doors slide shut.

In rising jerks, the train starts inching forward. Once it gains some speed, from a speaker mounted high, a hostile voice says, "We hate you, come back." It switches to sympathetic. "We don't hate you, go away." Then indifferent. "Come back every tomorrow the same you have every yesterday."

The train rolls down the track, clickety-clack, and endless white scenery creeps past. Stuck here with nothing to do, thoughts brew, thoughts that become increasingly solid. The beginning is so far back, it is impossible to know. And the end is so far to go, it is useless to hope that it ever arrives. No ends, at any end, ever. No reason, no purpose.

Again the speaker announces, "We hate you, come back. We don't hate you, go away. Come back every tomorrow..."

This is wrong. It feels as though I've made this trek a thousand times before.

I stand. "Stop the train."

The train slows to a stop, the doors slide open, and I step off. High in the dark sky, the spiral galaxy is still there, slowly rotating. But now it's snowing minuscule flecks of glitter.

Behind a stone desk stands a huge man with snowy mane and flowing beard. He's four times my size and glaring down at me. "You didn't finish the track."

"I'm not riding that thing anymore."

He reaches for a gavel and snaps it against the stone. "The misbehaved shall retrace the path of righteousness until goodness prevails."

Someone is here with me, and she's holding my hand. She smiles, all is well, and she pulls me along. A light breeze comes on, enough to unfurl a patch of clouds. The mist parts.

A dark red chair with square armrests.

"Sit down," she says.

There is this thumping, like a heart. But I don't have a body. Thumping like I have a body and a heart, and I should be scared.

Images form on the circling clouds. Forest, wildflowers, crashing waves.

I've seen this before. Déjà vu.

"Stuck in poo," a voice says.

I scan all directions. I am alone.

A faint band of glitter forms, circling me. Violet, pink and blue, translucent little diamonds.

"Who said that?" I ask.

"About time you got off that ride."

"Ride?"

"You know," he says, "round and round?"

Beyond the ring of glitter, the chair turns without me. Slowly, images on the clouds change from one to the next. No memory exists, but I know what happens in that chair. To stand aside and watch is different. I'm not forced to feel it.

The disembodied voice asks, "Are you going to meander through another life and get nothing done? One is bad enough, maybe even two, but this is ridiculous. How many times do you have to ride that thing before you figure it out?"

"I have before?" I watch the chair go round, and with it, the past runs down a drain. The voice from nowhere is right. Endless wasted lives.

"You've been stuck here for millennia, and you keep coming back to ride that mind-wash every time you die, so many times now I've lost count. Put it this way—Idan has land again, and has for many generations."

"What is Idan?"

Silence. Then the voice asks, "Do you remember anything?"

"I don't even know who I am."

Overhead, the spiral galaxy descends, spinning faster. Dark clouds sweep around the horizon and whip the sky into a swirling vortex. The cosmic disk drops lower and the center collapses in on itself to become a churning black funnel, tapering to a pinpoint far above.

"Time to go," the voice says. "See you on the other side."

The wind escalates to hurricane force and I'm hoisted skyward, sucked into the swirling vortex, then drawn into a narrow space, long like a straw, that stretches to infinity.

✷

This is one tight spot, no room to move. I want to stretch but everything is pressed up against me. It wasn't so cramped before. Time here has been warm and easy, but now I'd like to leave. To where, I don't know, just someplace else. I've outgrown this tiny home.

Sounds are dull, like being underwater. But one sound is clear, closer, that rhythmic thumping, rising to a faster pace.

The walls of my trap contract in a sudden jerk. And again, I'm being crushed. I don't like it here anymore. Another contraction, stronger this time, I'm squeezed and it hurts, but the sensation of moving along the canal promises escape from this prison. The passage is so tight that nothing should make it through, but somehow I do, as my little body deforms to fit. Muscles contract tighter, forcing me out too slowly, crushed and choking, the pain is unbearable. Then my journey becomes swift, propelled by one big push.

Outside, I'm free to move but there's nothing to hang on to. The giant open space is frightening. Blazing floodlights scorch my eyes. Great, now I'm blind. A cold breeze churns around my skin. I hate it here already. People shout, a woman is crying, and the washed-out blurry view jerks up, down, all around. Turn off the lights, be still, and please, someone please just hold me.

Smack! The surprising attack on my buttocks starts me wailing. Maybe if I cry loud enough they'll stop whacking me. What was that for? I know how to breathe.

Next is a bath in cold water, tubes rammed up my nostrils and in my mouth, then a horrendous sucking clamor as globs of phlegm are stolen.

At last, I am wrapped in a warm blanket. Someone carries me, I'm not sure who, the view bounces up and over with each footstep. I am set down near the familiar thumping, but now I'm on the outside. The steady rhythm is hypnotic. Go to sleep, my child, go to sleep.

A woman says, "You have a beautiful baby boy."

"Thank you."

The responding voice is clear, female, and very near. The familiar tone joins the thumping rhythm, and both resonate throughout my tired little body. Comforted by her soothing presence, I drift away, fading toward slumber.

"A handsome little devil. Have a name yet?"

"Yes," mother says, and soft fingers pet my head. "My son's name is Damian."

✳

Endless white. No ceiling, floor or walls, only white. Not too bright, a comfortable white. My naked body floats on nothing, struggling for a grasp of anything. The feet wiggle and arms move, but more like spasms. This baby doesn't understand what I want. Or I don't understand how to command it. So it only squirms in jerky little fits.

Something else is here, but it's blurry, a dark blob. I strain to focus. It's a tree, floating with me. Uprooted and dripping clumps of soil, it hangs in the white nothing. Leafy limbs spread out from a big trunk, on which sections of bark make the face of a grumpy old man.

"Welcome back," it says.

The wooden mouth moves. The tree is talking. Sure, and naked babies float across white nothings. Goofy dreams. Or maybe not.

"Am I dead?"

"Oh no," the tree says. "Just getting started."

"Didn't I just…"

"Many times."

I look off into the white nothing. It's all blank.

"I don't remember."

"A dreadful sentence," the tree says.

"Life is dreadful?"

"Oh no, not life. The chance to live is a glorious gift all must treasure."

"Then what's dreadful?"

"Not remembering it."

He's right. There is a past, I know there is, but it's all blank. Who am I, really?

The tree seems to know my thoughts. "You're fresh in from another Sol-2 mind-wash, now in a new body on Sol-3. Your latest mother named you Damian, if I'm not mistaken."

"I don't understand any of what you're saying."

"The Restricted Zone? Ring any bells?"

"What is that?"

The tree goes silent, eyes of bark staring at me. Then it says, "You cannot change that which you deny causing."

"Is that a riddle? I don't get it."

"If you ever hope to escape this trap, you must open your eyes and *look*."

"At what?"

"Your decision to forget."

"I decided?"

"Did you?" The tree creaks, twisting to one side, and gazes into the empty whiteness. "Let's refresh your memory."

Far off an engine roars, then a motorcycle materializes out of nothing. The rider is a young man in jeans, white tee and leather jacket, dark hair greased back. The bike zips across the white nothing, leaning side to side as the rider negotiates turns along an invisible road. A horn blares and tires screech. An automobile comes out of nowhere, fat rounded fenders and chrome grille like eyes wide and teeth bared. The sedan crashes into the bike and the rider is thrown.

The grisly image draws near as if being forced into my view. The rider's leg is folded back, snapped bone punctures flesh of his arm, and brains leak from his busted skull. His dead eyes stare at—*that's me.*

"*No!*" I scream. "It hurts!"

"Not many like that," the tree says. "Autos are relatively new around here."

The rider vanishes and a section of sidewalk materializes. A faint scream grows louder, then a bucket of rivets rain down, followed by a man slamming into the sidewalk. Blood pools around a pulverized bag of skin. *Me.*

"Ouch," the tree says. "Looks like that hurt."

"It still hurts, *stop it!* I don't want to see that."

The mess disappears. A soldier materializes, wearing a blue uniform. He pours powder into a long rifle and takes aim. Some distance off, in trees that have appeared, there's a pop and a puff of smoke, then sharp whistling comes quick. *THWACK!* Fragments of skull scatter and the soldier falls dead. Me again.

"I don't want to see any more. I hate war."

"Yes," the tree says, "quite an appetite they have for war. And brutal how they deal with rebellions."

Another apparition appears, this time a man on his knees, leaning forward with hands bound behind his back. A guillotine materializes around him and the blade drops. The head rolls near, dead eyes gazing. Me.

"Is it true?" the tree asks. "A quick death is painless?"

"*No!*" I scream. "It still hurts! It always hurts! Stop it!"

"Clearly," the tree says, "others are more difficult to bear, given the time it takes."

A man wears a hooded robe that hides his face. He is tied to a stake. Flames start at his feet and quickly grow to an inferno.

"What is wrong with people?" I stare into the amber glow. "I didn't dream up astromechanics. It's how it works."

"By the way," the tree asks, "how long does it take? You know, to char one heretic."

"Stop! Make it stop!"

The flaming stake vanishes, along with the sensation of cooked limbs.

The tree says, "Don't lose your head now. Oops, already did one of those."

A kneeling man is dressed in a colorful tunic. Standing over him, another warrior wields a curved blade. He raises it high, and in one quick thrust, beheads who I once was.

Though swift, the pain is clear, and with it, some memory of the shame.

"That was my own fault," I say.

"This too perhaps."

A lifeless old man is lying on a stone slab. His flowing hair and beard are as white as his robe. His arm hangs limp, a goblet slips from his fingers, and it hits the floor. Other men are gathered round, dressed in white gowns, some young, some old, all grieving.

"I should have kept my mouth shut."

"Less painful anyway."

"*You know nothing of pain!* Their pain is my greatest pain, forever."

"Then you remember your decision."

"Yes, and I'm sticking with it. I don't want to remember."

"Precisely the reason you do not."

"I don't care, I don't want to. Make it all end."

"Are you sure?" the tree asks.

"Yes. Make it all go away, forever."

"I must caution you. If you choose to forget, you will not remember anything, not even…"

A man and woman stand below steps buried in windblown sand, holding hands as they gaze skyward. She is crying. A sword is planted upright in the sand. The blade glows pale blue.

I know her.

"*Watch out!*"

She hears me and turns to look. She pulls free of my hand—the hand that was mine, when I was him—and she steps toward this me, the baby me.

A gust of nuclear wind roars past and my former self is vaporized. However, she has stepped clear of the blast and stands looking at me, the baby me. She wipes her tears and turns to see that he, who I once was, is gone. Then she turns back to see *me*, looking at her *now*.

Tender blue eyes that may never forgive me.

I promised to remember her.

I float closer, yearning to make contact.

She reaches out one slender fingertip.

Crackling. A spark leaps between our nearing embrace.

We touch.

A dazzling white brilliance ignites.

*

I thrash awake in Mommy's arms. She looks down at me and pets my head. "Quiet, Damian. Everything's okay." She stuffs a baby bottle in my mouth.

The television is going. I twist some, enough to see the wooden console, black and white screen, and crisscrossed slats over fabric covering the speaker.

"Pints of blood have been rushed into the room, for transfusion purposes, and two priests were called to the room."

Watching TV, at first Mom is concerned. Then she's horrified. Now she looks ready to cry. I want to ask what's wrong, but all I can manage is gibberish.

She shushes me and keeps watching. On TV, a man is seated behind a desk. He holds a sheet of paper that he reads to us. "There is the report in Dallas, you heard from our affiliate there..." The man wears glasses with thick black frames that he removes, looks up at us, then puts back on and reads more of his report. "The extent of his injuries, whether they are indeed critical or not, is not known, either. It was just an hour ago that the incident took place."

Mom starts crying. Please, Mom, don't cry.

The man on TV looks like he might cry too.

"...in Dallas, that he has confirmed, that President Kennedy is dead."

The adventure continues with *Resonance: Dead Forever Book 3*

CPSIA information can be obtained at www.ICGtesting.com
Printed in the USA
LVOW080853010612

?4135LV00001B/118/P